Since 2006, *New York Ti*
enchanted readers wi ... and
homecomings that have won several awards and been translated into over a dozen languages. She's worked as an administrative assistant, teaching assistant, in retail and as a stay-at-home-mom, but always knew her degree in English Literature would pay off, as she is now happy to be a full-time writer. Her new historical fiction tales blend her love of history with characters who step beyond their biggest fears to claim the lives they desire.

Donna currently lives in Nova Scotia, Canada, with her husband and two cats. You can often find her near the water, either kayaking on the lake or walking the sandy beaches to refill her creative well.

www.donnajonesalward.com

facebook.com/DonnaAlwardAuthor
instagram.com/donnaalward

WHEN THE WORLD FELL SILENT

DONNA JONES ALWARD

ONE MORE CHAPTER

One More Chapter
a division of HarperCollins*Publishers*
1 London Bridge Street
London SE1 9GF
www.harpercollins.co.uk
HarperCollins*Publishers*
Macken House, 39/40 Mayor Street Upper,
Dublin 1, D01 C9W8, Ireland

This paperback edition 2024
24 25 26 27 28 LBC 5 4 3 2 1
First published in Great Britain in ebook format by
HarperCollins*Publishers* 2024

A catalogue record of this book is available from the British Library

ISBN: 978-0-00-868875-2

This novel is entirely a work of fiction. The names, characters and incidents portrayed in it are the work of the author's imagination. Any resemblance to actual persons, living or dead, events or localities is fictionalised or coincidental.

Printed and bound in the United States

Prologue

October 12, 1918: Chester, Nova Scotia

I turned around and hobbled away, the tightness in my leg a reminder of where I'd been, of what I'd done, of things that could never be undone. All the choices I'd made in the last ten months, leading me to this one moment in time when I had nothing left. Choices? I didn't know if they were mine to make after all. I could say that another woman did those things, that I didn't recognize myself, but that would be absolving myself of responsibility. I couldn't do that. Couldn't make excuses. That was more shameful than what I'd done in the first place—acting like it was somehow justified.

I couldn't look back. Wouldn't. The door clicked quietly in the night as it closed behind me, shutting me away from the only future I'd ever wanted. My uneven steps took me down the hill, the black water of Back Harbour on my right, the fresh, salty air beckoning. The pale moon still hung in the sky, lighting my way, even as the rest of the town was sheathed in darkness. It was a relief to be alone. To stop pretending.

In the morning, the Zwickers would realize I was gone. There was not a single soul in this world who would miss me. The grief was now so deep, so profound, that even tears failed. Instead, I walked, one halting step after the other, toward the shoreline.

Were there U-boats lurking out there somewhere, lying in wait? Or had they retreated now that the tide of the war had turned? Oh, if only Frank had survived. Or my parents, providing a safe haven for me to heal and start over. But I had no one. No one but Winnie, and a friendship only went so far. Winnie would never understand this. She would never understand what I'd done in the name of love. How could she, when I could barely understand it myself?

Despite the autumn chill, I took off my shoes and my stockings, then lifted my skirts and waded into the icy water of the North Atlantic. The cold was like needles in my feet and calves, and I lifted my head to gaze at the solitary moon once more.

There was no one to miss me at all.

Chapter One

NORA

October 1917: Halifax

I leaned forward on the chair and wrung out the soft towel, then placed it firmly—but gently—on the angry scar left behind from an artillery shell fragment. Private Doucette winced and said something under his breath in French, but I just offered a little smile as I finished cleaning the wound and then started applying new dressing.

"*Merde,*" he breathed as I wrapped gauze around his arm. "That 'urts, Nurse Crowell."

"*Je suis désolé,*" I replied. I tried to work as efficiently as possible. My French accent was stilted, and I only knew a few phrases, but I'd picked up bits and pieces from the Acadian soldiers who came to the Camp Hill hospital to convalesce. As a

Nursing Sister, I tried to use the few words I knew to make the men feel more at home.

The soldiers were well enough to come home to Canada on a hospital transport ship, but not yet well enough to be discharged. Pvt. Doucette had been lucky he hadn't lost his arm. The wound had been deep and dirty. The trauma, paired with weeks of disuse, meant he couldn't yet straighten his elbow or use his hand.

"Tell me something about home, Private," I suggested, trying to distract him.

"Home? Ah, Chéticamp. Prettiest spot in Cape Breton," he said proudly, even though his lips were set in a firm, painful line. "*Ma mère et grandmère* make the best *tourtière* at Christmas, and Rappie Pie, too. Whole family gets together and—"

He broke off, turned his head away, and hissed in a breath.

I was nearly done, but I knew his reaction had little to do with pain from the bandage and everything to do with what was happening in his head and heart. I hadn't been at the hospital long—Camp Hill had just opened this fall—but it hadn't taken long for me to realize that some of the biggest wounds these soldiers suffered weren't physical ones.

"It sounds lovely," I said softly, finishing with the dressing and giving him a smile. "I've never had either of those dishes." I found it often helped to keep the soldier talking, keeping it light but not shying away from awkward moments as if their feelings were somehow wrong. Gentle understanding went a long way.

Doucette let out a breath. "I am 'oping that I get home for Christmas," he murmured. "Do you think I might?"

"It's only October. I can't say for certain, but if you take care and do everything the doctor says, you might be digging into that… what did you call it? Tort…"

"*Tourtière*," he answered, offering me a contrite smile. "*Je m'excuse*. I'm sorry I swore earlier."

I raised an eyebrow. "I've heard worse." I gathered up my supplies, preparing to move on. "But I appreciate the apology anyway, Private."

My next patient was not as cordial, however.

The sergeant was from Yarmouth and had no family close by to visit. He never spoke of his family, either. In fact, he barely spoke at all. He scowled sometimes, and occasionally startled us all with outbursts that made me nearly jump out of my skin. The rest of the time—like today—he stared straight ahead, his eyes vacant. Those eyes haunted me. Whatever he'd seen, paired with his devastating injuries, had turned him into a shell of a man.

How on earth could I put a positive face on that kind of suffering?

"Good morning, Sergeant," I said gently so I didn't startle him. The scar on his face ran from ear to eye, and it had healed adequately, though it would always be ugly. The bullet graze had damaged his eye and he couldn't see out of it now, and sometimes, if he were in a decent mood, he wore a patch over it. Not today, though. Today was not a good day. And the facial wound was the best of it.

Sergeant Hammond had lost both his legs and an eye overseas. I couldn't imagine how he must feel … but I still had to do my duty. I briskly shifted him to change his bedding, dealt with the bed pan, and gave him medication for his pain. Trying to do anything else was a miss. He was not compliant today. Not in the mood for any of the exercises that would help him with his strength and mobility. No words, just a few grunts.

But when I smoothed out his pillow and offered him a smile, I saw the tears gather at the corner of his good eye. It was during these moments my heart faltered. I knew words would do absolutely nothing, so I offered the only comfort I could: the squeeze of my hand on his shoulder.

He flinched away, and I lifted my hand as if it had been burned. Today was an especially bad day, then. Touching him had been a mistake.

"Don't do that."

I didn't know what to say, so I said nothing at all. Hammond turned his head away, shutting me out. I stood there, desperately wanting to help, trying to think of anything different to attempt that I hadn't already. I refused to believe that anyone was beyond help. At the same time, I was beginning to understand that if *they* believed they were, nothing I did would change it.

There were too many men like Sgt. Hammond. Too many who had left body parts in France and Belgium, too many who came home different from the men who'd departed, determined to do their part in the war. I saw them every day. I witnessed their pain and struggles. I knew the ones who were on the road to recovery and knew those who were not and never would be. I smelled blood and illness and bed pans, antiseptic and fresh sheets and bandages. There was laughter sometimes but also a lot of anger, worry, fear, despair.

It was a lot for me to process. I've always been focused on responsibilities and nursing and wanting to do more than be a wife and mother. Becoming a nurse in the medical corps was a dream come true. Like the soldiers, though, I hadn't truly understood what I was getting into, becoming a nurse in wartime. How could I paint a rosy picture of what lay ahead when all Sgt. Hammond wanted was to have died with his brothers in arms on the battlefield?

Life was a precious gift. And yet I felt the hopeless despair deep in my bones, and it unsettled me. It reminded me of the time I'd gone out in the dory with my brothers in Back Bay and we'd tipped the boat. My skirts had been heavy, dragging me down into the dark, cold water, no matter how hard I'd tried to stay afloat. If I felt the darkness of despair pulling me under now, how must the men feel who were actually experiencing it?

It made me long to get out in the fresh air and do something to feel utterly and blissfully alive. Anything to shake off the feelings of hopelessness and futility that threatened to drown me each day.

"Nearly done for the day?" came a chirpy voice behind me as I went to dispose of the contents of my basin.

I looked over my shoulder to see Jessie Smiley, another of the CAMC nurses, grinning at me. Jessie had an appropriate name. She never failed to make me smile when the job got a bit too much.

"Nearly. It's been a long one." I let out a heavy sigh.

"Always feels that way when Sgt. Doom and Gloom is on your rotation." Jessie shrugged. "I know, I know. I shouldn't say that. He's been through hell." I didn't blink at the use of "hell", either. We heard a lot of language, caring for military men.

"He has, and he's just so…" I sighed and dumped my bowl of dirty water. "He's a broken man, and I have no idea how to help him." I looked at my fellow nurse and admitted, "Sometimes I lie awake at night and worry about them. The patients, I mean. What will they do when they leave Camp Hill? Where will they go, and will they ever be happy again?"

Jessie's smile faded and her eyes filled with sympathy. "You have a soft heart, Nora. We just have to do our best and hope it's enough."

But what if it wasn't? I thought of it often. As much as I knew I shouldn't take work home with me, it was impossible not to. There was just so much pain.

"Anyway, it's a toss-up what's worse. Sgt. Doom and Gloom

or being treated like a glorified maid by the doctors." Jessie rolled her eyes. "Honestly. Some aren't bad, but we didn't train as nurses to go fetch coffee and sandwiches. It was on the tip of my tongue today to tell one in particular to either find a maid or a wife because I'm neither."

I gave an unladylike snort. It was no secret that we nurses faced some challenging attitudes at the hospital, from doctors and patients alike. The doctors tended to act superior, though the matrons ran a tight ship and protected us as much as they held us to a standard. But there were patients, too. Soldiers who thought a blue-clad bum was there to be pinched and that a smile would charm our nursing veils off.

"Well, I've been safe from pinches and barbs this morning, so I guess I should be happy to take Sgt. Hammond's frustration." I started gathering fresh supplies for my cart.

"Any plans coming up?" Jessie asked. "You're off shift tomorrow, aren't you?"

I nodded, happily moving my thoughts to my day off. "Alley and I are going walking. And maybe to a dance. I'm not sure." One thing was certain, though. I'd laugh and feel carefree. Time spent with the young soldier was a tonic against my melancholy moods.

"You and your Alley," Jessie said, replenishing her cart with rolls of bandages. She smiled widely at me. "Things are getting serious there, huh?"

"Oh, I don't know." A blush crept up my cheeks. It was true I liked Alley—Alton Vienot—a lot. But serious? I wasn't really interested in marriage. There were too many things I wanted to do first. "He's waiting to be deployed, and I'm busy here. It's too soon to be thinking about getting serious." I smiled and offered a little wink. "But he is a lovely distraction."

"He's a looker, all right," Jessie said with a chuckle. "And he has a twinkle in his eye. My ma would say he's some handsome devil up to no good. But ma'd say it with a wink. Your Alley-cat's been good for you, Nora. He makes you smile, and Lord knows we can all use a bit o' that after a long day here."

"Amen," I agreed, passing by Jessie and squeezing her forearm in silent thanks for the cheering up. No matter how bad a day got, the nursing sisters stuck together. I wouldn't trade that for the world.

Not even for Alley. It was true that he had swept me a little off my feet, but only because I let him. There was a war on. Maybe I wasn't serving in a hospital or clearing station at the front, but I saw enough to know that life could be short, and sometimes a girl had to grab at happiness with two hands—no matter how fleeting. But marriage? It wasn't for me. I wasn't sure it ever would be, either.

The next day, I shook off my doldrums and was ready for a day of autumn sunshine and laughter. I couldn't stop giggling. Alley's fingers skimmed along my ribs, hitting my most sensitive spots, and I danced away from him, the benevolent heat of the October sun beaming down on us both as we strolled through Point Pleasant Park.

We met almost a month ago after I'd had a particularly challenging day at work and was scrambling to run an errand before walking home in the middle of an early fall storm. My hat had flown clear off my head, and Alley had captured it tumbling down Barrington Street and brought it back to me. We escaped the rain and wind by popping inside a tiny café. Within minutes he'd had me laughing at his stories over a hot cup of tea and a slice of war cake. When the boys from his unit went by and jeered and laughed through the window, he merely waved a hand at them, turning all his attention back to me. No one was more surprised than me when I found myself utterly captivated.

Now outings with Alley dominated my off-duty hours. The date for tea had led to lazy walks in the park, a picnic in the Public Gardens on a warm fall day, and, much to my sister Jane's chagrin, dancing at the various socials held around the city by the IODE and Red Cross. Those organizations, and even churches, provided wholesome entertainment for the massive influx of men and the inevitable romances that resulted in a wartime port also in the throes of prohibition. I was thrilled to discover Alley could dance, all loose and limber and with a wide smile of enjoyment on his face. I enjoyed the music and laughter and being held in his arms, and two weeks ago, Alley had walked me home from such an evening and kissed me for the first time on the darkened doorstep of my sister's front porch on Henry Street.

Our courtship had taken me a bit by surprise. I'd never put much thought into romance. To my mother's dismay, I'd chafed against the expectations of leaving home to settle down and look after a family and a household, instead wanting more. I'd never been one to worry much over my hair or what I wore. That was Jane, though. Jane had done the expected thing and up and married, but when I showed no signs of following in her footsteps, my parents finally agreed to let me move to Halifax at the tender age of eighteen to train as a nurse—one of the few acceptable professions for a young lady.

Mum had tried to convince me to work in a shop, or perhaps teach school—something that didn't involve blood and, as she put it, "body parts". But that wasn't what I wanted. Medicine intrigued me. War broke out soon after I began my studies, and by the time I graduated, I was more than ready to enlist with the

Canadian Army Medical Corps to do my part as a nurse—a Bluebird, named after the blue-and-white uniforms we wore. I had just turned twenty-three and proudly held the rank of Lieutenant—though I was only ever called Nurse Crowell. Maybe I wasn't overseas like many of the nursing sisters, but I was happy to be able to help here at home. My entire focus had been far away from love and being romanced. Being useful held much more allure. Using my brain—and my hands—gave me satisfaction and purpose.

Except I hadn't anticipated how the pain and suffering would wear on me. I knew I shouldn't take the soldiers' troubles to heart, but I just couldn't seem to help it. How they'd left their loved ones and families, what they'd seen, the things they'd done… how could a person with half a heart not be affected? I looked forward to my stolen hours with my handsome soldier because they injected a bright ray of sunshine into the grey and heavy clouds that dominated many of my waking hours.

Like this afternoon, walking through the park nestled on the Northwest Arm of the Halifax harbour. The ocean gleamed to my right, sparkling blue, and the crisp red, gold, and orange leaves from the birches and maples crunched beneath my feet. Squirrels darted across the path, chattering at each other and zipping up tree trunks in a whirl of reddish brown. Despite the worry about the war, Halifax in the full throes of autumn was a sight to behold. The sky had never seemed so blue, the air so crisp and revivifying. It was my favourite time of year.

The gorgeous weather only added to my ebullient mood as I darted away from Alley's tickling hands, laughing as I smoothed my favourite burgundy wool skirt and then lifted my hands to ensure my hat was still in place and the smooth roll of my hair was anchored. There was fun and then there was bedraggled, and I took great care to never look untidy when we stepped out together. Besides, Alley looked so smart and handsome in his uniform. It wouldn't do for me to turn up in a workaday skirt and plain blouse.

The sun warmed me through my coat, while the musty scent of fall leaves mingled with the briny sea air. Alley gave up tickling and gallantly held out his arm in an exaggerated gesture that had me laughing all over again, charmed. I took it, leaning against his bicep and smiling up at him as we walked along the path.

I loved walking. Most days my walks consisted of hurrying between the hospital and my sister's boarding house. I was lucky to be able to billet so close to work and to be living with family. But the freedom to be out as I was today—in the fresh air and sun, with nowhere I needed to be—was wonderful. Even better when my companion was Alley. Jessie was right. He was a handsome devil, and he made me laugh.

My sister, Jane, wasn't so keen on him, though. Jane was my best friend, but sometimes having a "keeper" was a nuisance. Jane considered it her job to look after me, and the interference wasn't always welcome. Today, when Alley had shown up on the porch, Jane had frowned with sisterly disapproval, making the early moments of our afternoon awkward. Alley had been coming around more and more frequently lately, and I've encouraged it despite Jane's misgivings. Why shouldn't I walk out with him? We weren't doing anything wrong.

Yet.

My breast was pressed against the wool of Alley's sleeve, and I felt a little forbidden thrill. Our kisses were chaste at first, but lately they'd stirred a lot of unsettling feelings. I found myself wanting to feel his body close to mine, a jolt of excitement running through me when his hand stole from my waist to somewhere a little less appropriate. And then guilty that perhaps these urges made me somehow… bad. I definitely knew what my mother would say. What Jane would say: it's not how a *lady* behaves, and I must be careful not to get a reputation as a loose woman.

It boggled my brain how, if men engaged in such behaviours, they were lauded. Instead, I was constantly fighting a battle between acting like a dutiful sister and daughter and walking my own path.

Alley put his hand over mine where it rested on his arm. "Your sister really doesn't approve of me," he said, as if he could read my mind.

I shrugged, shaking away the thoughts that threatened to ruin my fun afternoon off. Jane's disapproval weighed heavily on my heart, even though I didn't want to admit it. We'd always been close and cared for each other deeply. We'd always shared confidences, too, keeping each other's secrets, but I couldn't talk to my sister about Alley. Jane was already properly married, and I found that she wasn't a willing listener to tales of my romance. I could have used some unjudgmental advice, but the few times I'd mentioned Alley, Jane's lips had pressed together in a thin, painful line. I wondered if it was because Jane really didn't like Alley, or if it was because her husband had gone to the front and talk about romance and intimacies caused her pain and worry. Either way, anything I wanted to talk about felt off-limits, so I kept it inside.

"My sister worries about me, that's all," I explained softly. "She feels responsible for me, since my parents aren't here." A fact for which I was eternally grateful. I wanted my own life, and not to be stuck at the family home in Chester with my two younger brothers who were chomping at the bit to do their part against the Huns, completely jealous that I held a rank and they couldn't even enlist. The war surely couldn't go on that long, could it? It had been three years already. It would be another two years before Willie could possibly be called up. Four for Stephen. The idea of either of my brothers ending up like the patients I cared for made my stomach turn with dread. "She worries about Jimmy, too," I said. "She has a lot on her mind." Jimmy was somewhere in France, and Jane single-handedly saw to the renting of three bedrooms and the preparation of two meals a day for her boarders.

Alley reached over and squeezed my hand. "You seem very capable of looking after yourself, Nora."

I was. There was a certain sense of accomplishment and confidence that came with my achievements. I quite enjoyed being a modern woman.

"Thank you." I leaned against his shoulder for a moment and took a big, restorative breath. "It's a lovely day, isn't it?" I wanted to change the subject. Thinking about Jane's disapproval threatened to spoil the mood. We didn't get many afternoons this glorious.

"Lovelier with you in it." He stopped on the path and stood back, then reached out and took my hands. My heart pitter-pattered in my chest as I tried to absorb everything about this moment. The autumn sun, the sound of the ocean breeze in the golden-hued trees, the smell of the salt air, and the way Alley was looking at me. His blue eyes were bright and focused on me so intently, I blushed. Distraction indeed.

"Have dinner with me tonight," he said, his voice urgent. "Nora, I… " His voice trailed off.

"What is it?" He looked so serious right now.

"I've been meaning to tell you something for a few days."

"Well, don't keep me in suspense." I smiled up at him, but a sense of unease curled around my insides. We were having fun together, weren't we? But Alley's face was so serious right now. I was horribly afraid he was going to ask me to marry him, and I wasn't ready for that. And yet the idea of turning a man down in wartime felt so cold and unfeeling. *Please don't let him propose.*

"I'm shipping out." His voice strengthened and he stood taller. "I'm heading overseas."

My stomach dropped to my feet as my smile faded. This was worse than a proposal—he was leaving. I had hoped against hope that the war would be over before Alley was called up. There was so much danger. Good heavens, just leaving the harbour was dangerous. There was a reason Halifax had become such a busy port on this side of the Atlantic: the deep water, Bedford Basin, and the fact that it didn't freeze made it perfect for convoys from all along the eastern seaboard to gather and then leave together with protection in numbers. U-boats were a constant threat when crossing the ocean, not to mention the danger on the battlefield once the men got there. I swallowed tightly and met his gaze. "Oh, no," I breathed, fear gripping my heart. Just because I wasn't looking for marriage didn't mean I didn't care for him. I did. More deeply than I'd planned.

"Don't say that." He linked his fingers with mine. "I want to go. I want to do my part, and that's not going to happen sitting around Halifax. All kinds of military presence here and nothing ever happens." He scowled. "I don't want to be one of those 'Safety First' boys."

I bristled at the name given to the soldiers who served at home, protecting the port. Most had been deemed physically unfit for overseas service, but they were much needed, in the same way my nursing skills were needed here and not just at the front. It infuriated me every time I heard the chant, "Compo-zite, they won't fight" aimed at the men stationed around the city. The coastline was guarded and the harbour even more so, with batteries along the coast, all the way to Sydney. The anti-sub net went up on either side of Georges Island each night. Blackout happened at 11 p.m. Maybe we weren't the European front, but Halifax was certainly still at war. "Maybe that's *why* nothing happens," I argued. "Maybe nothing happens here because we're prepared."

Alley stepped back and shook his head. "I'm ready to go. I want to, Nora. The boys over there… they need help. I'm proud to be going as a volunteer and not conscripted like those other fellas." Alley had enlisted earlier in the year, before conscription had come into effect, leaving the family farm outside Bridgewater and trading his hoe for a rifle.

I understood how he felt, I realized. I'd often wondered about serving at one of the clearing stations or hospitals over there, instead of nursing in a more convalescent role an ocean away from the action. Matron Cotton had spent time overseas and I'd been dying to ask her about it. I was serving, but was I doing enough? Was I staying where it was safe because I was afraid? What did that say about me?

He wanted to contribute, and I empathized. But I didn't have to be happy about it. I'd seen horrific injuries: missing limbs, scarred lungs from mustard gas, head wounds… everything. I'd heard the nightmares, too. Men calling out for sweethearts, or for comrades they'd lost. I didn't want to think of Alley as one of those broken men when he'd been my light and joy for the last few months. "You must stay safe," I said quietly, then stood on tiptoe and pulled him into a hug, something I normally wouldn't do in public. His arms went around me and squeezed me back.

"Of course, I will." He let me go and met my gaze again. "So what do you say? Dinner? Dancing? Let me treat my best girl like a queen."

"Best girl? I'd better be your only girl." I nudged his arm and made sure to smile though my heart was heavy. I didn't have the heart to say no to his request, though I knew Jane would disapprove. But I wouldn't let worry over my sister's opinion keep me from enjoying an evening with Alley. He would be gone soon, and I would carry this memory with me during the long weeks and months ahead until he was home again. In one piece.

"Dinner," I agreed. "And maybe dancing. But first, more walking. I need to feel the sea air on my face and enjoy the sunshine. We don't get enough of it." I gave a light laugh, trying to dispel my gloom. "When I walk to the hospital in the mornings, it's almost always foggy. And by the time I leave at night, it's already getting dark." I wasn't looking forward to the even shorter days of a cold, Canadian winter. "Soaking up the sun, drinking it in… " I sighed. "It's like it recharges me somehow."

"I'm sorry if you're upset. I didn't want you to be."

I stopped and looked over at him. "I'm not. I understand, I really do. I just worry. But let's not talk about it now. Let's enjoy the rest of the day."

We walked through the park, Alley chattering away while I remained mostly quiet. It certainly hadn't been part of my plan—getting involved with a soldier—but if I'd learned anything since coming to Halifax, it was that in wartime, plans were often just vague suggestions and hopes. If anything, we had to make the most of the time we had left. I tightened my arm around his as we strolled and looked at all the other couples also enjoying the rare afternoon of sun. I wondered how many of them were shipping out soon. How many were home again or on leave… or, as Alley called them, the "Safety First" boys who guarded the city? He might disdain them, but I was mighty glad they were here.

And what about the women on their arms? The sweethearts destined to be left behind? There were sure to be spouses, and new sweethearts, perhaps young ladies hoping for proposals. There were other women, too, women who dared wear a little too much rouge and coloured their lips, the kind who set up shop in the back of the cigarette shops around town that people pretended didn't exist, but everyone knew were there. Everybody seemed to be making the most of the time they had; time was the one thing that no longer seemed guaranteed.

We turned around and started the long walk back along Tower Road, past St. Mary's College, further into the centre of the city and toward the Public Gardens. Twilight deepened the sky as we approached Citadel Hill, the star-shaped fortification that dominated the hilltop and overlooked the harbour, out to Georges Island and beyond. I shivered as I stared at the cold, grey walls. British fortifications had been on this spot in one way or another for nearly two hundred years, long before Confederation had made Canada its own country. Up until a year ago, German POWs, mostly sailors, had been kept only steps away from where I now stood. Now they were sent to an internment camp over a hundred miles away in Amherst. It seemed impossible to think of the enemy being so close—even though they'd been under lock and key. It brought the war home to me just as surely as the ships in the harbour did, and the soldiers in the streets.

Alley squeezed my arm. "You've gone awfully quiet. Penny for your thoughts," he said softly.

I shook my head and tried to smile. "I was just thinking how life has changed so much. About the POWs. It seems so impossible to think of there being spies here in little old Nova Scotia."

Alley nodded, and the usual teasing glint in his eye dimmed. "There are a lot of Germans around the south shore." He took my hand in his and twined his fingers with mine. "It makes sense that people would wonder if they were spying for the fatherland."

"But Alley, surely we're all Canadians."

"It's better to be cautious," he replied, but that didn't settle with me. Neighbours spying on neighbours? I didn't believe it. Weren't neighbours supposed to help each other? Wasn't that what community was all about? It had certainly always been that way in Chester, the town where I grew up. One didn't even have to ask. Word would get out and help was given in food, chores, simple comfort. Whatever was needed. I couldn't imagine those families spying on each other.

"Come on," he said, injecting some lightness back into his voice. "I'm starving. You must be, too. We've walked all afternoon. I'd give my left arm for a milkshake."

We soon reached The Green Lantern restaurant on Barrington, and Alley ushered me through the crowd to a rare empty table.

The popular restaurant was teeming with soldiers and sweethearts and the noise was tremendous. I shook off the sombre mood of earlier and let my smile bloom as Alley paid me sweet compliments and said he was with the prettiest girl in Halifax. He reached across the table and took my fingers in his, rubbing his thumb over the top of my hand. I looked up at him and our eyes met, clung. I bit my lip, wishing we were somewhere private so I could kiss him again, like we'd kissed on the porch, partially hidden from prying eyes. It was so lovely when he did that… it made my toes curl in my shoes and my stomach got all swirly.

How long would it be before I got the chance to kiss him again? Weeks? Months? My heart wobbled. Years?

We ordered food and I ate, but it all seemed tasteless as I thought about what would happen next. My mind was swimming with him, the knowledge that he was going away, and that perhaps he might not come back. I was half in love with the way soft vowels sometimes snuck into his words, evidence of his south shore upbringing, and the way he was quick to smile at everyone, brightening a room just because he was in it. It was fully dark by the time we finished our meal, and I pulled on my gloves as we left the restaurant, hoping the night wasn't ending. A desperation settled in my chest, a need to live as much as I possibly could tonight, because with Alley's announcement, the days ahead were even less certain.

We joined up with a pal of Alley's and his girlfriend, and the four of us made our way to a church hall in the north end where his friend said a dance was on. By the time we arrived, the band had finished warming up and the music was in full swing, the crowd intense. I gripped Alley's hand and let out a jubilant laugh… there was nothing like the heat of a ragtime tune to clear away the doldrums, and the band was really good. He pulled me through the throng to the floor and took me in his arms, his quick smile warming me clear through as he led me in the steps. It wasn't long before I regretted wearing my wool skirt, but I wasn't about to let the heat slow me down. Alley was a fine dancer and I planned to take full advantage. This might be the last time I'd be in his arms until he returned.

His friend—Carl something, he'd said—produced a flask on the sly and everyone took a healthy slug before dancing off again. The liquor—I didn't really drink so I wasn't sure what it was—burned its way down my throat and into my belly, spreading a delicious warmth through my body. The band launched into a faster tune and our steps quickened, and so did my breath as little pieces of hair came out of my once-tidy roll. It seemed like the walls of the hall were heaving from the energy inside—the clang of the music with the punctuation of laughter and shouts, the heat from all the bodies and the overall *joie de vivre* of the occupants. A few more nips of whatever was in the flask, and I was pleasantly loose and limber when the band switched to a waltz. The dance floor was crowded once more, with bodies looped together as closely as they dared under the watchful eyes of mothers who stood on the sidelines like ospreys waiting for a fish to jump. As Alley pulled me close, I was glad I had no such chaperone here. Indulging in bootleg liquor was a first, but I quite liked the effect. Especially when Alley's arm slid around my waist and his lips fluttered against my ear as we took our first steps.

His body brushed against mine as we moved, and I liked it. It felt like every place we touched came alive, made me want to press closer even though I knew I shouldn't. And didn't dare, not here where anyone could see. His hand dipped just a little below my waist, grazing the sensitive spot just above my bottom, and I wanted more. When I looked up and met his gaze, his eyes dropped to stare at my lips and back up again and I felt the pull as surely as if he had kissed me.

Was this what desire truly felt like? I was a nurse. I knew what happened between a man and a woman, even if I had never experienced it myself. And I'd seen the way Jane and Jimmy had looked at each other, especially in the early days. Of course, their coming together had been sanctioned by marriage. But right now, I understood very well what it meant to want. To need.

Alley took my hand and we headed for the door.

He'd take me home now, wouldn't he? He'd leave me on the porch and go away and maybe I wouldn't even see him before he shipped out.

"Hey, Vienot," came the call. It was Carl and his girlfriend, also outside, and I noticed the woman's lips looked pink and puffy.

Carl offered us one last drink from the flask, which we took, stoking the fire already burning in my stomach and spreading pleasantly throughout my limbs. Then Carl took it back, took the last drink, saluted, and left, his arm around his girlfriend as they ventured away in the dark.

Leaving Alley and I alone.

My heart was beating fast, with fear and with something else I hadn't felt before. I wanted to tell him how I felt but of course I couldn't. A girl just didn't think it, say it, or actually do it. Except I wanted to, with every fibre of my being. I wanted Alley to kiss me over and over again, wanted to feel his strong body pressed against mine.

Impulsively, and ignoring the fact we were in the middle of the street, I stood on tiptoe and pressed my mouth to his.

He kissed me back with an urgency I'd never felt before, tasting of alcohol and the cigarette he'd lit when we'd left the hall. A thrill zinged down my spine as his hands pulled me closer. Good heavens. Our bodies were pressed together, and I put my arms over his shoulders and melted into his embrace. Nothing had ever felt as good as this… or as dangerous.

I stood back abruptly. What on earth was I thinking? It was scandalous, acting this way in the street where anyone might see. Nursing Sisters weren't actually nuns, but I felt the weight of a certain moral standard bearing down on me just the same. I pressed my gloved fingers to my lips… were they swollen? Alley's chest rose and fell as if he'd run a long way. My face was hot, and I suspected just as red as one of *those* women who'd been promenading today… Oh, I was so confused. My brain was telling me to be smart, but my heart—and my body—were shouting something else entirely.

"Nora… "

I looked up at him, his features shadowed in the dark, so strong and handsome, and my heart simply turned over. We had a connection, he and I. Not one I wanted to end in church, standing before a minister, but there was something that drew me to him, that made me feel so much better just being around his laugh and smile and charm.

He was unusually quiet, so much so, I started to worry. "What is it, Alley?"

He put his hands on either side of my face. Then he kissed me, slow and soft, until I melted into a puddle.

"Alley," I breathed against his lips. The first kiss had been surprising and passionate. The second, though, had been tender and loving. Like sliding down a rainbow. I couldn't resist him when he kissed me like that. I didn't *want* to resist him. I wanted to live, dammit. I was so tired of being told how a woman should act. That my identity needed to be tied up in being someone's wife or someone's mother, as if those were a woman's only contributions of value. A woman should be able to have a career she loved. She should have a say in her own life without needing a man's approval or permission. Women were pushing to get the vote, to have their say in government. Why, then, was this so forbidden when it felt like an absolutely normal, healthy urge?

Whistles sounded around us, and a few shouts, and heat rushed up my face again as I buried my cheek against the solid, rough material of his uniform jacket. He chuckled, then tipped my chin up with a finger. "Don't worry about them. They're all gassed. Come with me," he said, his voice lower than I'd ever heard it before. "Somewhere private. Where no one can see us. I want to… to be with you."

"I want that, too."

He pulled back and stared into my eyes. "You do?"

I nodded, sure of myself even though I was afraid, too. He dropped light kisses on my cheek. "I love you, Nora." His breath was warm in my ear, sending shivers down my spine. "I'll think of you every day. I'll remember what it's like to hold you in my arms. The touch of your skin. I need it so much… to get me through what lies ahead."

"I need it too," I admitted. "These last weeks, and what I've seen… being with you has got me through. When you kiss me… " My cheeks must have been flame-red now, talking so brazenly, but I was a bit jagged from the alcohol and aroused by his touch. "When things get difficult, I want to have this memory to look back on."

Even in the dark, I saw the light come into his eyes. He clutched my hand and quickly kissed my cheek. "Come with me," he said again, his voice huskier than I'd ever heard it, and that swirly feeling swept over me again, along with something forbidden and delicious.

I followed him with quick steps as we made our way closer to the harbour. A piece of hair got in my eyes, and I realized I'd left my hat behind, but cared little. Our steps echoed in the night as we trotted straight into the doors of the Queen Hotel. Despite the chill, my cheeks flamed as Alley procured us a room, and before I could breathe again, he was opening the hotel room door.

I began unbuttoning my coat with shaking fingers.

Alley took over that job, taking my coat and placing it over the back of a chair. Then he gently peeled off my gloves, put them on top of my coat, and with slow but sure hands, reached for the pins holding my hair. When he removed the last one, he sank his fingers into it, spreading it over my shoulders. His fingers grazed my blouse just on the side of my breast, and my breath caught. Alley dipped his head and touched his lips to the hollow below my ear, and my eyes slammed shut as everything in my body started to tingle again and it was difficult to breathe.

"Nora," he whispered, and I opened my eyes to find him gazing at me with wonder. "Your hair… it's so beautiful. Thick like a horse's mane but soft as a summer breeze. The colour of my uncle's maple syrup in the spring."

As much as I loved entertaining and light-hearted Alley, when he got all serious like this, he was irresistible. Maybe his words weren't fine poetry, but I didn't need that. I didn't need fancy words at all.

I had a choice to make right now. I was young and inexperienced. But I thought about all the challenges I'd already faced in the last few years, my determination to be an independent woman, and I lifted my chin.

I was scared, but what he was about to face at the front was a hundred times worse. For a short time tonight, we could cling to each other. And for once in my life, I'd know what this was like. What it was for a man to love me. Excitement raced through my veins, hot with desire. I might not have another chance; I wasn't like the women in the backrooms trading favours, after all. I cared for Alley. We were a… couple. It didn't mean I was looking for marriage—I had far more to achieve before that happened—but why shouldn't I be able to experience something so…

Alley's lips slid off my cheek and along the curve of my neck, and goose flesh erupted over my skin as I gasped, my thoughts scattered like the fall leaves in the wind. For tonight, I could touch a man's body and find it whole, without scars and grit and blood and disfigurement. I could feel his smooth skin, unmarred by bullets, hear his breath, untouched by the ravages of gas. The man before me represented pleasure and not pain, health and not heartache, and it would be months before I would find this relief again. Desperation clawed at me. How would I survive without Alley being the sun, peeking through the dark clouds of my days?

I would have to, but not tonight. Without another word, I reached for the buttons on my blouse.

Chapter Two

NORA

I snuck up the front steps feeling like a guilty child.

Alley had seen me into a taxi after we'd left the hotel. Staying out all night was impossible, of course. Jane's disapproval was one thing, but if I spent the night in a hotel there was certain to be a lecture. I didn't exactly have regrets about what happened, but I wasn't in the mood for a sermon. I was still trying to sort it all out in my mind. What I'd done. How it had felt. Looking back on that brief hour felt like looking at someone else I didn't know. I couldn't even decide if that was a good thing or not.

I took a moment to gather my wits before putting my hand on the doorknob. The sky was inky black, clouded over now, and the windows were dark as the blackout hour approached. Perhaps I could tiptoe inside and up to bed…

But as I stepped inside the entryway, a glimmer of light sliced into the hall from the parlour and my throat tightened. Guilt shivered down my body, leaving me cold. What we'd done… it had felt as natural as breathing, but now the enormity took over. I'd given myself to a man—without the benefit of marriage. It went against everything I'd been taught. Drinking, laying with a man wasn't something "good" girls did. And it was something that couldn't be taken back.

"Nora?" Jane appeared in the parlour doorway, her face lined with worry. "Oh, I'm so glad it's you. I've been beside myself."

"I'm sorry, Jane. We went to a dance over at St. Joseph's with another couple." I went forward and gave Jane a hug. "I didn't mean to worry you."

"The streets aren't safe at night, Nora. I don't even like you walking home from the hospital in the dark."

I smiled and stepped back. "I took a taxi home. No need to go all mother hen on me. I'm fine."

But Jane wasn't appeased. "You are now. But Nora…" She sighed. "Come into the parlour. I don't want to wake the girls."

I followed Jane into the cozy room. The furniture wasn't fancy, but it was the sturdy type that would last. The wallpaper was faded and a rug covered the middle of the floor, worn but serviceable, and there was a fire burning briskly in the fireplace, warding off the fall chill. On the mantel was Jane and Jimmy's wedding photograph, as well as one of me when I graduated from my nursing program. A book lay on a table, open about a third of the way through, and a little box of blocks sat by the end of the sofa, all tidy so they didn't get stepped on. What the room lacked in elegance it made up for in comfort and welcoming, just like my sister.

Jane sat on the chesterfield and patted the seat beside her. "I've been meaning to talk to you, Nor. About Alley."

I sat down, wondering if Jane could possibly tell what had transpired only an hour ago. Did I look different? I certainly felt different. Could she smell the liquor?

"He's shipping out," I said. "He got his orders." I twisted my fingers together in my lap, wanting nothing more than to climb the stairs and go to bed.

"Oh." Jane slumped a little next to me. "I'm sorry. I know you must be worried."

I nodded, abashed when a tear gathered in the corner of my eye and slipped down my cheek. I cared for him, deeply. And yet when he'd said he loved me, I hadn't said it back. Why was that? Because right now the thought of never seeing him again…

"How do you do it, Jane? How do you go every day, not knowing if Jimmy is all right?"

Jane's gaze met Nora's. "It's like that, then? You're not just flirting. You're in love."

I shrugged a little and frowned as guilt piled upon guilt. When you did what we'd done, you were supposed to love each other. Bad enough to do it without being married. But this was worse, wasn't it? "I'm not sure, Jane. But I do care about him very much."

"Oh, Nora."

I bristled at the sympathy and despair in my sister's voice. "What's wrong with that?" I asked, rather sharply.

"It's not bad, exactly." Jane pursed her lips. "It's just that… you're different lately. And different isn't bad, it's just, well, not you. And that worries me. This young woman who runs off for hours at a time, who focuses more on fun and a boy than work and family… that's not who you've ever been." She held up a hand as I tried to speak. "I'm not saying there's anything wrong with some fun or with a little romance. I'm just saying that it's like you've turned into a different person since meeting him, and it's concerning."

I took the criticism to heart. If there was anyone in the world I hated to disappoint, it was my sister. And yet I was a bit angry, too. Why did I always have to be the responsible one? "You know, for a number of years you and Mum worried I would never be interested in marriage. That I'd become one of those 'career girls'. Now that I am interested in a little romance, it seems I can't do that right, either."

Jane sat back, paling at the sharp words. "Nora, can't you see what I'm saying? Until the past few months, you would never have talked to me that way. Please, just be careful." She reached out and took my hand. "I know I got married young and had the girls. But marriage—and Jimmy—were what I always wanted. You always wanted to be more independent and have your own life. I never imagined you could even be silly—"

"Silly?" My irritation flared again. "Jane, I started seeing Alley right around the time I started working at the hospital. I spend my days caring for men who will never be the same again. The things they've done and seen, and the wounds they have that will never heal… It's so hard to watch. It hurts me… here." I pressed my fist to my breast. "Perhaps if I seem silly, it's because I need a little silliness in my life. Please don't criticize me for this. I see more of this war than you and it makes me more determined than ever to actually *live*."

Hurt shone in Jane's eyes. "My husband, my children's father, is over there. Don't tell me about being affected by this war."

She was right, and I sighed and dropped my shoulders. "You're right. I'm sorry. I don't want to argue. You're worried about me, and I know it's because you love me."

Jane's smile was soft. "I do. And if Alley is what you want,

I'm happy for you, Nora. Just make sure it's what *you* really want, and he's the right one."

I got up from the sofa and went to the mantel, shaken. What I really wanted… the right one… I could already feel myself resisting the very idea, just as I always had whenever anyone questioned when I was going to get married and start a family, as if it was the only thing I should aspire to. I looked at my photo, in my nurse's uniform, so proud and confident. I was still that woman. I was still determined to do my part in this war. Still dedicated to nursing and being independent—as independent as a woman was allowed to be in 1917, anyway. That hadn't changed.

"What do you really have against Alley?" I asked, bending to put another stick of birch on the fire, watching the flames lick around a curl of white bark, snapping and sparking in the quiet of the room.

Jane got up, went to stand beside me, and slipped her arm around my waist. "I'm afraid you'll get hurt. This war… It takes our men. It changes them. I know I'm probably overprotective, but Nora, it's only because I love you and want to protect you."

The fight went out of me then. My sister was only concerned because she loved me. There was no way I could be angry with Jane for that.

"I'll be all right," I said, putting my arm around Jane, too. "Until he comes back, I'll be here, working at the hospital. None of us can avoid being hurt, can we? But that doesn't mean we stop living. Would you trade any of your time with Jimmy?"

"Not in a million years," Jane answered. "You know that."

"So we keep on relying on each other. You manage this house, I do my work, and we carry on."

Jane nodded, then rested her head on my shoulder. "That's

the Nora I remember. Steadfast and true. Even from the time you were little. I remember when Mum had Stephen. I was eight and you were seven, and Willie was just two, and Mum was terrible weak after. I was the oldest, but you… you stepped in and told Dad that you would look after Willie so Mum could rest, and you did, too. For a whole week, you looked after our little brother, making sure he ate and stayed out of trouble."

"That's because family is everything," I said softly, and meant it. The story made me miss my brothers and parents something awful. "Just because I've been caught up in the hospital and my time with Alley doesn't mean I've forgotten that, Janie."

"Then you're forgiven for worrying me tonight."

My lips twitched with a smile as affection crowded my heart. "We should say goodnight, then. The girls will be up early, and I'm on nights starting tomorrow."

Jane banked the fire, then the two of us headed toward the stairs together and walked to the second floor, tiptoeing as quietly as we could and avoiding the creaks. But once on the landing Jane reached out and took my arm.

"Are you sure you're all right? You look different tonight."

"I'm fine. It's just finding out that Alley's leaving, is all."

"Well, goodnight, then."

We parted ways, but once I was in my room and in my nightgown, I sat on my bed and tucked my knees in close to my chest.

I hadn't exactly lied. I had a lot of feelings crowding around inside me right now. Love, fear, trying to sort through making love for the first time, as well as everything Jane had said tonight about how I'd changed. I couldn't dismiss the concern, because no one in the world knew me better than my sister. Besides, she'd only voiced what I was already thinking.

The best thing I could do was focus on my duty and my part in the war effort, and maybe not forget tonight ever happened, but leave it behind me. Gram always said that the reason you have eyes in the front of your head was to look to the future, not the past.

But that didn't mean I wasn't going to miss him.

Chapter Three

NORA

December 5, 1917

I hurried to dress in my uniform, dying for warmth now that I was outside the cozy quilts. Jane was up and I heard her adding wood to the fire, but the heat hadn't yet made it up the flue to my bedroom. I fumbled with a few buttons and rubbed my hands together. This was only early December. Come January and February, it was going to be positively frigid in here. I shuddered to think of it.

Blue dress, white apron, stockings, and shoes… all clean and pressed. I frowned into the small mirror as I tucked my hair back, fighting with the natural wave to form my usual roll so I could fix my nursing veil on top. I didn't mind my uniform, not really, but I hated that veil. Hated covering my head in general, if I were being honest. Now that Alley was gone, my social engagements had all but ceased to exist, and now I wore a hat to church on Sundays—if I was off duty—with my best dress and that was all.

My social life hadn't withered just because of his absence, either. I put my hand on my abdomen while nerves clustered in a knot just beneath my ribs. My monthly hadn't come. Not at the end of October, when I'd expected it, nor at the end of November. I was certain now that my night with Alley had left me with his baby. I'd been fairly sure when the middle of November had come around; my courses were never that late. But in the last two weeks, I'd been getting sick, too. And tired. I was so exhausted that I fell into bed at night and had to drag myself upright in the morning.

Work kept me so busy that I'd been able to avoid thinking of it too much, but soon there would come a day when I had to deal with the fact that I was a single woman expecting a baby. My stomach did a slow, sickening roll at the thought of telling Jane, and worse—telling my parents. It had only taken one time. One time of being impulsive and… half drunk and caught up in the moment for things to change irrevocably.

As disappointed as my family would be, I was equally disappointed in myself and devastated by the lack of judgment I'd shown. I was a nurse, for heaven's sake. I knew better and had thrown caution to the wind, thinking it wouldn't happen to me.

"Nora, are you up?" Jane's voice came down the hall. "I could use help with breakfast."

I sighed. Of course. There were two children to feed and breakfast for three big, strapping men to prepare. Jane set a fine table, too. There was usually fresh bread, hot porridge and coffee and, if she could manage it, eggs or bacon. For a little extra on their board, Jane packed the men a sandwich and anything she'd baked that week for a lunch, and at dinner time she managed, again, to somehow prepare dinner for seven.

It was a big job for a woman without a husband home to help her and with many goods rationed, in short supply, or outrageously expensive. Thankfully Jimmy had ensured the family had running water and an indoor bathroom before he'd gone overseas. As cold as my room was in the mornings, it was nowhere near as cold as it would be if I had to use a privy out back. It still felt like a luxury.

"Be right there," I called back, taking a deep breath. My stomach was flat and would be for weeks still, but eventually I would grow rounder and my secret wouldn't be so secret anymore. I gave my uniform one last tug and then put my hands to my hot face. What would Jane say? Would she want an unmarried, pregnant woman under her very respectable roof? Acid burned in my throat as I thought of all the secrets I'd been keeping from my sister, beginning with that night I'd come home from the Queen Hotel.

But there was no time to think of that now. Since I paid less board than the other tenants, it was my duty to help where I could. That often meant kitchen duty, even though I was not a good cook by any stretch of the imagination.

My shoes made dull sounds on the floor as I left my room, leaving the door open so any heat could circulate. The girls were already downstairs. At four years old, Evelyn was big enough to carry plates, so she put them around the table while baby Clara sat in her highchair and played with a few blocks Jane had put on the tray to keep her busy. She threw one off onto the floor and giggled, then grinned a toothy grin when Evelyn picked it up and gave it back. They continued the game while Evelyn put forks around the table, too.

"Morning," I said, smoothing my skirt and stepping into the blessedly warm kitchen. "Sorry I'm late. What can I do?"

"I managed to get some ham yesterday and I'm frying that up, and eggs. Could you start frying the eggs? The boys will be down any minute."

The boys meaning the boarders. I put another apron over my uniform, grabbed a cast-iron pan, and put it on the range. Eggs I could manage without burning them. I added a little fat to the pan—precious bacon grease that we'd saved in a jar—and then started adding eggs, each hitting the pan with a sizzle. One for each of the girls, one for Jane, and two for each of the men.

I saw Jane counting. "None for you today?"

Since cooking them was already making my stomach precarious, I shook my head. "Not today," I said lightly. "Use mine in something special."

"Are you sure? You have a long day ahead."

I nodded. "I'm sure." The idea of eggs made my throat feel strangely thick.

One by one the men came to the kitchen, and for a few minutes there was the comfortable noise of good mornings being spoken and the clatter of cutlery on plates. I swallowed against sudden extra saliva in my mouth when I poured coffee; this too was a scent that seemed to turn my stomach. And I avoided looking at anyone else's plate with bright-yellow, runny yolks. Just the thought was enough to make me want to gag.

"Everything okay, Nora?"

I lifted my head, startled out of my thoughts. "Oh… oh, yes, of course." I smiled and reached for the jam jar. Toast and jam was filling and non-offending.

"You're just very quiet."

I looked around the table. Everyone was staring at me now, so I put down my knife and lifted my chin, pasting on a smile.

"Well, I've got a lot on my mind." I made a point of looking at the little girls across the table, Evelyn in particular, and wiggled my eyebrows. "You know Christmas isn't that far off. I've been thinking about my shopping list for a couple of very good little girls." I was hoping to find them each a new doll. The ones they had now had been mended several times.

"Will Daddy be home for Christmas, Mummy?" This from Evelyn.

"I don't know, sweetheart," Jane answered softly. "But we can pray for the war to be over so he can come home."

Evelyn nodded soberly. "I pray for Daddy every night."

Heavens, the girls were so sweet and loving. I resisted the urge to touch my stomach again, but my heart gave a pang anyway. I wondered what this baby would be like, mine and Alley's. Life was going to be so incredibly complicated. I'd been so swept up in him that night. I bit down on my lip. Now I was half wishing he had proposed. On the back of that thought came anger, because it seemed unfair that the only way to legitimize my pregnancy would be to give up everything I'd worked so hard for.

If he would just write to me, respond to my letters…

Jane had received a letter just this week from Jimmy. I kept looking at the mail and hoping. But there'd been nothing. Nothing since Alley had boarded the *Justicia* in October and left the harbour—and me—behind. Nearly seven weeks now without a single word, even though I'd written each week, sometimes twice, wanting to cheer him with news from home.

"We'll make sure you have a big Christmas tree," said John, one of the boarders who worked as a taxi driver. He looked around at the other men. "Won't we, boys?"

"You bet, Mrs. B," answered Milton. He always called Jane Mrs. B, rather than Boutilier, but Jane never seemed to mind.

Indeed, while Jane was their landlord, it seemed to be an unspoken pact that they'd all look out for her while Jimmy was serving. The third boarder, Harry, merely grinned as he bit into his toast. Harry was a man of few words, but he was the first one to see something that needed doing around the house. When he wasn't working on the docks, he could be found with his tools, fixing this or that.

It wasn't long before the men were up from the table and getting ready to head out for the day. I had to as well, but I had time to help clear the dishes away before the short walk to the hospital.

"Evelyn, go on up to your room now and make your bed," Jane ordered. There was something steely in her tone that put me on edge. The girls noticed it, too, because they gave their mother a wide-eyed look. Evelyn trudged dutifully to the stairs while Clara resumed playing with the crusts of her toast on the highchair tray.

Once they were gone, Jane put down her stack of dishes with a thump and turned to me. "When were you going to tell me?" she asked.

Panic rushed, icy-cold, into my extremities. "Tell you what?"

Jane's gaze was not warm and comforting as she faced me, and I felt the weight of her condemnation. How could Jane possibly know? I'd tried to hide things so well…

"I've had two of my own, Nora. Don't you think I recognize the signs? You're tired. You turn green when faced with certain foods, and"—she lowered her voice—"you haven't had your monthly since earlier in the fall."

I reached out for a chair and sat heavily. "I'd hoped you hadn't noticed."

Jane pulled out another chair and sank into it, her body slumping. "Oh, Nora. Why didn't you come to me? I didn't think it was like that between you two. I should have done something to stop it." Her lip wobbled. "I haven't been a very good big sister."

"Don't say that!" I leaned over and squeezed Jane's hand, heartsick at her distress. "I knew you didn't approve of him. I-I didn't know how to tell you. And then it just… " As Jane's eyes filled with tears, so did mine, blurring the shape of my sister in front of me. "I'm so sorry, Jane. I know I've disappointed you."

Jane squeezed my fingers. "You're my sister. I love you. Besides, it wasn't that I didn't approve of him, exactly. He seemed very charming and entertaining. It just… well, wartime has changed so much. Everything happens so fast, and soldiers leave girls with broken hearts behind. I didn't want you to be one of them."

That just made me cry more, and I reached for my handkerchief to wipe my eyes. "It's not like that. My heart's not broken. It was just one time, and now I'm in such a mess… " Did that make it worse somehow? That I wasn't head over heels in love with him? That I'd given my body to a man before I'd given him my heart? That wasn't the usual order of things, was it? Or at least… not the acceptable order.

"The night you came home late." Jane phrased it as a statement, not a question, her mouth set in a firm line.

"Yes, but… He's a good man… I'm sure he'll marry me when he gets back." My heart sank. Maybe it wouldn't be so bad. It wasn't as if I didn't care for him. I did. We had so much fun together. But a lifetime…

Jane waited for me to finish, then sighed. "Nora, a good man would have married you first. Or… taken precautions. There are ways, you know." Jane sniffled, her lips turned downward.

"I do know." And I'd known better.

"We should have talked about this when you started stepping

out with him, but I kept telling myself that it would be all right. That you were… " She shook her head. "Then when you said he was shipping out, I told myself my worry was for nothing."

I blew my nose. "It's as much my fault as his, Jane. I don't know what to do. I go to work and it distracts me from my own troubles. And when I'm here… I look at your girls and how sweet they are, and I know I'll figure it out somehow."

"Life is awful hard for an unmarried mother, Nora."

I nodded, a tear splashing on my nose. Awful hard, yes. Impossible… maybe. Society looked at unmarried mothers differently than widows or wives whose husbands were serving.

"Does Alley know?"

The wave of nausea came back full force, and I swallowed against it, trying to will it away. "I told him in my last letter. I've written every week since he left, but… but I haven't received one reply." Instead, I'd taken to going downtown to check the casualty boards each day, looking for his name, hoping I wouldn't find it.

Jane reached out and put her hand over mine, giving it a squeeze. "I'm sorry, Nora. I'm sorry he's disappointed you."

"He hasn't!" I leaped to defend him. "Maybe letters aren't getting through."

But I knew that was just wishful thinking on my part. Quiet settled over the kitchen, and then Jane simply said, "Oh, Nora." As if this were the end of everything.

And maybe it was. Jane ran a boarding house… how would this look? Not to mention my enlistment. Nursing sisters weren't married, and they certainly weren't pregnant, either. Would I be dismissed—and disgraced? Would I still be allowed to work at the hospital? What if I had to go back home? The gossip would be horrible… While a part of me cherished the life inside me, I couldn't deny that this was the end of so much I'd worked for.

Oh, how ironic that I had chosen a career over marriage—already flouting the norm for girls my age—and now I wouldn't have either. Underscoring it all was the knowledge that I'd disappointed my sister, the person I most looked up to in the world.

"Mum and Dad are going to be so upset." Yet another thing to worry about.

Jane patted my hand and straightened, her mouth taking on a determined set. "You have time yet, and you're right. We will figure it out, together. You don't need to tell them right away. And you will always have a place here. I promise. I will not turn my sister out, no matter what."

I hadn't realized how much I needed a crumb of encouragement. Just having that bit of support, having someone to share the burden with, felt so much better, and tears of relief stung my eyes.

"But that brings me to something else, Nora. Mum and Dad are coming today. I got a letter from Mum yesterday. They're leaving the boys at home for a few nights and coming into the city. Mum says she wants a visit before the winter weather sets in, so she can pick up a few things for the holidays." Of course. The shopping in Chester was limited and driving up to Halifax made sense, especially when there was family to be seen.

But what normally would be a cause for celebration made cold dread settle in my stomach. "You aren't going to tell them, are you?"

Jane's face flattened with surprise. "Of course not! It's not for me to tell."

I nodded, relieved. "I know I'll have to. I was thinking… maybe if we could get the holidays over with. In the new year. Besides, I might have heard from Alley by then."

"Nora… " Jane began in a halting voice. "I've suspected for a few weeks now, and I've been doing some thinking. God willing, Jimmy will be home soon. We could… we could raise your baby with the girls. As our own. If you wanted."

I sat back in my chair, my mouth open in surprise. The offer was genuine and generous. It wouldn't be the first time a family did such a thing. But how could I hand my baby to my sister to raise and forego my own role of motherhood? How could I watch my child grow and change each day, while keeping such a secret? And yet I knew no one would make a better mother than Jane. I could continue nursing, perhaps. A world of conflicting emotions settled behind my breastbone. I'd been brought up to bear responsibility for my own actions. It would feel like shirking to let Jane take this on. And yet… what if I didn't have to give up the life I loved so quickly?

"I… I know I should say thank you. I'm just so overwhelmed."

"Of course you are. And you don't need to decide now. Just know that the offer is there. I would love him or her as my own, Nora. You must know that."

"Oh heavens, of course I do!" My lip wobbled. "You're a wonderful mother, Jane. I only hope I can be half as loving and patient as you." I looked into Jane's eyes and tried not to feel like I was a failure, tried to push back the shame, but it lodged there, under my ribs, a reminder of how indulging my desires had brought me to this point. "You are the best sister I could ask for. Better than I deserve."

"We're in this together." Jane gave a firm nod. "I won't leave you, Nora. Just you mind that. Don't be scared. We've got a roof over our heads and food on the table and each other. It'd be greedy to ask for more." A pretty smile curved her lips.

"We're rich," I agreed, giving a soft laugh, though it was heavy with emotion. What would I do without my sister?

"All right." Jane clapped her hands on her knees. "Evelyn will be down again soon, and I have so much to do today." She offered a small smile. "Two extra tonight means supper for nine. I'm going out today to see if I can find something good. Mrs. Thompson next door is going to watch the girls for an hour or so."

The older widow had taken a shine to the little girls, and they popped over often. She had a cat that was a brilliant mouser and the girls had taken a real liking to the calico beast.

"Mum and Dad can have my room tonight," I offered, feeling much lighter than I had in weeks. "I can sleep in with the girls."

"Don't be silly. It's too cramped. You can stay in with me." She smiled, her eyes warming. "We can have a sister night like we used to as children. Curl up in the quilts and whisper so we don't keep anyone awake."

Tears gathered in my eyes again—heavens, I was so emotional! "Jane, thank you. For your offer and for not turning me out. For still loving me. I know I've disappointed you. I've disappointed myself." Every time I looked back on that night, it felt like I was viewing a stranger. I was an independent woman, but I'd never been reckless. Not like that.

Jane reached out and held my hands. "You're my sister. I'll always love you and I would never abandon you." She squeezed my fingers. "Besides. Evelyn arrived just shy of nine months after our wedding. I know how easily it can happen. We're living in strange times, Nor, where we feel as if we have to reach out and grab every precious moment because we might not have another."

I thought back to that night, the way he'd smiled at me, the warm burn of the liquor, the feel of his body, knowing the time to his departure was ticking down… and knew that was exactly what I'd done. I'd grabbed onto a moment with both hands. And now I was the one left to deal with the consequences. Frustration burned. Men could do what they wanted. They didn't have to fight for the right to work and vote or even be considered an actual person in the eyes of the law. And men weren't the ones to "get in trouble" and face hardship and social censure when a baby came along, even though they bore half the responsibility.

Then my annoyance dissipated when I remembered that those same men were the ones on the front lines and in the trenches, fighting right now. Dying right now.

Nothing made sense. I simply felt… lost. As if the whole world was topsy-turvy and would never go back to "normal" again.

Sadness flickered in Jane's eyes, but then she let go of me and stood. "You've got to get to the hospital, and I've got things to do before company arrives. I'll see you back here for supper?"

I nodded, anxious to get to work and focus on something else. I was thankful Jane hadn't made a big time about the baby, but there would come a time when this wouldn't be so easy to brush off. How on earth would I manage then?

Chapter Four

CHARLOTTE

December 5, 1917

"Hurry up with them dishes, girl. You're slower than cold molasses."

"Yes, Mrs. Campbell."

I held back a sigh and picked up my speed, wiping the plates from breakfast and stacking them neatly on the shelf while Alice, my fifteen-year-old sister-in-law, slouched at the table, reading a magazine before leaving for school. "You could help, you know," I muttered darkly.

Alice looked up, snorted, and looked down at her magazine again. It was clear as the nose on her face that Alice didn't like me, though she should since my presence meant she was absolved of housework.

Aileen sat in her highchair in the cluttered kitchen, smacking her hands on the surface, but I knew it wouldn't be long and she'd tune up her little lungs and voice her displeasure at being restrained for so long. Keeping her out of the way was necessary, though. She'd just started walking, and her stumbling steps had her bumping into all sorts of things or falling and being vocal about her displeasure. This might be our house, but it certainly didn't feel like *home*.

There was nothing wrong with it, of course. It was like many other houses in the working-class neighbourhood of Richmond: two storeys, adequate construction, warm and dry. But Mrs. Campbell subscribed to the theory that *more* was *better*. A large table and chairs dominated the kitchen, while the parlour was jammed full of little piecrust tables, upholstered chairs, heavy drapes, and one long, tufted sofa that was incredibly uncomfortable. There was barely a space on the wall without a picture or sampler on it. Knick-knacks and crocheted doilies adorned every surface. I knew what my mum would say about it all. She'd say that Mrs. Campbell was putting on airs. Trying to be someone—something—she was not.

That parlour was a hazard to Aileen. How could a child, just walking, not reach and grab at tables and figurines? And then I would be the one to bear the brunt of my mother-in-law's anger. It was better to just keep Aileen out of the parlour as much as possible. Which meant she was under my feet as I hustled to keep the house to my mother-in-law's exacting standards.

It also meant we spent our time either in the kitchen—the warmest room in the house—or our attic bedroom. The coldest. The latter afforded us some privacy. The former meant sharing space with family members, including Alice. That girl was what Frank would have called "slack assed." With six of us living in the house, there was plenty to do, but she never lifted a finger. Instead, she looked at me with this little smirk that told me we would never truly be family. The only time I saw her smile was when Aileen did something particularly cute. And if I caught her at it, her smile was replaced with a scowl so fast, I wasn't sure I hadn't imagined it.

If I'd shown that sort of attitude growing up, I would've been whupped. But Mrs. Campbell was just as bad. The apple didn't fall far from the tree, it seemed. Oddly enough, Frank had always described his little sister as sweet and fun. I wasn't sure what to make of the difference.

As a war widow, living here was the best option for me and my daughter. I loved Aileen to bits. She was the sweetest baby and the single bright light in my life. Living with Frank's parents, however, was an exercise in patience and humility. Most days I was treated like an indentured servant. Frank would have hated this for me. Thinking about him made my heart ache. He had the loveliest wide smile and twinkling eyes, like he was always just about to tell a joke or tease. But those sparkly eyes would never twinkle at me again or see his daughter. Learning he'd died at the Battle of The Somme had taken the earth from beneath my feet. My grief had been soul deep. I'd lost my husband and my best friend, and it was as if someone had reached inside and pulled everything out of my chest, leaving a gaping hole where he used to be.

I was the widow left behind, but I'd been somehow made to feel my pain was self-indulgent. I'd known Frank for less than two years; his family had loved him his whole life. Their message was clear: they had earned their grief. I hadn't. As if time was the sole measure of love, or misery was somehow a competition.

I hung up the drying towel and let out a sigh. Frank's family hadn't liked me from the start and hadn't even tried to hide it. I never quite understood why. I was Catholic, like them, from the same neighbourhood. I wasn't lazy. I always got the impression

Mrs. Campbell thought he could do better; the first thing she'd asked me was who my "people" were, and learning I was an orphan had shown her to be more prejudiced than sympathetic. They hadn't liked that Frank married me in a hurried wedding before shipping out, either. And with smiles pasted on their faces, they'd promised him they'd care for me in his absence, because I was now "family." It soon became clear that "care" meant a roof over my head and little more. What I cost in food I more than made up for in good old elbow grease.

With the dishes finally done, I reached for Aileen and took her out of her chair. The girl lifted her chubby little arms and the love for her inside me bloomed like a spring flower. Honestly, my daughter was the sunny centre of my life. Maybe I suffered from a dearth of affection from my in-laws, but Aileen gave me the unconditional love I craved. The two of us now made a family, even if Frank would never be a part of it.

"Did you sweep the floor?"

The sharp question came from the parlour, where Mrs. Campbell sat, knitting needles clicking. She spent her days knitting socks and rolling bandages, helping the war effort. It was admirable, but it had been made plain as plain that she was doing it in memory of her son and for "them boys over there." All her positive energy went into her causes. None was left for me, her widowed daughter-in-law she'd never wanted.

At least she loved Aileen. I know that's because Aileen is half Frank. Mrs. Campbell could love that half and ignore the fact that her granddaughter was half of me, too.

There was a snicker from Alice, whose head was still stuck in her magazine, though I suspected she wasn't reading as much as trying to be a pest. I ran my free hand down my plain skirt and went to the parlour door, holding Aileen in my arms. "Not yet. I'll do it right away."

Emmeline Campbell put down her knitting and waggled her fingers. "Give the child to me. I'll mind her while you finish your chores." She lifted her chin. "Alice! You get on to school, now." She sighed. "That girl," she grumbled.

Your chores, she'd said. As if I were the hired help, though without the benefit of payment. Indeed, I contributed to the household from what I got from the Patriotic Fund. My widow's portion went directly to Mrs. Campbell for expenses, but I refused to hand over Aileen's smaller portion. I used it as frugally as possible for Aileen's needs and managed to squirrel some away for a rainy day. When I have enough, the two of us will find a place of our own. I'll find a way to support both of us somehow and get out from under Emmeline Campbell's thumb.

I understood what Frank meant when he said he'd joined up to get away from home. The Campbells were not happy people and resorted to blaming others for their misfortunes instead of using any gumption to improve their own lot.

I reluctantly left Aileen in Mrs. Campbell's care, praying that she didn't get into anything she shouldn't in the cluttered parlour. Alice slammed out the door, leaving a trail of dirt from her boots as she left. Then I swept the kitchen floor as quickly as I could and went out onto the front step as well. My breath made white puffs in the clear, cold air, and my fingers stiffened on the handle of the corn broom, but the weather would be much colder in the weeks ahead, once the snow came and stayed for good. It would become more difficult for me to take Aileen out, as well, so once everything was ship-shape, I went back inside to retrieve our coats and mittens for our daily escape.

"I'm going to take Aileen for her walk now," I announced. Getting out of the house for our walk was the only time of day I looked forward to, and I often made it last as long as possible. "If you need anything, I'm happy to pick it up." Wasn't I just the generous, accommodating one? I took another deep breath. Being resentful didn't solve anything, though sometimes I couldn't help it. I might as well offer, because if I didn't, Mrs. Campbell would be sure to mention how I'd been off gallivanting and wasting my time. Running errands during our walks kept the criticism to a minimum.

Mrs. Campbell looked up, her dark eyes flinty. "Need? I need everything, between the rationing and the shortages. But still, better for it to be going to the boys still over there. I'll get you the coupons." She heaved a put-upon sigh and hefted herself up from her chair. "And a little money, but don't waste it and I expect an accounting for every penny." She went to the kitchen and took out a tin can, then withdrew a few dollars, holding it for a moment before giving it to me. "Every penny, you mind."

"Yes, Mrs. Campbell." For heaven's sake. As if I would steal. Besides, some of that money came from me.

In record time I had Aileen bundled up, pulled on my own coat and home-knit mittens I'd made for myself in the fall, and tucked a warm blanket around Aileen in the carriage that had once belonged to the Campbell children. Mr. Campbell and Frank's brother, Joseph, worked at the sugar refinery close to the waterfront. Joseph still stayed in the room he'd shared with Frank, and Alice had the luxury of her own room, which meant Aileen and I were cramped together in the attic, with sloped walls and little light. I put Aileen's crib closest to the brick flue from the woodstove, so she had a little extra warmth as winter approached.

For a fleeting moment, I wondered what my life would be like if I hadn't got pregnant right after the wedding. For one thing, I'd still be working at Dominion Textile, putting in long, hard days. But I'd have my independence, and the circle of friends I'd gained over my years there.

I looked down at my daughter's sweet, pudgy face and toothy grin, and knew I wouldn't trade her for all the independence in the world. Aileen was a blessing and that's all there was to it.

The December air was brisk and cold, and I took a deep, restorative breath and let it out again. The tinge of woodsmoke scented the fresh, salty air from the harbour and the brisk north wind brushed against my cheeks, stinging a little. The air smelled of freedom. I refused to let our situation overshadow the one pleasure I took each day: our walk along the cobbled streets of Halifax, out of the working-class neighbourhood of Richmond and to my favourite view in the whole city. From the slopes of Citadel Hill, I could look out to sea past Georges Island, or in toward The Narrows and the Bedford Basin. Looking down at the grey-blue water and seeing all the ships coming and going made me feel as if the world really was bigger than the claustrophobic existence I led in the plain house on Russell Street.

Aileen was happy to be in the fresh air, and beneath her blanket her legs kicked excitedly as I turned right off Russell and onto Gottingen Street. From there we'd walk straight on toward the Citadel, to stand by the clocktower and watch the ships come and go. I did so the morning after Frank said goodbye, my heart heavy with fear and pain at his leaving, wondering if he'd make it back to me. But there'd been pride, too, that he was stepping up to do his part for king and country. That morning I'd sat for hours, watching the orchestrated activity on the water, trying not to think of the future, or even what waited for me at home. Now, even though Frank was gone, the grey fortress on the hill still made me feel somehow safe and strong. Like life was bigger than my little corner of it. That someday, my life might be more than it was at that moment.

I'd been over the moon with happiness when he proposed.

We'd talked about the future, and what we were going to do after the war was over. We'd have our own house and raise our little family. I wouldn't have to work at the factory, and he'd come home to me each night where we could whisper to each other in the dark after the children were in bed. We didn't want much—just our family and a little security.

That dream had sustained us, until it disappeared somewhere in France.

Aileen and I reached our destination, and I lifted my daughter out of the carriage, cradling her on my arm. "See out there, Leenie? Your daddy went away on one of those ships. He was a hero." I pointed toward the harbour, where the dark-grey Navy ships were docked. Supply and relief ships dotted the water, too, in addition to the regular port traffic. Over the past months we'd seen hospital ships return as well, with big red crosses painted on their sides to ensure safe passage. Wounded soldiers returning home...

Bittersweet grief pierced my heart. I'd have been more than happy to welcome a wounded Frank home rather than no Frank at all. A piece of my heart was missing without him. "He was the best man I ever knew," I whispered to her, "and he loves you, wherever he is."

Aileen patted my face with her little mitten. "Bah bah."

"Papa," I said, kissing the mitten and vowing that Aileen would always know she'd had a father who loved her.

"Bah bah."

The port was doing a brisk business this morning, with tugs and ships dancing through the harbour, following protocols with the precision of a ballet. Two blasts echoed on the air; what looked like a supply ship adjusted its course to cede the right of way. Frank had once said proudly that he thought the harbour pilots in Halifax were the best in the world, to guide all that traffic without incident.

Frank. It had been over a year since his death, and still he occupied my every thought. How a man as loving and kind and funny had come out of the Campbell house was a complete mystery to me. The only thing I could fathom was that he'd had good friends to balance out the sombre home life. From what I could tell, Mrs. Campbell was miserable and wanted everyone else to be as well. I'd since come to the conclusion that Mrs. Campbell and Mr. Campbell did not love each other, so marriage was a trial rather than a blessing. How sad! Mr. Campbell didn't speak at dinner, and the children were brought up under the old adage that they should be seen and not heard. There were no fun nights playing cards at the kitchen table, or much laughing at all. It was utterly different from my own upbringing, and not how I wanted Aileen to be raised. She deserved to be brought up surrounded by love and laughter.

Aileen began to fuss, so I put her back in the carriage and we continued our walk. We headed down the hill a little, a few blocks closer to the waterfront, then turned left to head back toward Richmond again. All the businesses and shops were busy, bells above doors jingling merrily in the clear air. Christmas would soon be upon us, and I thought of the presents I wanted to buy for Aileen. She was old enough for a little doll, perhaps, and I'd saved bits and pieces of fabric and yarn to make her some new clothes.

Conversations blossomed around us, and I momentarily felt on the outside, distanced from everything happening in my own city. Before Aileen, I'd worked at the textile factory. It hadn't been a glamorous job, but I'd made ends meet, and it had kept me fed and housed since I'd turned eighteen and had suddenly become orphaned. The other women at the factory had become my surrogate family until Frank came along. I still missed them. We often caught up on Sundays at St. Joseph's for mass, but only for a few moments. I was expected to sit with my husband's family, not with friends.

I'd brought up the topic of going back to work a few months ago, half-hoping that my mother-in-law would offer to watch Aileen for a portion of my wages. It wasn't that I particularly wanted to go out to work; I loved being home with Aileen. But it was about finding the means to set up our own household. Mrs. Campbell had looked at me over her glasses and insisted that a woman's place was in the home looking after her family. It was immediately apparent that to Mrs. Campbell, looking after my "family" meant being at my in-laws' beck and call. She'd been so sharp about it that Alice had actually winced in sympathy, one of the few moments of solidarity we ever shared.

The carriage bumped its way back to the north end and once we were back in Richmond, we made a stop at Upham's General Store, where I was able to procure a dubious cut of steak and some bacon, then the ubiquitous potatoes and some onions. I'd be able to cook the beef in a rich gravy with onions to make it tender and more importantly, make it stretch to feed all six of us. I had a little of Mrs. Campbell's money left so I added a turnip and a small bit of cheese. Constant Upham himself wrote up my receipt and I paid with cash—the Campbells refused to use store credit.

"We're going to have a feast tonight," I said to Aileen as we strolled along, the items tucked into the cloth bag I took each day for just this reason. "There might even be a little sugar left for me to make something sweet for dessert." I had to take the bright spots where I could find them. I'd lived in a boarding house for three years before we got married, and I did like having the run of the kitchen. Mrs. Campbell would find something to complain about, naturally, but I ignored her. I knew I could cook.

On our return to the house on Russell Street, I passed by my old address. My childhood home had been torn down after the fire, a new one built in its place with a new family living in it. I faced it with a lump in my throat, just the same. So many memories were buried here in the ash beneath the new house. So many hopes and dreams, and so much love.

I hadn't been home when the house caught fire. I'd spent the night at a friend's as a treat to celebrate her birthday. It was likely the only reason I was alive, as the fire had burned fast and hot. Sometimes I could still smell the singed, sharp scent of the ashes left behind. Everything I had known and loved had lived in that house, suddenly gone and I was left alone.

My memories of that time were piecemeal and felt… random. For a while I was numb. I wondered if I could have saved them if I'd been home instead of having fun; then alternately wondered if I would have died too. I remember crying for my cat more than my parents. Thinking about my clothes hanging in the small closet in my room. The smell of my father's shaving soap, the taste of my mother's molasses cookies. My friend's family took me in until I turned eighteen; a collection was taken up at the church and I was given charity. But through it all it was like half of me had been ripped away and I didn't know how to go on. I just went through the motions. I existed, but I wasn't alive.

But then I'd found Frank…

"Oh, Mum," I whispered. "I wish you were here now, to see Aileen, to give me a hug and let me know it's all going to be all right."

Maybe my memories of the fire were fragmented, but the ones of my childhood were not. My home had been as different from Frank's as sun was from rain. An abundance of love, rather than criticism. Fewer things, but more warmth and affection. Whenever my thoughts about the future were bleak, I just remembered my mum's warm smile and how she'd made our home such a comfort. I was determined to do the same for Aileen, come hell or high water.

I still missed them, though. I missed them, and I missed Frank with an intensity that stole my breath. He was my sun and my moon, and if it weren't for our daughter, I would have been plunged into darkness.

I'd been standing there so long that Aileen started to babble, so I let out a breath and smiled at the sweetest sound in the world—the sound that gave me a reason to keep going each day. As long as I had my baby, I'd be fine. The two of us could face anything… as long as we were together.

Chapter Five

NORA

December 6, 1917, 6:32 a.m.

I scrubbed my face and gave my hair a glance. What I wouldn't give for a hot bath, but that would have to wait. With seven of us in the house, hot water was dear. Right now, Jane needed help with breakfast. There were two extra mouths this morning, and a busy day ahead for everyone.

Jane had just gone down to get the fire going again, leaving me to dress in the cold and dark. Last night she had put on a beautiful meal, even with some items in short supply. She'd made a huge pot of baked beans and a batch of still-warm brown bread for dinner, and then treated us to a rare dessert of gingerbread with fresh whipped cream—a real extravagance. It had been wonderful having Mum and Dad visit, or would have been wonderful, except all I could think about was telling them about the baby and imagining the look of dismay and censure on their faces. Jane had sent me encouraging smiles all evening, but by the time we'd fallen into bed and huddled under the quilts, I let out a sigh and Jane turned over and gave me a hug in the dark.

"We will figure something out, Nora. I promise. If I can run this boarding house without Jimmy, then together we can get through."

"I don't deserve you, Jane," I whispered.

"You're not the first girl to get caught, and certainly not the first in this war." Jane's voice was hushed but firm. "Though I agree about waiting to tell Mum and Dad until after the holidays." She gave me a supportive squeeze. "They're planning on coming back with the boys and we'll have a full house on Christmas morning. Won't that be nice? And by then, maybe you'll have had a letter from Alley. Maybe you two can come up with a plan. Have some faith, Nora."

"What if he doesn't write?" I asked, and then voiced the nagging fear that had been plaguing me for the last few weeks. "What if he never meant to write at all? What if he just… got what he wanted, and left?" I didn't want to think I'd been that gullible, or that Alley had been that callous. But his silence spoke volumes. I didn't want to be tied down, either, but I couldn't just pretend my predicament didn't exist.

"Oh, Nora." Jane's hand reached out and smoothed my hair in the dark, the touch gentle and reassuring. "Don't you worry about that yet. He did say he loved you, didn't he? Hold onto that. I'm sure he'll marry you." She gave my hand another reassuring squeeze. "Instead of worrying, why don't we start planning your wedding in secret? Like we used to as girls. You could be married at home, in Chester. Wouldn't that be nice?"

Yes, but when we'd playacted, it had always been Jane

playing the bride. She'd wanted nothing more than to get married and start her own household. That wasn't my ambition. In an odd way, Jane's switch from despair to optimism caused me more worry, not less. Jane was trying to make a silk purse out of a sow's ear here, and it felt a little… desperate. My options were limited, and we both knew it. Jane wanted to plan an imaginary wedding, but what I really wanted was to not have got pregnant in the first place. I wanted my independence. To be a nurse. Maybe, if I dared, go on to medical school. Those dreams died the moment I realized I was carrying a baby. I was one of those "modern" girls, I supposed, and the term wasn't usually said in a complimentary way.

As I finished dressing in my uniform, doubts crept in again. I prided myself on being a smart woman. Strong and determined. I couldn't have accomplished everything I had in the past few years if I weren't. I wasn't feeling so strong these days, though, and Alley's continued silence only fed into my fears. I couldn't get Jane's offer out of my mind. Could I actually do it, and live with that decision if I got to keep my independence and career? Could I let my sister raise my child as her own? Or would my conscience prick me every time I heard my own child call me "Aunt"?

That was a worry for another day; right now, I had responsibilities to face. When I entered the kitchen, I discovered Jane had put a pot on for porridge, something cheap and easy that would feed the nine of us for breakfast. We bustled around and were soon joined by our mother, Maggie, who greeted us with a warm smile. "It's so good to see my girls again. Look at you both. You're lovely, strong women and I'm so proud of you."

Her words made the guilt in my heart that much heavier.

"What are your plans for the day?" I asked, getting out bowls for the meal. I did a quick sidestep to avoid bumping into

Evelyn, who'd run downstairs at the sound of her grammie's voice.

"We're going down to the waterfront this morning," Mum answered, a hint of excitement creeping into her words. "Your father wants to see all the ships in the harbour. Then a little shopping and we're going to treat Jane to lunch. Do you want to join us, Nora?"

I wished I could. It sounded like a lovely morning. "I'm sorry, Mum. I'm due at the hospital."

"I'll go, Grammie!" Evelyn popped up and looked at her grandmother with dancing eyes.

"Oh, that would be lovely, dear. But how can I find your Christmas present if you're with me? I heard you're visiting with the lovely lady next door today. Your mummy told me she has a cat?"

The only thing more enticing than a rare meal at a restaurant was the idea of Christmas. Evelyn chattered away about the cat, Buttons, and moved on to what she hoped to get for Christmas, and then there was a clumping of boots as the men came down to breakfast. There was a lot of talk and laughter around the table as Jane served hearty porridge and fresh cream, and I sat back for a moment and soaked it all in. This was my family, too. Not just my parents and sister, but my nieces, and even the men who boarded here. When breakfast was over, one of them headed outside to bring in more wood for the day. Jane didn't even have to ask. The boarders were protective of Jane and the girls and of me, too. Would they still be that way when the truth came out? Would they even still want to live here? How could I do that to Jane, when she relied on the extra money to make ends meet?

Before I could change my mind, I excused myself to go upstairs. It only took a moment to retrieve pen and paper, and I sat down and wrote a brief but emotional appeal to Alley, one more plea that he write back, tell me what I should do about our baby. The more I thought about it, the more I realized there were only two options. I could marry Alley when he returned, or I could let Jane raise the baby and work to provide for him or her. In this day and age, the very idea of raising an illegitimate baby on my own was impossible. How could I work with a small child at home, and would I even get hired in the first place? Even if I had my family's support, there'd be so much gossip and humiliation. I could just imagine the curtain twitchers back in Chester, peeking out from behind their drapes and whispering about that loose Crowell girl who got herself in trouble.

There was no hope of marriage now for months. But if Alley were to write back, if he were to just write the words that he would make us a family when he returned, I could bear the difficult months ahead. I did care about him. We got along like a house on fire. Maybe marriage wouldn't be so bad… The thought threatened to overwhelm me again, so I folded the letter and addressed it, then hurried downstairs and cornered Jane in the pantry.

"Jane, will you mail a letter for me this morning?"

Jane looked up, startled. "Of course, I will. Is it…?"

"Yes." I looked over my shoulder, not wanting to be overheard. "About the baby," I whispered.

Jane tucked the letter in her skirt pocket and gave it a pat. "Of course, I'll mail it. Don't you worry. You've been a bag of nerves about this, I can tell."

I gave a small smile and tried to sound more positive than I felt. "It's knocked me for a loop, but we'll figure it out. About what you said yesterday… about raising the baby…" I let the thought hang, still unsure.

"I meant it," Jane said firmly. "We can talk about it later.

You've got to get going or you'll be late for your shift. I'll see you at supper tonight."

"Have fun with Mum and Dad. I wish I could go with you." I gave my sister a quick hug, then went to get my heavy coat to bundle up. It was a clear day, but a Nova Scotia December always held a chill, the winter air the raw sort that seemed to cut right into the bones.

After saying a hurried goodbye to my parents and the girls, I made my way down Morris Street with quick steps. Regardless of my rush, I was going to be a few minutes late and hoped I wouldn't get in trouble with the matron for my tardiness.

There was no time to waste when I arrived. I went straight to my duties, attending to the wounded. Some of my job I didn't enjoy—like bedpan duty. But other things were so fulfilling. I had a gentle but firm touch, and I changed dressings and tended wounds with a steady but kind hand. Sometimes what was truly needed was a soft voice and a hand squeeze—compassion. Sometimes it was reading a letter from a loved one—or writing one. There were times, though, that I wished I were a doctor and could do some of the more complex medical procedures that intrigued me. Occasionally I'd been able to assist the doctors with the more challenging cases and I'd found it utterly fascinating. But I wouldn't complain; I had a fine job in a brand-new hospital, and I was doing my part for the war effort. There was a lot to be said for that.

It felt like I'd only been working for a short time when I heard a commotion from a cluster of nurses. Since Alley's departure, I'd stopped engaging in those fun and frivolous conversations with the other girls. At first, I'd been a bit melancholy, missing the fun distraction he provided, and then after I discovered I was pregnant, I'd felt… well, set apart. I certainly couldn't tell them the truth, but the idea of gaily taking off to socials and outings as if I weren't burdened with this secret poked at my conscience. I'd be lying if I said I didn't miss the laughs and camaraderie desperately. This group of women… we were a community. We were working women, we were nurses. We saw the devastating effects of war first-hand and that was something no one else could understand. Because of one lapse of judgment, I'd removed myself from that sisterhood.

Today I found I needed it. Maybe it was all the talk about the baby and feeling like everything was about to change, but their excited voices were like the beacon of a lighthouse, showing me the way to safety.

I tidied the bowl I'd been using to clean a leg wound and washed my hands, then went over to see what the fuss was about.

"And it's on fire! Oh, I wish we could go see! Nothing exciting happens up here!"

"What's happened?" I asked, leaning into the group.

Jessie Smiley gestured with her hands as she replied. "We just heard from one of the delivery men. There was an accident in The Narrows. One ship going out, one coming in, and both determined to keep their course, apparently. The waterfront is crowded with people watching. They say the crew has left the boat. If they've left it, who's going to steer it and fight the fire? And here we are, stuck up here. We miss out on all the fun." She affected a pout.

I felt a renewed jealousy for my sister's day of shopping with our folks. They were probably down by the docks right now, watching the excitement. Dad would be sure to have a fine story to tell the boys when he returned home. Longing filled me. Our times together these days were so few.

"I'm sure it'll be fine," I replied, straightening my apron. "Listen, girls, my parents are visiting tonight, but do any of you want to do something tomorrow night?" Tomorrow was Friday and there was bound to be something on. "I feel like I haven't been out in ages."

"Not since your Alley-cat left," said Joan, one of the nurses I'd studied with at the Victoria General Hospital. She gave me a wink. "It's about time you stopped moping. I'm sure we can scare up a little bit of trouble."

Joan didn't really mean trouble. She was a nice girl with a jolly laugh, but a devilish gleam in her eye now and then. "I'd like that." I wiggled my eyebrows. "You still seein' that Corporal, Joan?"

Joan laughed. "That boy is too struck on himself. Hardly a bit o' hair and he spends more time on it than I do." She gave her hair a mock bob with her hand. "I have a rule, Nora. I can't go out with a guy who's prettier than me."

We all laughed.

Another nurse, Irene, squeezed my arm. "Girls? What do you say? Nora's ready to stop wallowing over her handsome soldier. Shall we take her out tomorrow night? There's bound to be a social happening somewhere. Where's the best dancing? And by best dancing, I mean the best place to find good partners."

We were just discussing possibilities when my chest cramped, and I couldn't breathe. There was something… like all the air had been sucked out of the room. It was a horrible, heavy sensation that something was terribly wrong.

When the air came rushing back, it was unleashed with an unbridled fury and boom that threw me to the floor. Glass shattered and steel pans and instruments went flying, while people were thrown off their feet and beds by the impact.

Instinctively I covered my head with my hands as supplies and shelves toppled, landing with a deafening crash. Cries of terror and breaking glass filled the dusty air. But once everything stopped, the deafening silence was worse than the commotion, as if something had irrevocably changed. I gingerly moved my hands off my neck and ran them down my body, making sure I didn't have any cuts from the broken glass.

"Nurse Crowell. Nurse Crowell, are you all right?"

The voice sounded far away, as if I had cotton in my ears. I had to get up, didn't I? But I couldn't seem to make my arms and legs work as they should. What had happened? Fear crowded my chest. Had we been bombed? Had the Germans come here, all the way across the Atlantic?

The room spun as firm hands helped me up and guided me to a chair. "There we go. Nice and easy. Are you hurt anywhere?"

I shook my head. "No. Just…" I put my hand on my diaphragm. "Breathe."

"You've had the wind knocked out of you." I recognized Matron Cotton's voice now, firm and comforting in its practicality. "Give it time and your breath will come back. Let me check you for cuts."

My head swam, but I was finally able to focus my gaze on the matron's face. I held out my hands and the matron did a quick examination. "Very good. Take a moment now, Nurse Crowell, but only a moment. We're about to get very busy."

"Were we bombed?" The words caught in my throat, fearful and incredulous. This was *Halifax*. And yet there was a reason for all the fortifications around the city and harbour…

"I don't know, Nurse Crowell. But our patients need us now. And more will be at our door within minutes. That I know for sure."

The matron kindly pressed a cup of water into my hands. It was only after I'd taken the first sip that I looked up and finally understood what was happening around me.

The hospital was in chaos. Soldiers who had been on the

battlefield were panicked and needed settling. Beds were overturned, mattresses tumbled and needed to be righted. Broken glass and fallen items littered the floors. One of the nurses I'd just been chatting to—Irene—stumbled by with a bloody dressing pressed to her head, needing medical attention. Others—doctors and nurses—scrambled around, either barking or following orders, trying to create calm out of the pandemonium.

"We must prepare," the matron said loudly. "Many of the injured will come here, and we will be ready," she decreed, as if any other outcome was unthinkable. Matron continued handing out orders, her time served overseas in the clearing hospital holding her in good stead. Nurses scrambled to fulfill their duties. I finally stood on shaky legs, took a deep breath, and placed a hand on my stomach.

I'd been thrown to the floor most violently. Was there a chance the impact had hurt the baby? For a brief moment, I thought maybe it would solve all my problems. And then in the very next second, I shook my head. Wrong or right, I wanted this baby. Even with all the trouble it was bound to cause, I didn't want anything to happen to him or her. The protective feeling was so new and strange, I wasn't sure what to do with it.

"Nurse Crowell! Get moving!"

I jumped to attention and hurried to help one of the orderlies right a row of beds, shoving the mattresses back onto the metal frames. We worked to get the men settled again, handling them gently but efficiently, knowing time was of the essence. Private Doucette looked at me with wild eyes. I said his name three times and gave him a gentle shake before his gaze cleared and he was able to focus on me. "Private, please go back to your bed. You're safe." I hoped it wasn't a lie. When I was assured he was fine, I moved on to the next... and the next... trying to bring some organization to the ward. When I got to Corporal Jenkins, I put a calming hand on his arm, knowing he was prone to panic and that sometimes a gentle touch helped anchor him. "Corporal," I said, trying to be gentle but having to raise my voice over the commotion. "Corporal Jenkins, you need to get back into bed."

His eyes were panicked, his muscles corded with tension. He'd been pacing, his limp noticeable. My heart ached for the men who carried the effects of the battlefield home with them, but there was little time to waste. "Corporal, look at me! It's Nurse Crowell."

His dark eyes met mine. "Breathe," I ordered. "You must breathe. Slowly, in and out."

He nodded, rapid shakes of his head, but in a few moments his chest rose and fell a little more regularly. "Corporal Jenkins, you must get back in bed. I know you're frightened, but there are new patients arriving that desperately need my help."

He gripped my fingers so tightly it was painful, and I thought I might have bruises on the tops of my hands later. I waited half a heartbeat, and then he nodded again.

"I have to do something," he said. The wound on his leg was improving, though I suspected he'd always walk with a limp. Right now, he was waiting to have a piece of shrapnel removed from near his hip, which caused him regular pain. "Please," he said, more forceful. "Let me help. It's better than watching."

I understood that. Keeping busy kept one from thinking too much—wasn't I guilty of losing myself in my work so I didn't have to think about my troubles? I gave a brusque nod and beckoned to an orderly. "Corporal Jenkins wishes to be of some use," I said. "If there's anything he can do to help, give him orders." If what Matron said was true, we could use all the help we could get.

I darted away before either man could respond, but when I

looked back a few minutes later, I saw Jenkins following the orderly. His limp was pronounced, but he was moving with purpose and determination.

Hammond was sitting on his bed, blank gaze forward, body rigid as if paralyzed. My heart ached for him, knowing he'd disappeared to somewhere else in time. There was nothing I could do for him right now, even if I wanted to, for the first of the wounded had started to arrive.

I stared at the bodies coming in the door. They were covered with dust and dirt and blood, and their faces… oh, their faces. For the first time in my life, I truly understood what terror looked like through the eyes of another. They were the walking wounded, and they were everywhere.

"It had to be the boat in the harbour," one of the doctors said as he passed by my shoulder. "Oh, God. The docks… we need to prepare for so many casualties."

I froze as dread and fear raced down my body in a cold, electrifying line, threatening to weaken me at the knees. The docks would have been crowded with workers and with Haligonians going about their day. Jane was down there. My parents were down there. My God. *Clara* was down there. Jane had said Clara was too much for Mrs. Thompson today and took her with them… My whole family. Had they been watching the ships? Were they safe? The urge to run and find them was overwhelming. What if they were dead? What if they were hurt and needed my help? I had to… I had to…

"Nurse? Nurse!"

I jumped at the sharp yell. I couldn't think about them now. There were wounded here. Mothers and fathers, daughters and sons. And they were relying on me. I shook my head and pushed myself into the fray.

Within minutes, the hospital was overrun.

Chapter Six

CHARLOTTE

December 6, 1917, 8:22 a.m.

Mrs. Campbell was in rare form this morning.

I had already fed the family, washed the dishes, and made all the beds, all while trying to keep an eye on my increasingly mobile daughter. It wasn't like Alice was any help. The Campbells were not well off, but honestly, the two women acted as if they were above any sort of manual labour. What on earth had they done before I arrived? They certainly hadn't been able to afford household help. And they definitely enjoyed having me there to take the menial duties off their hands so they could act like "fine ladies". Alice didn't even need to be off to school for another hour, but today she'd taken her things and met her friends rather than staying and helping—or even simply picking up after herself. She was in great danger of becoming a spoiled brat. But then, if I had a chance to escape her mother, I'd likely take it too. That woman was a pill.

"Charlotte," came her whiny voice, "you need to return to Upham's this morning. Why you only got enough meat for last night's supper is beyond me."

I rolled my eyes as I reached for my coat. Ah, the ever-present criticism. Maybe if Mrs. Campbell had given me adequate coupons and money, I might have been able to procure more than the tough cut of steak for last night. Even my cooking skills hadn't been able to make the gristle palatable. But I held my tongue—something I was getting used to doing. I'd learned from experience that nothing good would come from being sharp in return. Or as my mum would say, it's an ill wind that blows no good. If I gave Mrs. Campbell any lip, guaranteed it would come back to me in spades.

Mrs. Campbell huffed her way into the kitchen just as Aileen started to wail, protesting about the mittens I was trying to shove onto her hands. "Gracious, can't you keep the child from screaming like a banshee? I swear you have no mothering instincts at all."

Most of my mother-in-law's comments rolled off me like water off a duck's back, but this one cut deeply. Everything I did was for Aileen, and my one joy in life was trying to be the best mother I could. I bit my tongue yet again and snatched the money from Mrs. Campbell, tucking it away. I didn't trust myself to say anything, so instead I sailed out the door with Aileen on my arm, grabbed the carriage, and made a quick business of tucking my daughter inside and setting off down the street at a punishing pace. The further I could get away from that house, the better. One of these days I'd take my savings and leave—never to return.

Guilt crept through me, though, at the thought. As much as I disliked Frank's family, and they disliked me, Aileen was all they had left of their son. It didn't feel right to think about depriving them of a relationship with her, no matter how surly they were.

Maybe "never to return" was a bit too far. Maybe a visit now and again… but the fact remained that I was looking forward to the day I could finally get out from beneath that woman's thumb and have a place of my own.

I let out a huge breath, trying to shake off my resentment. Aileen had stopped crying now and was far more contented in the fresh air and the change of scenery as we followed our usual route. I rolled my shoulders, determined to leave the toxic home environment behind and enjoy this daily respite.

The atmosphere was different today somehow. There was an energy in the air that felt pulled tight like a string, as if the city collectively sensed something big was about to happen. Good news, perhaps, from the front? Maybe we could make our way down to the waterfront and catch any news or gossip, or at the very least get today's *Chronicle*. There was more foot traffic than usual, too, and clusters of people stood on street corners, facing the harbour and pointing. By the time I got to the corner of Gottingen and Cornwallis, there were more people looking toward The Narrows and pointing than actually walking. Perhaps a big ship had arrived, carrying more wounded soldiers, or maybe even a German vessel had been captured! We could certainly use some good news.

"Pardon me," I said to a cluster of ladies who were talking animatedly, "but what's all the commotion this morning? Has something happened?"

"There was a collision in The Narrows," one woman explained, her face bright with excitement. "And now one of the ships is on fire!"

"But another ship is out there trying to fight it, see?" The second woman pointed toward the activity on the water.

I looked out toward The Narrows, the area where the harbour narrowed like the curve of a woman's waist before emptying into the broader Bedford Basin. The basin had proved to be the perfect place for ships to wait safely until they were ready to head out to sea, crossing the Atlantic in the protection of convoys. But this morning, safety seemed elusive as a ship—I couldn't make out the name on the side—burned, little explosions bursting into the air at random intervals, rather like fireworks. While crew from another ship attempted to put out the blaze, the ship on fire kept drifting closer to the pier. "They won't let the boat hit the pier, will they?" I asked, worried. There were dozens of dock workers down there, and a burning boat with no one at the helm was a dangerous thing.

"I don't know," answered another woman. "My husband is down there, working at Pier 6. I wish I could ask him what's happening." She looked at me, concern lurking behind her polite smile. "I'm Mrs. Abbot. These are my neighbours, Mrs. Langille and Mrs. Morrison. We all live just here"—she pointed behind her—"on Charles Street."

"Mrs. Campbell," I answered, holding out my hand. "Pleased to meet you all. I've seen you at St. Joseph's, I believe."

"Yes, that's right," Mrs. Langille said with a smile. "I used to see you at some of the social events." She looked down at the carriage. "Looks like maybe you have your hands busy these days. Congratulations. She's beautiful."

I swallowed against the lump forming in my throat. "I haven't felt much like dancing," I admitted. "My husband was killed at The Somme."

"Oh, I'm so sorry, my dear." Mrs. Abbot's face softened. "If you need anything, the ladies at the church are very good at providing support." She reached out and squeezed my arm. "And friendship. We have a little knitting circle right now to make things for the soldiers. There's always room for one more."

The invitation touched me. It was true; I'd been horribly lonely since Frank left for France. Maybe I'd take her up on her offer. If my mother-in-law—my warden—considered it appropriate. Which really meant as long as it didn't inconvenience her.

Mrs. Langille nodded. "We're going to walk down a little closer. Would you and your little one like to join us?"

I considered for a moment. The friendly overtures were so very welcome, since I felt increasingly isolated these days. But what I really wanted was to go to my usual perch and get a better view from farther up. "I must get on my way, but thank you. It was nice to meet you. I'll think about joining you on Sunday. It was so nice of you to offer."

I gave a nod and a smile and started walking again, listening to Aileen babble in the carriage. Every few steps I stopped and looked over my shoulder toward the activity on the water. Unease settled over my body, heavy and disturbing. Haligonians were treating this as some sort of entertainment, but it was dangerous too, wasn't it? There were men trying to put out the fire, men trying to keep the docks safe and undamaged. And while the little explosions seemed to delight others, I couldn't help but wonder what was causing it. What was the ship even carrying for cargo that would create such a flurry of flashes?

I hurried along. It was nearly nine and Mrs. Campbell would expect me home shortly after ten, and I still had to stop at Upham's. Perhaps tonight Mr. Campbell and his son would be able to tell us more about the accident. They were close to the action, after all, down at the sugar refinery. And soon I'd have a perfect view from the Citadel.

Aileen grumbled, and I stopped for a moment to peek down into the carriage and offer a soothing reassurance that we would be able to see all the ships in the harbour in just a few minutes.

I'd just straightened when the world fell silent, then a rumble shuddered beneath my feet and a terrible force pressed on my body, the blunt punch of it delivering me into blackness.

Chapter Seven

NORA

The wounded never stopped coming.

I finished bandaging a gash on a woman's arm and let out a breath as I looked up for the first time in what felt like hours. What I saw defied belief, yet I knew it must be true because I was seeing it with my own eyes. Any earlier thoughts about wanting to be serving closer to the front seemed laughable as I stared at the broken bodies around me. Men with haunted eyes. Women carrying children—God, the children. A numbness descended over me at the sight of them all, as if my brain couldn't quite believe what it was seeing. I needed that curtain of distance, I realized, to do my job. To focus on the injury and not the person behind it.

The victims crowded the portico entry that faced Summer Street, a horde of walking wounded coated in dirt, oil, and blood. The tang of it was acrid and unfamiliar, and for a moment I turned my head and pressed my nose into my shoulder, drawing in the fading scent of fresh laundry and starch from my uniform. Smells were a sensitive spot for me, but I had to put aside my peculiarities and deal with what was in front of me: people in desperate need of help. I sent the woman on her way—thankfully her injuries had been minor—and stood, stretching, preparing for my next patient, ignoring my own discomforts. My back and feet ached, and I could use a trip to the lavatory, but those were minor considerations.

Stretcher-bearers never stopped bringing the wounded who had injuries too serious for them to walk. Some of the staff doctors were triaging, the others, along with the nursing sisters, tried to keep a sense of organization in the middle of the chaos. Any ambulatory soldiers had now given up their beds for the wounded, but it would never be enough. Each of the hospital pavilions was going to be crammed with patients as the convalescent hospital transitioned into one of primary treatment. The more serious cases were taken to makeshift surgeries; others wouldn't survive and were made as comfortable as possible. I'd spent the last three hours carefully plucking splinters and glass, cleaning and disinfecting wounds and bandaging them up as efficiently as possible. Hadn't I just been wishing for more complicated cases? Dear Lord, not this way.

I moved on to the next patient. I had to, because if I stopped for a moment my thoughts would shift to my mother, father, sister, niece. Even Harry, who had left for the docks early this morning. The boarders. I hadn't stepped outside, so I didn't know if the house on Henry Street was even still standing or not. All I knew was that other than a few blown-out windows, Camp Hill had remained structurally unscathed, and I had a job to do.

"Here now," I said gently, guiding a man to a chair. "You have a sit down right here, sir. We're going to get that bandaged up nice and neat."

The man stared at me with vacant eyes. "My wife…"

My throat tightened. The one downside to working with minor wounds was that the patients were conscious, and they were in shock and grieving. The fear and confusion came off them in waves, rolling over me and weakening my own defences. I prided myself on being compassionate and comforting, but today those qualities failed me. I had no platitudes to offer; if the patients were any indication of what was outside, there was no way I could guarantee anyone was surely alive and that they'd find each other soon. A sharp cry filled the air from somewhere to my left; I flinched at the haunting sound and then straightened my shoulders, bracing myself against feeling any more emotions. "There now," I said as softly as possible through the din. "We're going to get you fixed up, right as rain."

I began removing the splinters and glass. There was a particularly large splinter in his neck; I probed around it with careful fingers, ensuring it hadn't hit an artery before carefully removing it with tweezers. His wool coat had kept the shrapnel from piercing his torso, thankfully, but there was a shard of glass in his thigh that was worrisome. It was deep and long enough that it would require stitching, and I called for a doctor.

He gave the wound a cursory examination and looked me dead in the eye. "Can you suture, Nurse?"

I nodded hastily, surprised. This particular doctor was one of the worst for making me feel I needed to be kept in my place. Today, though, it was all hands on deck. I knew how to suture. There wasn't much call for it in my current assignment, but I was deft with a needle and thread and confident in my abilities. "I can, sir."

"Then do it."

I knew without him saying so that suturing would spare the

doctors for more crucial cases. He rushed away with long strides, leaving me with my patient.

I removed the glass, cleaned the wound thoroughly, and prepared to stitch.

The needle was threaded and in the needle holder and I took a breath, let it out, and prayed for steady fingers. It had been a long time since I'd practiced, and certainly not in a situation such as this. With forceps, I lifted the edge of the wound slightly and slid the needle through the flesh, feeling the resistance up the instrument to my fingertips, and I swallowed thickly. Then I pierced the other edge, pulling the thread through until there was a small tail out of the first side.

"Two loops," I said under my breath, wrapping the thread twice around my needle holder, then grasping the tail and pulling it through to secure the first knot. *Another loop, pull through, second knot. Both ends together, snip.*

I'd made my first stitch. On a human being.

The man clenched his teeth but said nothing as I prepared for my second stitch. I placed my tongue behind my teeth as I repeated the steps a second time, then a third, fourth, fifth. When the sixth stitch was done, I sat back and admired my work. They were good, strong stitches. Amid the horror around me, pride filled my chest. I took a moment to feel the accomplishment, a tiny bright spot in a horrific day. I was so good at this. Couldn't imagine giving it up.

"All done," I said kindly. "You have more fragments for me to remove, but no more stitching."

He gazed at me, the vacant expression fading and replaced with one of anguish, and not from his wounds. It was a look I was too familiar with; the same one I saw day after day in the faces of the soldiers under my care. The pain of this day would take longer to heal than simple stitches. "Thank you, Nurse," he said hoarsely.

I desperately wanted to ask him about the docks and what he'd seen. Being shut in the hospital meant not knowing anything that was going on. But to ask might cause him more pain, so I held my tongue and reapplied myself to removing pieces of glass, dropping them with little clinks into my bowl. It seemed an age before I finished and his clothing was back in place, and I squeezed his hand when I was done. "Good luck to you," I said quietly.

His expression turned bitter. "No sense looking for luck. Not when we're in the middle of hell." He rose, favouring the leg I'd just stitched.

"Go easy on your leg. You don't want to rip your stitches, now."

But he said nothing, just hobbled his way out of the hospital. I knew he wouldn't give a thought to his stitches. Nor would I in the same situation. I'd be desperate to find my family. I was terribly tempted to get up and walk out of the hospital to search for them. But of course I could not. My duty had to come before my heart, my fear. At least in this moment.

I was just in the middle of treating my next patient when word came down that there was a chance of another explosion, this time at the nearby armoury. Fear cramped my chest, but only for a moment. When the order came to evacuate, I looked around at the other doctors and nurses. No one made a move; they simply kept treating their patients. Surgeries had been set up in the kitchen and dining rooms, using whatever meagre supplies were on hand. Camp Hill was woefully unequipped for this kind of mass casualty event, but we were making do in an effort to save lives. Evacuate, and leave these suffering people behind? I couldn't do it, and apparently neither could my colleagues. We all kept working.

I was moved into a curtained area and now had a bed at my disposal, which made things infinitely easier. I went to fetch clean water and antiseptic and caught sight once more of the massive number of wounded. There was not a single space in the hospital that wasn't occupied. I bit my lip as my gaze landed on a woman lying on a mattress on the floor with her arm blown clean off just below the shoulder. Another, next to her, unconscious and with a large wood fragment protruding from her leg. I paused for a moment, looking at the woman's peaceful face. Her hair had come out of its twist and lay tangled around her shoulders, covered in grime and that oily substance that seemed to be everywhere. But she was pretty. As I watched, two stretcher-bearers picked up the woman and carried her off, presumably for treatment to remove the fragment. I hoped she would be all right and that she wouldn't lose her leg.

And so the afternoon went on, with no stopping. The threat of a second explosion passed, and I hardly looked up. I focused on splinters, shards, stitches, burns. Treated them all, one after another, breaking only to resupply before seeing the next patient. My neck started to ache from bending over so much, and my eyes burned from my intense focus. During my resupply breaks I caught glimpses of horrifying injuries… faces sliced open, the skin in flaps; limbs missing, horrible gut wounds that weren't survivable. Somewhere nearby there were scores of the dead. My lip quivered and tears stung my tired eyes, but I blinked them away. I couldn't think about it now. If I did, I'd fall apart, and my job wasn't to collapse. It was to work. To nurse. To treat the wounded. That was all—and it was everything.

For the first time, the phrase "we're at war" took on a real, true meaning, and I felt it from my heart right down to my toes.

It was no longer some nebulous, far-away idea. It was right here in Halifax, the little Canadian city with the big port, that had for hundreds of years survived battles between the French and English. And yet today, in a matter of a few seconds, the city and its people were shattered. If I weren't in the middle of it, I wouldn't believe it was possible.

The stretcher-bearers brought my next patient. "Unconscious, but she needs stitches."

I examined the woman, looking for other wounds. Other than a few pieces of glass in her hair that were completely superficial, I saw no cuts or signs of swelling other than two gashes, one on each forearm. Stitching her up while she was unconscious was a blessing. I wondered how she got two such identical wounds. Had she been watching from a window, like so many stories I was hearing?

"When I'm done she'll have to be moved to a bed."

"Yes, Nurse."

I went to work. The wounds were deep and laid to the bone. Swallowing the sudden bile in my mouth, I cleansed the right arm and prepared to suture. I'd put in three stitches when I sensed someone standing behind me.

"Sorry, I won't be done for a while," I said without looking up.

"You've a fair hand at suturing."

I glanced over my shoulder and saw a doctor there, but not one I recognized. "I'm sorry, sir… you are?"

"Captain Neil McLeod," he said. "I'm a doctor at Aldershot. I've come to help."

"You should report to Major Morris," I replied, returning to my work. "He'll assign you."

"I've already seen him. Where did you learn to stitch like that?"

My cheeks heated as I looped and pulled and snipped and started again, falling back into a rhythm. "To be fair, sir, I've had a lot of practice this morning."

"It's late afternoon, Lieutenant."

It was so rare that anyone called me by my rank that I startled and dropped my forceps. I stood to retrieve them and swayed on my feet.

His hands gripped my upper arms, steadying me. "When did you last eat? Have something to drink?"

I stepped away from his hands. The weakness and unsteadiness persisted, though I tried not to show it. "It hasn't been a priority."

"It is now. You can't treat patients if you faint, Nurse…"

"Nursing Sister Nora Crowell," I replied, steady enough to retrieve the forceps and drop them into disinfecting solution. "Sir."

"Finish with your patient, then have one of the VADs find you something."

"I'm fine—"

"That's an order."

I bristled. He was a captain in the CAMC and a doctor, but he wasn't a Camp Hill doctor. Yet he marched in here and started giving orders…

Except he was right, of course. And if he was here, it meant he had come to help because we were overwhelmed. I suspected every hospital and doctor's office in the city was probably overwhelmed at this point.

How many dead and wounded were there? How was it they were still coming?

Once more I pushed aside the thoughts and focused on my suture kit. "Yes, sir," I replied, threading the needle.

He left then, and I saw him later when I'd finished with the patient and called the stretcher-bearers to take her to a ward. He was at the front of the hospital, triaging patients, sending them this way and that. He looked over his shoulder and caught sight of me, his blond hair now dishevelled and his jaw set. But he lifted an eyebrow at me, as if holding me to my word to get something to eat.

Wooziness threatened again, and I knew I had to obey. Not just because it was orders, but because of the baby. For the first time, my pregnancy was affecting my ability to do my job. The thought sent conflicting emotions crashing through me… consideration for my unborn child, resentment that my life was changing, guilt for harbouring the secret and for not being… better, I suppose.

I'd traded the traditional domestic life for a professional one, and because of that I realized I'd felt pressure to be perfect at it. To prove that my choice was worth it and the right path for me. It was a punch to the gut to know that I couldn't give it my all right now, and that I had no one to blame but myself.

Gram's voice came through my mind again, as it usually did when I needed shoring up. *Nora Margaret Crowell. You listen to me. What's done is done. You're ready for this. Now hunker down and get at 'er. People need your help.*

I spluttered out a little laugh at the thought of Gram's no-nonsense wisdom. I was doing the best I could under the circumstances. I found a volunteer—a VAD—and miraculously a cup of tea and a few slices of bread were produced. It wasn't a meal, but it was enough, and I felt much better afterward.

Except for the hole that seemed to widen in my chest with every passing hour. Treating patients had kept me from thinking too much, but in between patients worry seeped in. Eventually I would have to go home and find out the fate of my family.

The worst for me were the eye and facial injuries. So many

people had gone to their windows to watch what was happening in the harbour that when the explosion happened, glass had embedded in eyes, sliced eyelids… So many people would never see again. As the hours wore on, I found myself blinking a few times to clear my own vision before resuming treatment. Fatigue was setting in, and I needed to fight it. But I also needed a drink of water and to relieve myself, so I took a short break. As I moved through the cluttered hall, I passed a doctor I didn't recognize—a civilian—working over a patient's head. I couldn't see the patient, but I saw the bucket of eyeballs on the floor next to them.

I had seen horrors all day long. Blood, bile, excrement… the smells had assaulted my nose and I'd withstood it. But seeing those eyeballs did something to me. My throat burned with bile, and I rushed to an exit, pushing my way outside into the cold air where I bent over and retched onto the hard ground.

There was nothing to come up. I'd had so little to eat since morning that I dry heaved, the bitter taste of bile in my mouth as my head went light. I would not faint. I would not. Instead I gulped in air, put my hands on my knees, dropped my head a little, and waited for the dizziness to pass.

This was just so wrong. Soldiers… when they were wounded, it was horrible too, but they'd signed up. Been trained. They weren't innocent civilians going about their day, changed forever by some random accident. The people of Halifax had got up this morning as I had, ate breakfast, read the newspaper, said goodbye to loved ones, not knowing that in mere minutes their lives would be altered. It was so unfair. It wasn't just the eyeballs and knowing those people wouldn't see again. It was everything. It was the loss of security. Of being in a war without seeing the horrors of war. Now I'd seen it, and while I wasn't injured, I would never be the same, either.

"Nurse Crowell?"

The kind voice was at my elbow—Captain McLeod. Embarrassment burned my cheeks. I didn't want anyone to see me like this. Didn't want to appear weak and unable to do my job, and certainly didn't want anyone to know about the baby. I immediately straightened, fighting the dizziness. "So sorry, sir. I'll be right back in."

It was dark outside now, and little snowflakes had begun to fall. Shadowy figures shifted around the hospital entrances, wounded who still waited for treatment. At present there was just enough snow that it barely dusted the ground. It melted on my uniform that was now blotched with dirt and rusty, dried blood, but the air had the feel of a storm to it, not just a light flurry. The sounds of pain in the air were a haunting echo, sliding over my skin, and I shivered. The air, while cool and bracing, was tinged with the acrid smell of smoke. Whether it was from wood stoves or structures burning after the explosion, I didn't know. What I did know was that out there—in a city I could no longer see—human beings were dead, wounded. Thousands were without shelter, food, or water. And for what?

I had not been outside since arriving in the morning, and now the entire city was changed. While I couldn't see it, I could feel it. It was as if the landscape had gone through a tectonic shift, taking the people of Halifax with it, never to be the same again. The devastation started to sink in. When I visualized what kind of an explosion could cause this many casualties, I started to shake, unsure if it was from the cold or delayed shock. "Do you know what caused the blast?" I asked him finally, my teeth chattering.

He nodded. His face was in shadow, but I saw the movement, saw the grim light in his eyes as he met my gaze. "The ship that was on fire in the harbour. It was carrying munitions. When it blew, it leveled the whole north end of the city."

"Leveled?" I breathed, horrified. "All of it?" But that was... massive. Impossible.

"The train tracks... we had to stop at Rockingham. It's..." He turned his head and looked away. "It was unlike anything I could imagine."

The lump in my throat grew. "One of the soldiers who was helping said it was worse than anything he'd seen at the front." I paused. "I didn't believe him."

We let that thought sink in for a moment. It was a relief to know it hadn't been an enemy attack, but to think of the boisterous, vital city I loved being the scene of such destruction... If I weren't in the middle of it, I wasn't sure I'd believe it.

"Are you all right now?" he asked, touching my elbow again.

I nodded. "It was the eyeballs," I said, shuddering at the memory. "I'm not usually squeamish."

He chuckled a little. "Don't be too hard on yourself. Not many of us here have seen anything close to this before. You're doing fine."

I felt anything but fine but appreciated the sentiment just the same. His reassurance bolstered my confidence. "Thank you, sir. I should get back."

"How long have you been here today, Nurse Crowell?"

I met his gaze. "What time is it now?"

"Nearly nine."

Heavens. I had worked nearly non-stop all that time. "Thirteen, fourteen hours?"

"You should go home, get some rest." Suddenly his face changed, softened. "I'm sorry. Where is your home? I hope it's not in Richmond... I don't mean to be thoughtless."

"No, not at all. It's not far. On Henry, on the other side of

Robie Street. But my family… they were all going to the docks this morning."

"And you don't know what has happened to them?"

I shook my head, my throat closing as the trembling started again and a pit of dread settled in my stomach. *Jane was to mail my letter,* I thought numbly. *Jane's going to help with the baby.*

"I'm sorry," he replied. "You should go home, get some rest," he said again.

"But there are so many patients… "

His lips thinned and his jaw tightened. "Nurse Crowell, we are looking at days of treating the wounded, not hours. It might seem cruel, but we need to look after ourselves, to have the stamina to see it through. Too tired, and we start making mistakes."

I knew he was right. Now that I'd stopped, I was ready to drop. "Only if Matron sends me," I said firmly. I would not be the one asking to be relieved. As anxious as I was about my family, I understood that this was not my own unique circumstance. Was there anyone in this city who wasn't wondering about the fate of a loved one? And then there was the part of me that wanted to put this off a while longer, just in case the news was bad.

The moments in the fresh air had cleared my senses, so when we went back inside, the smell was the first thing that struck me again. Metallic blood, burning flesh, and the underlying scent of antiseptic and disinfectant bit at my nose. I breathed through my mouth a few times so I could adjust.

Captain McLeod disappeared from my side, and I returned to my duties: assess, cleanse, treat, bandage. My stomach growled but I ignored it. I was the one alive and in one piece. I was the one with skills to help. And I would stay as long as I was needed.

I was on my third patient since returning inside when Matron

Cotton approached with a young woman behind her. The girl—definitely younger than me—wore a nurse's uniform, but not the pale blue of the CAMC Nursing Sisters. "Nurse Crowell, Miss Murray will take your place. I want you to go home, get some food and sleep, and report back in the morning."

I snipped my stitch and looked up. "Are you certain? I will stay. I'm needed."

The matron gave a brisk nod. "Dalhousie University has sent over students to assist us."

I looked at the girl. She was perhaps twenty, her face pale but her eyes bright and determined. A rush of exhaustion swept over me, and I put down my needle holder.

"It's not a request, Nurse Crowell."

"Yes, Matron," I answered. I ran my hands over the skirt of my apron as I faced the two women. Hands that were now red and raw following so many washings and disinfections; hands that had, in a matter of a few hours, sewn hundreds of stitches. "I'll be back first thing." One did not argue with the matrons, though I knew if I had the energy I would have pushed to stay. My easy capitulation was evidence of my fatigue, and I went to retrieve my belongings for the dark walk home.

I was used to walking home in the early evening, near suppertime, and it usually didn't make me uneasy. Tonight, though, was different. In the space of thirty seconds the world had irrevocably changed, and the stress of the day, added to my worries about my own family, made me uneasy about the journey. There was nothing to be done, though. Others were in far worse situations than I tonight. I buttoned my coat and prepared to head outside into the darkness.

"Wait, Nurse Crowell!"

Captain McLeod's voice reached me, and I turned. He was pulling on a coat and trotting after me, and my heart gave a strange thump at his appearance. Twice today he'd shown up at my side, offering the support I'd desperately needed. It was odd for me to be glad to see him—a relative stranger—but it eased my tension just that little bit, feeling like perhaps I wasn't so alone. That I wasn't just a cleaning, bandaging, stitching machine.

"Let me walk you home," he said. "To be sure you're safe."

"That's not necessary, Captain." I pulled on my mittens. "Surely you're needed more here."

"I am, and I'm coming back. If I need a few hours sleep, I'll find a corner somewhere." We both knew that was a lie. There were no corners to be found. Every available space was being used.

I looked up into his face, noting the firm set to his mouth. "I'm not going to change your mind, am I?" I asked.

He shook his head. "I'm afraid not. You said it isn't far. I'd like to ensure you get home safe and sound. Tonight… It's late."

I could have said no, but I'd just been dreading the walk, feeling as if I were stepping out into the unknown somehow, even though I'd been walking these streets for months. "I could use the company," I admitted. I pushed away the guilt crawling through me at leaving behind people who needed my help so much, as we stepped outside once more. Perhaps it was a blessing it was dark and flakes had started to fall, as the snow formed a fragile white blanket over the brokenness of the city. But as we walked away from the hospital and started toward Jubilee Road, our heads tucked into our collars against the biting wind, the thoughts I'd shoved aside all day began creeping in, bringing with them the beginnings of fear and panic.

He was a stranger, but right now he was the only friend I had, and I had a great need to voice my fear before arriving at my sister's doorstep. "I'm afraid of what I'm going to find when I get home," I confessed, my words shaking. "I'm frightened to death."

The skift of snow had covered a patch of ice and I slipped. Captain McLeod reached out and caught my arm, saving me from falling, and then tucked it safely into his elbow. "This snow is going to hamper the rescues," he murmured. "And I hope your family is all home again, cozy by the fire and waiting for you." He reached over and squeezed my mittened hand.

"They went to the docks to see the ships this morning." My voice caught. "Dad wanted to go. Then Mum wanted to pick up some things for Christmas. My sister and the baby went, too. They were all going to have lunch together." Another slight hiccup. "I couldn't go because I was on shift…"

He said nothing, and I supposed that was because there was nothing he *could* say. We turned left onto Henry and my stomach clenched with nerves and fear of what I would find on the other side of my front door. I thought about what Captain McLeod had said about rescue efforts and realized that while I'd faced the stark brutality of injuries all day, I'd been spared the view of wider destruction. Henry Street looked mostly unchanged. Lamps glowed in windows, weak yellow light through the inky darkness. As we got closer to the house, I saw the outline of my father's car that he'd bought in '16. The sight of it made me want to weep, and I sent up a prayer that they would be there to welcome me home, safe and sound and whole.

"Miss Crowell?" Captain McLeod called me Miss this time instead of Nurse. As a friend or acquaintance would, not a fellow officer. "Whatever happens, it will be all right." He paused, and I turned to face him at the end of the walkway. "You are here and alive. You survived. And you will not be alone."

I nodded, my throat so clogged with fear and trepidation, I couldn't speak until I swallowed it away. When the tightness eased, I looked up at him. There were a few flakes of snow on his cap and his eyelashes, and his face was sombre and yet kind. "This is presumptuous to ask of you, but… would you come inside with me?" I asked. "I know you have to get back, but I—"

I halted, my lip wobbling. Normally I was the staunch, stalwart one, but right now my hands were shaking so much that I shoved them into my pockets. Jane had to be on the other side of the door. She simply had to. My parents would greet me with hugs and kisses and they would be so thankful to be spared. Any other scenario was unthinkable.

"You don't want to go in there alone. I understand. Of course I will."

We made our way up the walk together, our boots making soft sounds against the hard ground. There was a light coming from the parlour, and I pressed my hand against my stomach before reaching out and opening the front door with trembling fingers.

It was quiet. So quiet, and… heavy.

Captain McLeod stepped in behind me and shut the door. The noise must have roused the occupants of the house, because only a few moments later Mrs. Thompson came racing from the kitchen through the hall and to the front door, her eyes strained with worry.

Mrs. Thompson. Not Jane. Not Mother.

"Oh, my dear, I'm that glad to see you," Mrs. Thompson said, her mouth working.

"My parents? Jane?"

Mrs. Thompson shook her head, tears welling in her eyes. "No news," she said briefly. "But we're hopeful."

If Mrs. Thompson had seen what I had seen today, there would be very little hope in her eyes. But perhaps she was right to grab onto hope. Maybe my family was injured, being treated at one of the other hospitals in the city. Maybe they were seeking refuge somewhere for tonight. I mustn't give up. I couldn't.

"Auntie Nora!" Evelyn came barreling out of the parlour dressed in a long flannel nightdress covered with a knitted sweater, and thick wool socks on her feet. "Auntie Nora, where is Mummy? Where is Clara?"

Mrs. Thompson gave me a look that I interpreted as *I've been answering this question all day.*

For a prolonged moment, I struggled to find the words, but I knew I must for Evvie's sake. I faced my niece, with her sweet, anxious face, and felt such a wave of love, it nearly took me to my knees. This beautiful little girl who prayed for her daddy every night before she went to bed, hoping he would be safe. It was inconceivable to think that she might have also lost her mother and her sister…

Sister. The ache in my heart intensified as I thought about Jane and all the secrets and confidences we'd shared over the past few years. What would we all do without her? My only sister. The one I relied on through thick and thin. The one person I knew would never forsake me, always make me laugh, support me no matter what.

Evelyn was facing a life without her family… and it occurred to me that I was facing the exact same. A gulf of emptiness, as cold as the winter sea, opened up inside me. Right now, in this moment at least, Evelyn and I only had each other.

I bit down on my lip, determined to hold myself together for her sake, then took a shaky breath and knelt down, still in my coat and mittens. I pulled off the mittens and held out my hands. "Come here, darlin' girl."

Evelyn came close and put her little cold hands in mine.

"I don't know about your mummy or baby Clara. But tonight,

when we go to bed, we're going to say a prayer for them and your daddy, all right?"

A tear slipped out of Evelyn's eye and down her little cheek. "I want my mummy," she whispered, and the sound of her small voice broke my heart for the hundredth time that day.

"As do I, sweetheart. Would you like me to tuck you in?" It sounded like an absurdly ordinary question, but Evelyn still had to go to bed. It was already hours past her normal bedtime.

Evelyn rushed forward, wrapping her arms around my neck, oblivious to the melted snow on my coat. "Don't leave too, Auntie Nora! I don't want to go to bed! My window is broken, and I'm scared."

Right then and there, I made a decision. "If my room is still in one piece, you can sleep in with me. You are not alone, Evelyn. I promise."

I looked up at Captain McLeod, who'd been standing silently in the entryway. He'd said those exact words to me only minutes ago. I realized that in the days ahead, we were all going to have to lean on people… friends, strangers, neighbours. It was the only way Halifax would be able to rebuild.

"I'll be along soon," I promised. "I need some supper and to talk to Mrs. Thompson. But you can go get into my bed." I tipped the girl's nose with my finger. "Maybe you can warm the covers up for me?"

"You won't leave?"

"No, sweetheart. I have to go back to work in the morning, but I'm not leaving you."

Evelyn nodded. "Will you take me up to bed?"

"Of course I will." I stood and looked at Mrs. Thompson. "Mrs. Thompson, this is Captain Neil McLeod, a doctor from the valley who's come to help. He needs to get back to the hospital, but I wonder if there's anything we can offer for a quick meal?"

"Of course." Mrs. Thompson cleared her throat and lifted her chin. "If you'll come with me, Captain, I'll rustle up something in a jiffy."

"I really should get back. There's no need—"

"It's the least we can do after you saw me home safely," I protested. "You can't look after others if you don't look after yourself," I reminded him.

He smiled a little at that. "All right. Just for a moment."

I took Evelyn's hand, and we started toward the stairs together. But as we began climbing the steps, my tenuous hold on my emotions began to slip. Fatigue and worry were overwhelming. I wondered how long I could continue before I broke.

Chapter Eight

CHARLOTTE

December 7, 1917

I heard, rather than saw, when I awoke. It was impossible to open my eyelids; they were so very heavy, and my head pounded. But there was no mistaking the moans and cries surrounding me. I desperately tried to sort out where I was, but nothing felt right. Not the air, not my body, not the smells or the sounds… all unfamiliar and so very disconcerting. The last thing I remembered was leaning down to talk to Aileen in her carriage…

Aileen.

Panic slammed into my chest, stealing my breath. I bolted upright, gasping for air as my eyes flew open and my head felt as if it were splitting right down the middle.

I was on a cot of some sort, dressed in only my underclothes.

All around me were cots and mattresses, crammed with poor souls who were bloodied and bandaged and in pain. I couldn't move my leg; there were bandages on my arms, and a cursory examination of my pounding head revealed more bandages, soft beneath my fingertips.

Where was Aileen?

I threw off the covers and tried to get up, but immediately a nurse approached, her blue-and-white uniform and starchy veil a contrast to the torn and tattered people occupying the ward. "You mustn't get up," she called as she ran forward. "Please, ma'am, lie back. You'll tear your stitches." I was in a hospital… a military hospital, of all things, for this was one of the medical corps' Bluebirds, the nickname for the nurses with the blue uniforms.

I didn't care about my stitches. "My baby," I cried, looking frantically around for the carriage or a little bed or any sign of my child. "Where is my baby?"

The nurse arrived at my side and touched my arm gently. "I'm sorry, ma'am, but there was no baby brought in with you. Please, lie back. I'll answer your questions as best I can, but you must lie still." Her voice was compassionate, but very firm with no room for negotiation.

Lie still. As if I could, and Aileen missing. My entire body went numb as I stared up at the nursing sister, now noticing that her uniform was stained with blood and sweat. I searched my brain for pieces of memory, trying to knit them together into something that made sense. We'd been going to the Citadel to look at the burning ship. The street corner, Aileen fussing, the strange feeling… nothing after that. Without Aileen in my arms, it was as if someone had ripped my heart out of my chest, leaving a hollow filled with fear and loss. I stared at the nurse, but I was screaming on the inside. Screaming in terror. I was a mother, and I did not know the whereabouts of my child.

My head hurt so badly that grey spots swam before my eyes, so I allowed the nurse to ease me back onto the cot. "That's it," the nurse soothed. "You've had a shock now, but you're all right."

"I'm not all right without Aileen," I whispered, my face wet with tears I was unable to stop. A raw, agonized moan sounded, and I realized it had come from my own throat. Oh, God. My daughter. My precious baby… the last part of Frank I had. I couldn't go on, not without the only family I had in the world. I would rather die.

"There was an explosion," the nurse said, taking my hand gently and rubbing it between hers. "In the harbour. You were found and brought in. The doctor removed two large splinters—one from your head, and one from your left leg. Both have been treated and stitched. You also have a concussion." Her soft voice was soothing, and I began to breathe again. "You probably have a horrible headache and you might experience some double vision. What you need now is rest and time to heal."

"But my baby…" I struggled to sit up again. How could I rest without having Aileen with me?

The nurse cleared her throat, her firm tone returning. "Ma'am, the city is in ruins. Even if you wanted to, it's snowing right now. When you've healed better, you can try to find her. She might have been rescued and taken somewhere else. I know this is awful, but I'll pray that you find her safe and sound."

Safe and sound… The words sounded so lovely and optimistic, but they couldn't erase the knot of grief and panic sitting on my breastbone with the weight of an elephant. I turned my head, blinking back hot tears, and saw the figure of a man on the cot next to me. Most of his arm was missing, and he had bandages over his eyes. The level of devastation started to sink in. "People have been killed," I whispered, turning back to the nurse. I noticed now that the woman was perhaps a little older than myself, with dark-blond hair tucked under her nursing veil and circles under her eyes. "What time is it?"

"It's around two thirty in the morning. December seventh."

I'd been unconscious for hours. It hadn't even been nine o'clock when I'd set out with Aileen, just to escape the house. If only we'd stayed inside, waited…

"Ma'am, what's your name? We didn't find anything with you that told us who you are."

"Charlotte. Charlotte Campbell, and I live on Russell Street." I started to cry again, the ache in my chest building. "I should have stayed home, where it was safe… instead of going walking. Oh, I killed my baby," I sobbed, putting my trembling hands to my face.

Gentle hands enveloped mine. "Mrs. Campbell, all reports are that Richmond is gone. Completely leveled. You are probably alive *because* you were out walking. Hush, now." She rubbed my upper arms lightly, where they weren't bandaged, the touch soothing and anchoring. "Will you rest now? You'll be no good to your daughter when you find her if you tear your stitches. The piece of wood the surgeon removed barely missed an artery. You're lucky you didn't lose your leg."

The only words that made any sense were the ones reminding me that Aileen would need me to be healthy and strong. As agonizing as it was, I couldn't leave this hospital bed. I was too weak, in too much pain. I nodded, just a little, each movement like a hammer banging away from inside my head. I let the nurse ease me back onto the pillow. "There," she soothed. "Get some rest. I'll be back to check on you soon."

My eyelids closed again; it was such a chore keeping them

open. I needed to rest and get well for Aileen. As the nurse's footsteps receded, I whispered a prayer for my daughter's safety. Prayer was, at the moment, the only thing in my power to do. I prayed for God to keep her alive, to keep her safe. I prayed for Him to let me find her. And I prayed for Frank, her father, because if ever I'd needed an angel, it was now.

Then I imagined Aileen's warm little body in my arms, safe and secure, and I fell back into a dreamless sleep.

Chapter Nine

NORA

When I woke in the morning, the first thing I registered was Evelyn's body pressed into mine. It was freezing in the bedroom. A few of the windows in the house had been broken, and despite the men doing their best to board them up yesterday, the cold seeped into me with icy fingers. There was barely any light creeping through the curtains, and when I slipped out from beneath the covers and went to the window, I was greeted with a swirl of icy white.

The timing couldn't have been worse. But the weather, like everything else in the last twenty-four hours, was out of my control.

I rushed to dress in a clean uniform, both because I needed to get back to work and because it was simply too cold not to hurry. The fire from last night had surely burned down to only embers, and it would need tending. But when I reached the kitchen, I stopped in the doorway and my mouth fell open in surprise.

Mrs. Thompson was there. She'd already put wood on the fire, and it was burning briskly. There was a kettle on top of the stove and the older woman was filling a pot with water.

"Mrs. Thompson, you're here... I... I don't know what to say."

The older woman spun around. "Oh, heavens, you startled me." She put the pot on the stove and brushed her hands down her skirt. "Now, just where else would I be, tell me that? Seems you're going to be needed at the hospital and there's a little girl that needs carin' for."

"But for you to come over here so early... you're a godsend, Mrs. Thompson. I wasn't sure how I was going to manage today."

Mrs. Thompson came and took my cold hands in hers. "Don't fret. I slept on the chesterfield in the parlour. John and Marvin will be up shortly—" She broke off and gave my fingers a squeeze. "And maybe we'll hear from Harry today, too."

It was unlikely. The quiet, gentle man worked at one of the piers. Just yesterday he'd sent me a wink over breakfast. He never said much, but when he did, it was generally kind.

"I don't expect you to—that is—" I stammered, trying to cast a net over the thoughts swimming in my head. "Oh, there's just so much." I sighed. "I hardly know where to begin."

"Which is why I'm here. You just let me take care of things." Mrs. Thompson's dark eyes held worry in their depths. "Truth be told, Nora, I need to keep my hands busy. If not, I think too much about the poor souls—"

She broke off again, cleared her throat, and reached for the crock of oats. "I hope you don't mind porridge."

I went over to my dear neighbour and enfolded her in a hug, no longer caring if I cried or not. Tears slid down my cheeks, tears of sadness and worry but also of relief at knowing someone was here to help shoulder the burden.

"Having you here makes me feel so much less alone, so I'll eat porridge for breakfast, lunch and supper if that's what there is," I whispered. I sniffed, so very grateful for the older woman's presence but feeling a keen sense of loss at the same time. It should be Jane here. All of my family crowded around the kitchen table, talking and laughing. No matter what happened from this day onward, it would be a long time before any of us laughed again. None of this felt real. *I* didn't feel real. Instead, I felt almost disembodied, as if I were caught in a nightmare and had yet to wake up.

Mrs. Thompson squeezed me back. "You're not alone, dear. You're needed at the hospital, and you can contribute in ways I can't. But if I can keep things going for you here at the house… well, goodness." She pulled away and tried a weak smile. "Keeping you all fed and watered and caring for Evelyn is the least I can do. And the boys, too. They did the basic repairs yesterday, but you can rely on them to fix what needs fixin'. John's handy with a hammer."

I smiled a little at Mrs. Thompson referring to the two grown men as "boys", something Jane had also done. "And I'm that thankful, Mrs. Thompson. I'm not going to say no, because I have no idea how I could handle everything." I met her gaze. "Especially Evelyn."

"She slept last night?"

"I think so." I gave a rueful half smile. "I was so tired that I fell asleep right away and didn't wake at all until a few minutes ago. She's still sleeping."

Mrs. Thompson went to the stove and poured in the oats, setting them to cook. While she was stirring, I went to the breadbox, took out a loaf of bread, and sliced off four pieces. I topped each with a tiny smear of precious butter and some of Jane's strawberry preserves, then packed them away along with four molasses cookies. I tried not to think that they were the last of the batch that Jane had made before our parents had arrived—that sort of thinking was sure to bog me down. Instead, I thought of Captain McLeod, and how he'd gone back to the hospital to work all night instead of resting.

"I hope it's all right that I'm taking something for Captain McLeod," I said, looking at Mrs. Thompson over my shoulder. "I doubt he's had breakfast."

"My dear, this is your food. You don't need to ask permission."

But it wasn't. It was Jane's food. Jane used everyone's coupons and money to buy food for all. Jane was the one who ran this household, not me, and I'd been glad of it. It had left me free to devote my time to my work. Now though… now it would fall to me, another giant task I felt ill-equipped to take on. I nodded quickly, but once more hoped that my family would somehow walk through the door again and I could wake up from this nightmare.

"It feels odd, that's all," I confessed, tucking everything into a bag. Then I sat at the table while Mrs. Thompson brought me my oatmeal, steam curling up from the bowl. I used less sugar and milk than normal—I did like my sugar on my porridge—because who knew what the food situation was going to be in the days ahead? We were already conserving and economizing. Things were going to get tighter now. Supplies would be harder to come by. Prices were bound to rise.

I was just about to eat when my stomach turned, and the feeling that was growing so familiar burned the back of my throat.

In all the upheaval, I hadn't had much time to think about my baby. The spoon shook in my hand as all my feelings started to crowd together. Work, my pregnancy… that had been distressing enough. But now, with this disaster, I literally did not know where to begin to try to put the pieces back together. Wasn't sure I could. Never in my life had I been this terrified.

"Is everything all right?"

"Oh y-yes, fine, thank you. I-I'm just a bit tired, still, and dreading the day ahead."

"Of course you are. And it's some storm outside. I hate to think of you walking to the hospital in it."

I didn't much like it either, but there was nothing else to be done. I'd bundle up and go because I was a nurse in the Canadian Army Medical Corps. This was my duty, my job. Reminding myself of that fact helped shore up my strength and focus my mind. I tried a bite spoonful of porridge, and the nausea subsided a little. If I could just keep it down…

I did need my strength this morning. Captain McLeod had said this would take days, not hours. Could I expect more of the same today? Removing glass and splinters, stitching with little disinfectant and no morphine to spare, or anesthetic?

I made quick work of the porridge and hurried to get ready. It was already seven; I should have been at work earlier. I wrapped a scarf around my neck and went to retrieve the bag with my lunch and my nursing veil—with the storm raging outside, I was bundling up in my grandmother's knitted hat and mittens. When I went to retrieve my bag, I noticed Mrs. Thompson tucking something inside it. Duty or not, knowing my neighbour was handling things here at home took a load off my mind.

Mrs. Thompson straightened and handed me the sack, the drawstring now pulled tight. "I put in some hot tea for you and your captain."

My cheeks heated. "He's not my captain," I answered,

reaching for the bag. "He merely showed me a kindness yesterday. Mrs. Thompson, I… " I let out a breath and looked up. "I have someone overseas, you see." My throat tightened. If I were being honest, I missed Alley. I missed his smile and the way he teased me. The way he was able to make me forget my worries. I could certainly use a bit of that right now.

"Oh, that young man from last fall? I didn't know you were still… I'm sorry, Nora. I didn't mean to stick my nose in where it doesn't belong."

"It's all right," I assured her, but inside my emotions started roiling again. Alley… Had news of what had happened made it to the men overseas? Was he still safe… alive, even? And Jimmy… My God, Jimmy. What if Jane and baby Clara were truly gone? What would he do?

I dragged my thoughts back to the present, determined not to get sucked into the whirlpool of what-ifs. "Captain McLeod is just one of many who has volunteered to help. He's left his home to come to Halifax. There was a doctor last night who came down from New Glasgow, and nursing students from the university… Oh, Mrs. Thompson, I do think the only way we're going to get through this is if we all stick together."

Mrs. Thompson squeezed my hand. "I'm sure you're right about that," she replied. "Now, you go on. I'll see to everyone else this morning."

"I hope to be home this evening. But be sure to tell Evelyn that I am coming, will you? The poor little mite is so scared."

"Of course I will. Stay safe in the storm, now. It's blowin' a gale out there an'll take you right with it."

I stepped outside into the swirling wind and snow and gasped in a breath. The cold bit at my cheeks and my boots sank in the snow, up past my ankles. It showed no sign of letting up, so I hunched my shoulders and started to trudge through the drift along the walkway. Once more I was thankful that I lived so close to Camp Hill. The walk took longer than usual, but it was still only a matter of minutes and I'd arrived, covered in snow but none the worse for wear.

Not much had changed from the night before. People still waited to be seen, though the stream of wounded being transported to the hospital doors had tapered off, the rescue efforts hindered by the force of the storm. I took a few moments to tidy my hair, then I pinned my veil into place and straightened my clean apron, relieved to have something to focus on and distract me from my own worries. There was barely anywhere to walk; cots and mattresses with wounded filled every nook and cranny, and the air was tinged with that same metallic scent of blood, dirt, and despair. My first stop was to check in with the matron and get my assignment for the day.

To my surprise, I was being sent to help the surgeons. "You did exemplary work yesterday," the matron said with a brisk nod. "Your abilities will be very useful in surgery today."

A warm jolt of pride filled my chest at the word "exemplary".

"In surgery?" I repeated.

Matron gave me a sharp look. "You will be able to close incisions, Nurse Crowell. Faster surgeries mean more people getting the help they need as soon as possible."

"Of course," I replied, standing straighter. I was eager to get started—I'd been longing to work on more complicated cases for ages—but I had something to ask first. "Matron, before I begin… may I check to see if any members of my family have been brought in?"

The woman's eyes softened. "You're missing people?"

I nodded, trying to keep my emotions locked away. I wanted to check, but I didn't want to appear as though I were too distraught to do my job. "My sister, my parents, and my baby niece."

Matron nodded. "I'm so sorry, Nurse Crowell. Of course, you may do a quick check, and then report to the dining room." Her face hardened. "Never thought I'd see the day our dining room and kitchen were used as operating theatres."

"Yes, ma'am. Thank you, ma'am."

I scurried away, hurriedly checking the list of patients and scanning the wards, but no one matching my family's names was on the list, nor did I see any of them among the treated patients, though there were so many, it was impossible to see every face. Disappointment and worry were heavy in my chest, but I pushed the feelings aside and made my way out of the main pavilion to where the surgeries were located. While I was in this building, I would do my sworn duty. I just hoped that wherever my family was, they were getting the same attentive treatment.

My morning was spent assisting with some of the worst injuries I'd ever seen. Cuts laid to the bone, some requiring amputation. Removing shrapnel of all kinds, repairing internal damage… so much destruction. But I met each challenge as staunchly as I could, a task made easier as my nausea subsided the more the morning went on. Not every patient made it. More than once, the surgeons stepped back from the table, their eyes dulled with weary frustration. Had any of them slept at all? Not that I would presume to ask. My only job was to follow orders.

One doctor complimented me on my suturing skills, and I thanked him, though restrained myself from telling him the sum total of my actual experience had been gained only the day before. Sometime in the early afternoon I had a small break. I'd just helped with an amputation and had the opportunity to step away for a few precious minutes. I washed my hands for what felt like the hundredth time and retrieved the thermos and little bag of sandwiches, then hurried to see if I could find Captain McLeod, marveling to myself that after all I'd seen that morning, I was still able to respond to hunger in my belly.

I found him in another pavilion, tending to a head wound. There was a cut in the man's head that ran from just above his ear to the crown, and Captain McLeod was busy removing all the pieces of foreign material before closing the wound.

"Ah," he said, his voice tired but light. "Nurse Crowell. I hope you rested well?"

"Yes, sir," I replied. "I've been in surgery all morning, but I brought you something from home." I felt silly saying it, so I added, "To thank you for walking me home last night. It's just bread and some jam."

"Food is food at a time like this, don't you think? Not that I wouldn't love to have a fried egg sandwich." He looked at his patient and offered a tired smile. "What do you think of that, Gerald? My grandmother used to make them when we would go for a visit. There's nothing like a fresh, fried egg on bread that your grandmother baked just that morning."

"No sir," Gerald answered, holding perfectly still but wincing when Captain McLeod pulled out a rather large shard of metal. I admired the way he kept a stream of easy conversation going. It helped to relax and distract the patient as he was treated.

"Mrs. Thompson also sent tea," I added.

"She seems like a nice woman." He prepared to stitch, then looked Gerald in the eyes. "This is going to sting a bit," he apologized.

"I don't need nothing for pain, doc. Save it for the poor souls who need it," Gerald replied staunchly. But I knew there was nothing to save. Many supplies were dwindling, if they hadn't already run out. Rumour had it aid was on the way, from other Canadian cities but also places like New York and Boston. It couldn't come soon enough, and the storm was likely hindering efforts.

I watched as Captain McLeod made tiny, neat stitches, taking great care even though the wound was in the man's hair and wouldn't be visible for long. He was much faster than I, stitching in a line rather than tying and cutting off each one, and I watched him intently, looking for ways to improve my own novice technique.

After he finished and gave Gerald instructions for care and when to see someone to get the stitches out, he turned to me with a smile. "There. I can't take long, but tea and bread sounds like it will hit the spot."

"You must be exhausted," I said, as we turned to find a quiet spot away from patients. It seemed every available space was taken, but we finally found a corner near one of the supply rooms. I poured tea into the single cup and handed it to him, along with the bread and jam I'd wrapped up this morning.

"It's been a very long twenty-four hours," he admitted. "We worked clear through the night and there's still no end in sight. The snow is hampering rescue efforts, too." He frowned. "I'm afraid this is soon going to become a case of recovering people instead of rescuing them."

My eyes stung as I nodded. "I know. I haven't given up hope yet, though." His words reignited my fear, and an image of my mum and dad freezing beneath the snow raced through my mind. Focusing on work was a blessing, but in between times, the thoughts hit me with a bitter punch.

Captain McLeod's face instantly flattened with dismay at his blunder. "Oh, Nurse Crowell, I'm so sorry. I didn't mean…" His cheeks coloured. "Still no word from your sister?"

"No," I replied.

"I shouldn't have said what I did. It was thoughtless of me."

I appreciated, though, that he didn't offer me false assurances, which would somehow be worse. "You're exhausted," I said, excusing him. "Besides, I know you're right." I swallowed around the lump in my throat and took a bite of bread. It suddenly seemed dry and stale, and I struggled to chew and swallow. "I try not to think about it too much, but at some point, I must." Oddly enough, it was that realization that scared me the most. If I gave up, if I let in the grief that was bubbling outside the walls of my heart, I was afraid I'd never be whole again. It was as if I were held together with one, tenuous thread and if it snapped…

He refilled the teacup and handed it to me, our fingers brushing. It seemed rather intimate, sharing the same cup, but considering the circumstances…

"You could use a bit of this too," he suggested.

I took a sip, then a second, the hot liquid feeling like love and care from a woman who'd stepped up when she was needed out of the goodness of her heart.

I pushed the cup back towards him. "Mrs. Thompson sent that for you," I said, trying to smile. "She said so specifically."

He smiled, and I realized again what a pleasant face he had, even though there were dark circles under his eyes and lines on either side of his mouth from fatigue. "And your niece? Is she staying with Mrs. Thompson today?"

I nodded. "Mrs. Thompson has said she will stay as long as needed, to look after Evelyn so I can work. She'll care for the boarders, too. She's an angel."

With their brief snack down to crumbs, Captain McLeod brushed off his hands. "That hit the spot. But I'd better get back."

"You are going to sleep eventually, aren't you?" I asked.

He nodded. "I am. I've been up and doctoring for over thirty hours now. I'll need to rest sometime. I thought I'd try to find a hotel room. All I need is somewhere to lay my head for a bit."

I shook my head. The captain had hopped on a train, volunteered to help in the disaster, and had worked through the night saving lives. He deserved much more than a place to "lay his head".

"That won't do at all," I said primly. "Even if you could somehow manage to find a room." I thought of Harry who hadn't made it home last night, and felt the sting of that loss, too. The entourage at Jane's… they were my surrogate family. It hurt to think of losing any one of them. But I also had to be practical. We had room. Hadn't I told Mrs. Thompson that we all had to stick together?

"To put matters bluntly, one of our boarders is unlikely to make it home. There is a bed, food, hot water, and as you know, the location is perfect. You'll stay with us."

He stared at me, then chuckled. "That's the voice you use with your patients, isn't it?"

I couldn't help but smile back, though it felt strange to be able to do so in the midst of so much pain and chaos. "Was it convincing?"

"Maybe."

"Good. And even if Harry, by some miracle, makes it back, there's room for you, Captain." Right now, there was Jane's room sitting empty, and if push came to shove, we could arrange Evelyn's room into something suitable and Evelyn could sleep with me.

His eyes cooled the slightest bit at my last word. I'd chosen to address him by rank deliberately; I certainly liked the captain, and he was kind and considerate. But that was all. Despite offering him what would normally be considered a paltry lunch, our association was a professional, not a personal one. At the very best it was friendly. After all, he was the only one I'd really spoken to about my family. Somehow talking to a stranger was easier than speaking to one of the other nurses I considered friends—and truthfully, we'd all been much too busy to be chatty. I'd noticed Irene working, her head stitched and bandaged, and Jessie and the others had all been bustling around, treating patients as quickly as possible. There'd been no time to chat at all.

"If you're sure Mrs. Thompson won't mind, it does sound better than trying to find a hotel room."

"I don't think she'll mind at all." I smiled at him again. "In fact, I think she'd give me what for if I didn't offer."

"Then I accept."

I gave a brisk nod. "Good. I'll send a note over, so you can go whenever you're ready. No need to wait for me."

"Thank you, Nurse Crowell."

"Of course." I packed up the thermos again and rolled my shoulders. "Now, I've got to get back."

"As do I."

I worked non-stop for the rest of the day, my weariness growing by the hour. Our "big" hospital, which had once seemed so busy with convalescent patients, was now heaving with wounded; it felt as if we'd treated thousands. Some of the nurses and doctors working now I'd never seen before, replacements from all over the city and province, including Dr. Cox, the oculist from Pictou County that I'd seen last night. He was still working, treating eye and facial injuries.

My feet ached and I found myself blinking repeatedly, trying to moisten my dry eyes as I closed an incision and moved on to the next patient. Sustained by only a few slices of bread and a single molasses cookie, I found my stomach rumbling as I finished and went to wash my hands, the raw skin stinging from so much soap, water, and disinfectant.

The storm had finally stopped but it was fully dark when I was instructed to go home for the day. When I inquired, I was told that Captain McLeod had gone around four. He had been on his feet and treating patients for over twenty-four hours and awake for many more than that. But I was glad he hadn't waited for me and had gone on to the house. He needed rest, and I… well, tonight I wanted to make the walk alone. I'd been around people all day. Heard the horrible stories that the wounded couldn't help but share as they all tried to make sense of what had happened and how the shape of their families had suddenly changed. And at home there would be more to face—more questions I didn't have the answers to, more worry and fear. But for ten short minutes, I could be quiet with myself. I needed it desperately, because there was one job I had yet to do that I couldn't put off any longer.

I had to send a letter to my grandparents and… my brothers.

All day I'd worked at saving people, but now I would become the blunt instrument that delivered the kind of news that broke people's hearts. My dear grandparents… Gramp with his soft smile and the patience of Job, and Gram, who bustled around like a buzzing bee and came up with absurd sayings that made us all laugh. And my brothers… not quite men, not quite boys… how could I be the one to light the fuse that would blow their lives apart?

Anger shivered through me. I hadn't lit the fuse. This damned war had. And it was costing so many so much.

There was no way to telephone; Gram and Grampie had no phone at their house, and as news filtered through the hospital I was not surprised to learn the telegraph and telephone lines were down. A letter would take time, too, and I briefly considered waiting. It had snowed all day. Surely the mail was also delayed, but waiting would only make it harder. Instead, I found a corner, as well as a sheet of paper and a pen, took a deep breath, and began the missive that would surely break my family's hearts.

The burden of it sat heavy on my shoulders, but there was no one else.

There was no one else.

Dear Gram and Grampie,

As I am sure you have heard, yesterday there was a horrible explosion. It has been so very busy at the hospital, and this is my first chance to write.

I paused. How could I possibly couch this in gentle terms? There was no soft way to explain what had happened, what I knew and didn't know. My throat tightened as the pen hovered above the paper, a teardrop of ink plopping onto the corner and leaving a black stain. It jolted me back into the moment and I put nib to paper again.

Yesterday, Mum and Dad, Jane and Clara went to the harbour to see the ships. We have not heard from them since, but I have not given up hope. We hear of rescues happening every hour, so I hope to write to you with better news soon. As soon as I can, I shall start looking at the other hospitals.

I am working long hours at Camp Hill treating the wounded. Our neighbour, Mrs. Thompson, is caring for Evelyn and the boarders in my absence and has offered to do so until Jane returns. I am writing this at the end of my shift, so perhaps they are already home and waiting for me. Please give the boys my love and try not to worry. I will write again as soon as I can, and the moment I have any news.

Love to you all,
Nora

I ran my fingers beneath my eyes as I finished. Was I wrong to give them false hope? Or did I truly believe that somehow my family could still be alive? I wanted to. Oh, I wanted to hold onto the fraying cord of hope. But deep in the very depths of my soul, I knew it wouldn't come to pass. Perhaps it was seeing all the carnage in the hospital. Perhaps it was the increasing number of bodies that no doctor could help. Either way, it was a bone-deep knowing that I couldn't shake. I folded the letter and tucked it into my pocket.

The snow was deep, over the tops of my boots, and the city was nearly dark as I left the hospital behind and trudged toward the post office, hoping someone would still be there to receive the letter, hoping mail trains would be running and that my family would soon have some news. I thought about Alley, and his silence over the past seven weeks. Knowing the worst couldn't possibly be worse than not knowing, could it? My imagination often got the best of me when thinking about him. What if he were killed, missing? What if I'd missed his name on the casualty lists? How was it that I had given up hope on my family but still held onto the tiny fragments of hope that Alley would come back?

The dark streets and melancholy mood weighed me down as I reached the post office. It had been damaged in the blast, too, but I was gratified to see two clerks still working as I stepped inside. They looked at me kindly, and somehow it was almost worse to see kindness and sympathy; the smallest bit of gentleness threatened to break the dam of my emotions. Instead, I set my lips and kept the transaction as businesslike as possible, putting my mittens back on as I left the post office and headed back up the hill toward home, each step on the incline heavier than the last.

Even though the city was blanketed in snow, it felt changed. Sad and grieving, but also afraid; yet in the midst of the destruction and loss I met people with purpose and a strange sort of optimism. Those who had survived were prepared to help their neighbours. The tinny thud of hammers echoed thinly through the winter air. A wagon passed me, loaded with wooden caskets, and I shuddered, but also felt a sliver of gratitude knowing that the bodies of those lost were being treated with care. However, I refused to envision any of my loved ones in the new pine.

So much had changed in less than a day. Last night I'd been desperate to see if my family was home safe and sound; tonight, as I trudged through another snow drift, I abandoned hope. Not that I could say that out loud. I could just imagine the looks on Evelyn's and Mrs. Thompson's faces if I said such a thing. But the truth was, the longer time went on, the less likely it was that any of my family would be found alive. It was a cold, hard truth I needed to accept.

My chest tightened and I halted on the corner of Jubilee and Henry, bending and putting my hands on my knees as I struggled to draw in a breath. Cold and pain knifed through my lungs, heavy grief sitting just behind my breastbone. For this moment, I let it in—the gaping maw of loss that had been waiting to suck me in at the first sign of weakness. I realized that for a day and a half I'd felt things, but they'd been wrapped in a layer of numbness to protect me. That layer was now gone, and everything rushed in and took me to my knees.

My sister, my best friend… Our last conversation ran through my mind. Jane was the most unselfish person I knew. For her to offer to raise my baby… to love him or her… She'd offered to do it without condition or question. Jane had always been on my side. To think we'd never speak again… Oh God, if Jane were dead, I prayed she hadn't suffered. And sweet baby Clara…

I sank into the snowbank, thinking about Clara's toothy smiles and belly laughs, or the way she liked to snuggle on my shoulder, her warm face tucked into the crook of my neck. Over the past thirty-six hours I'd seen my share of dead bodies, children included, and until now, I'd pushed the shock and horror of it into a little box inside myself just so I could keep going. Now, though, a corner of the box opened, and nausea burned the back of my throat as I imagined little Clara's still, grey face. I turned and retched until there was nothing left to come up and I could only heave. So much blood, and brokenness, and death.

Remorse washed over me, heavy with regrets. I hadn't even said a proper goodbye to my family that morning. I'd been running late and had rushed, offering a called-out goodbye, saying I'd see them all at dinner. If I had only known it would be the last time…

Family was everything. Mum had always told us that. Now, unless there was a supreme miracle, I would never see them again.

Cold, wet snow bit through my clothing as I knelt, pulling for breath, and wanting to erase the past two days and go back to the moment when Jane had offered me such unconditional support. When she'd announced that together we'd manage the changes to come. When the idea of our parents visiting had brought a rush of excitement to the house, and the laughter during that final supper, when we'd all sat around the table, talking and making plans for a big family Christmas. We'd prayed for Jimmy to come home safely, and Mum had read the girls a bedtime story. A big, happy family… gone. Now I was in

Halifax alone, with two younger brothers back in Chester who… The breaths came faster now as I struggled for air and my head went light. My little brothers, who so desperately needed parenting still as they made the journey from boyhood to manhood. Who would provide that? Not me. I was a woman and single and pregnant. I was the last person to set an example and guide anyone to adulthood. Our grandparents, I supposed…

So. Much. Loss. I didn't know how to begin to make sense of it all.

So I sat in the snow until I couldn't feel my knees any longer. The street was dark and quiet, everyone inside their homes seeking the illusion of safety and comfort. Cold, wet, exhausted, and anxious, I finally pushed myself up and wobbled for a moment, then started the final steps to take me to the house. The car was now a snow-covered lump; Dad's pride and joy, abandoned to the storm. Most of the curtains were drawn, lending an eeriness to the evening. I climbed the steps to the door and paused on the porch for a moment, garnering the strength to go inside. This porch, where Alley had kissed me for the first time. Alley, whose presence I missed every day, a beam of light in the darkness. If he were here, he'd hold my hand, flash his ready smile, and tell me it was all going to be all right. I would have someone to lean on, instead of being so horribly alone and scared.

It would never be all right again. Not with this gaping hole in my heart. I could work my fingers to the bone trying to avoid facing the truth, but eventually I'd have to stop running and face the tragedy that was my life. I was alone. Not just alone, but responsible for a four-year-old child and this big house and my work and the baby growing inside me. This had never been the life I'd wanted. It was Jane's life. And now I had no choice but to step into it. The weight of that responsibility warred with my grief for the right to overwhelm me.

With a worn sigh, I stepped to the door and let myself in.

The house was warm and welcoming, and I shut the door as quietly as possible so I could take a moment and let the desperately needed comfort wash over me. Voices came from the kitchen, the words muffled but the tone easy and somehow… light. Mrs. Thompson's higher voice, followed by John's gruffer one and a laugh that was unfamiliar… Captain McLeod's? A door opened and closed upstairs… that had to be Milton, unless Harry had somehow made it back. But I saw no evidence of my family's return, and felt guilty that I didn't expect it, either. What would they think of me, giving up on them so easily?

I unbuttoned my coat, took off my boots, and tiptoed upstairs. I wanted to change out of my dirty uniform before going to the kitchen to find some supper. I had to eat—for myself and for the baby. I could only get through this a minute at a time. One small chore at a time. Right now it was changing my clothes and feeding my physical body. With a hollow laugh, I realized I was actually triaging my own care.

After I had changed, I stepped to the kitchen doorway and paused for a moment to absorb the scene in front of me, hungrily drinking in the small bit of normalcy.

Mrs. Thompson was at the sink, washing up some dishes, and Milton was beside her, a dishtowel in his hand, drying the plates and stacking them together. John and Captain McLeod sat at the table, both relaxed and leaning back in their chairs. Captain McLeod looked slightly more rested than he had earlier today, and an easy smile was on his lips as Milton made a joke. John looked exhausted, lines appearing at the corners of his eyes and edges of his mouth. But even without Jane and the children, there was a sense of family that eased the knot in my chest the tiniest bit. Captain McLeod's words from last night echoed in my head again. *You aren't alone.* I wasn't, not entirely. I put my hand on my belly, thinking of the child that rested there. I wasn't alone now, but would that change when they found out I was expecting?

John looked up and saw me there. "Nora." His weary smile brightened his face. "It's good to see you home."

Captain McLeod turned and caught my eye, sending me a smile, though concern darkened his eyes. "They let you go for the day?"

I nodded. "Yes. It's still so busy, though." I sighed. "The people just don't stop coming."

We both knew eventually they would, though. And when that happened, the process of rebuilding would begin.

"Sit down, Nora, and I'll get your supper. I saved it for you. You're white as a sheet and as my mum used to say, a bird can't fly on one wing." Mrs. Thompson fluttered around, retrieving a bowl, fork, and knife. Before long, I found myself seated at the table with a bowl of stew and dough boys and a cup of bracing hot tea. It smelled delicious and tasted even better, and I wasted no time at all digging in. I was starving. There was some momentary guilt about being able to eat when my emotions were in such turmoil, but I quickly pushed it aside.

As I ate, Milton and John filled me in on what was happening around town. It seemed the entire province and beyond had mobilized to address the dire need for help. The Halifax Relief Committee had been formed the day before, to help residents with the immediate needs of housing, food, and safety. Trains had begun arriving with medical supplies and personnel, food, and clothing. All this had happened despite the storm raging outside. Temporary housing had been set up on The Common, but it was the soldiers sleeping in the tents, having given up their barracks to those left homeless. The 63rd Rifles provided a mounted guard all night, after working at rescues all day.

The Chebucto School had been established as a mortuary in addition to Snow's over on Argyle. I bit my lip as Milton described coffins stacked like crates outside of Snow's funeral home and said empty coffins had come from Christie Brothers in Amherst, filled with food.

Outside of Camp Hill, the entire city was abuzz with activity. The hospital was my world, but there was so much going on outside of it. I took in the information but didn't say anything about my trip to the post office. I wasn't ready for the looks of sympathy I'd get from the others about having to write the letter. They were already careful around me, probably because it was hard to disguise the fact that I'd been crying earlier.

Mrs. Thompson collected my empty bowl and gave my shoulder a squeeze. "Evelyn is asleep on the chesterfield," she said softly. "She didn't want to go to bed without you."

"She can sleep with me again," I said. "She's scared, and I think it reassures us both."

John looked at me, his brown eyes serious and sad. "About Mrs. Boutilier and the baby… and your folks, too, Nora…"

"It's okay, John." I took a deep breath and prepared to speak my truth. "I think we all know it's unlikely they're going to walk through that door." My voice broke on the last word. "I'm trying very hard not to fall apart about it."

"Oh, my dear," Mrs. Thompson said, squeezing my shoulder again.

But what I really wanted was a reassuring hug from my mother. To see Jane's face and have her say that we would get through anything together. Mrs. Thompson offered comfort, but it wasn't the same.

I was twenty-three years old and now, with Jimmy still away, the one person responsible for Evelyn and the two remaining boarders at the house. I mentally pushed aside the supportive touch. I had to, so I didn't fall apart in front of them all. For now, I had to treat home the same as the hospital. By dealing with what had to be done, and not dwelling on everything else.

Throughout all of it, I sensed Captain McLeod's gaze on me, as if he could read my thoughts.

Milton hung up the dishtowel—it was so strange to see one of the male boarders helping with household chores—and leaned against the counter. The older man was gruff and slightly grizzled, but he had a heart of gold. Both men had promised to look out for Jane when Jimmy had gone overseas, and in the years since he'd been gone, they had proved themselves considerate and honourable. Milton's wife had died of typhoid years earlier and he'd never remarried, and his job driving the street cars seemed to provide him with a sense of contentment. And John… well, John was a dedicated bachelor, though no one knew why or even if he had any family. He kept to himself, but he was kind and a hard worker. Jane had relied on them; now I must as well.

"Nora—Miss Crowell—I hope you know that John and me… well, we'll pitch in and do whatever needs doin' to keep things runnin' smooth here. You just say the word."

I smiled faintly. "Thank you, Milton. I appreciate it more than you know."

John cleared his throat. "I'm hearin' about miracles all the time, you know. Heck, today they found a little girl safe and sound, all because she'd been covered by an ash pan. Imagine that. Don't give up all hope, Nora."

Bless John and his optimism, but I had discovered something about myself yesterday and had it confirmed today. I understood why Jane had worried about me when I'd started stepping out with Alley. It was a side of me no one had ever seen before, one that I hadn't even known existed. I could suddenly see Jane's perspective with absolute clarity, because now, faced with a crisis of gigantic proportions, my true character was taking over. That strong, practical side that made me a good nurse was suddenly front and centre. It didn't mean I didn't have a heart. But I had never been one for flights of fancy, and despite John's words of hope and encouragement, I knew, deep inside, that my family was lost to me. And that somehow I'd find a way to go on.

But before I could do that, I had to find them. I couldn't just accept that they were gone. If my family had perished—and surely they had—it was up to me to find them and ensure a proper burial. They deserved that last thing.

"Thank you, John," I said softly. "Thank you to all of you. We all need to stick together. And Mrs. Thompson… I don't know how to thank you."

I looked up at Captain McLeod. "And Captain… you are welcome to stay here as long as you need." It was strange, making that decision in a house that wasn't my own, but they were all looking to me in this moment, and I could not let them down.

"I feel odd, being in Harry's room," Captain McLeod admitted, looking around the table at everyone. "His things…"

"Poor old soul," Mrs. Thompson murmured, her mouth turned into a sad, inverted U. "I don't suppose there's much hope for him, though. Not with him working on the docks like he did. The paper today… it said the sugar refinery is just gone, and so's everything else on that stretch of the waterfront. Dominion Textile's roof and second floor collapsed with those poor workers inside. Even across the harbour… Dartmouth had its share of destruction, too."

Milton sat down at the table. "Tuft's Cove is washed away.

The wave after the blast demolished it. The Oland factory was damaged, too."

Tuft's Cove. The native people who lived there called it Turtle Grove. There'd been some controversy lately about them being moved to a different reserve, and now it seemed it was all moot. If there was nothing left of their homes… The ache in my heart deepened. So much senseless destruction.

As I finished my tea, the trio at the table filled me and Captain McLeod in on what details they knew. By the time they'd finished, my brain was swimming. More information about the two ships colliding was revealed, and now there were even rumours of German sabotage. I remembered talking to Alley about it once, about the possibility of German spies among us. At the time it had seemed so far-fetched and unbelievable. Now? It wasn't so difficult to fathom.

Captain McLeod took a drink of tea and put his cup back on the table, letting out a deep sigh. When he discovered everyone looking at him, he chuckled. "Sorry," he offered, a smile curling the corner of his mouth. "I think the good food and pleasant company has allowed me to relax, but I'm ready for bed." He pushed away from the table. "Thank you all for being so welcoming and you, Nurse Crowell, for opening your home."

"Of course." I smiled, though it took effort as my own exhaustion was overwhelming. "I think I'll head up as well."

"Evelyn is sleeping in the parlour," Mrs. Thompson said. "I hate to wake her, but…"

Captain McLeod cleared his throat. "I can carry her up, if you like. If you don't think she'll mind, that is."

"I doubt she'll wake," I admitted. "She's a very sound sleeper." It occurred to me, however, that Captain McLeod would be entering my bedroom, something that was definitely not appropriate.

An unexpected surge of anger flared in my breast. Why on earth did appropriateness even matter right now? It didn't. He was simply doing a kindness, which I appreciated because I was indeed ready to tip over, and the idea of carrying the girl up the long flight of stairs felt like climbing a mountain.

Evelyn was asleep, curled up on a pillow with her soft flannel nightgown tucked around her feet. My fiery temper of moments ago dissipated into nothingness at the sight of my niece, and a swell of guilt took its place. It didn't seem right that Evelyn had had to endure the last few days with a neighbour and two middle-aged but well-intentioned men. I wished I could be in two places at once—helping the wounded at the hospital and caring for my niece at the same time. Jane would want that, wouldn't she? Mrs. Thompson was a godsend, but she wasn't *family*. And I loved Evelyn dearly. Yet how could I abandon my post? I couldn't. I was part of the army. I'd worked hard to be there, and I was good at what I did. I didn't *want* to give it up. But suddenly that felt so very selfish when compared to a motherless child.

Captain McLeod slipped his hands beneath Evelyn's slumbering form and lifted her easily into his arms. I brushed a silky lock of hair off Evelyn's face, but the little girl never moved, she was so fast asleep. With soft steps, we climbed the stairs to the upper floor, my heart breaking anew with each tread. With every hour, every minute that passed, the likelihood that anyone from my family would return home disintegrated into dust.

Jane should be here. Our parents should be here. Alley should be here. But right now, a stranger was carrying my niece upstairs, and not a soul knew that I was pregnant. I had absolutely no one to turn to about so many of the things rioting around in my head and heart. Pain centred, sharp and sure, in the middle of my chest. How I wished Jane or Mum would walk through the door downstairs and tell me it had all been a horrible dream. For the briefest of moments less than forty-eight hours ago, my heart had been at ease, thinking that with Jane's help I could navigate having this baby. But now Jane's help—and her offer—were gone.

I hesitated at my bedroom door, then stepped inside. "I hope you don't mind if I don't turn on a light," I whispered. "I don't want to wake her if I don't have to."

"It's fine," came his soft voice from beside me.

"She's sleeping with me for the moment. It's… comforting."

For both of us, I realized. Evelyn's presence was life-affirming and frankly gave me a reason to go on beyond the fact that I was needed at the hospital. I turned down the neatly made covers and stepped aside so he could place the child on the soft mattress.

Evelyn's eyes flickered open. "Mummy?"

"Shhh," I soothed, stepping in and sitting on the edge of the bed. "It's Auntie Nora. It's time for bed now."

"I want Mummy."

I swallowed tightly. "I know, Evvie. So do I. But you get under the covers now, and I'll be back in two shakes of a lamb's tail. All right?"

Evelyn nodded and burrowed into the cold covers, but I saw a tear slide out of the corner of her eye and I wasn't sure how much more I could take today. I was still raw from my earlier cry in the snow; seeing my niece crying for her mother plucked painfully at my heart. "I'll be right back," I whispered, trying to keep my voice from cracking, and then I slipped from the room, Captain McLeod behind me.

"Thank you for carrying her upstairs," I murmured, as we stood out in the hall. His room was only steps away, the bathroom in between the doorways. "We should both get some sleep. Another long day tomorrow."

I avoided looking into his face. I didn't want to see pity on his features. Or worse, understanding. Keeping emotional distance was the only way I was holding things together.

"Nurse Crowell… " This time it was his voice that cracked. "I'm very sorry there's been no news of your family. It's unfathomable to think of that little girl without a mother."

I lifted my chin. "She's got me," I replied firmly, but then the import of verbalizing my earlier thoughts cut me off at the knees. "Oh, heavens. Me. If Jane doesn't return, Evelyn…" Panic crept through my chest. "Her father's overseas. Until he returns…"

"You're her mother."

"I'm her mother." Before I could think better of it, I put my hand to my belly, thinking of my own child there. How on earth was I going to be able to parent two children, all on my own? How could I do it without the support of my family?

Tears started to fall again, running out of my eyes in hot streams that I was helpless to staunch. Mortified, I turned to rush away, but he reached out and gripped my wrist, stopping my progress.

"It's all right," he said gently, and then he did the most surprising thing. He hugged me.

The intimacy was utterly improper. He was a captain, I a lieutenant. He was a doctor, I was a nurse. He was a single man, and I was a single woman, pregnant with another man's child, and he was holding me in a tight embrace while I cried pitifully on his shoulder, my salty tears soaking into the wool of his uniform.

"I'm so sorry," I squeaked, appalled at my behaviour, even as I was unable to stop the flood of emotion.

His wide hand rubbed my back. "It's all right," he repeated.

"It's all right to cry. You don't have to hold it in. You're still here, and you're safe, and from what I've seen the past two days, you're incredibly strong. I promise you, Nurse Crowell, that your strength will see you through this. And when you begin to feel alone, you've just to ask your friends for help." He released me a little and tilted my chin up to look at him. "I hope you will count me as one of those friends."

I stepped back and wiped my cheeks with my hands. "That is all we can ever be," I said, my face hot. "I have a… a beau in—" I broke off. Where was Alley now? France? Belgium? How would I know? Still, the lack of letters didn't stop me from hoping. He was the father of my baby. That fact alone made any intimacy with Captain McLeod awkward and inappropriate.

"—at the front," I finished.

"Friends," he repeated, his blue gaze warm. "That is all I want, too. You don't need to worry about that."

Having a friend sounded rather nice right now, so I nodded in agreement, though something inside told me this was not as uncomplicated as it sounded.

"Get some rest," he suggested. "We've another long day tomorrow, but we can walk over together if you like."

"That might be nice."

He gave me a nod, then turned and headed into his own room, going inside and shutting the door with a light click.

I scuttled back into my room and didn't even bother changing out of my skirt and sweater. Instead, I crawled into the bed with Evelyn, curling around her tiny body to give us both warmth, and fell into a dreamless sleep.

Chapter Ten

CHARLOTTE

December 8, 1917

My eyelids felt gritty as they slid open, but for the first time since arriving at the hospital, I woke and my head didn't throb, and I no longer saw spots in front of my eyes.

My leg ached so much, I felt it clear up to my hip. I ran my fingers down my thigh and encountered a heavy bandage beneath my slip.

Several times over the past few days I'd awakened, roused by the sounds of pain and distress around me, trying to shut out the awful noise by putting my hands over my ears. Being awake meant thinking about Aileen, and that was torturous enough without listening to everyone else's grief.

I vaguely remembered nurses tending to me, and once I'd

been alert enough to drink some tea before falling into oblivion again.

But this time felt different. I was awake. Alert. And still with that horrible, horrible emptiness, knowing that my baby was out there somewhere, waiting for her mother. Was my daughter wondering where I was? Were strangers caring for her? I refused to believe that she was dead. If I had come through alive, Aileen could have as well. She *had*. Anything else was incomprehensible.

"Nurse? Nurse?"

My voice croaked after two days of not using it and not having food or much to drink. One of the sisters, a pleasant-looking one in her blue uniform and starched apron, approached the bed. "Mrs. Campbell. How lovely to see you awake! How are you feeling?"

The answer was ridiculously complicated, so I kept it simple. "Thirsty," I replied.

"Let me get you some water and see if the doctor can check you over."

The nurse slipped away, and I wondered how she was able to move without making a sound. I shifted on the cot, trying to get comfortable, and winced as a few of my joints and muscles twinged.

When the nurse came back, a tall doctor followed. He had a kind face, with blue eyes and blond hair that had just a little wave, reminding me of Frank's and creating another deep ache in my breast. The nurse held up a cup and helped me drink, and then smiled. "Mrs. Campbell, this is Doctor McLeod. He's going to look at your wounds."

The doctor stepped forward. "Good morning, Mrs. Campbell. It's very good to see you awake." I stared at him as he examined the stitches on my head and took my pulse. "I must check your leg wound," he said kindly. "We'll remove the bandage, have a look at the stitches, and then rebandage it for you. All right?"

I curled into myself a little. He was a doctor and here to help, but the idea of him looking under my slip… I'd never considered myself overly modest, but there was something improper about it somehow. I'd had a midwife when I had Aileen. And… there were so many people around.

"Mrs. Campbell?" He looked down at me, and I noticed that his eyes were kind and patient. "Would you be more comfortable with the nurse removing your bandages? I do have to have a look, but she is very capable."

I reminded myself that when I'd been unconscious, a surgeon had not only seen my leg but had operated on it. He was a doctor, for heaven's sake. I gave a tremulous nod, then squared my shoulders. What was modesty in times like this? "That would be fine."

The nurse's hands were gentle but confident as she removed the bandage from my thigh. When she lifted the leg to slide the old bandage beneath it, the muscles resisted, and I caught my breath as pain darted the length of my leg. "You're sure to have some stiffness and pain for a while. That's natural while it heals, and then when you get the muscles working again." The doctor's voice was smooth and reassuring. "You're very lucky, Mrs. Campbell. You should make a full recovery, I think."

Lucky? A full recovery? Without Aileen? Impossible. How could I live when my heart was ripped out of my chest?

I looked up into his face. "Do you know if a baby has been brought in, about a year old, with light curly hair and blue eyes? She was in a dark-blue carriage and wearing a pink coat and mittens. Her name is Aileen… " My voice cracked, and I pressed my lips together. I was afraid to start crying. Afraid that if I started, I might never stop.

Sympathy etched his face. "Not that I'm aware of, but I'll have one of the nurses check to see if we have a young patient that fits your description." He squatted down beside my bed and met my gaze. "Mrs. Campbell, there are many hospitals overflowing with patients right now. If she isn't here, it's possible she's at one of the others."

"Or that she's—" I broke off, a sob clogging my throat. I couldn't bring myself to say the word, but it bounced around in my brain. *Dead. Dead dead dead.*

"Yes, that's possible as well." His voice had softened even further with sympathy. Somehow it made things worse.

I shook my head, even though the movement hurt. "No, I'd know if she were. I'd know in here." I punched my fist to my heart. "I need to find her. Perhaps the papers..."

The nurse tucked away the old bandage. "I can bring you a paper, Mrs. Campbell, but it... well, it might be a bit overwhelming."

More overwhelming than not knowing where my daughter was? I doubted it.

"All right, let's have a look at these stitches," Dr. McLeod said, shifting the sheet to examine my wound.

His fingers were gentle but even so, the touch hurt, and I winced as he seemed to probe in all the tender spots. "It's healing well. There was significant trauma to your leg, Mrs. Campbell. But you didn't lose it, so there's a blessing."

Blessings. Well, wasn't that right up there with being lucky. I wasn't feeling particularly blessed at the moment. How much more loss was I supposed to take? First my parents. Then, after such a brief happiness, I lost Frank. The only reason I'd kept going at all after his death was because I had Aileen to love, and who loved me back. What reason did I have now, if Aileen was gone? Grief ballooned inside me, a huge ball of it sitting on my chest, making it hard to breathe. I started to picture what might have happened to her… what might have happened to her little body, and suddenly I was gasping for air. Oh God, was this how she'd felt? Suffocating? Afraid?

"Mrs. Campbell… Mrs. Campbell. It's going to be all right. You're just having a bit of a panic, that's all. Try to breathe slower. Deeper breath in… full breath out. That's it."

It wasn't it. Breathing slower eased the ball of grief but replaced it with a pain so sharp, I thought I might die from it. "My baby," I wheezed. "I can't go on without my baby."

I knew, in that moment, that without Aileen, I couldn't do this. I couldn't live. If she were dead, then so was I.

"Mrs. Campbell." The doctor's voice was firm but not cruel. "There's a chance your daughter is not dead. But if you are going to try to find her, you'll need your strength. That means healing so you can walk. It means doing what the nurses tell you. Then you can begin searching for her." He leaned down and squeezed my hand. "Mrs. Campbell, it's possible that she's already home with your family, isn't it?"

It felt like this was his way of giving me false hope, but I was desperate enough to reach for it. I gave a small nod, focusing on his eyes. He didn't look away, like people did when they were lying. "My husband's family…"

"There, now." He let go of my fingers and straightened. "Good luck to you, Mrs. Campbell. I hope you find your daughter and your family safe and sound."

As much as I disliked my mother-in-law and most of Frank's family, the thought that Aileen could be with them right now gave me something to focus on. Regardless of what they thought of me, they did love Aileen. Especially Alice, even if she didn't like to let on. There were times I thought Alice might be a nice girl if she could just get away from her mother's bitterness and need to control everything. If Aileen were with them, she'd be waiting for me to come home. And if not—if she were in the hospital, like me—I needed to get well to start to search for her.

"Good girl," the nursing sister said to me, her lips upturned. "Let's start you on some broth and start rebuilding your strength."

If it meant I could see Aileen again, I'd eat every spoonful and do whatever she told me.

Aileen was waiting for me. I just knew it.

Chapter Eleven

NORA

December 11, 1917

Once the initial influx of wounded eased, the hospital remained a hive of activity, but it at least felt more organized. Or perhaps *contained* was a better word. The emergencies became fewer, and I found myself involved in the continuing care of serious cases or checking on those who returned to the hospital for ongoing treatment. Still, conditions were incredibly cramped.

It also meant that it was time to begin the grim task of looking for my family.

In those first few days, my eyes burned from scanning the lists of the dead in the newspapers. Encouraged that their names were not listed, I then spent a precious day off going from hospital to hospital, searching for any sort of clue. Even if they'd passed through… I had shaken my head at that thought, knowing it was folly. If they'd been seen and released, they'd be home already. My job now was to find out what had happened to them to… what? Have a proper burial? I supposed so, though it felt incomprehensible. But what else was there to do?

There was no sign of them at the Victoria General, nor at the hospital set up by the team from Harvard at Bellevue House. I checked with the military facilities but came back with nothing, my steps weary and my heart heavier. I even paid a call to Dr. Ligoure's clinic on North Street. The Trinidadian-born doctor had no hospital privileges in the city, but I'd heard some of the doctors talking about how he'd treated victims for free after the explosion. It was unlikely, but I had to check every possibility before giving up. There was still a tiny flicker of hope, deep inside me, that wondered if there might be a miracle.

Throughout it all, I was witness to the devastation in the city, worse the closer to the north end I got. It would take weeks to clear the debris. Longer than that to rebuild. No soldiers were to be deployed during the emergency period; all leaves were canceled. Places like The Green Lantern had transitioned into distribution sites for clothing and footwear. Food lines formed at City Hall.

The idea that things could ever return to "normal" was ridiculous. The job ahead was gargantuan. It wasn't just brick and mortar that needed fixing, either. The personal costs were so much higher. How did people put lives back together when families had been blown apart? How did you put a price on that sort of loss?

As the hours went on and I grew more and more weary, I longed to see my brothers and grandparents, to have some connection to family, to band together and find solace. But authorities were asking people not to travel to the city, with its already strained-beyond-belief resources, and it was my duty to stay. So far we'd made do with a few paltry letters. It wasn't the same as a hug.

I finally staggered home and stood outside the house for a good fifteen minutes, staring up at the windows. I couldn't feel my toes, they were so cold, and my lips were chapped from the brisk wind. Yet the cold was preferable right now. Inside was so difficult. I kept expecting to hear Jane's voice. Everything reminded me of her.

"Nora? What are you after doing outside?"

I spun around to see Mrs. Thompson coming up the walk, Evelyn at her side, both of them bundled in knitted hats and thick mittens. Mrs. Thompson carried a bag in her hand.

The older woman bent down and gave Evelyn something out of her pocket, then whispered something in her ear.

Whatever she'd said, Evelyn darted off happily. Mrs. Thompson chuckled after her as she awkwardly turned the doorknob and then slammed the door behind her. "My land, she's a cute one," she said. "We were coming up Spring Garden just now and a boy went arse over teakettle in the snow and I thought she was going to fall over from laughing." She looked closer at me. "Nora, you look a fright. What's wrong?"

I stared at the door. "I don't want to go inside yet. Oh, Mrs. T, I've checked all the hospitals. No one has seen them at all." I shuddered. "Next I'll have to check the morgues."

"Come inside, dear. You're worn clear out. I'll make us both some tea and you can sit by the fire to get warmed up. You're not going to solve anything sittin' out here."

I knew she was right. With a weary sigh, I followed her into the house, hung up my coat, and sank into a chair in the kitchen while Mrs. T put away the items she'd bought, chatting to break the silence.

"I had a bit of a time at the grocery," she remarked. "Some of the goods are scarce as hen's teeth and sugar was awful dear. But I'll make do." She smiled and put a small packet of coffee in the cupboard. "My mum was a champ at making a meal stretch. And it didn't matter what it was, she could throw it all in a fry pan and make it come out tasting good." She gave me a wink. "I think her secret was to always add a bit of onion for flavour."

I tried not to picture Jane as she used to bustle around the kitchen, humming and cooking for everyone, and instead focused on the warmth from the fire. Mrs. Thompson pulled out a chair and joined me with her own cup of tea, unsweetened but with the smallest dollop of milk turning it a muddy brown. I noticed, though, that she'd added a full teaspoon to mine. Funny how a spoonful of sugar felt like love.

Mrs. T took a first sip and then gave me an eagle eye. "Nora, you're going to work yourself sick, that's what."

"I'm fine, Mrs. T. I promise."

"You're taking on too much. Workin' all day at the hospital, looking after those soldiers and all the people who were hurt… and on top of that, searching the other places for your folks. You come home looking like you've been through the wringer."

"It's not too much," I insisted. "We're all tired right now, but don't ask me to stop. I need to know what happened, if I can. I need to find them and…" I stopped, took a breath. "They're not at the hospitals, Mrs. T. If they are at one of the morgues, I need to find them and make arrangements. I need to do that for them."

"All right, all right," Mrs. T soothed. "Far be it from me to stop you. You've always been so determined, ever since you arrived here, about to start your nursing studies."

That had been years earlier. I had still been a girl. And Mrs. Thompson's husband had still been alive. The two of them had been surrogate parents to Jane and me. Now Mrs. Thompson and I only had each other.

And because of that long-standing connection, Mrs. Thompson had known exactly the right thing to say. Perhaps life was a shambles right now, but I had always prided myself on knowing my mind and being one to act rather than shy away. Perhaps that determination had also caused me some problems—my current state being one—but it provided a reserve of strength for me to draw upon. Having Mrs. T understand and not fight me on that meant the world.

"What would I do without you?" I asked softly, a little tremor in the words.

"Oh, you'd muddle along, I expect. But I'm awful glad I can help. Besides, I'd be lonely without you, too."

"I've written to Jimmy," I confessed. I'd penned the letter last night and mailed it this morning during my hospital search. "A man goes off to war and must worry about his own life, not the ones of the family he left behind. Now half the family is gone…" The ache was back in my chest again. Clara's little giggles, Jane's smile and gentle but firm mothering. For the millionth time I wondered how I could get through life without my sister and parents.

Mrs. Thompson just shook her head; there was nothing she could say that made any of this any better.

"Mrs. Thompson?"

"Yes, dear?"

"I'm going to have to step into being Evelyn's mother." Once the words were out of my mouth, the weight of them settled heavy on my shoulders. The other secret sat on my tongue, but I couldn't bring myself to say the words. I needed the older woman so badly right now and was so afraid that if Mrs.

Thompson knew the truth, she'd pack up and head back next door.

"That little girl loves you, and you love her. And you're family. You have a good heart, Nora. You can do this."

"I don't know if I can be a nurse and a mother. I can't keep imposing on you to watch her. And I feel horribly guilty leaving each day. I feel like I should be home with her."

And soon my own situation would become noticeable. I wouldn't be able to keep nursing then. Once more, I wished Alley were here to make everything right, then frowned at the thought. It rankled that I *needed* a husband when I didn't *want* one. That somehow my life and choices could only be legitimized by a man's actions. With every day that passed, that unalterable fact chafed more and more.

He'd already had nearly two months to respond. Expecting him to waltz in and make everything right was a dream, wasn't it? I could be waiting a very long time. Forever. And in the meantime, I had a child to think about… two children. It wasn't that I wanted to stop believing. But I had to be practical, now that earlier options no longer existed.

"Between the two of us we'll manage, just like I told you before," Mrs. Thompson said.

"Would you consider moving in here?" I asked. "You can't keep sleeping in the parlour. It's not right. Not when there's a perfectly good bed upstairs."

The bed being Jane and Jimmy's. Mrs. Thompson sighed, then finished the cold tea in her cup. "You're right, of course. Although I don't want to give up my house. Bertie and I… " Her lips softened in memory. "It's still my home. But for the time being… " She grinned a little sheepishly. "Oh, Nora. I did something today that I need to confess to you. I hope it's all right."

I brightened at Mrs. Thompson's humorous tone. "I can't imagine you having to confess anything."

"I brought my cat over today. Evelyn was having it a bit rough, and I know how much she loved playing with Buttons when she came over, and I felt badly leaving him home all alone. Dollars to doughnuts she's up in her room right now, playing with him."

"I wondered why it was so quiet. I thought maybe she was tired from your walk and she was napping."

"She probably is by now. This morning she took him upstairs with a little ball of yarn and a feather and when I checked on them, he was lying on his back getting his belly rubbed. That silly beast."

Imagining Evelyn happily snuggled with Mrs. Thompson's cat warmed something in me that had been cold for the past several days. It was an odd feeling, like somehow life would find a new normal again, when things were still so uncertain. Like December sixth had swept the rug from beneath my feet—beneath all our feet—but there was a small spot where I could put my toe and find it firm.

"Of course, it's all right. I'd been telling Jane we needed a mouser around here for ages. She kept saying she wanted to wait until Clara wasn't crawling on the floors…"

And now Clara wouldn't be crawling anywhere. Just like that, my little foothold disintegrated.

Since my hospital search had turned up nothing, it was time to begin searching the morgues. My family's names had not turned up on the list of victims in the papers, but many bodies were unidentified. My already delicate stomach churned at the thought of walking through rows of bodies, examining each one. It wasn't as if I hadn't seen dead bodies before, but it was different thinking of those bodies being my loved ones. And while my sickness had begun to ease a bit, each morning I still got that odd feeling in my mouth, the pool of saliva under my tongue, a warning before I got sick and gagged. I tried to be quiet about it, as Mrs. Thompson had moved into Jane's room temporarily, and there were still three men sleeping in the rooms around me.

But this morning was particularly bad. I woke with nausea crowding my throat and the urge to vomit was so strong, I grabbed the basin in my room instead of rushing to the bathroom. When I was done, cold sweat had pooled along the back of my neck, curling the wisps of hair there, and my knees were weak from the exertion of vomiting with nothing in my stomach but bile.

I knew my body needed food, and yet the thought of it nearly made me reach for the basin all over again.

A quick glance showed the bathroom was free and I rushed to go inside and shut the door. I rinsed the basin and washed my face, taking deep breaths, but my legs were unsteady, and my face was pale. It was almost as if taking one day off had given my body permission to let go. Whatever the reason, it was going to be a massive challenge to get through my shift. And soon I'd be taking my turn at night shifts again. I couldn't expect to get the daytime shifts forever.

Cleaned up and marginally refreshed, I opened the bathroom door to find Captain McLeod waiting outside.

"Oh, I'm sorry I've kept you waiting." I clutched the front of my robe together with one hand while the other held the now-clean basin. "It's all yours, Captain."

His gaze settled on me, and my cheeks heated beneath his sharp examination. "Are you all right, Nurse Crowell?"

I nodded. "Of course! Excuse me. I'll see you downstairs for breakfast." I could already smell the bacon frying. My stomach turned again. But I scuttled aside and hustled back to my room to dress.

I would get through this. I would.

At breakfast I avoided looking at anyone's plates and focused on the plain toast I was trying to choke down. Mrs. Thompson was so busy moving back and forth that she didn't seem to notice, thank goodness, but I felt Captain McLeod's gaze on me as the meal progressed. As soon as I could, I rose from the table and dropped a kiss on Evelyn's head as I wiped a little bit of jam from around the girl's mouth.

"I'm off to work soon. You'll be a good girl for Mrs. Thompson, yes?"

"Yes, Auntie Nora. I'm going to play with the kitty. He slept with me last night, you know."

I did know, because it had been the first night Evelyn had slept in her own bed since the explosion. Oddly enough, I had missed having Evelyn beside me last night, but it wouldn't do to make a habit of her sleeping with me all the time.

When I went back downstairs, Captain McLeod was ready and Evelyn was by the front door, practically dancing as she waited for her goodbye kiss. I shrugged into my coat and retrieved my mittens from the pockets, then noticed the lace was untied on my right foot. I bent to tie it, but when I stood again, black spots appeared before my eyes, and I weaved a bit as dizziness swept over me.

"All right, Nurse Crowell?"

Why did Captain McLeod have to be everywhere? He noticed

everything. I pasted on a smile. "Of course. Evelyn, I'll see you later tonight. Be a good girl."

"I will."

I kissed Evelyn's head, but then Evelyn shoved the cat up into my face. "Kiss Buttons, too," she demanded.

I laughed a little and dutifully placed a kiss on the cat's head. The cat did not look impressed, but it seemed he would tolerate it for Evelyn, the purveyor of belly rubs and yarn balls. Even Captain McLeod smiled and gave Buttons a quick pat before we headed out the door.

"She's a sweet child," he observed as we set off up the street.

"She is. Always has been. Sunny and a bit stubborn, like her mother." The words opened the pit of achiness inside me, but I figured I had to get used to it. I couldn't ignore the grief forever.

"I was going to say, like her aunt," he offered.

"Jane and I were very different, but also very alike, if that makes sense."

He laughed a little. "It does. I'm the same with my brother." A shadow swept over his face as he said the words.

"Your brother?"

"He's overseas," he said shortly. "We're just hoping he makes it home."

"Same with Jimmy, my brother-in-law," I said, but in my mind I added, *and Alley, too.* Still, he hadn't mentioned a brother before. He must be worried, too.

"Nurse Crowell, can I ask you a question?"

"Of course." The conversation helped take my mind off my discomfort, as did the fresh air. Perhaps keeping occupied today would be my salvation.

"I don't know how to put this delicately, so I'm just going to say it." He stopped and faced me, forcing me to stop as well. "Are you expecting?"

Why was it so obvious? Jane had sussed it out and now Captain McLeod. A flush went from my neck to my ears as I burned with embarrassment. "Captain McLeod, I—"

I halted, words failing me, until I finally whispered, "I am."

He let out a breath. "I see."

I lifted my eyes and met his gaze. "I highly doubt that, but I get your meaning. Yes. I'm a single woman, a CAMC nurse, and I'm pregnant and alone."

"Especially with your sister gone."

Tears clogged my throat and I swallowed against them. "Yes, especially that. Jane was the only person who knew. She figured it out the day before the explosion."

"And the father?"

"At the front, as I mentioned before. I don't have to ask how you put it together. This morning was the worst morning I've had so far." A sudden thought struck me, and a twist of panic wrenched in my belly. "You're not going to report me, are you?"

He looked at me for a long moment. Then he sighed and his gaze softened. "No. You're a tremendous nurse. You're needed." He paused, and then added, "And I think you might like to take some time to figure out what to do next?"

It was an unexpectedly generous thing for him to say. I turned away and started walking again. We couldn't stand in the middle of the street forever and be late for work. "Jane and I had just spoken of it, had decided to not tell our mum and dad until after the holidays. I was so relieved she knew, and she said she'd help me decide my next steps. And now—" I broke off, wishing some of this sadness and emptiness could abate for just a little while.

"I understand."

I doubted that and was irked he said so. There was so much he didn't know about, including Alley's continued silence. I was an unmarried woman expecting a baby. I could expect to be shunned. Have whispers behind my back. And then the problem of supporting both myself and a child—two children, at least until Jimmy got home—how was I supposed to do that?

"I appreciate you trying, but you can't really understand. After all, no one would tell you that you couldn't work if you were having a baby." I'd stopped again, forgetting to keep going in my frustration.

He stopped too. "At risk of stating the obvious, men don't have to deal with the… peculiarities of being pregnant."

I stared at him for a moment, supremely annoyed, and tired enough that I wasn't sure I had the patience for this kind of conversation. I took a calming breath, though, and measured my response. "Of course. And perhaps I shouldn't complain. This is partly my fault. I made my own decisions. It's just… I love nursing. It feels like the price to pay for one moment in time is quite steep."

I looked away, sure he was going to walk away now. Men didn't seem to like it when women were so honest. I'd probably just ruined my chances by my bluntness. He was likely to report me. Any other doctor at the hospital would.

"I'm sorry," he said simply, surprising me. "You're right. I don't understand. What I do know is that you must take care of yourself. Get enough rest. Eat well. Even when it's difficult." He angled me a look as we began walking again. "Are you sick only in the mornings, or all day?"

I was grateful to return to discussing what he called the "peculiarities".

"Mostly in the mornings. Dry toast seems to be all right, and plain porridge. Other than that, sometimes just a smell is enough to turn my stomach."

"And have you had dizzy spells like the one this morning?"

I shook my head. "No, that was the first time."

"Your blood pressure dropped when you stood. When that happens, just wait a few moments and it will pass."

"I am a nurse, you know."

He chuckled. "Of course. But nurses and doctors don't always make the best patients." His smile faded. "I take it Mrs. Thompson doesn't know."

"Of course not!" My body tensed. "Honestly, I'm so afraid she'll find out and leave, and then where will I be? I need her. Evelyn needs her. I'm sure I don't have to tell you what a mess of a situation this is."

"Surely your… the baby's father," he corrected, "will do the right thing?"

The right thing. The only meaning for that was marriage, but I couldn't even seem to get Alley to write a letter. With every day that passed, I lost a little more faith that he'd be back for me at all.

I looked over at Captain McLeod. He'd turned out to be an unexpected friend this past week, kind and pragmatic, and I appreciated the steadiness and fairness he seemed to bring to every situation. *In for a penny, in for a pound,* I thought, and let out a breath. "He hasn't written since he shipped out. Not one reply. I haven't given up all hope, but…"

"I see." The captain's voice hardened.

I sighed. I couldn't admit that I didn't love the man I'd slept with. How would that sound? "Do you?" I asked. "Because I don't."

"It explains why you're prickly," he remarked, stepping back a little when I aimed a heated look in his direction. "You're carrying the weight of all of this, plus your family, while he is free as a bird."

"Except he's fighting a war. It's hard to hate a man who is putting his life on the line."

"But you can still expect him to do the right thing. And it looks like he's not. For that I'm really sorry, Nora. You're a good person. You don't deserve that."

I snorted. A good person wouldn't be in this position in the first place, but I wasn't about to say it out loud. What I really wanted was for this conversation to end.

We were almost at the hospital now. I rounded my shoulders against the north wind as we crossed Robie Street. On the other side of the hospital doors was the job I loved—nursing. I'd worked so hard, and now I would have to give it up. None of this was as I'd planned. "I just need some more time to figure out what I want to do," I said, chancing a glance up at him. "I can trust you to keep my secret, can't I? At least for now?"

"Friends look out for each other," he answered, squaring his shoulders. "You've had so much to deal with already. Of course you need time. There's just one thing, though." He stopped me with a hand on my elbow. "If anyone asks me directly, Nora, I won't lie."

My stomach twisted, but I nodded. "Of course, you can't. I would not expect you to."

We were at the doors now, and he hesitated. "Nora, have you seen a doctor?"

I shook my head. "No."

Our eyes met and I knew that when the time came for me to be examined, I didn't want him to be the one doing it. "Everything is fine right now."

He didn't question my answer. Instead, he gave me a brusque nod. "If anything changes, promise me you'll let someone examine you."

"I will," I said. But so far everything was right on schedule. Not that he needed to know, but pinpointing conception was no problem.

We were stepping inside the door when I said, "Captain?"

He turned to face me.

"After my shift today I'll be heading to the morgue at the Chebucto School. Don't wait for me. Just tell Mrs. Thompson I'll be along."

His face softened. "Would you like company? It's a hard thing to do alone."

It was, but I felt deep in my bones that I needed to. "No, but thank you. I want to go by myself."

He didn't insist. Instead, he reached out and squeezed my arm, and then walked off. My gaze followed him, a new tension settling in my breast. Now someone else knew my secret. And while I wanted to trust him, it felt wrong. We'd only known each other for a few days, and now he held my career in his hands.

Chapter Twelve

NORA

I arrived at the Chebucto School when it was nearly dark, dread settling like a stone in the pit of my stomach. For the past several days, I'd seen my share of dead bodies. I'd seen horrific wounds and burned flesh. But this was different. This time I was looking for familiar faces, and while I wanted—no, needed—to know what had happened to my family, it was a very different thing thinking about being faced with loved ones who hadn't made it, and what wounds or scars they might bear. For several minutes I stood outside in the cold, looking up at the red-brick structure that just a week ago held laughing, energetic children learning to read and write, playing games at recess in the frosty air. Now everything was silent as the building held the bodies of the dead. I was afraid to go inside. Afraid of what I might find… afraid of what I might not.

Eventually I let out a breath and made my feet move. Inside, I waited my turn as someone was already below, and I shifted from foot to foot with nerves. Coming inside had been a challenge, but now, being inside and forced to wait was a different kind of stress. A man came back up and out the doors, eyes red-rimmed, a cloth bag in his hands. My heart ached, but I had no time to think about it as Professor McRae, apparently the person in charge, motioned to me and led me downstairs. I followed him, my steps automatic and wooden.

Some of the windows had been blown out, and the cold crept through my heavy coat with chilling fingers. With a shock, I soon realized that there were three "classes" of remains: those that were easily identifiable, those beneath white sheets, hiding disfigurement, and then just… personal effects, in small cloth bags marked with a number.

The back of my throat burned. Perhaps I should have asked John—

No. This was *my* family. *My* responsibility.

We moved slowly amongst the bodies. There were so many of them—and so many of them children—that tears rolled silently down my cheeks as I moved from place to place. With each still face, I experienced both relief and distress that the features were not familiar. Looking for those I loved was more of a torture than I ever could have imagined. And yet my feet kept moving, following the professor, one body at a time.

I didn't want Mum and Dad to be here. Didn't want to find Jane and Clara among the still, grey faces. I wanted them home, warm, laughing, loving. This felt so… oh, Lord. It felt so very, very wrong. Like a nightmare that wouldn't end, even when I desperately wanted to wake.

We were nearly to the end of the first section of bodies when my insides froze, and a cry escaped my throat.

It was Jane. Jane in her pretty blue dress and coat, now covered in black grime and blood. Jane, her face still in death, without pain, without life. My beloved sister, the closest thing to another half of myself I would ever have. I covered my lips with my hand and took a shuddering breath, then shuttered away the emotion out of sheer necessity. I gave Professor McRae Jane's details and collected her personal items, tucking the mortuary bag inside my coat pocket. There wasn't much. A little money. A tiny rattle that Jane gave Clara when she fussed. Her wedding ring, and the necklace she always wore with two hearts linked together. I had an identical one. We'd received them from our parents when I was twelve and Jane was thirteen.

I looked at McRae and somehow managed to say, "My sister would have had a baby with her. Nearly a year old, female, light hair." My voice came out with a rough croak, and I cleared my throat, the sound harsh and breaking the odd sanctity of the room.

McRae answered me softly. "Mrs. Boutilier was brought in just this morning, found..." He consulted his records. "Ahem. Found in the rubble on Brunswick Street. I don't recall there being a baby with her, but..." He kept his voice gentle. "There are those who still need identifying, Miss."

I nodded and a curtain of numbness descended over my body. *Good,* I thought, dazed. I'd need to stop feeling to get through the rest. To be honest, I could have used a nip from Alley's friend's flask.

Over and over again McRae lifted sheets so I could look into the faces of the dead. Each one scored my soul as I searched for familiar features through the soot and blood-stained bodies. Then they were there, side by side, my mother and my father, their bodies broken and faces disfigured but discernible. I stared at them a long time, trying to make sense of it all, understanding that on some level my brain had shut down, or at least closed a part of itself away. "Mum," I whispered, my voice raw and pained. "Oh God, Mum."

"I'm so sorry, Miss," McRae offered, his voice barely above a whisper. I turned to him and realized what a horrible, horrible job he had. At the hospital, I put lives back together, at least most of the time. But he… he was the killer of hope. What a toll that must take. I reached out and squeezed his arm, and he looked at me with surprise. Did his lower lip wobble just a little? If so, it was gone in an instant. I dropped my hand, not wanting to distress him further.

"Thank you," I said, struggling to keep my composure. Once more I was the recipient of their personal items, also in mortuary bags. It felt wrong, somehow, that human beings were reduced to numbers on a piece of fabric, even though I understood it was the best way to organize the belongings of those who were not identified. The practice had begun after the last tragedy to affect Halifax—the sinking of the *Titanic*. How devastating to be using the system again so soon.

With my heart in tatters, I still had one more body to look for. The hardest of all—Clara.

But in the remaining bodies, there was none resembling my niece. Nor did I find anything familiar among the personal effects. I stopped and traced my finger over a sooty pink knitted blanket, something that had clearly been crafted with such care. This was so wrong. So very, very wrong. The world had gone mad and was taking me with it.

How could I possibly lay my family to rest, not knowing Clara's fate?

After giving what information I could, I left the morgue, the three mortuary bags tucked into my pockets. They weighed heavily there, these final pieces of my family, and I trudged my way toward home in the darkness. I'd been determined to find my family to lay them to rest properly, and now, instead of focusing on that, I just seemed to be putting one foot in front of the other.

The walk was not an overly long one, but when I reached the house on Henry Street I stared at the car and now knew for certain that my father would never sit behind the wheel again, his smile wide beneath his thick moustache, his eyes dancing with delight as the engine roared and chortled. I reached down and grabbed a fistful of snow, hurling it at the car, letting out a shout. Anger bubbled up inside, anger and fear and sadness and emotions so overwhelming, I could not stop them, nor did I wish to. Instead, I threw fistfuls of snow at the hateful vehicle that had brought my family to town and would not return them to their home, to the boys who still needed them, to the house with the rose bushes and back garden where Mum grew peas and beans every summer.

This house, where Jane would never laugh and bake and tease Evelyn and kiss the soft skin of Clara's neck. This damned house that wasn't mine, the house where Jimmy would return to a single child who needed him, but no wife and baby. I picked up another mittful of snow and hurled it at the front porch. Goddamn this war, those ships, goddamn everything to hell!

And then there was a pair of arms around me, holding me from behind, the drab wool familiar and the scent of antiseptic and soap reassuring.

"It's all right, Nora. It's going to be all right."

It was hearing my name that took all the starch out of me. I wilted against the embrace, dropping to the ground as all the hurt and pain I'd felt in the morgue, but shuttered away, fought its way out of my body and mind.

Neil knelt behind me, supporting my weight in his strong arms. I realized that cold, melting snow was seeping through my stockings and skirts, but I didn't have the energy to care. Nor did I care that I was outside where anyone might see. I'd simply lost the strength to give a damn about anything right now, and it all came out in a keening sort of wail that frightened me with its intensity.

"I'm sorry," he said softly, his voice low and pained. "I'm so very sorry."

"They're gone," I gasped. "Oh, Neil, they're gone. Mum and Dad and Jane, and Clara is missing. I… I don't know what to do. I can't move. I can't breathe."

His broad hands gripped my waist and shifted me the slightest bit, and then he slid his arms beneath me—one under my back, the other under my legs, and he got to his feet, holding me against his body as he made his way to the house. I was too surprised to say anything. Too shocked. Grief and anger still rippled through me, so I said nothing as he got to the door, fumbled with the doorknob, opened it, and stepped inside the entryway.

I expected him to put me down, but he didn't. Instead, he wiped his feet on the doormat and then headed straight for the stairs. His tread was heavy on the steps as he carried me like a child, just as he'd carried Evelyn to bed only a few nights previously, and I started to cry all over again, burrowing against the front of his coat. I would have to tell Evelyn now, have to tell that adorable, loving little girl that her mummy was never coming home again. How could I do that?

Neil went straight to my bedroom, carried me inside, and sat me on the bed. Once there, he knelt before me and unlaced my boots, removing them from my feet, and then sliding each of my buttons from the holes in the front of my coat. I was too numb, too shocked to stop him, and wordlessly he took my coat, put it over a chair, then eased me down onto the bed and covered me with a blanket.

"Rest," he said gently. "You've had a shock, Nora. I'll be back in a moment."

His boots sounded on the floor as he crossed the room, then I heard a door open and then close again.

When he returned, he slipped a bottle and a small glass out of his coat. He poured a small amount into the glass and held it out to me. "You look like you could use this."

I sat up. "What is it?"

He smiled a little. "I would have preferred a nice brandy, but rye was what was available."

I tossed the bootleg liquor back, then gasped as my throat turned to fire. Still, the warmth that spread through my chest was not an unwelcome sensation. I handed him back the glass. "Thank you."

He took the glass, poured another generous helping, and then tossed it back himself, his face grim.

My lip trembled. "I feel so… numb. I don't— I can't—" My breath started to hitch again.

"Shh." His voice was so soothing. "You're overwhelmed. It isn't surprising, Nora. You've been working so hard since the explosion, and you're exhausted. Now you have shock and grief for your family. A person can only take so much."

He poured another splash of rye into the glass and handed it to me.

"You're coping fine," I said, almost an accusation, before accepting the drink. This was all, though. The last time I'd had alcohol had been the night with Alley. It was one thing to calm the nerves. It was another to lose my good judgment, especially when I was already so distraught.

"You think I'm fine?" He gave a bitter laugh. "You'll notice this bottle isn't full. In the last week I've seen so many horrific injuries. Ones I still see when I close my eyes. Sleep doesn't always come easily, even when I'm so tired I can hardly see straight."

I stared at him. He always looked so calm. So competent. But now that I looked, I realized the bottle was two-thirds empty. I dragged my gaze back up to his face, noticing the shadows under his eyes. We were all falling apart in one way or another.

"Now, I think you've probably had enough. I'm guessing you're not used to it, and you probably haven't eaten all day, either." He plucked the glass from my hand, and I wondered if he was going to have another swallow after he left. "Get some rest. I'll send Mrs. Thompson up with a tray."

"But I have to tell Evelyn—"

"There's time for that," he soothed. "Nothing is going to change if you wait a few hours. Get your feet beneath you first."

I nodded, knowing he was right. Besides, I was already woozy from the alcohol and my eyelids started to droop with exhaustion.

"I'll check in on you later."

"There's no need—"

"I will anyway. Doctor's orders."

He left me then, sitting on my bed with a quilt pooled around my hips, alone with my grief and anger and numbness. I lay down and put my head on the pillow, closing my eyes, wanting so desperately to just stop feeling anything at all.

But then I thought of how he'd gallantly carried me inside, cared for me, and called me, for the first time, by my first name.

And how I'd thought of him as Neil. Not Captain McLeod.

Chapter Thirteen

CHARLOTTE

December 12, 1917

The doctors didn't think I was ready to leave, but I'd spent so much time in bed wondering about Aileen that I was going crazy. I'd followed the doctors'—and nurses'—instructions to the letter, with the promise that I would be released as soon as I was up and about. That had been my sole focus: heal for Aileen. Her toothy, smiling face was the only thing I saw as I did everything that was asked of me. And in the end, Dr. McLeod didn't make too much of a fuss. The hospital was still crammed with wounded. One less body to worry about.

Now here I was, standing outside Camp Hill hospital, my leg aching and the stitches pulling, dressed in unfamiliar clothes that had been provided by some sort of relief effort. The cotton dress wasn't half bad, though the material was thin, and it was slightly too big. Or perhaps I'd lost weight while in the hospital. For the first few days I'd eaten nothing at all, then I'd moved on to broth and toast. The meals got slightly more substantial, but my stomach growled now, and I was suddenly overwhelmed with what to do next. Where to go. Where to start.

Leaden clouds hung over the city, as if drawn down by the weight of the tragedy still rife in the air. But there were noises that proved there was life: the purr of motorcars on the streets, the clang of the streetcar far below me on Barrington Street, hollow on the damp, cold air. People bustled along, weaving in and around me, and here I was, standing still.

I turned and looked at the hospital again, almost wanting to go back where I knew it was warm and dry and certain. But Aileen was waiting for me somewhere. I couldn't stay frozen to the spot forever.

The first thing was to go home, I supposed—if the house was still standing. The news that the North End had been flattened just didn't make sense in my mind, and I wondered if it could possibly be as bad as everyone said. I huddled into the strange coat that smelled of cedar and must—probably donated from someone's old things—and took my first few steps, catching my breath as the muscles in my thigh pulled and caught. I knew I should find a taxi, but I had no money and only the clothes on my back. So I started away from the hospital, inching my way closer to the house that had become my home.

Normally I walked this city with ease. Now each step was a pain-riddled feat.

By the time I reached the corner at Agricola, tears blurred my vision. Perhaps I hadn't been ready to leave after all. The pain was like a knife stuck into my leg, the blade of it turning with each movement.

"Ma'am? Can I help you?"

I turned to find a middle-aged man getting out of his car. It wasn't a brand-new model, and there were a few scratches and dents, but it seemed to be running just fine. I stared at him, considering the folly of accepting help from a perfect stranger, wary that certainly some would try to take advantage of Haligonians who were down on their luck. The loss of trust saddened me, but after dealing with the Campbells for over a year, I knew that what people said was often very different from their actions.

"No, thank you. I'm fine."

"This is my cab, ma'am. My name's John. I'd be happy to take you where you need to go." He doffed his hat, which surprised me.

I hesitated, examined him. He seemed nice enough, neat and tidy, and he met my eyes, which made me think he was honest. "I don't have any money to pay you," I explained. "I've just left Camp Hill."

His face softened. "Oh, I'm sorry. But glad you're all right. Don't you worry about the fare. Let me take you home. Where is that?"

I limped across the street, following him to his car. "Russell Street," I said, and watched as his face fell.

"Ma'am, I don't know how to tell you this, but—"

"I already know," I replied, taking a breath and squaring my shoulders. "I'm up the hill from Gottingen. I'm hoping the house has been spared."

He gave a quick nod, then opened the door for me. My leg throbbed as I got inside, but I was grateful for the ride all the same, and the generous driver who was willing to take me free of charge.

John manoeuvred through the cacophony of cars, horse-drawn carriages and wagons; foot traffic dwindled the further toward Richmond we drove. While nothing had seemed changed when I left the hospital, the more we moved toward the North End, the more evident the destruction became. Buildings were boarded up, roofs and walls damaged, debris littering the yards. I realized, too, that down the hill from us was ever so much worse. It was completely leveled—buildings, telephone poles, nothing was standing. My mouth dropped open. It hadn't been an exaggeration. It was just… gone, reduced to a pile of matchsticks. I could see clear to the harbour—not a single building blocked the view.

The Halifax I had known my whole life was no more.

It didn't take long before John stopped the car and turned in his seat to meet my gaze. "I'm sorry, ma'am. I can't take you any further. Richmond is closed unless you have a permit to enter."

"But I live here."

He nodded. "Talk to the soldiers there. They might let you through."

I nodded in return, thanked him for the drive, and got out.

John drove away, and when I turned and looked at the community that had been my home, I recognized nothing. It looked like a war zone.

Was the Campbells' house still standing? Were my in-laws even alive? I'd been holding out hope that perhaps they already had Aileen and were keeping her safe, but that hope dwindled with every step I took toward my community. My leg pained but somehow I became numb to it as I approached the soldiers monitoring the comings and goings.

"Good afternoon. I live on Russell Street and would like to check on my home." I tried to sound confident, but inside I was quaking. I needed to get back there, to see for myself what had happened to the house, to… to Frank's family. Then there was the little box I kept under my mattress, the one where I squirreled away Aileen's portion of the Patriotic Fund. It wasn't much, but it was more money than I had in my pocket right now, and if the house wasn't livable, I'd need a place to stay and God, something to eat. My stomach was hollow already.

"I'm sorry ma'am, there's no admittance without a permit."

"I haven't had time to get one," I said, and my voice broke a little. "I've been in the hospital since the sixth. Please. My baby girl is missing. My husband's family live there. And it's toward the top of the street." I tried a smile. "It's safer up that way, isn't it?"

I knew I must look a fright, in an out-of-fashion, ill-fitting wool coat, my hair not done, and the last time I looked I still had the bruise along the side of my face, though it was more yellow-green now than purple. Still, I tried a shaky smile. "Please. I promise I'll be careful."

Something must have softened them because the next thing I knew, I was walking my old route, along Gottingen and then turning up Russell. All I could do was stare at the wreckage surrounding me. Some houses were down to the foundations. Others stood, but oddly enough the walls were blown out rather than in, making them appear bloated and sore, all the windows gone. It looked like one good puff of wind would send it all crashing to the ground, like the house of cards Frank used to like to build on Sunday afternoons, when his mother had said there were no cards on Sunday, and that was how he got around it and entertained himself—and me.

The closer I got to the house, the more my hope dwindled. While it was clear crews had begun digging through the rubble, the Campbell house seemed untouched and eerily vacant. The porch leaned crookedly on the front of the house, while the north wall was buckled. All the windows were gone. The shed in the back was a pile of boards. It was clear there was no one here, but where were they?

I went to the porch and put my hand on the railing, then tested each step as I painfully climbed my way to the front door. The walls were off-kilter and the door swung open with a small creak. There was dust everywhere. Dishes had come off the shelves and shattered. Mrs. Campbell's prized Blue Willow platter was in pieces, the shards littering the floor. All the frames on the walls had come off their nails, and as I tiptoed to the parlour, I saw every single knick-knack scattered on the now-dusty rug, broken and alone. Mrs. Campbell's parlour, her pride and joy, reduced to rubble.

I cautiously made my way to the stairs, praying that they wouldn't collapse beneath my weight. I had no idea how stable anything was, or if one wrong step would send it all crashing down with me in it. There was no family here, no Aileen, so the only thing for me to do was retrieve anything I could that had some value and get out. I had never liked this house, and it had never felt like my home, but I was sad just the same to see it now, a ramshackle shell.

On the second floor, I limped my way down the hall to check the bedrooms. I poked my head into Mrs. Campbell's room and a gasp rent the air—mine. I trembled all over as I looked past the bed to the window. The glass was gone and a large, oddly shaped chunk of it had lodged in Mrs. Campbell's throat. Beneath her, on the floor, was a black, dried pool of blood.

I'd heard stories of patients arriving at the hospital with glass to be removed because they'd been watching the fire from their windows when the ship exploded. But this shard was so large it had become a deadly projectile.

I stared, trying so very hard to slow my breath. I'd never seen a dead body before. Even the horrific injuries I'd seen in the hospital were not as gruesome—as final—as seeing Mrs. Campbell's lifeless, grey body on the bedroom floor. I sat on the dusty bed, stunned. The woman had done nothing but grumble at me from the beginning, picking apart every task and finding fault, ordering me about and treating me like something stuck to her shoe instead of her son's wife and mother to her only grandchild. I did not like this woman. I certainly didn't hold any love for her. But this… I hoped she hadn't suffered. She hadn't deserved this. No one did. To die so violently and then be left alone… I hated the thought of her lying there, with no one to care for her remains, or pay their respects. I closed my eyes and uttered a short prayer.

I couldn't stay here. But I couldn't leave her, either. The only thing I could do was alert the authorities and let them take over.

"All right," I finally whispered to myself. "All right. I will get my things and… get out." I turned my back on her body and made my way to the steep stairs leading to the third floor.

The climb to the attic was frightening. The floor seemed to sway beneath my feet, and I wondered how long that buckled wall could possibly hold, and if the whole house would teeter over in a cloud of lumber and dust, taking me with it. It was difficult being both quick and cautious, with my paining leg adding extra challenge, but I grabbed a small leather bag and shoved what I could fit inside. The windowless attic was dark and dreary, but at least that meant that nothing was wet or covered in glass. In the gloom I saw that the single dresser was on its side and Aileen's crib was twisted and against a different wall.

Aileen.

In addition to the underclothes, single nightdress, and day dress I put into the bag, I rooted around and gathered some of Aileen's things as well. She would need them when I found her.

Under the crib I found the rattle that Frank had whittled and sent home once I'd told him I was pregnant. It was the only thing she would ever have from her father, and I ran my fingers over it for a few precious seconds before tucking it into the bag. She wasn't here, but she was somewhere.

The bag was now getting quite heavy, and I was sore and weak. I wouldn't be able to carry much more.

My bed was mostly untouched from the blast, and I felt beneath the foot of the mattress and took out the small, flat box that held my savings. I would count it later. Right now, I needed to get out of this house and somewhere safe. Besides, it gave me the willies to know I was alone in the house with a dead body.

It took me some time to get back downstairs. Going down the steps hurt worse than going up, which surprised me, and I held onto the banister even though it wobbled in my hand, loosened from its moorings. Once I got back to the kitchen, I hesitated for a moment and then went to the cupboard where Mrs. Campbell kept the household money and ration coupons. I took out the tin can and looked inside, then hesitated. This money was for the whole family. But no one was here, and surely if anyone were still alive, Mrs. Campbell would not still be alone upstairs.

With the force of a hammer, the delayed realization hit me. Mrs. Campbell was dead and her body had been upstairs for six days. Six. In all that time, there were no signs that anyone had been here. Not Mr. Campbell, not Joseph or… or Alice. My God, was Frank's whole family gone? They weren't a cheerful bunch, but the idea of his entire family being wiped out in a single moment…

I righted a kitchen chair and sat in it, letting that possibility wash over me. I hadn't liked his family and I certainly hadn't liked living here, but I never wished the Campbells dead. The men had gone to work at the sugar refinery, which had been leveled. Alice had gone to school that morning, walking with friends… Guilt swept through me. I should have tried harder with her. Frank would have wanted that. I might eventually have had a sister. Now that chance was gone.

I sat there a long time. Then, when I noticed it growing darker as the afternoon waned, I got up, went to the tin can, and took out everything inside. I needed to live somehow. I needed to find a place to sleep and eat and heal and search for Aileen. It made no sense to leave perfectly good money behind.

When I left the cold, empty house, I tried to shut the front door behind me, but it wouldn't latch, the frame skewed from the blast. The spot on the porch where Aileen's carriage usually sat was empty. I gripped the wood railing with one hand and the leather bag with the other, gritting my teeth as I went down the five steps to the ground.

And when I reached the street I turned and looked at the wretched house that had been my home for nearly two years.

I'd lived in two houses and had two families in Richmond. This time when I walked away, I vowed I was never coming back.

Chapter Fourteen

CHARLOTTE

By the time I reached the perimeter of Richmond again, I was in so much pain I wasn't sure how much longer I could go on. One of the soldiers took pity on me and helped me fetch a cab, but I had no idea where to go. My stomach growled again, and I knew I needed food. My next job would be to try to find a hotel room for the night. I didn't care if it wasn't much; warm and dry would do me just fine. Anywhere I could get off my leg.

So I told the cabbie to take me to Barrington Street and the Tally-Ho, where I might first get a good cup of tea and something warm to fill me. Surely someone there would know where I could find a place to stay. Even though panic started to crowd my chest, I told myself I only had to do one thing at a time, and I remembered the kind nurses reminding me that I needed my strength to find Aileen.

Aileen. I now realized that if we'd been home and not out

walking, we probably would have been killed, too. But I was here, and if I'd been lucky enough to survive, I was sure she had, too. I just had to find her.

I'd have to make my money stretch, so I counted out coins to pay the driver before getting out of the car, my leg so stiff now it was hard to move. With small steps I entered the restaurant, the tantalizing scent of meat and vegetables heavy in my nostrils. The hollow feeling in my stomach intensified, and for a moment I was rooted to the spot, overcome with the sound of voices chattering, the clang of silverware, and the bustling about of the waitresses. It sounded so… normal.

"You lookin' for supper, dear?"

I turned to my left, where a waitress in a white apron smiled at me. "Oh… yes. Please." I must have looked startled because her face softened and despite the fast pace and the din, she put her hand on my arm and gave it a reassuring squeeze.

"It's all right, dear. Everyone's a little out of sorts. You look like you could use a good bowl of somethin'. You're a bit pale."

"That sounds lovely," I replied, relieved as she led me away to a small table that was miraculously empty. I whimpered as I sat down, happy to be off my feet but wishing I had something to help with the pain. I'd got up and walked at the hospital, but certainly nothing like the strain I'd put on my leg today.

"I'll be right back," she said, patting my shoulder.

I realized after she bustled away that I hadn't asked for tea, but it was as if she were a mind-reader because when she returned she had a steaming cup for me as well as a bowl of heavenly smelling chicken soup and warm, fresh bread. I nearly wept with gratitude. The last home-cooked meal I'd had was the steak and boiled potatoes I'd made the night before the explosion. And while the menu here wasn't exactly home cooking, it was a very close second.

"Thank you," I said, picking up my spoon. Oh heavens, there was even butter for the bread.

I was alive. I was sitting in a restaurant having a meal. It was so much more than so many others had at this moment or would ever have again. Mrs. Campbell's face appeared in my mind, and I fought to dismiss the gruesome image. No. I had another chance, and I was going to take it. As soon as I found Aileen.

I'd eaten every bit of the soup and had saved half a slice of bread to savour for last when a familiar voice said my name.

"Charlotte? Charlotte Campbell, is that you?"

The tears that had been sitting just behind my eyes all day couldn't be held back. Winnifred Slaunwhite came toward the table, her glossy black hair swept back from her face and her lips in a wide smile.

"Oh, Winnie! It's some good to see you." I smiled through my tears as she leaned over and kissed my cheek in greeting. I sniffled as she slid into the chair across from me. "I'm sorry I didn't get up. My leg…"

She blanched. "Did you lose it?"

"No, but I have a nice line of stitches and it hurts like the devil. Oh, it's so good to see a familiar face."

Winnie reached across the table and gave my hand a squeeze. "So many people lost… I haven't heard anything from any of the other Dominion girls." We'd both worked in the textile factory, but Winnie had "married up" and moved out of Richmond right after I married Frank, and we'd lost touch. "They say many of the girls were killed when the roof collapsed. I'm afraid to look at the list. There's bound to be people we know."

I didn't want to see those names, either. "I haven't seen anyone at all. I just got released from the hospital today and managed to get into Richmond to check on the house, but…" I stopped and took a sip of the cooling tea to steady myself, though my hand trembled. "I think Frank's whole family is gone. The house is definitely unlivable. And…" I bit down on my quivering lip and tried to regain my composure. "My baby daughter is missing."

Tears of sympathy shone in her eyes. "Oh, no. I'm so very sorry. Where are you staying?"

"I don't know. This was my first stop after leaving the house. I'm hoping to find a hotel room, but something tells me they're scarce as hen's teeth." I looked up at her. "Do you know of anyone taking in boarders?"

"Don't be silly. You'll come stay with Ed and me."

I stared at her for a long moment, a bit speechless. But I shouldn't have been. Winnie had always been kind and generous. "At any other time, I'd say no, but I really don't know what to do next. But just for a few days, until I'm able to sort things out." I didn't want to take advantage.

"You can stay as long as you like. There's lots of room. Other than Ed and me there's just the baby…" She cast a worried look at me. "Oh, will that be too difficult for you? I understand. I don't know what I'd do if…" She broke off, her cheeks colouring.

She wasn't entirely wrong. Seeing a healthy baby—just thinking about it—caused an ache in my chest. But I needed a place and couldn't afford to be choosy. Besides, Winnie was a friend. I shook my head, resolved. "I'll be fine. I'm sure Aileen is alive. I just need to find her."

Winnie's eyes changed, concern darkening their depths, and I knew what she was thinking. That it was unlikely that a one-year-old missing baby was going to be found alive. But miracles happened all the time. I'd heard lots of strange stories about people being found in rubble or waking up after being thrown from the blast with their clothes missing… nothing sounded impossible anymore.

"Then that's what we'll do."

"I'll pay you for board."

"You'll do no such thing." She said it with such finality that I couldn't help but smile. Winnie had always been chatty and fun and generous to a fault when we'd worked together. It was nice to know that marriage and children hadn't changed her. Oh, how I wished Frank and I would have had that chance…

She was going to pay for my dinner, but I refused, saying I had some money. It was a relief, though, when she took over fetching us a ride to her home on Beech Street, near the university.

"What were you doing downtown, anyway?" I asked.

"Volunteering. The Green Lantern is set up as a relief centre. Clothing, household goods… donations have been flooding in. Ed and I are so fortunate. I told him that if he can serve on committees to help, I can be of use, too."

Winnie had always been a hard worker with an unflagging spirit. Just seeing her buoyed me and gave me a bit of hope. "Winnie, I can't tell you how much I appreciate this."

"Nonsense," she said, smiling. "When a friend needs help, you help them."

We arrived at her Beech Street house, and I stared at the lovely brick exterior. I knew Ed worked at the bank, but I hadn't realized that this was how Winnie now lived. Perhaps I should have; she dressed differently now, in a stylish skirt and polished shoes and a fine, heavy coat that looked as if it was in its first winter. And here I was, in my cast-off dress. We couldn't be more different.

"Come inside," she offered warmly. "I'll draw you a bath and prepare your room."

I followed her inside, staring around me at the dark, polished woodwork and elegantly papered walls. There was no clutter here like at the Campbells'; a few pictures on the walls, a couple of knick-knacks on the mantel I glimpsed in a parlour to my right. She took my bag and led the way upstairs, my progress painfully slow. "I'll make some tea and bring it up, so you don't have to use the stairs again. And the bathroom is next to your room."

Hot running water and an indoor toilet. I felt as if I'd landed in a palace. Winnie stepped inside a small but beautiful bedroom. "This will suit, yes?"

The same dark woodwork framed the window and the door and was matched in the bed frame. There was blue wallpaper, and the bedspread was a shade deeper blue. It was the nicest bedroom I'd ever seen.

"Winnie, I don't know… I can't tell you…" I was utterly overwhelmed. When I left the hospital, I had never imagined this was how the day would end. The only thing missing was my daughter, and tomorrow I would begin my search.

She put my bag on a chest at the end of the bed, then turned around, her dark eyes soft and sad. "So many are lost," she whispered. "I'm so happy to be able to help a friend. And I will help, Charlotte. I'll help you look for your daughter, too."

She came forward and hugged me, and I held on tight.

With each day that passed, it felt as if I'd been sent a miracle in the form of Winnie. I had a plush bed, and my aching body cried out in relief when I settled on the mattress, soft and forgiving. She found better-fitting clothing for me during her hours volunteering at The Green Lantern. At night, Winnie put salts in my bath to help my leg heal, and her housekeeper, Marion, cooked me delicious meals. There were eggs and toast in the mornings, "to build up your strength," Marion said, and soups and stews that were rich and flavourful despite the rationing and the shortages. The older woman seemed to smile all the time, with crinkles at the corners of her eyes. It was such a change for me, this happy, contented kind of household. It made me homesick for my parents and my own upbringing that had never been as well-to-do as this but had been equally as peaceful. The kind of household that was so very different from the Campbells'. It was what I wanted for me and my daughter. Oh, not the money, but the love and warmth and harmony.

Ed spent long days both at work at the bank and on a relief committee working on housing those who were homeless after the disaster, which meant Winnie and I had plenty of time to catch up. My heart did this strange hitch every time I caught her holding her baby boy, Eddie (named after his father, of course). I tried not to let it show, but resentment burned like a hot coal in my chest when I saw them cuddling or heard his coos and babbles. I should have been snuggling my own sweet baby, hearing the sounds she made, listening to her laugh and feeling her hot breath on my neck as she fell asleep on my shoulder. Sometimes, if I closed my eyes, I could still feel the weight of her in my arms, the fresh-baby scent of her after her bath.

Sometimes I thought I might go mad with it, this overwhelming sense of fear and loss. I became even more desperate to find Aileen. The certainty that she was still out there waiting for me had never wavered, at least. And if, for a moment, I considered that she might have died, my heart and soul instantly dismissed it. A mother knows when her child is lost, doesn't she? I would *know*.

That first day we began by scouring the papers and the lists of the wounded and dead, focusing on children and babies. There had been nothing in the carriage to identify Aileen's name or address. In addition, we put ads in several publications giving her details—her age and features, what she was wearing, the carriage, our location… anything that might help, with Winnie's address as a contact.

And yet the ads went unanswered.

Within a few days, my leg had vastly improved. The stitches no longer pulled as the swelling in my flesh eased, and though I still limped, the pain was far more bearable. I was ready to begin an actual search of hospitals and other organizations that were caring for "unclaimed" children. The list was long.

On the first morning, fortified with hearty porridge and fresh cream, I called for a cab to take me to the Victoria General as Winnie had volunteer commitments. It had been nearly ten days since the explosion, and it was possible that Aileen had been injured and still required care. I entered the hospital with hope centred in my breast. Imagine, if tonight I could kiss her sweet face and tuck her into bed alongside me! The very idea propelled me forward.

It had not been long since I left Camp Hill, but as I stepped inside the VG hospital, I was slapped with sights and smells that burned my eyes and the back of my throat. The hospital was packed with victims, and the acrid scent of disinfectant was seared on my memory. Patients were wrapped in bandages, walking on crutches, confined to their beds. Nurses bustled around tending to various needs, and doctors walked the hallways with purpose, the skin beneath their eyes purple with fatigue from long hours. The odd, cloying smell of burning oil clung to the air, mingling with the iron tang of blood, and I put my gloved hand over my mouth and nose. How quickly I'd become accustomed to fresh air and the perfumed bedding at Winnie's.

For over an hour I walked wards and waited for answers to

questions, until ultimately, I came away unsatisfied. There were children being treated, but none that matched Aileen's age and description.

Next I went to the Red Cross hospital that had taken over the YMCA on Barrington, and from there the relief hospitals at Bellevue and St. Mary's College, each with the same disappointing result. By the time I left the college, my leg was so painful that I could barely stand, and I still had not found my daughter. Any moment that my hope flagged, I shored it up by telling myself that it was perfectly believable that she was no longer in need of medical attention and was being cared for elsewhere in the city. I had to believe that. The alternative was unthinkable.

I didn't want to go home, but I knew I must. I could not logically search every single place in the city in a single day. I was disheartened but determined. I would *never* give up.

Back at Winnie's, however, my nerves frayed at little Eddie's antics. Winnie was thrilled that he'd said "Mum" a few times, and I wanted to snap at her that Aileen had been saying my name for months now. Eddie was sweet, but he was not the only child in the world, and did Winnie not understand how tired and afraid I was?

No, not afraid. I could not be afraid. "She's out there," I whispered to myself, repeating it over and over in my head until the panic in my breast eased. Still, dinner seemed to drag on forever, Winnie and Ed chatting about all the relief efforts going on in the city, as well as the rumours of German sabotage aboard the colliding ships and the debate over which ship had been at fault. I wanted to plug my ears against the animated voices, but of course I could not. The moment dinner was over, I begged fatigue and went to my room with the latest evening paper. Perhaps there was a new notice, or one that we'd missed.

Anything to escape the reminder that my arms remained horribly empty.

The next day I made the rounds to the military hospitals and any other dressing stations that were still active… anywhere wounded had been taken and treated. I saw children, but none were the right age, and as I turned to walk away at one station—I cannot remember which—I saw a mother reunited with her child, a boy of around four.

It broke something in me, seeing that. The relief on her face, the unbridled joy, the tears… and the way the little boy clasped his arms around her neck so tightly, as if he would never let go. My arms ached with emptiness, and for the first time, despair took hold, leaving me breathless and with my legs quivering. When I returned to the house on Beech Street that night, I only picked at my dinner before excusing myself again. It wasn't that I was ungrateful to Winnie; she was a good friend and so incredibly generous. But as the days wore on, the pain of seeing her happy family bore a hole right through the middle of my chest, leaving behind an emptiness that was dark and all-encompassing. Winnie smiled at her husband over dinner and kissed her child goodnight. Meanwhile, my husband was buried somewhere in France, and my child… Worse, I knew I should be grateful and not resentful of her happy life, and the guilt piled on top of my anger and sadness. It was easier just to avoid her.

As the Slaunwhites finished their dinner, I sat on the edge of my bed and wiped tears from my eyes; no matter how often I swiped at the hot drops, more followed until there was simply no stopping them. I cried for hours, curled up on top of the bedspread, utterly lost. If I couldn't find Aileen, what was I to do? How was I to go on? Oh, it would have been better if I'd just been killed, if I was never to have my daughter back!

It was dark now in my room, and no one had knocked on my

door or checked on me. Probably because I'd been crying for so long, but that last thought gave me the clarity I needed again. Because I hadn't been killed. I'd been spared, and if my life had been spared, it had to be for a purpose. It had to be! That purpose was Aileen, and I would do whatever it took to bring her home with me again. I would not stop until I found her. Not ever.

That night I woke in the darkness and heard her crying—pitiful, distressed wails that reached in and wrapped around my heart. It was clear as day to me, and I got up out of bed and went to the nursery, needing to comfort her and assure her that it was all right and we were together. I held her solid body close to mine and swayed back and forth, humming with tears streaking down my cheeks.

Then Winnie came into the room, pulling her robe around her before halting at the sight of me. I saw the look on her face, the shock and dismay and… it looked like fear. I held onto the baby and kept rocking back and forth. Why would she be afraid? I loved this baby. I would do anything for her.

"I'll take Eddie now," she said, her voice soft, creeping into my consciousness. "Please, Charlotte, give me the baby."

Because the baby was Eddie, not Aileen, and I was in her house, and Aileen was missing, and it had been his cries waking me from my troubled sleep, not my daughter's.

"Of course," I whispered, the baby's cries now reduced to the odd whimper. "I heard him crying, was all. I thought to… to let you sleep."

I put the weight of him into her arms then stepped back, trying not to look as shaken as I felt, because then she'd know She'd know that I had thought her baby was my own. That I'd held Aileen in my arms, and until she'd come into the room, hadn't realized any differently.

I went back to my room and crawled into the bed, pulling the covers up to my chin as I stared at the ceiling.

I was losing my mind.

With that last thought, I let out a sigh and crumbled into sleep.

Chapter Fifteen

NORA

December 17, 1917

On the day that so many unidentified victims were buried in a mass service at Fairview Cemetery, Neil and I instead made the journey to Chester for the funerals of my family. The day was incredibly long and yet seemed to be over so quickly, and now we left my grandparents' house, walking side by side to the station to catch the train back to Halifax. Our breaths formed puffs in the wintry air, and we didn't say much, but I was honestly talked out. And to my surprise, I was glad for the company. That Neil seemed to understand I didn't wish to hold up my end of a conversation was a relief.

It had been the issue with the car that had prompted Neil to offer to accompany me. I never learned to drive, and it made no sense for the car to remain in Halifax. But I was sure my

.er could use it, or perhaps the boys would drive in a .wo. Or they could sell it, since my grandparents would .ve two extra mouths to feed. I'd voiced my concern about .esence of the car one evening at the kitchen table, where . gathered since it was the warmest room. Neil had offered .he spot to drive me to Chester for the service and return with . on the train.

I'd been slightly uncomfortable with the idea, because Neil was a young, handsome doctor and I was sure there'd be speculation—there always was in a small town. And yet I had no real other alternative, and he *was* good company. He'd kept true to his word to keep things friendly between us, and I had got used to seeing him both at work and at home. For the most part, he was a steadying presence, like the calm in the midst of a storm. But occasionally he'd disappear for a while and when he returned I could smell liquor. I never asked him where he got it or made any comment at all. Far be it from me to criticize how people handled the stresses of their days. It wasn't like I was in a position to judge.

But today he'd been a rock, which was a blessing, as my emotions had ridden so close to the surface time and time again. Seeing the three caskets side by side broke something inside me —just when I was sure there was nothing more left to be broken. It had taken all my emotional reserves to not break into weeping but stand stoically as the coffins were removed from the sanctuary, but Neil had reached over and taken my gloved hand in his, an unexpected anchor keeping me tethered. After that, I was completely numb. It was as if going through the ritual of the funeral emptied every last bit of feeling out of me, leaving me a shell of the person I'd been before.

As the last of the mourners had passed by, I'd been surprised to feel Neil's hand at the small of my back, guiding me forward.

It wasn't unpleasant, and I briefly felt guilty about it. I was carrying Alley's child, for heaven's sake. But then I pushed the thought aside. It had been eleven days since the explosion. Two months since Alley's departure and he'd not sent a word. Nor had he appeared on any casualty list. He'd simply… vanished. As if what we'd shared hadn't even existed, except I had the proof that it had.

We turned left off my grandparents' street and headed north toward the station. I stole a look at Neil's profile. There was no denying he was a handsome man. He had a fine, strong nose and nice lips, crisply edged and not too full. His lashes were longer than they appeared, I realized, because they were a sandy shade that matched his light hair, but seeing them from the side was different. He didn't smile as much as Alley, and his energy wasn't the infectious sort, but he was reliable, and that was something I needed in a friend right now.

"I can't thank you enough for coming with me today," I offered, just to break the silence. "I know it was to drive the car, but to go through the funeral and then after at my grandparents'… it was above and beyond."

"You're welcome. I like your family. They remind me of my own, a little. It was no trouble, I promise." He offered a slight smile.

I looked away again, not wanting to stare. "Well, I appreciate it just the same. I like to think I'm a strong woman, but the last few weeks…" I let out a sigh and shook my head.

I felt his eyes on me again. "You're probably the strongest woman I've ever met," he replied. "But if I've been any help at all, I'm glad."

The compliment went straight to my heart. I'd always considered myself strong and determined. After all, I'd moved to the city and completed my studies and signed up with the medical corps. Of course, I'd had Jane, but the accomplishments —those were mine. Maybe I'd wobbled in the last few weeks, but who wouldn't? No one really knew what they'd do in extraordinary circumstances until they were tested.

The weather was clear and cool but not too cold, and as we kept on, I found the walk rejuvenating, helping bring me back to my normal self bit by bit. "Do you know, when I walk, I seem to be able to work out all my troubles," I mused. Gram had given us a lunch to eat on the train, and I held the parcel of food close to my coat. "If it weren't so far away, I think I'd walk all the way to Halifax."

"Because you have so many troubles to solve?" Neil looked over at me, that same little smile playing on his lips.

"Well, you know one of them. I couldn't bring myself to tell Gram. Today was…"

"Today was about your parents and your sister," he supplied easily.

I'd wanted to tell her, though. I'd looked around the table at what remained of my family and placed my right palm against my still-flat stomach beneath the table. The words sat on my tongue, particularly when I looked at my grandmother. I longed to share my news, longed to talk to another woman about the life growing inside me, about what to expect. I missed Jane and my mother with an unbearable ache. And yet the words remained unspoken. This wasn't joyous news. It was my… shame. Today was not the day. My news could wait. I was more worried about Will and Stephen, and said so.

"Your brothers are good lads, Nora, and well looked after," Neil assured me. "Your grandparents are wonderful. They were very welcoming and kind to me."

"It's where Mum gets it," I said, then swallowed hard. "I mean, where she got it."

"And her granddaughter, too," he reminded me. "You didn't even blink before offering me a place to stay."

What he said about my grandparents was true, though. Gram had welcomed Neil like an old friend, inviting him to join us at the house following the service. She'd wanted me to stay longer, but I didn't like leaving Evelyn alone and didn't expect Mrs. Thompson to take on everything in my absence. Besides, Neil was due back to work, and I had night shifts starting. When I'd apologized, Gram had said how proud she was of what I was doing, told me I needed to rest, and make sure I ate. The concern was so familial it thawed a corner of my heart that had been frozen since the sixth.

We passed a few other townspeople out on the street, which interrupted our conversation as we nodded a greeting and I accepted condolences. Neil picked up the conversation again once we were alone. "What do you think you'll do with the house?" he asked.

The house. That cozy house with the front porch and the garden in back, with the window frames that sometimes stuck in humid weather, the pitched ceilings of the bedrooms upstairs with the beds tucked beneath them. The house where all six of us had been so happy. It was now mine, to my surprise, but what would I do, rattling around in a house all by myself?

Except I wouldn't be by myself. I'd have my baby.

"I don't know. Maybe I'll come back someday, or maybe one of the boys will want it. There's no rush." I was still trying to sort out what my life could potentially look like. As much as I loved the house, there were problems coming home to a tiny community with a baby and no husband. And what if I did want to work somehow? The opportunities in Chester were so limited. "Right now, I have to stay in Halifax. Evelyn is there, and the house, and my job. As long as I have a job, anyway. I have to start making decisions, Neil, and every time I try, it feels as if everything that's happened crowds me and I end up not deciding anything at all."

He said nothing, just listened, which I appreciated.

"I'm now responsible for Evelyn. I will have to resign my commission." Tears stung the back of my nose. "I wish I could do both. I love nursing, and it's been so important to me that I've been able to help with the war effort."

"There are other ways to help," he said softly. "But I don't mean to make light of your feelings. They do you credit, Nora."

But I didn't want to help in other ways. Once more, the unfairness of it all prickled. This was not a choice Neil would ever have to make—between his work and his family. He could have both and no one would bat an eye.

I knew I should be more grateful. I had a house to live in and there was also a little money; enough to pay Mrs. Thompson a small wage if she continued helping at the house and perhaps a bit to keep me going while I figured things out. While I hated taking it, right now I was committed to caring for Evelyn until Jimmy got home. It wouldn't be fair to uproot her from the only home she'd known. And when I'd asked Will and Stephen if my plans were all right, they'd both got teary. In the end, neither wanted to go back to the house without Mum and Dad there. They'd stuck together, brothers to the end.

We'd reached the small station now, and there were others around, waiting, some faces familiar, many not. I stayed to the side, not wanting to be social or repeat the platitudes I'd given and received all day long. I'd spent the last few weeks working and searching for my family and making arrangements, but now the funeral was over, decisions had been made, and I couldn't lose myself in those details any longer. When my feelings had snapped this morning, it had felt so very final. I couldn't wallow in my emotions anymore. There were important things to be done.

"Neil, about my time at the hospital…" I sat on the hard, cold bench and folded my hands in my lap. "There are still so many patients. I'd like to stay on a while longer."

"Nora, I—"

"Please don't say you can't keep my secret." I turned my head to look at him, my throat tight. "Please, Neil. Work is what is keeping me going right now."

He frowned, then sighed. "It's not about it being a secret. I just… well, generally speaking, pregnant women don't go out to work. I don't want you to put yourself at risk. Or the baby."

"Is that all?" I laughed, relieved. "Oh heavens, Neil. Women don't go out to work but if you think washing and cleaning and cooking and hauling wood and water is less exertion than what I do day to day, you're mistaken. I'm strong as an ox. At least I am when I've managed to eat. But I will make you a promise. If I start to feel poorly at all, I'll quit."

He chuckled. "You're a stubborn woman, Nora."

"Thank you." I brightened. It was just the kind of compliment I liked. It was lovely, of course, to hear that my hair looked pretty, or my dress was sharp, but admiring me for my determination was something that went right to my heart. In the distance, the rumble of the train coming up from Bridgewater vibrated through the air, along with a faint whistle at a crossing. "I would like to work until the end of January before resigning," I stated. "It's still so busy, and I'm needed." After that my condition would become evident. But another six weeks… I could manage another six weeks easily enough.

It felt good to make a firm decision, and I looked up at Neil. He had a pensive look on his face, as if he were thinking about saying something but holding back. Still, this wasn't his choice. If I had to quit, I wanted to do it on my terms.

"That's six weeks away. Maybe…" He looked into my eyes, his face softening. "Maybe you'll have some good news by then, about the baby's father, or about your brother-in-law. Lord knows you deserve some."

I clenched my teeth for a moment, deliberating on how to reply, since once again the situation apparently depended on the appearance of a man in my life. Then I let out a sigh and accepted the inevitable. "I'm not holding out for anything from Alley. I'm afraid I was a fool, Neil. A predictable fool taken in by a uniform and a smile." I softened, though, when I thought of Jimmy. "However, I would love it if my brother-in-law came home and Evelyn had her father back. That would be the greatest Christmas gift. Unlikely, as the holiday is only a week away."

"So you've given up on… this Alley fellow?"

I shrugged. "I think so. I've tried to keep this smidge of hope that there's a good explanation why he hasn't written. I do check the casualty boards as well. I would understand if he'd been wounded, or… or killed. But not one single word since his departure?" I shook my head. "I don't have much faith. I need to figure this out without him swooping in to rescue me."

"Not all men are as fickle, Nora."

"Oh heavens, I know that. I'm more mad at myself than anything." I chanced a look up at him and gave him a wry smile. "I was a fool. The only one to blame for that is me." And if Neil thought I meant a fool for falling for Alley, so be it. I knew the truth. My foolishness had been trying to escape my day-to-day stress by indulging in reckless behaviour. Alley wasn't to blame for that.

The train chugged into the station and before long we were boarded, seated, and on our way again. My appetite had returned—it was always better in the afternoon—and I opened the bag with the lunch inside. "Mmm. We'd best not waste Gram's milk rolls. You won't have anything like them in Halifax." I handed him a buttered half and with dainty fingers added a slice of ham and a bit of cheese. Tiny little sandwiches of love and thoughtfulness.

We ate companionably for a few miles, and then I rested my head against the back of the seat as the train swayed back and forth on the tracks, the vibration rolling beneath my feet, a gentle lull that relaxed me after the trying day. Tomorrow night was the beginning of night shifts, my least favourite rotation. Then Christmas would be upon us. I looked over at Neil, resting his head against the seat with his eyes closed. Another time, another circumstance, perhaps I would be interested in something more. I was about to become an unwed mother, however. Neil was... well, he was not without flaws—the bootleg liquor and occasional reticent moods troubled me, as well as his working far too hard—but he was good and noble. But it didn't matter anyway because my feelings didn't run to love where he was concerned. Instead, I was very grateful to have his friendship.

Another thought crossed my mind as we chugged toward the city that was still in utter ruins. In a week it would be Christmas Eve. Evelyn certainly deserved a good Christmas, and we all could use a bit of cheer. Despite my exhaustion, what I wanted most of all was to be able to show my cobbled-together "family" how much I appreciated them.

And as I closed my eyes, I began to plan.

Chapter Sixteen

CHARLOTTE

December 23, 1917

Christmas was two days away, and I was not above praying for a miracle. I honestly did not know how much longer I could go on. What little bit of hope I had dwindled with each day I spent without Aileen.

I hurried to button my blouse and noticed that it fit looser than it had a week ago when I went to The Green Lantern looking for essentials. Winnie offered to buy me new clothes, but I already felt beholden to my friend. I'd been staying here nearly two weeks already, and Winnie wouldn't take a dime for my lodging or meals. I didn't like the feeling of being indebted to her, but I didn't exactly have much choice, either. In searching for Aileen, I'd also looked for the names of Frank's family. There was nothing of Alice. His brother's body had been pulled from the wreckage of the Acadia Sugar Refinery, but it would be weeks before everyone would be recovered. I was certain that my father-in-law hadn't survived. Perhaps I should have gone to the morgue to check, but that was one thing I couldn't bring myself to do. I just couldn't walk among all those dead bodies. My sanity was hanging on by a tenuous thread as it was.

I was determined to be as small a burden on Winnie as possible, so I left every day, searching for Aileen, which meant I wasn't in the way at the house. I'd checked each hospital twice, as well as all the places that might house an infant: St. Joseph's Orphanage, the Halifax Infants' Home, Brookfield House, the Home of the Guardian Angel… even the City Home, which was really the poor asylum. One day I got my hopes up as there were three unknown babies at one of the houses, but none of them were my Aileen. After that, I sat in the cold on a bench near the Public Gardens and wondered if I would ever find my sweet baby. A gentleman asked if I was all right—it felt like I'd only been sitting a moment but when he spoke to me I realized it was nearly dark, and I had no recollection of the past few hours. I got up and walked home again. Except it wasn't home. Despite the comforts and friendship within the walls, it was not my home, and I was acutely aware I didn't belong there. I didn't belong anywhere.

I stared at my reflection in the mirror as I prepared to go out again today. My cheeks were sunken and my complexion sallow, my eyes tired from sleepless nights lying awake in the dark, alternating between imagining our joyful reunion and despair at the thought of never finding her again. I tidied my hair as best I could, but it was lifeless and dull, and somehow a shade darker than it had been before. The oily film that covered the city after the explosion seemed to cling to my hair, too. Everything weighed me down. It took every ounce of energy I possessed to go out each day and search. My stomach was constantly in knots so that I had trouble eating, and the small sliver of hope that remained was all that kept me putting one foot after the other. I was terrified of what would happen if that sliver disappeared.

With a final pat on my hair, I let out a breath and prepared myself to go downstairs. I would have to do. Today was the day. Today was the day I was certain I'd bring my baby home. There was just something that told me this was it. It had to be, because I wasn't sure how much longer I could go on.

Ed had already departed for the day when I entered the dining room. Winnie was there, of course, perfectly neat and tidy, with her hair in its elegant roll and her lips turned up in a smile. "Good morning, Charlotte. Let me call for some breakfast for you."

It was still so very strange that I was not the one stirring the fire and making breakfast for everyone else. I'd never been waited on in my life, except the time I came down with croup when I was twelve and Mum brought me everything while I remained in bed. But here at Winnie's, the housekeeper brought meals to the dining room table and then picked up the dishes after we'd finished. I looked at Winnie. "Do you ever feel like this is too good to be true?" I asked.

She chuckled. "Every day, Charlotte. I feel like the luckiest woman in Halifax. And there's been a lot to learn. Sometimes I have to accompany my husband to business dinners." She shuddered, then smiled. "I'd much rather spend my evenings home with a cup of tea and some knitting or a book."

I tried to smile back. I was working so hard at not resenting Winnie's good fortune, but I was not always successful. Sometimes I wanted to scream and just get all the feelings bubbling around in me out. I was so… angry. And afraid. God, the fear was crippling. And when Winnie went on like everything was an ordinary day, I felt like I was going to explode like that ship in the harbour and never be put back together, the pieces of me flung across the peninsula like the remains of the *Mont Blanc*.

But today was a better day, because I'd awakened with *that feeling*. The one that said tonight I'd be rocking my little girl to sleep, and we would be reunited, never to be parted again.

It was a big feeling, so big I could barely contain it. But I let out a slow breath and asked to see the daily papers.

I still scanned the announcements every day. My hand shook as I ran my finger down the columns. Many were notices that I had already seen and investigated, and my heart sank lower and lower as I turned the pages. The cavern of darkness threatened to overcome me again. *Please, God, I need some good news. Just a crumb. Please.*

Then I saw one I hadn't seen before.

Information Wanted

Unclaimed Baby at N.S. hospital, from 1 year to 18 months. Long, fair hair when admitted; since cut; blue eyes. Not much injured. No record kept of clothing or place from which she was brought.

That was it. There was no indication which hospital she was at, or who to contact. The pages shook in my hands as I looked up at Winnie. "This is her. I know it is, Winnie." I turned the paper her way and tapped on it with my finger, my insides a mess of knots. "What do I do?"

Winnie stared at the advertisement and then turned her gaze up to me. "Charlotte," she began cautiously, "don't you think that—"

"No!" I snapped, then let out a sigh. "Sorry, Winnie. I don't mean to be cross. I just… have a feeling. I have to find out. What if it's her and I didn't bother to check?" The tendrils of panic began winding around me and I gave my head a shake. "I just… where do I start? There's mention of a hospital but not which one."

Winnie's eyes still held her concern, but she came through anyway, just as she had been for two weeks. "You start at the newspaper office. I'll go with you. Surely they'll have more information about who placed the ad."

But would they? So many ads were placed by people looking for missing friends and relatives. I snatched the paper back and stared at the ad again. "It says 'N.S. hospital', not Halifax. Does that mean she could be somewhere else?"

Winnie pushed away her plate and slid her chair closer to mine. "Some of the wounded were taken out of the city on trains, to Truro and Windsor. Remember the story we heard about the boys ending up in Truro and the glass and oil in their hair?"

I did remember. Hundreds had been sent out of the city, and more left later when they were left with no place to live. The boys had been taken to a barber, who'd found their hair full of shattered glass.

"It's possible this baby could have been taken elsewhere," Winnie said. "There was so much confusion on the day…"

All I had for memories of the day were vague sensations. I couldn't remember any sort of chaos because I'd been unconscious. I didn't even remember how I got to the hospital. Maybe that was a blessing. Maybe not seeing that pandemonium was what helped me keep my hope alive. All I knew was that I had to get to the bottom of this ad and find my girl.

I forced myself to eat a little breakfast—I choked down a piece of toast and a coddled egg that the housekeeper brought me, as well as a hot cup of tea. The moment breakfast was over, I was ready to leave for the newspaper office. It was a Saturday, and with everything closed tomorrow, and then Monday for Christmas Day, I felt the frantic need to hurry. Like if I didn't find Aileen today, I would never find her, and all hope would be lost.

Winnie brought Eddie with her, bundled into the carriage. She'd agreed to come with me to the newspaper office, though the air was heavy and smelled like rain. How she could look so calm and stroll along as if she had not a care in the world was beyond me, as I was itching to get to the office on Argyle. Big flakes of snow drifted down around us as we went, though it melted as soon as it hit the ground, and the air was mild enough that I was certain I'd be caught in the rain later and had no umbrella. Gritting my teeth against the pain, I measured my steps to hers. Aileen was waiting and I didn't want to lose a single minute.

The baby started to fuss, and I looked down into the carriage, seeing the pink blanket I'd knit for Aileen in those first few months after she was born, and pink cheeks and blue eyes. I reached down into the carriage to soothe her and then stopped as Winnie moved in front of me, tucking the blue blanket around her son and speaking to him softly.

I stood there for a moment, my insides quivering, shaken at what had just happened yet again. The blanket was blue. Her son's eyes were brown, like hers. It wasn't Aileen in the carriage, but for that brief moment, I was back on our daily walks again.

My head turned from side to side, searching. All around me were people walking to and fro, there were other carriages, other babies who could be my Aileen, and my chest tightened as my breaths quickened. What was happening to me? It was like the other night, when I'd heard the crying in my sleep. But I was wide awake now. I had to get a hold of myself. It was the stress of the days and weeks following the disaster that had me discombobulated, that was all. In a nearby window, I saw my reflection and barely recognized myself. A new panic fluttered in my chest. What if Aileen didn't recognize me? What if she didn't know I was her mother? I pulled off my gloves and tried to tuck stray hairs away, but they wouldn't stay in place. Little pieces stuck out by my ears, at my temples.

"Charlotte? Charlotte, are you all right?"

I turned my head, a bit too quickly, and it took a moment for Winnie's worried face to come into focus. She was frowning at me, holding her baby in her arms—in that blue blanket—and I forced a smile to my lips. "I'm fine now," I assured her, though I felt anything but. "I just had a little dizzy spell."

"You haven't been sleeping, and barely eating. You're not yourself." Her face was creased with worry. "You must take care of yourself, Charlotte."

Why must I? I wanted to ask. If my search came to nothing today, what did I have to live for? Despair came crashing in again, my frequent companion, and I fought against it, trying to remember the feeling of hope I'd had when I saw the ad in the newspaper. "I know, and I will. I didn't mean to worry you. Let's keep on." I smiled again, the feeling unnatural. Winnie looked at me strangely, then put Eddie back in the carriage and we walked on.

When we reached the newspaper office, we both went inside to make the inquiry. But when I was faced with the man behind the counter, I suddenly couldn't speak. I looked at Winnie, and my expression must have been wild because her eyes widened and then she turned and smiled at the gentleman.

I listened as she made her inquiries, but the words jumbled around in my head. It was only moments and Winnie was back at my side, her hand on my arm. "The Aberdeen Hospital in New

Glasgow," she said, squeezing my forearm. "I'm sorry it's not here in Halifax…"

"It's fine," I said, and my voice sounded a long way away. "I checked all the hospitals here. I need to go to New Glasgow."

"Then let's get you there," Winnie said, putting her hands back on the handle of the carriage. A man opened the door for us to leave the office, and once again we found ourselves out on the busy Saturday street. My leg was aching already from the walk from Beech Street, and now we had to make our way to the North Street Station. I didn't even know the train schedule. But I carried all the money I had in the world in my purse, and it would be enough—I hoped—to get me to New Glasgow and back.

We began our walk and my steps hitched as my leg resisted. I'd had the stitches out earlier in the week, but the muscles were still healing beneath the skin. I bit down on my lip and Winnie must have seen because she stopped me. "I'm getting you a taxi," she said. "You need to save your strength."

"I can walk—" I started to protest.

"This will get you to the station faster. Here." She reached into her purse and took out a few bills. "Take this. Just in case."

"I have money," I protested.

"Then if you don't use it, give it back to me when you return." Her dark eyes were firm on mine. "I wish I could go with you, Charlotte. I'm worried about you going alone, but I haven't got things for Eddie and—if you wait, I can go too. Maybe the day after Christmas."

"It's all right. I'll be all right," I insisted, which was possibly a lie, but I was going to go, come hell or high water.

She must have heard the determination in my voice because she gave a brief nod. "Then take the money and go. I'll be praying for you that this baby is Aileen and you'll be reunited. Please, Charlotte." She pushed the money into my hands.

I tucked the bills into my purse because she was right. A few extra dollars gave me some insurance so I wouldn't have to worry about the fare home.

Home. I didn't have a home. But I had Winnie. And she'd stuck with me. A true friend.

"You are an angel," I whispered, drawing her into a hug. The baby started to fuss again since the carriage had stopped, and we each gave a watery laugh. Within two minutes she had bundled me into a taxi and the big snowflakes were starting to feel more like rain.

The North Street station was drastically changed. All the windows had been blown out by the explosion, and they'd been boarded up until they could be repaired. The train shed roof was completely destroyed. But miraculously, within a few days of the disaster, the rubble had been cleared and the trains were running regularly again. The roof was being rebuilt and new glass installed in the windows. I bought my ticket and sat down on a hard bench to wait, both excited and unsure. The only time I'd been on a train, Frank and I had gone to Bridgewater and spent the night when we were married—a brief honeymoon. I'd never traveled alone. It felt odd, being at the station as a single woman, even if I was widowed. I didn't exactly feel unsafe, but I wasn't comfortable, either. It felt as if everyone's eyes were on me and my second-hand coat and hat. I shifted and tried to get more comfortable, wishing the minutes away, feeling exposed. Tucking my hair again, smoothing my gloves. All the while vacillating between hope and fear of what I'd find at my destination.

When boarding was announced, I quickly rose and made my way to the waiting train car and slid onto a black bench seat. As the other passengers boarded, the seats filled, but being on first meant I'd chosen a spot at the front with no facing bench, so I didn't have to look at someone else or make conversation. I didn't want to talk to anyone. I cradled the knowledge of what was happening today deep inside me, protecting it, as if speaking it would let it loose and all fly apart. As if putting voice to it would somehow shatter the possibility of finding Aileen like glass. Instead, I looked out the window.

But that proved to be a mistake, because as we pulled away from the station, all I saw was a wasteland. Buildings leveled so they resembled a pile of matchsticks. Others partially standing, neglected, abandoned to tumble and die. People had perished here. My heart wrenched as I realized that there were still bodies entombed in the rubble. The sugar refinery… my father-in-law could be in there right now, dead, even as the train took me past the wreckage toward Bedford. Alice, too, on her way to school, out in the open… She'd had the whole of her life ahead of her. All that potential… gone. She'd been smart as a whip and perhaps not the friendliest toward me, but as the tracks took me past the destruction, I mourned the loss of all the chances we might have had to make things different. The full impact of what had happened finally reached in and grabbed me by the guts in a way it hadn't when I'd gone to our house on Russell. Perhaps I'd still been in shock then; I certainly had been when I'd sat with Mrs. Campbell, and the image of her lying there would be embedded in my brain forever. Now, from the window of a railway car, I saw the utter annihilation of what my world had once been, and I rested my head against the train window as tears slipped down my cheeks. So much pain. So much loss. So much grief. It threatened to drag me down, and only the thought of Aileen kept my head above water.

New Glasgow was much smaller than Halifax, but its station was a lovely, large building untouched by disaster. I cautiously disembarked, and then asked directions to the hospital so I could go there directly. I needed to stretch my legs and get my thoughts in order, so I walked to the large brick building on Hospital Avenue, one halting foot after the other, trying not to hope too hard because I knew the disappointment would finish me. And yet I couldn't escape the feeling that this was it—that I was walking closer and closer to my daughter, my baby that I hadn't held in over two weeks, and my lone surviving family.

My heart clubbed inside my chest as I neared the building. My leg pained but I didn't care. Inside my purse was the little rattle that I'd found in the house, the one that Frank had carved and sent home before he'd been killed. I carried it with me every day. Somewhere, behind these solid walls, was my child, and I'd put this rattle back in her little hand, right where it belonged.

I stepped inside the hospital and my head swirled for a moment, I was that giddy with anticipation. For all Mrs. Campbell had said I had no mothering instincts, I knew she was wrong. I was a good mother. A loving mother, and I believed in my intuition. Not once in my search had I felt such certainty as I did today.

"May I help you? Do you need assistance?"

The kind, clear voice brought me back to the moment, and I looked up to see a pressed and polished nurse looking at me with assessing eyes. "I-I'm here because I saw your notice in a paper in Halifax. In the *Evening Mail*. About the baby from the explosion."

The nurse's gaze softened. "I see. I'm Nurse Fraser, ma'am. And you are?"

I started to breathe again. "Charlotte Campbell. I was taken to Camp Hill Hospital after the explosion, and my baby has been missing ever since. She's just over a year old, with light hair and eyes."

"And you came all this way today?"

I nodded. "I'm a mother, Nurse Fraser. I'd move heaven and earth to find my child."

"The baby's name?"

"Aileen. Her father was killed in action and the rest of his family…" The image of Mrs. Campbell with the glass through her neck intruded into my thoughts, shifting immediately to the carnage I'd witnessed from the train car just this morning. I bit down on my lip and closed my eyes as the horror of those pictures paraded through my mind. I couldn't think of that. The spectre of an image was lurking, one of Aileen with that same deadly shard of glass embedded in her tiny body. I dropped a mental curtain on it. I would not think of her that way. I refused.

"Mrs. Campbell, please sit down." The nurse took my arm and helped me to a chair. "You're looking quite faint. Are you sure you're all right? Let me get you some water. Have you eaten?"

"I'm fine," I assured her, clearing the images from my head. Why wasn't she taking me to my child already?

"You were saying, about your husband's family?" she prompted, her hand still on my arm.

"I was going to say the rest of Frank's family were killed in the explosion. Or at least I think so. His mother was still in the house and his father and brother worked at the Acadia Sugar Refinery. His brother's body was recovered, but his father's…" I paused. "I haven't seen any news of his sister, Alice, either. She was fifteen and on her way to school." A smidge of guilt coiled through me. For all my regrets, I hadn't exactly looked that hard. What if she were alive? The sudden thought of her navigating the world alone bit into me. But that wasn't why I was here.

Somewhere in this building, my child waited for me to take her home. What was taking so long?

"May I see the baby, please?" I forced what I hoped was a serene smile on my face, even though my insides were trembling.

"Of course. I'll be right back."

I waited on the hard chair, my hands folded in my lap, trying not to twist my fingers together. A small part of my mind cautioned me that this baby might not be Aileen, that I shouldn't get my hopes up, but my heart didn't listen. It beat as if it had wings, trying to fly its way out and to the little girl who was here. It seemed to take forever for Nurse Fraser to return with another nurse and a doctor. "Mrs. Campbell, will you please come with us?"

I rose and followed. I couldn't even really feel my legs, and my breath shortened with anticipation. I had the strange thought that it was the excitement of the moment mixed with how utterly exhausted I was from the last few weeks, but the odd energy propelled me forward as I followed the hospital staff.

And then suddenly there she was, and cold raced down my spine and my arms and legs as my head swam and my vision blurred.

"Mrs. Campbell." The voice sounded far away, and I turned my head this way and that, trying to follow the sound.

I was on the floor, I realized, with the doctor supporting my weight. Things began to return to focus. "I'm so sorry," I apologized, still a bit dazed, embarrassed that I'd fainted. Perhaps it was the shock. "I suppose I haven't eaten much today…"

I looked up and saw the sweet little blond head in the crib and I started to cry.

I took in her little face, blue eyes, and the cap of curls, shorter than I remembered, surrounding her head like an angel's halo.

The doctor and nurse helped me to my feet, and I went forward, stronger now, gathering the baby into my arms as I sobbed.

She was different—lighter, perhaps, as I settled her weight into my arms and drank in the sight of her. Her cheeks had roses and her eyes were bright and inquisitive as she lifted a pudgy hand and played with a flyaway piece of my hair. She had certainly been well cared for here, and gratitude flooded my heart as I stared at the nurses and doctor through watery eyes.

"Thank you. Oh, thank you so much for caring for her." I slid my gaze over to the baby and looked into her wide eyes, staring solemnly at me as if she couldn't understand all the fuss. I noticed now a cut on her scalp, healing, and I kissed the spot, so overwhelmed with relief and love and gratitude, I wasn't sure what to say or do. "Was she hurt?" I asked, holding her tightly. Too tightly, since she began to squirm as if she wanted to be let down. I put her back in the crib reluctantly—I wanted to hold her forever and never let her go again.

The doctor stepped forward. "Mrs.… Campbell, is it?"

"Yes, sir." I let out a breath and met his gaze.

"You're certain this is your child?"

I frowned. What sort of question was that? "Of course I'm sure! I've been searching for her since I was released from Camp Hill." I gave her date of birth and any other information I could think of as I reached into my handbag and produced the rattle that Frank had made. "Here's Daddy's rattle, sweetheart. Yes, there you go." Aileen grabbed the toy in her chubby fist and shook it, a smile finally breaking out on her face, her two front teeth looking adorable as she grinned and waved her arm. "I'm afraid we lost everything," I said. "We lived with my husband's family in Richmond, you see."

"Oh, I'm so sorry." Sympathy etched his face. "You should know, the child sustained some minor injuries in the blast. There is the cut on her head that gave us some worry. But I feel fairly certain now that there shouldn't be any long-term effects. She had a number of bumps and bruises, as well, though really it's a miracle she survived mostly unscathed."

"Her name is Aileen," I told him, my voice stronger now. "She was in her carriage when it happened. Perhaps that protected her." Tears welled in my eyes again. I couldn't believe this was happening. "Oh, this is the best Christmas present I could have ever hoped for." Just hours ago, I was wondering how I could possibly go on, my thoughts so dark and grim they'd frightened me. I didn't dare give them any more space in my mind. And now here I was, with my little girl, my reason for everything.

"Mrs. Campbell, if you'll follow me, we can look after the details about releasing Aileen, as well as recommendations for her care. You do have a place to live, don't you?" She gave me a strange look, and I lifted my hand to my hair. I knew I didn't look my best. How could I, when I'd been frantic with worry for days?

"A dear friend has taken me in, and I know I'm welcome there for as long as I need." Oh, Winnie was going to be so happy for me. "There's plenty of room for Aileen. The house wasn't damaged, and her situation is quite…" I searched for the right word. "Her husband does well, works for the bank. We won't want for anything, I promise." A sudden panic filled my breast. What if they didn't think I could care for her? What if they didn't let me take her home?

"If you'll follow me…"

I looked back at the baby. I didn't want to move a step without her in my arms, but the nurse touched my arm and smiled. "She's not going anywhere," she said softly. "You and your daughter will be just fine."

I looked at Aileen, sitting in the crib gnawing on the rattle, and my heart filled with a love so big and pure, I thought I might burst with it. She was here. She was alive. She was mine.

"I'll be back, Leenie. I'll be back as soon as I can and we're going to go home."

Chapter Seventeen

NORA

December 24, 1917

I stood back from the table and admired my handiwork while a great hole of loneliness opened inside me. Christmas was tomorrow. John and Marvin had, as promised, set up a tree in the parlour and Evelyn, Mrs. Thompson, and I had put Jane's decorations on it. Mrs. Thompson had even dug out her crochet hook and crafted some dainty snowflakes and bells and presented them to Evelyn to put on the sweet-smelling branches. I wasn't sure how I would have managed without Mrs. Thompson. She'd quickly become a surrogate mother and grandmother to me and to my niece. What might have been an afternoon full of tears had instead been a few hours to come together and be thankful for each other.

Despite everything—the war, the devastation—a little

Christmas spirit prevailed. Thousands of children had lost their homes or families, and after seeing a plea in the *Daily Echo* for the Sunshine Fund, I took Evelyn to purchase little gifts to donate to the children in need throughout the city. Evelyn had enjoyed buying for other little girls and boys, and for once I hadn't counted pennies. I would happily go without extras for a while just to see that rare smile on Evvie's face.

But tonight, there was no escaping the empty places at the table.

Jane. Jimmy. Clara. My mother and father. And yes, even my brothers and grandparents, who'd decided to remain in Chester, no longer enthusiastic about the previously planned "big family Christmas". And I didn't blame them. Nor did I wish to travel to Chester—even though I'd been invited—and see all the old places without the precious faces I cherished. The funeral had been hard enough. Instead, my "Halifax family" would have breakfast here, I'd nap, and then report in for the night shift on Christmas night. There wasn't even a tree at the hospital, for space was still too snug to have room for it. To say holiday spirit was in short supply was not an exaggeration.

Neil was with us for Christmas Eve, though he was taking the train to Kentville in the morning and visiting his family briefly for the holiday. It surprised me to realize I was going to miss him. Marvin and John were nice men, and Mrs. T was a godsend, but Neil was closer to my age, only a few years older, and we were both in the medical profession. We had a lot in common, and he'd quickly become a good friend.

But that was all. Despite everything, there was still that spot in my heart that hoped for a letter from Alley. I'd even considered writing to his family on the South Shore, but what would I say? How could I explain that he hadn't written a word since his departure? And what if his parents admitted that he'd been writing to them all along? Every time I thought about it, I wasn't sure which would feel worse. It would be awful to find out he'd been killed, but thinking he'd abandoned me was a different but equally devastating thought. Grief was one thing, but at least his silence would have a reason that had nothing to do with me. The thought that I'd been discarded cut me deeply. For a man who'd said he loved me, he had an odd way of showing it. Alley had always been ready for fun, but when I needed him to take some responsibility, to do the "right" thing—society's solution, not mine—he was nowhere to be found.

"The table looks lovely, dear."

Mrs. Thompson came into the kitchen, a covered dish in her arms, and I pushed my depressing thoughts away. Tonight we were all going to be together for dinner. Mrs. Thompson had promised to make something for dessert, and she'd done it over at her house so it would be a surprise. There were fresh loaves of bread cooling on the counter, and Neil had come home with a mess of seafood and refused to say where he'd got it or how much it had cost him. Despite my lack of prowess in the kitchen, I had dug out Jane's recipe book and found our mother's recipe for chowder. Tonight we would eat like kings.

"Thank you, Mrs. T. I went through Jane's linen closet. I thought we needed something festive."

I'd draped Jane's finest snow-white tablecloth on the table, then had gone outside and cut spruce and pine boughs and placed them in a pretty vase. Each place had a teacup beside it for hot apple cider, seasoned with cinnamon sticks, nutmeg, and whole cloves—a change from the usual plain tea. I'd even unearthed Great-Grandmother Mabel's soup tureen for the chowder, adding a real sense of occasion.

Clara's highchair had been tucked away, though I touched my tummy and tried to think happy thoughts—next Christmas, my own child could be in that chair, making spirits bright and happy. There were things to look forward to. A future. It might be uncertain, but it was there, and I needed to remind myself of that when I got too glum. Yes, I was sad and frustrated about leaving my vocation. At the same time, I did like children. I loved Evelyn and Clara, and I knew I would love my own child, too. This was not the life I'd envisioned for myself, but I would make it work somehow. I rolled my shoulders back and lifted my chin. Yes. I was a smart, resourceful woman, and I would figure this out.

But today… today I was struggling to feel festive amidst so much loss.

Mrs. T put the dish down on the counter and came to my side, wrapping an arm around my shoulders and giving me a squeeze. "It's bound to be difficult, no matter what," she said. "No sense trying to pretend otherwise, dear. We've just got to be thankful for what we have left and honour the ones we love."

I put my hand over Mrs. T's. "You're right. It's so hard to know they're gone, and they're never coming back." Indeed, I had shed plenty of tears at night, missing my family with a brutal ache that seemed worse in the darkness and quiet. "But I am thankful for all of you. We've stuck together, haven't we?"

"We sure have." The older woman nodded. "And you're doing fine, love. We'll all just keep looking after each other."

For the millionth time, my secret hovered over me. I hesitated, considered bringing Mrs. T into my confidence, but just then the front door slammed, and a deep voice called, "Ho ho ho!"

"That'll be Captain McLeod," Mrs. T said, her face lighting with a smile.

Everyone liked Neil, and it was no secret that Mrs. T's glances often went between the two of us. Perhaps it would be simpler if I found myself with romantic feelings for him, and there were times when our conversations seemed… intimate. But in the end, I appreciated him as a friend. Nothing more. Moreover, that friendship had become important to me, and I hoped it would not be spoiled by romantic nonsense.

"Merry Christmas," he exclaimed, coming into the kitchen. He was in his uniform but had removed his boots and was in his stocking feet. There was a small stack of packages in his arms, too, wrapped in simple brown paper and string. Gifts. He'd thought of gifts. I thought of the little basket of packages I had upstairs, too, and was glad I had bought the items instead of letting my dread of the holiday weigh me down.

"Merry Christmas to you, too, Captain," Mrs. T said warmly. "And what have you got there?"

"Just a few things for everyone. As a thank-you for making me feel so welcome here, in such awful circumstances." He gave a winning smile, and a sudden wave of irritation came over me. Maybe that was the problem with Neil. Everyone loved him. He always seemed to know the right thing to do and say. How could anyone ever live up to his example?

Evelyn came running into the room, her curls bouncing and her eyes sparkling. "You're here! That means we can eat! I'm hungry."

My irritation fled and I burst out laughing, and it felt good. There was too little laughter these days, but Evelyn's excitement was contagious, and it did my heart good to see my niece smiling. Evelyn had showered attention on Buttons, but the cat didn't make up for losing her mother and sister. There were plenty of moments when I saw sadness shadow Evelyn's face, or I heard the little girl whispering to Buttons about Clara and Jane. Maybe Neil was "perfect", but if that meant a jolly household for the holiday, I would paste on a smile and pretend.

Neil touched Evelyn's nose with the tip of his finger. "You only want to eat because you know there are presents after."

"Mummy lets me open one the night before Christmas." Evelyn bounced on her toes. "But everything else has to wait."

Neil knelt before her, and I thought of Jimmy, far away from his daughter for another Christmas. There hadn't been a letter from him lately, either. Not since that last one Jane got before the explosion.

"Maybe you can open my present tonight, since I'm going to visit my family tomorrow."

She nodded, curls bobbing again, and everyone laughed.

"Let me put these under the tree, then. Maybe you can help me?"

He couldn't have asked a better question. Evelyn held out a trusting hand and there was a pause before Neil took it, meeting my eyes. I softened a little bit, seeing him holding Evelyn's small hand.

"Oh, my goodness. Just a moment, Evelyn. I nearly forgot." He reached into his pocket and withdrew a letter, handing it over to me. My heart skipped a beat as I met his gaze. Was it from Alley—finally? I took the envelope into my trembling hand and glanced at the writing. Not Alley, then. But it was from Jimmy.

Disappointment rushed from my head to my toes, though a little part of me warmed to know that Jimmy was still out there and able to write. "Thank you, Captain," I said quietly.

"Of course. Come on, Evelyn. Let's go see the tree." Then the two headed toward the parlour.

"That man needs a wife and family," Mrs. T mused quietly.

"Mrs. Thompson…" I warned.

"I'm just saying it's as clear as the nose on your face that he likes you, Nora. And he's awfully good with Evelyn."

"Evelyn has a father. And this letter is from him." I hastily opened the short letter, scanning the writing quickly. I didn't want Evelyn to know there'd been a letter if there was bad news inside. But my worries were unfounded. Jimmy was tired but well, sending holiday wishes, missing home and sending his love to Evelyn with a hope that the war would soon be ending and he'd return. Relief filled the spots where disappointment had lived just moments ago. Evelyn still had a father, at least, who loved her dearly.

"Is everything all right, Nora?" Mrs. Thompson hovered anxiously, the lines in her face deep with worry. "Is Mr. Boutilier well?"

"He is," I answered with a smile, looking up. "Homesick, of course. And I'm sure he's heartbroken about Jane and Clara. He kept the letter positive, probably for Evelyn's benefit. We just have to pray he stays that way." Especially since the letter had actually been penned a few weeks earlier. So much could happen in that time…

Mrs. Thompson let out a sigh, then pressed her hands against the apron tied at her waist, protecting her dress. "Well, thank the Lord for that." Then she grinned. "Now, back to the handsome doctor in the parlour…"

There was no deterring my well-meaning neighbour, and there wasn't a lot of time before dinner, either. But I knew I couldn't hold onto my secret any longer. "Mrs. T, I need to tell you something. Sit down, won't you?"

A frown formed a crease between Mrs. T's eyebrows, but she pulled out a chair and sat. I did the same, nerves making my stomach churn. Confessing my problems was so tough. Still. This wasn't going away. I was going to have to start dealing with the consequences. And that began with Mrs. T, come what may.

"Are you all right, Nora? I thought you said Jimmy was all right."

I nodded, then cleared my throat. "He is, and I'm fine. Truly. And before I say anything more, you need to know that you've been an absolute angel to us, and I can't imagine doing without you."

Another frown. "Then why does it sound as if you're going to have to?"

I lifted my eyes and twisted my fingers together, searching for the right words that wouldn't ruin everything. "Remember when I told you I had a beau? That he'd gone overseas?"

Mrs. T nodded. "I'm sorry if me teasing you about the captain has made you uncomfortable."

"It's not that. It's just…" I sighed and decided to just say it. "Mrs. T, around the middle of July there's going to be another baby around here. I'm around ten weeks along."

Mrs. T's mouth dropped open, but no sound came out.

"I know it's a shock. It was just once…" Heat rushed up my neck to my face, making my ears burn.

"Good heavens, child. I'm not judging you, it's just the shock, that's all. Lord knows, it happens often enough." She reached out and took one of my hands, patting the top. "In wartime, everyone's desperate to grasp every bit of life, I think."

My throat clogged with tears. "We should have waited, but we didn't, and now here I am, and Jane was going to help me, but now she's gone, and I have Evelyn and this place and I'm just —" I stopped, a bit embarrassed that my last words had tumbled out.

"You're tired and you're scared. Oh, ducky. I wish you'd told me sooner. Does anyone else know?"

"Neil," I whispered. "He guessed when he noticed the signs."

"I knew you weren't eating well, but I thought it was just the grief of everything. My mam always said grief killed the appetite," Mrs. T answered. "Oh, Nora. A woman needs her mother at a time like this. I'm so very sorry."

Tears slipped down my cheeks and I lifted my hands to swipe them away. "At the end of January, I'll have to resign. I just couldn't bring myself to do it now, when the need at the hospital is so great. And then I don't know what I'm going to do. Thank God Jimmy is all right, and at least Evelyn still has a father."

"And what about this young man of yours? What does he say about the baby?"

That was the question, wasn't it? "Nothing. None of my letters have been answered." More tears tumbled out and ran down my cheeks into my collar, not just of sadness but of anger, at him for not writing and me for sleeping with him in the first place. "He hasn't written since he left. I wrote several times a week at first, and not one reply. I've been such a fool, Mrs. T. For a smart girl, I was very stupid."

Mrs. Thompson let out a big breath and straightened her spine. "Well. You're certainly not the first to fall for a handsome soldier, and not the first to trust that someone means what they say, either. If he's left you high and dry, that's his loss, because you are a wonderful young woman. You're smart and caring and generous. And he's the fool, not you."

The stalwart support had the tears coming faster. "I keep thinking maybe he's hurt and hasn't been able to write. How can I be angry at him when he's off fighting a war?"

Mrs. T's face softened. "You fell in love, dear. And you're right. There could be a perfectly good reason he hasn't written." She patted my hand again.

Except I hadn't fallen in love. A part of me was still ashamed of that, as if love was the reason that would make everything understandable and less… tainted. What I wanted most of all was to legitimize this baby, so that my mistake didn't ruin both our lives—me as the mother, and this baby growing up the child of a woman with loose morals.

"I was so scared to tell you," I admitted. "Scared you wouldn't want to associate with an unwed mother." Just saying the word *mother* felt foreign, but I would get used to it in time. I had to, didn't I?

Mrs. T waved a hand and made a *pshhh* sound. "I'm not in the habit of abandoning people I care about, Nora. And a bit of gossip doesn't bother me. For heaven's sake, if we shut out every woman who had a baby less than nine months from her wedding, hardly anyone would have friends at all."

I laughed at that, a watery chuckle. I remembered that my grandmother had been a premature baby. There were stories about her first few weeks being in a breadbox close to the wood stove. But even doing the math, it was clear that my grandmother had been present at her parents' wedding… by about two months. It was simply not discussed, that was all.

"Everyone makes mistakes," Mrs. Thompson continued, "and I'll tell you a little secret." She leaned forward. "It's often the women who bear the brunt of them. We need to stick together. So nothing's changed for me. I'll be here as long as you need, so just you mind that."

It was the best Christmas present I could have asked for. "Then let's pray extra hard tonight for this war to end and Jimmy to come home soon. Evelyn needs her father here. And… oh, it would take a lot of pressure off me too, I guess."

"And we'll pray for your young man to write." Again Mrs. T patted my hand—her usual comforting gesture—and then pushed on her knees and got up from the table. "Now, let's get this Christmas Eve dinner on the go. That chowder smells delicious. I'll cut the bread."

I rose and went to the stove to tend to the chowder, which

had been on low heat, letting the flavours seep through. My appetite had suddenly returned—maybe the old adage was true. Maybe confession was good for the soul. I took a taste and then snuck a little more of the precious butter into the broth. John and Marvin came in as well, having finished work for the day, their jovial conversation lighting up the space. The warm, family atmosphere left me feeling oddly bereft, wishing Jane were here with her smile and motherly care; wishing we were indeed having the big family Christmas we'd planned, with the boys and our parents smiling at everyone's antics as presents were opened. Those days would never come again, and no surrogate family could make up for the loss.

And then Evelyn and Neil came back in the kitchen, still hand in hand, and I forced a smile to my face. I would not be maudlin. Not now. There was still so very much to be thankful for. I'd make this a good Christmas for Evelyn, even if I couldn't quite make it a good one for myself. It would have to be enough.

The mood around the table was jovial as we dined on the rich soup and soft bread, sopping up the last of the broth with the crusts. The cider was a real treat, but the best part was when Mrs. T took the cover off her baking dish, revealing an actual chocolate cake with boiled frosting on the top. "I only had one egg left, so I'm sorry there's not more frosting. But it's sweetened with maple syrup."

It was absolutely decadent, and the look on Evelyn's face when she tasted the sweet, boiled icing made us all smile. When the meal was done, we stacked the dishes for washing later, as Evelyn was fairly dancing with excitement to go to the parlour and see the presents before bedtime. We all filed into the cozy room, a brisk fire burning at the grate, the tree standing slightly lopsided yet regal in the corner. It was all so bittersweet, a bit of light in the midst of the darkest days I had ever known, and my emotions had been seesawing all day, leaving me raw and perhaps a bit vulnerable. But as everyone settled into a chair or on the chesterfield, second cups of cider in their hands, I made the decision to simply be thankful. I had so much more than some people in Halifax this Christmas.

"Auntie Nora, which one can I open?" Evelyn appeared before me, jittery in her excitement.

Neil leaned forward. "If it's all right with your aunt, maybe you can open mine, Evelyn."

The fact that Neil had gone and got gifts for everyone in the midst of his grueling schedule made me like him even more. In a few short weeks, he'd become a part of our ragtag family, almost as if he'd always been here. He always had a kind word and a smile, sometimes weary but always when it was needed. He joked with the other men, carried wood for Mrs. T, and was a support to me.

Evelyn took his hand, and he went with her to the tree, plucking out a small package and putting it in her palm. He returned to his chair, but to my astonishment, Evelyn followed and innocently climbed up on his knee.

He looked up in surprise. Evelyn was not this familiar with either John or Marvin, of course, and it was inappropriate. And yet I didn't have the heart to tell her to get down, though perhaps I should and save Neil the trouble. Before I could decide, Neil settled her more firmly on his lap and helped her untie the knot in the string holding the paper together. I watched with a lump in my throat. It should be Jimmy here right now, or Jane. Or even my own father, bouncing his granddaughter on his knee. It was lovely for Neil to step in, but this wasn't something he could fix like setting a broken bone or stitching a wound, no matter how hard he tried.

"I'm not used to buying presents for little girls," he said. "But the lady at the shop helped me."

Evelyn tore at the paper, making them all laugh, and then opened the little cardboard box. Her mouth made a little "O" as her little fingers reached inside.

"They're so pretty."

"What is it, Evelyn?" Mrs. T leaned forward, trying to see inside.

"A bow for my hair. And ribbons! Look, Auntie Nora!" She held them in her little fist, the colourful satin trailing from her fingers.

There was one large bow in blue, Evelyn's favourite colour. Other lengths of ribbon in red, brown, cream, and a vibrant green created a rainbow of hues. Pretty ribbons were an extravagance, and not something Jane had indulged in while trying to run a frugal household.

And yet Captain McLeod had thought to spend his money on something pretty and frivolous, which was exactly what a Christmas present should be for a four-year-old.

"You must thank Captain McLeod for the thoughtful gift," I said.

Evelyn turned to Neil, her face beaming. "Thank you, Captain McLeod." And with childhood guile, she shifted on his lap to kiss his cheek before sliding to the floor. "Auntie, will you put one in my hair? I want to wear it all night!"

I was still shaken by the familiarity Evelyn had just displayed. It didn't seem to bother Neil at all, and it had been completely innocent, of course. But it did drive home just how much Neil had become interwoven into our household, and it also showed me how much Evelyn missed having a father figure around. Neil was far closer to Jimmy's age than the other two men, so it was only natural for Evelyn to gravitate toward the young doctor.

"Of course, I will," I answered. "You pick which colour, and I'll weave it into your braid so you can wear it to bed." I gave Evelyn a meaningful look. "Little girls have to go to sleep so Santa Claus can come."

Evelyn picked the green, because it was the same colour as the Christmas tree, she said. Then she stood mostly patiently while I wove the fine ribbon through her braid and tied it in a little bow at the bottom. "There," I said, giving the bow a final tug. "It looks very pretty."

Evelyn beamed. "I'm ready for bed now," she announced.

Everyone smiled at that. The reference to Santa Claus meant there'd be no resisting bedtime tonight or begging for one more story. "Then let's go get your nightie on and I'll tuck you in."

Evelyn raced off toward the stairs, making everyone chuckle.

Mrs. T stood. "There's more cider, and I might have a little nip of something to put in it, if you gentlemen are interested. Nora?"

It was Christmas. It surprised me that Mrs. T might have bootleg alcohol hidden away, but a little spiked cider sounded quite celebratory and harmless. "Regular cider is fine for me, Mrs. T," I replied. "But you are all certainly welcome to have a Christmas tipple. I'll go tuck Evelyn in and be back shortly."

When I got upstairs, Evelyn was already struggling with her buttons. Together we got her into her soft flannel nightgown, and I slid a pair of warm knitted socks over her little feet. Buttons the cat was a permanent fixture now, and he was curled up on the bed, opening one eye as Evelyn slid under the covers and I tucked the quilts up under her chin.

"Merry Christmas, sweetheart," I said softly, kissing Evelyn's forehead.

"Merry Christmas, Auntie," Evelyn said in her sweet voice. There was a moment's pause, and then she said, "Do you think there's Christmas in heaven, Auntie?"

My throat tightened and I blinked against the sudden stinging in my eyes. "Since it's Baby Jesus's birthday, I think there must be a big birthday party."

"With cake?"

I chuckled, the sound thick. It should be Jane here, answering Evelyn's funny questions. Instead, I was, for all intents and purposes, Evelyn's mother now. It all fell to me, and the responsibility was heavy. And yet it was beautiful, too. Perhaps it wasn't the path I'd envisioned for my life, and I was plenty fearful about the months to come, but these were still precious moments. If I had learned anything from this war, and from the past few weeks, it was that life was fleeting. And family was everything.

"Maybe with cake," I whispered. "Just like Mrs. Thompson made."

"Mmm."

Evelyn still held onto my hand, though her eyelids were growing heavy. "Auntie, do you think Mummy and Clara will have presents in heaven?"

Oh, Lord. Innocent questions that had the ability to reach in and tear my heart to shreds. I smoothed an errant piece of hair away from Evelyn's face. "I'm sure they will, sweetheart. And Grammie and Grampie, too." I didn't know what heaven looked like, but it was comforting to think of them all together. Comforting and yet sad to be the ones left behind.

"I prayed Daddy would be home for Christmas. But he's not."

"I know, sweetheart. But it was lovely that he was able to send a letter, wasn't it? He loves you so much. We just have to keep praying that he'll be home soon, and the war will be over."

"I miss Daddy. And Mummy. And Clara. I liked having a sister."

I wasn't sure how much more I could take. "I miss them, too. But we have each other, right?"

"I love you, Auntie Nora." Evelyn sat up and threw her arms around my neck, holding on tight.

I hugged her back, closing my eyes, drawing in the soft scent of the clean flannel nightgown and soap from face washings before bed. Caring for Evelyn wasn't just a duty for me, no more than working at the hospital was. Both were labours of love, just in different ways. There was something to be said for that.

There was no way I could stop the tears from filling my eyes now. "I love you too, Evvie. Now go to sleep so Santa Claus can fill your stocking, and I'll see you in the morning."

Evelyn nodded and burrowed into the covers.

I kissed her hair and left the room, shutting the door behind me.

I disappeared to my room for a few minutes to have a bit of a cry and then dry my eyes. The holiday without my family was hard, even though everyone was trying to be jolly and making the best of it. Evelyn's honest and innocent questions were the hardest, and it felt good to have a little weep and get it out. I went to the bathroom and splashed a little cold water on my face, then straightened my clothing and prepared to go back downstairs.

Mrs. T was nearly done tidying the kitchen, with Marvin once more wielding the dishtowel. "Oh, Marvin, let me do that." I reached for the towel, which he relinquished with a smile.

"I don't mind, Miss Crowell."

I grabbed a bowl and began to dry it just as John entered

through the back door, his arms laden with wood for the night. Captain McLeod had momentarily disappeared, but for right now it felt as if we were a family, all pitching in.

Mrs. Thompson gave me a curious look, and I wondered if my eyes were puffy, but I smiled and soldiered on, putting the dishes away. A new round of apple cider was poured, with a tot of rum in each except mine, the scent burning my nostrils a little. Neil returned, and I wondered if he'd snuck upstairs for his own tipple; his eyes looked slightly glossy and there was the scent of rum in the air, though that might have been from the cider. We all sat at the kitchen table again, Marvin and John setting up the cribbage board to have a game before bed.

The warm, spiced drink made me relax, and I let out a slow breath. We cheered the game on and when the first was over and a second started, I put down my cup. I'd had enough, and there was still one more chore before bed.

"I'm going to fill Evelyn's stocking," I said quietly. "And then I'll bid you all goodnight."

"Mind if I join you?" Neil's bright-blue gaze met mine, and my stomach gave a little twist, both in recognition and apprehension. He did have extraordinary eyes. Any fool could see that. And right now, there seemed to be a hidden meaning in them, though I couldn't say for sure what it was. All I knew was that it put me on my guard.

"Not at all," I replied. What else could I say?

"I'll just head upstairs," Mrs. T announced. "I'll see you all in the morning for breakfast."

With the game in full swing in the kitchen and Mrs. T and Evelyn upstairs, the parlour felt very intimate as we entered. The fire had burned down to embers, giving the room a soft, cozy glow. The little pile of presents sat under the tree, but to me it was a sign that there were people here who cared about each other enough to give little gifts, even with goods and money dreadfully short in wartime.

A sock hung by the mantel, and I retrieved my knitting bag—which hadn't been used in some time—and took out the little items for Evelyn's stocking.

Neil held the sock open while I put in a little bag of marbles, a chocolate bar, and a package of peppermints. Then there were the few items that Jane had already put aside. A new pair of soft mittens in dark blue to match Evvie's coat. A new dress for Evvie's doll, stitched out of fabric scraps in a way that only Jane could manage. I despaired of ever acquiring Jane's mothering skills and domestic talents; I was far better at stitching wounds than tiny doll dresses. I reached into my pocket and took out three shiny pennies and put them inside. By the time everything was added, the sock was full. Tomorrow morning, I'd present Evelyn with the new doll I'd bought.

I stepped back and sighed. "There." I looked up at Neil. "What you did for Evelyn tonight… Thank you. She shouldn't have climbed up on you like that, but opening your present made her evening."

"It surprised me, but I didn't mind. She's very sweet."

"That's all down to Jane. She was a fabulous mother." And didn't it hurt, referring to her in the past tense.

Neil reached out and took my hand, and a frisson of unease rippled over me at how very intimate it felt. "It's not just Jane. It's you, too," he said. "Since meeting your family, it's clear you come from a kind and loving place. You're doing fine, Nora." He hesitated. "Every time I see Evelyn's curly hair and smile, I think of how much she's lost and it breaks my heart. I'm a poor substitute for family."

"Not at all," I reassured him. "We've all had to come together, and we're all missing loved ones tonight. You must be happy to be seeing your folks tomorrow."

He nodded, but his eyes took on a distant look. "My brother's been wounded. He's going to be fine, which is a blessing and a curse. They'll patch him up and send him right back out there again."

"You're upset. Of course you are. The worry won't end."

He met my gaze. "I worry for my parents, too. Cameron is… We all love him. When he enlisted, my mother made me promise to serve on this side of the ocean. She couldn't bear the thought of both her boys being on the front." He looked away. "I resent her a little for that. And I've never breathed that to another living soul."

I felt honoured and also a little uncomfortable that he'd shared something so personal. But it made him seem slightly more human, rather than the paragon he appeared to be, and it prompted me to confide similarly. "I sometimes wonder if I didn't take the easy way, too, nursing at Camp Hill rather than going over to one of the hospitals or clearing stations."

"Over the last three weeks you've seen your share of horrors. And saved your share of lives."

It was odd to feel a sense of pride and accomplishment when it had come at the cost of so much pain. "As have you, Captain. Perhaps we… perhaps we are where we're meant to be. If I were over there, what would have become of Evelyn?"

"We certainly wouldn't have met. And that would have been a shame."

The earlier frisson of unease became a rolling tide of nerves. His eyes plumbed mine, and he was looking at me differently right now, in a way I didn't want. He was looking at me the way Alley had, the day he'd told me he was being shipped out.

As if he cared about me, but also with worry about what he

was about to say. It showed in the tense set of his jaw and the tiny furrow between his eyebrows.

"Nora, these last few weeks that I've come to know you…" He stopped, cleared his throat, and started again. "That is to say, the coming months are going to be difficult. Especially with you on your own—"

"I'm not alone," I replied, my pulse quickening. Oh heavens, where was this leading?

"You're going to have a baby, Nora, and you have Evelyn now, too."

"She still has Jimmy. The letter he sent—"

"And I pray he comes home. You are a strong, determined woman, but raising a child… children…"

I knew what he was getting at. It kept me up at night sometimes, being overwhelmed by the responsibility of it all. Still, the conversation in general fired up my indignation and my stubborn streak, and I lifted my chin. "How many women are raising families without their husbands right now? Their men are off fighting, and for many of them, their husbands won't come home at all."

Neil slipped his hand away from mine but did not look away. I was not the only stubborn one here. "That's true," he said quietly. "But those women are also entitled to his pay… or widow's benefits."

Neither of which I could claim. Once I resigned, my income was gone. By rights, anything that was made beyond keeping the household afloat from the money the boarders brought in belonged to Jimmy. Not me. I didn't need reminding. It was a good part of what kept me awake at night.

"I think…" He sighed, and I caught the faint, spicy scent of cider and rum. He looked down, and then up to meet my gaze once again, his blue irises so earnest, it made my chest catch. "I can't believe I'm fumbling this so badly. I'm asking you to marry me, Nora."

Oh gracious, there it was. I took a step back. A thousand emotions rushed through me in the flash of a second, but none of them were filled with the euphoria a woman should feel when she's received a proposal. The world was supposed to open up, not feel as if the walls were closing in.

I had no idea what to say.

"Captain McLeod, I—"

"Neil," he corrected me.

I swallowed tightly and tucked my hands together at my waist. The tension around his eyes increased. Perhaps if he'd looked more like a happy man in the midst of proposing, it might have given me pause. But he didn't look anything like a man preparing for a life of contentment with the woman he loved.

Because he didn't love me. And I didn't love him.

And that sobering realization crystallized everything.

I tucked my hands together. "Neil," I said softly, "while I appreciate the gesture—really, I do—I can't marry you. And you don't want to marry me, either."

"I do," he insisted. "Nora, you're lovely and kind and smart and a heck of a nurse. I enjoy being with you."

"And you'd be taking on a baby not your own," I reminded him painfully, and turned away to face the fire.

He put his hand on my shoulder. The glow of the coals grew blurry at the comforting gesture. "I want a family, Nora. It doesn't matter to me about the baby. And Evelyn, too, even if it's just for the time being. She's lovely."

I spun back around. "You can't possibly be this perfect," I accused, overcome by all of it. "Why on earth would you want this when you could have any woman you wanted with the crook of your finger?"

He winced but didn't answer.

"You don't love me, Neil. Please don't say otherwise. We've known each other a few weeks. You told me—*told me*—that you were only offering friendship. We don't have…"

I stopped, my cheeks heating.

"Passion?" he supplied. "We've both had that, though, haven't we? And been burned by it."

He was standing too close to me, and his gaze dropped to my lips. I took a step back. I thought about that night with Alley and tried to imagine it with Neil and couldn't. I was sure my face was aflame, and it had nothing to do with the heat from the fire in the grate. At least he wasn't insisting he cared for me *that way*. And what did he mean, he'd been burned by it? I wanted to ask, but at the same time, I wasn't sure I wanted to know. The more I knew, the more I might come to care for him, and that wouldn't do at all. My life was already complicated enough.

"You need to remember that the fathers of these children are overseas fighting in the war. They're not… *gone*," I retorted.

"You still love him." He stepped back.

"I don't know!" I exclaimed. But I did know. And the truth was, I didn't love Alley. Not as a wife should. But once more, I couldn't say it, because then what did that say about me? I kept hearing the words "loose morals" echoing around in my brain in my mother's voice.

"There's still Jimmy. I'm Evelyn's aunt, but she has a father. When Jimmy comes home, he'll want her with him, and she *should* be with him." I let out a sigh. "Oh Neil, I appreciate the offer, I do. Please don't think I'm ungrateful. I just think it's for all the wrong reasons. And I don't need a saviour. I just need a friend."

The hurt that darkened his eyes went straight to my heart. I hated that I'd wounded him somehow. He was a good man. But

I'd spoken the truth, too. I'd been sharp about it, but none of what I'd said was wrong. And really, why was he still unmarried? The nurses were all crazy about him. I'd heard the gossip in the rare moments we got to stop and catch our breath. When it came right down to it, I didn't trust his kind of perfection. Certainly not enough to understand *why me*.

I didn't trust anything anymore, I discovered.

"You don't hate me for asking?"

"Of course not. How could I hate someone for wanting to take care of me?" I didn't hate him, but I did resent him just a little bit, because now our lovely friendship was going to be tainted by this moment, made awkward. "I guess I just don't understand why. You don't owe me anything. We hardly know each other."

"Marriages have been based on less," he mused.

I angled a look up at him. "That still doesn't tell me why. And while my current situation does have me in a pickle, I still believe that marriage should be based on—" My voice halted, and I looked away. "More," I finished.

He stepped to the fireplace and stared into the glowing coals. "I've had more, Nora. But in the end… We're alike in that way, I guess. Both of us have been left behind. It's not all it's cracked up to be."

But we weren't alike. My heart wasn't broken. Oh, I was disillusioned, there was no doubt about that. But my heart—at least where romance was concerned—was still intact.

After an uncomfortable silence, he moved away from the fire. "I'll say goodnight, then." Already there was a wall between us, changing things, and it made me sad all over again, because in the absence of family, I relied heavily on my friendships and didn't feel I could afford to lose any. Oh, why did he have to go and make it all awkward?

"Merry Christmas, Neil. I hope you enjoy your time with your family." I softened my voice, meaning the words.

"Merry Christmas to you, too," he replied, his voice stiff. And then he turned, leaving me in the parlour alone.

I stepped toward the fire, putting one hand on the mantel and resting my other hand on my tummy, which had started to thicken. I'd already had to move some of my buttons to accommodate the shift in my figure. In the weeks ahead, it would be harder and harder to hide my condition.

But Neil was willing to marry me.

It was the gesture of a friend, not a lover. A convenient agreement that would solve almost all my problems. But it didn't matter. I'd been impulsive once, thinking only of myself, and that had got me into this mess.

I wouldn't be so irresponsible again.

Chapter Eighteen

CHARLOTTE

December 24, 1917

"Would anyone like some more tea?"

It seemed impossible that it was Christmas Eve, that I was staring at a Christmas tree, with candles glowing and holding my daughter in my arms once again. Last night we'd suffered a bumpy, jolting train ride back to Halifax, then caught a taxi to take us to Beech Street. It was late when we arrived, and we'd fallen straight into bed after a quick meal. There was no crib for Aileen, but I didn't care. We slept together in my bed. In fact, I wasn't sure how I was ever going to be able to let her out of my arms—let alone my sight—again. She'd changed so much in the days we'd been apart.

But then I'd awakened this morning with Aileen beside me,

and it felt as if Christmas had already come. After weeks of pain and loss and fear, I was delirious with joy.

Giving her a bath was a long-awaited pleasure, and the smell of her clean hair now mingled with the sweet scent of the spruce tree taking up the corner of the room. I held her close, and she put her little arms around my neck. A lump formed in my throat. I'd been so afraid I'd never feel this again. Never feel whole.

Aileen felt smaller somehow in my arms, and I worried that perhaps in her time in the hospital she'd lost weight, as I had. No matter. She was here now, and Winnie was so thrilled that after she'd hugged us both on our arrival, she'd set about adjusting Christmas plans.

We all dressed up in our Sunday best for the occasion. A second stocking hung by the fireplace, and Winnie had somehow conjured presents out of thin air, tucking them into the little sock for Leenie to open in the morning. There was a Christmas pudding, and after dinner Winnie had cut into the moist, fruity goodness and given us each a slice with real custard and celebratory cups of tea. Then, for a brief time, Ed had sat down at the piano and played carols while the rest of us sang… dubiously, and not always on key, but to me it was the best sound in the world.

"I'll have a little more tea," I said, not wanting the evening to end. It had been so joyous and fun, something I'd been missing since Frank died. Winnie filled my cup and offered me another cookie. I broke off a little piece and gave it to Aileen, grinning as she gave me a toothy smile before taking the morsel in her chubby hand and shoving it clumsily into her mouth.

My heart squeezed as I looked down at her soft curls. She hadn't *really* changed, had she? It was just me, fretting, worrying after being separated for so long. Winnie said that a person couldn't go through what I'd been through without being changed on the other end. I took comfort in that and decided she was right. My concerns of the past seemed so trivial and silly now. I thought back to my life with the Campbells and realized that despite everything, they had been good people. Now Aileen wouldn't know her father's family at all, and the thought made me unexpectedly sad.

"She's fallen asleep," came a soft voice at my elbow, and I turned my head to see Winnie watching us with shining eyes. I blinked back tears.

"Winnie, I don't know how to thank you. For everything. For taking me in. For helping me find Aileen, and just being… wonderful. I could not have survived this without you." Winnie would never know how close I'd come to not surviving, how close I'd been to giving in to the darkness. Finding Aileen had come just in time.

"It's been my pleasure." She came forward and touched one of Aileen's curls. "It does my heart good to see you reunited. She's beautiful, Charlotte." Winnie gave a watery sniff. "To be honest, after the explosion I felt guilty for being spared. I needed to do something. To help, or else why was I here? The people who died… so many of them were our people, Charlotte."

I knew what she meant by "our people." The part of the city that had been most affected was the working-class area, where we came from. Some had even been the girls we'd worked side by side with. I hadn't been back to Richmond since that awful day I got out of the hospital, not even to see the fate of St. Joseph's. For some reason, I suddenly thought of the women I'd met that morning, inviting me to go with them, closer to the waterfront. My stomach gave a sickening lurch. If I had, Aileen and I would most certainly be dead.

I couldn't conceive of going back to my old neighbourhood

with Aileen, but I knew I'd have to do something. I couldn't trespass on Winnie's generosity forever.

But right now it was Christmas, and I would save that worry for another time.

"I'll always be in your debt," I said, reaching out with my free hand and taking hers. "You're the best of friends, Winnie."

She squeezed my fingers. "I'd better check on little Eddie. Morning will come soon enough."

Before long, the house was quiet and dark. Aileen was tucked into bed beside me, and I realized I was matching my breaths to her soft ones echoing lightly in the darkness. She hadn't called me Mum yet. Hadn't really said much of anything at all, but after all she'd been through…

At least she'd enjoyed playing on the carpet in the parlour tonight. She'd crawled along and giggled, playing with Eddie and a set of blocks until she tossed one and hit him in the head and the game was over. He started crying, she started crying, and it was all so blessedly normal that Winnie and I both laughed as we consoled our babies. But Aileen hadn't made any attempt to walk, either. Before the blast, she'd been pulling herself up on furniture and scooting around on unsteady but strong legs. I supposed I would never know all the peculiarities of her injuries, but the doctor had assured me she'd make a full recovery. Perhaps she just needed time. After all, I was still limping.

Her little body was warm against mine, and as my eyelids started to close I thought about the future we'd have together. A place of our own, and maybe a job for me somehow—my widow's benefit wouldn't get us far. Frank and I had dreamed of a home of our own, with him supporting us and me staying home with our babies. This cursed war had changed everything, but for the first time I was confident I would figure it out.

"She's home, Frank. She's home. And she's going to know all

about her brave daddy, and"—I took a breath—"and about his family, too. I promise."

And as I fell asleep, I knew that was a promise I'd be able to keep.

Chapter Nineteen

NORA

January 28, 1918

With Christmas over, I was flung right back into work again. As winter settled firmly into the city, blast victims were still being treated at various hospitals—sometimes continuing care, some never having been discharged at all, others rehabilitating from their injuries. The temporary hospitals established during the crisis were now shutting down. Emergency housing was being constructed for displaced families at a record pace, and the relief efforts showed no signs of slowing. Food allowances were cut from $3.50 to $2.50 a week.

But the war was not over, nor did it look like it would be anytime soon. Ships came and went from the harbour almost as if the explosion had never happened, heading for the front with crucial supplies and men, gathering in convoys and steaming their way across the ocean, hoping to dodge German U-boats. And with each day that passed, my anxiety grew. I was so needed at Camp Hill. I was a good nurse. And the time was coming very soon when I'd have to hand in my resignation.

Alone for a moment in a supply cupboard, I pressed my hand against my tummy. There was a little bubble, just the tiniest thing, but my baby was growing in there and I smiled as I thought of it. The coming months were going to be awfully hard, but that didn't erase the little ripple of excitement I felt each time I considered the life growing inside me. Even the morning sickness had improved the last week, which came as a massive relief.

Sometimes I felt like a study in contradictions. I wanted to continue working, not just to do my part, but because I loved nursing. And yet another part of me was falling in love with my unborn baby. It gutted me that I could not have both. The worry of how I was going to support myself and my child hung over me like a perpetual dark cloud. I'd been thinking about Neil's proposal lately, wondering if I should reconsider. He wasn't wrong; it would solve many of my problems. Honestly, the one hesitation I had wasn't to do with me at all, but with him. I kept thinking he deserved better, and how could I sentence him to a life in a loveless marriage? Was friendship truly enough?

"Nora, whatcha doin' in here?" A grinning Nurse Smiley dipped her head into the room, her white veil bobbing. "I'm going to the mess to grab some lunch. Do you want to come?"

I did, desperately. I was hungry, and not just for food. Acceptance was on the tip of my tongue when I realized that I'd likely have to leave these friendships behind, too, and there was little point fostering greater camaraderie only to miss it in the months ahead. "No thanks, Jessie. I'm not quite done yet." At

Jessie's crestfallen face, I offered a compromise. "Snag me a sandwich, maybe?"

"Nora, are you all right? You've been acting so distant lately." When I went to speak, Jessie held up a hand, her mouth set with determination. "I know a lot has happened, but even before the explosion something was different about you. You can talk to me, you know."

I knew the news would get out eventually, but it must not before I'd had a chance to resign. "Don't worry, Jessie. I'm all right." I tried a smile, hoping to reassure my friend.

"Best cure for a broken heart is jolly friends, you know." Jessie offered me a wink. "I do wish you'd come out with us some night. We miss you."

"I miss you, too." An ache pressed against my heart. "But I have the boarding house and my niece to care for now. It hasn't left a lot of spare time."

Jessie leaned against the door frame, her kind face wreathed in worry. "That sounds like a lot for one person. If you can, get away with us some evening. Oh, nothing too racy. Just some much-needed laughs. You need to look after yourself too, you know. Have some fun. Goodness knows we can all use it from time to time."

The concern went straight to my heart. "I'll think about it. Thank you, Jessie."

"Of course. I'll grab you a sandwich, but I can't guarantee it won't be chipped beef." She made a face, then winked.

We both laughed, and then Jessie was on her way.

But after she was gone, I put my supplies on the cart and stood a long while, pondering the future. Thinking about Neil's proposal again. He'd come back on the afternoon train on the twenty-sixth, smiling and with a Christmas cake wrapped in cheesecloth, a gift from his folks. We'd cut thick, rich slices and had them with tea around the table, and it was as if the awkward moments in the parlour had never happened… except to me, it seemed. On Christmas Eve he'd looked at me with such earnest eyes. As if he truly did care… Perhaps he was as good an alternative as any when it came right down to it.

"Nurse Crowell, are you going to stand in here all day?" Matron Cotton stood in the doorway, her face firm but not unkind.

"Oh, of course not! I'm so sorry, Matron. I'm coming." I hurriedly finished stocking my cart and got back to work, leaving my thoughts of Neil behind. Thankfully this week we were on opposite shifts, so we crossed paths morning and night but were spared working together or putting in long winter evenings in the warm kitchen or by the fire. Instead, I had resolutely taken up knitting with Mrs. Thompson. Right now I was knitting a simple-patterned blanket for the baby, but at the rate I made my stitches, it would take me until July to finish it.

The rest of the day followed the pattern of the others lately: work, walk home, eat supper, clean up, spend time with Evelyn and read her a story before bed, then knit by the fire until I also went upstairs.

The next morning, though, I woke early, before dawn. The fires had burned low, of course, and my room had a distinct chill. The sun didn't rise; instead, the light from the grey dawn cast dismal shadows, letting me know daybreak was near. A restlessness had me rising from the precious warmth of the bed and scooting to the bathroom to wash my face and tidy myself before anyone else was up. When I'd finished putting on my uniform and fixing my hair, I checked the time. It was just after six; everyone else would be downstairs for breakfast soon. I didn't want to see any of them. I wanted to walk. Clear my head.

See if I could make sense of my thoughts and feelings, for my heart was so very heavy.

I'd written my resignation letter just before crawling into bed last night. It stared at me now, not accusing, exactly, but reminding me that my carelessness was the reason I had to leave behind the job I loved. The tragedy that had befallen Halifax was not my fault, but my leaving had everything to do with my choices, and it was a bitter pill to swallow. After today, I would no longer be a Bluebird. I would take off my uniform and exchange one life for another, creating my own before and after. It was one more in a long line of things to mourn.

I hastened to the door and buttoned up my coat, bundling against the January cold. It bit at my face as I stepped outside, but I took grateful lungfuls of it as I started down Henry Street. I had time before needing to be at the hospital, and I desperately wanted to get my thoughts in order.

Even in the cold, a thin fog rose up from the harbour with chilly, damp fingers. It carried on it the deep, hollow calls of ships readying to depart, the slightly higher-pitched ones of the smaller steamers. The streets were busy in the early Monday morning, people and cars and horses rumbling over the cobbles and the *ding ding ding* of the streetcars echoing through the fog like an otherworldly invitation to hurry. Halifax might be damaged, but she was definitely determined to remain a going concern, battered but not broken. I inhaled a great breath and let it out in a gust, rolling my shoulders, thinking about the paper I carried in my coat pocket.

I'd come through the explosion, and I would survive this, too. I was alive and I was resilient. I wasn't ready for motherhood, but it was finding me anyway, and I'd be up to the challenge because, I reminded myself, that was who I was. I was managing the house, albeit with a great deal of help. I was a strong, smart woman. With a bit of luck—and at this point I figured I deserved a little luck—Jimmy would be home soon.

Oh, that this war would end, and Jimmy would come home and the noose that kept tightening around me could ease. Being responsible for so many lives was wearing on me. But there was no sense putting things off any longer. I was over three months along and I was tired. On top of that was the guilt of knowing I'd been keeping this secret for weeks. I would far rather resign than be dismissed from service.

When I got to the hospital, Neil was still finishing his shift. He looked up at me and smiled; I smiled back but turned away, wanting to get this task over and done with. My whole reason for leaving Chester, for moving to Halifax, for studying hard and working even harder for my commission was ending today. Years of effort coming to an abrupt end. I was going to need some time to grieve for yet another change in my life before pulling up my socks and getting on with it.

I found Matron Cotton in her office, her spectacles resting on her nose as she tended to a stack of paperwork on her desk. I knocked and was bid to enter; my hands shook with nerves just as they had my first day reporting for duty. "Yes, Nurse Crowell?"

I held out my letter, placed it on the desk.

"And what is this?"

"My letter of resignation, ma'am."

Her lips twisted in consternation. "You're not serious."

"I wish I weren't, Matron." My voice shook. Her gaze pierced me, then she gave a brief nod.

"Sit."

I did as I was ordered.

She opened the paper, scanned it briefly, then sent her piercing gaze up to me again. "Nurse Crowell, you are one of the finest nurses on staff here. I understand you suffered many personal losses, but your skills are very much needed."

The compliment was one I knew I'd always treasure. That as much as this hurt, I could at least remember that I had been good at my job. "Thank you, ma'am. But you see, I'm now guardian to my small niece. I can't expect my neighbour to parent her indefinitely. And…" This was the hardest part. "This summer there will be another baby."

Matron had dropped her eyes to the paper again, but when I said those last words, her gaze snapped up and her lips thinned. "You're pregnant."

"I am, ma'am. Since October."

"And you're just telling me now."

"I was trying to sort out my future, and then the explosion happened, and there was no question of me walking away. I only do so now because soon it will be evident. I am incredibly sorry to be leaving you. This has been"—my voice broke—"the greatest honour of my life."

"I'm disappointed, Nurse Crowell."

"No more than I, ma'am."

"And does this mean you'll be getting married?"

I knew she meant the father. My thoughts went to Neil. "It's not quite settled yet," I caged.

"I see." She stood then, and held out her hand. "Well, I wish you the best of luck, Nurse Crowell. I'll see your resignation goes up the chain."

"Thank you, ma'am."

"Dismissed."

And that was it. It was over. I would work my shift and then the after would start. There was a small sense of relief to have it done, but a much bigger sense of loss.

Eight hours later I shut the door at Camp Hill Hospital behind me for the last time. A heaviness weighed in my heart, mocked by the fading sunshine that had appeared once the fog had burned off mid-morning. I turned and looked at the structure, so white and new. I'd lost so much since coming to work here. Alley, deployed; my family, killed. Patients, too, who hadn't made it. And yet this place, this job, as grueling and heartbreaking as it could be, had been my constant through it all. Now I was saying goodbye, and I reached up with a mittened hand and wiped a tear away. Then I let out a sigh, turned on my heel, and headed toward home. I'd share the news at supper tonight and tomorrow I would begin a new normal.

As I made the walk in the waning afternoon, I let my thoughts drift to what I might do to fill my days. I supposed Mrs. Thompson might want to go back to her house, which meant I would be busy running a household for five. Or perhaps Mrs. T would stay, and I could find some sort of charity or cause that needed my help—there were certainly plenty of them. Maybe I wouldn't be a Bluebird anymore, but I could still help the war effort.

In fact, I came to the decision that I *needed* to help the war effort. I still had to do my part somehow if I were to feel fulfilled at all.

Evelyn met me at the door with a bounce in her step. "Auntie Nora! You're home!"

The exuberant welcome started to chase away my glumness. "Hello, sweetheart. Yes, I am. How was your day today?"

As we went inside, Evelyn chattered ceaselessly about how she'd filled her day, while I listened with half an ear. I hung up my coat and removed my boots, then Evelyn trailed behind me on the stairs—still talking—as I went to change out of my uniform for the last time. I hung it up with a lump in my throat, then reached for a plain blouse and skirt, throwing a warm sweater over top. Perhaps if I thought of today as a new beginning rather than an ending, that would help.

I went into the kitchen, expecting to see Mrs. Thompson at the stove cooking supper, but the range was cold and the older woman was sitting at the table looking as if she'd aged ten years. "Evelyn, my darlin', why don't you take Buttons upstairs to play for a bit? I want to talk to your Auntie Nora."

Evelyn knew that tone of voice; it was the tone that said there were grown-up matters to discuss. "All right, Mrs. Thompson," she agreed, sliding her hand out of mine and going in search of the cat, who was most likely in his customary spot in front of the fire.

"What's wrong?" I asked, sliding into the chair next to my friend.

Mrs. T's face was drawn as she reached inside her apron pocket and took out a small envelope. I knew right away what it was. A telegram. And there was only one reason why we'd be receiving such a communication. Only weeks ago, I'd learned what fear and panic really felt like: the icy-cold rush through my veins, the clamminess that broke out over my skin, the tangle of nerves centred right in my belly. It all raced through me in a fraction of a second, and I was glad I was sitting down.

With automatic motions, I took the paper from Mrs. T's wrinkled hand and unfolded it.

"It was for Jane," Mrs. Thompson said into the utter silence. "They must not know… though how they couldn't…"

My hands were steady, which surprised me. Now that the initial rush of panic had passed, I felt oddly calm.

"Have you read it?" I looked up, met Mrs. Thompson's sad gaze, and knew the answer.

"We regret to inform you..." I read the rest in my head, though I didn't need to. Jimmy was gone, killed during a patrol somewhere near Vimy on January fifteenth, only three weeks after his last letter had arrived. I swallowed around a lump in my throat and my chest tightened. God, Evelyn. She was an orphan now. Jimmy—fun, smiling, responsible Jimmy—would not be coming home to claim his daughter or his house. I didn't even know who would own the house now. Evelyn was only four. I had the thought that perhaps I should be more upset. And then on the back of that, the thought that perhaps I'd seen and felt so much death over the past weeks that I was somehow numb to it, or at least some of it. Would I ever truly be able to feel again?

"That poor lamb," Mrs. T murmured, sighing.

I nodded, folding the paper again. For the past several weeks, I'd held onto the idea that Jimmy would return, and I wouldn't have to carry the burden of my family alone. Now that hope, the one that had burned like the flame of a candle every time I got overwhelmed, was forever extinguished. This house needed to be run. Evelyn was orphaned and I was the only parental figure the girl had left. I had a baby on the way, no husband, and just this morning I'd lost the income that might have eased some of this a bit. As Jimmy's daughter, surely Evelyn would receive something similar to a widow's benefit, but I had no idea how much or how to access it. Suddenly that horrible weight was sitting squarely on my shoulders, heavier than before.

And I would have to tell Evelyn. I'd rather do anything else than break that little girl's heart again. It was so unfair.

"Would you excuse me, Mrs. Thompson?"

"Of course, dear. What can I do to help?"

I got up and looked around the kitchen, my fingers clutching the telegram once again. "I don't know. If we could just keep on as we are until I know more…" Lost, I bit down on my lip and met Mrs. Thompson's sympathetic gaze. "Oh, Mrs. T, I don't know how to navigate any of this."

"We never do," the older woman said softly. "Until we have to, and then we just do. One step at a time."

"I resigned my commission today," I whispered.

Mrs. Thompson went to add wood to the stove, then reached for the kettle, her solution for everything. "You need some tea. You're worn clear out, Nora, and I know leaving the hospital was hard, but gracious, you need to give yourself a bit of a rest. You were already working hard and since the explosion you haven't stopped. Things will work out in time. Don't try to solve it all now."

But that wasn't my style. When things had to be done, I generally did them. That work ethic had powered me through my studies and through getting my commission; through long night shifts and through the learning curve that was treating emergency wounds and assisting in surgery during a tragedy. It was going to take more than fresh tea to solve my problems.

I truly didn't know how I was going to do this alone. Because it wasn't just myself I was responsible for. It was a household, two children… even my brothers, in a way. I had a responsibility to them, too. Perhaps the answer had been sitting in front of me since Christmas Eve.

"I'll be back down for supper," I said, smoothing my skirt. "First, though, I need to see Evelyn. I need to tell her. Waiting changes nothing."

Mrs. Thompson's understanding nod and damp eyes only added to the rock sitting on my bruised heart as I left the warmth of the kitchen and headed to the stairs.

I found Evelyn in her room, with the ever-present Buttons

curled up on the bed beside her. She was turning the pages in the little alphabet book that John had given her for Christmas, a truly generous gift, and I was pleased Evelyn was eager to learn her letters.

Now her parents wouldn't ever see her learn to read, or grow up, or get married, or all those precious moments in between.

But I would. I vowed right then and there that I would witness all those things in Evvie's life. That I could never take Jimmy and Jane's places, but I would ensure that Evvie always felt loved and secure. I would do absolutely anything to make sure that happened, no matter the cost to myself.

"Hello, sweetheart."

Evelyn looked up. "Hi, Auntie Nora. I was readin'." Her little voice was sweet as maple candy, the kind my daddy used to make poured over fresh snow.

I went further into the room, gathering my strength, trying to protect myself from breaking down while still being open enough—compassionate enough—to do what was necessary for my niece. I sat on the edge of the bed, took a breath, and reached out for Evelyn's hand.

"Evvie, I'm afraid we've had some news today."

Evelyn looked me right in the eyes, the blue so penetrating, it was almost like looking into Jane's. "Is it Daddy?"

I swallowed. "Yes, it is."

"Mummy told me, but she said Daddy is happy." The fingers of Evelyn's other hand were buried in Buttons' fur. "But I'm sad."

"Me, too." I rubbed my hand over Evelyn's knee, absorbing what Evvie had just said. "What do you mean, Mummy told you?"

Evelyn shrugged. "Last night, when I was dreamin'. She was there, and she patted Buttons, and then she told me that I had to..." She puckered her brow, as if trying to recall the words. "I had to be strong because Daddy wasn't coming home."

I sat back, unsure of what to say. Who was I to argue, whether it was a dream or otherwise? It was too timely to be random; too odd to really think about too much.

Either way, it didn't change things. "I'm so sorry, Evvie."

Evelyn nodded, but I noticed a few little tears on the crests of her cheeks, and I pulled the little girl into my lap, settling her on my knee and cuddling her in my arms.

"You won't leave me, will you, Auntie?"

The innocent question was tinged with doubt that reached in and grabbed my heart. "No, sweetheart. You and I are going to have to stick together. And we'll get by, just you wait and see." I sniffed and set Evelyn back a bit so I could look her in the eye. "Evvie, Jane will always be your mummy. She was such a good mummy, and a wonderful sister to me. And I loved her dearly, and I love you with all my heart, so I promise that I will do my best to be a good auntie to you. I promise to love you and care for you just as she would want me to. All right?"

Evelyn started to cry now, soft, heartbreaking tears. That little girl had lost her entire family unit—parents and sister all in the space of six weeks. I cuddled her close again, and we sat that way for long moments, two orphans holding on to each other. I had meant to offer comfort to Evelyn in these moments, but I found myself likewise comforted by the trusting and honest embrace of my niece.

In that moment, everything else fell away and I knew only one thing: I was, from this moment, a mother. To Evelyn, to the baby inside me. The resentment I'd been feeling for weeks now began to fade, eased by the sheer size of the love inside my heart for these two little beings.

Every decision I made from this moment forward would be in

the best interests of the children. I no longer came first. And while a big part of me lamented leaving nursing behind, knowing I was solely responsible for two lives gave me a sense of awe and purpose. It also, as I took out a handkerchief and wiped Evelyn's tears, gave me an additional sense of clarity.

Evelyn crawled off my lap, scattering my thoughts. "Auntie Nora, I'm hungry."

I gave a watery laugh. Gram always said strife either stole an appetite or created it, and while I had forgotten all about supper, Evelyn apparently had not. At least tomorrow, when the rest of the household woke, I would be able to put on regular clothes, perhaps have a second cup of tea, and spend time with Evelyn. The little girl needn't feel alone. Yes, Mrs. Thompson was here, but it wasn't the same.

"Then let's go see what Mrs. Thompson has cooked up tonight, shall we?" I stood and held out my hand.

Evelyn placed her little one, small and trusting, into mine, and we left the bedroom together.

Chapter Twenty

NORA

January 31, 1918

I'd spent the last three days trying to adjust to life without nursing. It was harder—and easier—than I'd expected, to be honest. For over three years now my days had been governed either by my studies or by my shifts at the hospital. Now I was free to do as I pleased. The first day I had a nap in the middle of the afternoon, having fallen asleep while reading to Evelyn on her bed while a warm, soft Buttons curled up beside me. I'd awakened feeling delightfully indulgent. But since then, I'd rolled up my sleeves and thrown myself into heavy cleaning to keep busy. Mrs. Thompson kept the kitchen running and the basic household chores were done like clockwork, but the explosion had left dust and dirt in all sorts of corners, and I went at them with a vengeance.

And while I cleaned, I considered the future, my chest tightening with worry. I had yet to navigate the paperwork concerning Jimmy's death, and the task hovered over me. When I'd told the "family" that I'd resigned at the hospital, I'd also been compelled to explain why, and the widening of John and Marvin's eyes had made me feel small and… well, soiled. The men had mostly recovered, but there was no question they were treating me differently now. Like a stranger, almost, and perhaps a little bit like glass, as if I were going to break.

If that were true, I would have broken before now. Heavens, I'd gone through the explosion and the aftermath, all while being pregnant. There was no need to treat me with kid gloves. But it was more than that, too. They didn't meet my eyes as often, sliding their gazes away and leaving uncomfortable silences. Mrs. T tried to fill the gap with chatter, and though things had been tense with Neil, I appreciated how he acted as if nothing had changed.

But it was the future that worried me. I went around and around, thinking about my limited options. I had no source of income other than my portion of what was left from Mum and Dad, and the thought of using Evelyn's money for myself was distasteful. Yes, a certain amount could certainly be used for Evelyn's needs, but not for my own or for my child. I could stay here in Halifax or go to the house in Chester, which was certainly an alternative but wouldn't solve all my problems. I simply didn't have it in me to lie about my marital status and make Alley a false husband fighting overseas. Chester was a small town. People there knew me, had known my parents, knew my grandparents and brothers. If word got out, which it surely would, I'd be the subject of whispers and conjecture. And so would the children.

There was one solution that was obvious, and I'd scoured my

mind for other options just as surely as I'd scoured the house, not quite ready to accept the inevitability of it. Neil was a good man. A doctor. He would give me respectability and security. We liked each other and I thought—if we could move past this awkwardness—that we could get along well. I would bring a little money and a house to the marriage, so it wasn't as if I had nothing to offer. But…

But.

But we didn't love each other.

It was time I faced facts. Alley had been gone over three months and not a single word. It was not how a man acted when he was in love. He'd been gone twice as long as we'd courted, for heaven's sake. I was done waiting for a miracle.

That night, after John and Marvin turned in, I pulled Neil aside.

"Might I have a word, Captain?"

His blue gaze struck mine. It was the first time I'd addressed him directly in several days; I'd resorted to addressing the room in general as we all talked over dinner.

"Of course, Miss Crowell."

Miss. Not Nurse, or Lieutenant. I missed the titles so much, it physically ached.

We went into the kitchen and sat at the table. Mrs. Thompson had discreetly gone upstairs as well, so it was just the two of us, sitting by lamplight as the blackout was just about to start, and even with the curtains in the house drawn, our habit was to keep the lights dim.

"Captain—Neil…" I met his gaze and folded my hands on the table, trying to find a way to ease into the conversation. "I'm in over my head, I'm afraid."

"What can I help you with?"

I explained how I didn't know what to expect as far as

Jimmy's property was concerned. "I don't know what happens to his pay, or the house, or anything else. I don't even know if he had a will. With Jane not here…" I bit down on my lip. "Jimmy and Jane's things should all go to Evelyn. But of course, she's too young."

"Well, I can perhaps help you with a bit of it. What was Jimmy's rank?"

"Corporal."

He nodded. "Well then, he likely did a will because there's a sample in the back of the paybook carried by enlisted men. If you like, I can look into it for you."

"I can do it, if you tell me where to go or who to write to."

A ghost of a smile curved his lips. "I can do that. I know by now you don't like to be rescued."

I didn't want to smile, but I found myself doing so anyway. "I don't. But that leads me to something else, and it's not as simple."

He didn't reply, just lifted his eyebrows, questioning.

"What do I do next, Neil? Assuming the house is Evelyn's, do I stay here and run it as a boarding house? John and Marvin are like family. I don't want to… I don't know, sell it from under them. On the other hand, I could sell it and put the money away for Evvie when she's older. It could give her a good start in life."

"It could give you a good start, too."

"But it's not mine."

He sighed. "Nora, I never met your sister, but I've met the rest of your family. I think every single one of them would say that you should have the money from the house to raise Evelyn. Surely no one would begrudge you that."

"I would," I answered firmly, and he pursed his lips and sat back.

"All right. What's the next option?"

"I could move us to Chester and into the house. Since it's mine."

"You sound hesitant."

"Oh, Neil." This time I sighed. "I'd be going back to my hometown, unmarried and pregnant. I have the house there, but no means of supporting myself. Oh, I know I could sell this house and keep the money. But I already said my conscience won't let me do that. And I can't sell the house in Chester. Not with the boys still living close by… it was our home."

"Have you considered staying a nurse? I don't know how feasible it is to hire someone to care for the children, but…" He leaned forward. "You're a tremendous nurse, Nora. A doctor or clinic would be lucky to have you."

The compliment went straight to my heart with a bittersweet pang. "I know I am. But if I stayed a nurse, I'd have to have someone care for the children. I can't ask Mrs. Thompson to take that on. Jane and I…" I swallowed around a lump in my throat. "Jane offered to raise my baby as hers, you know, so I could continue to nurse. I was seriously considering it when…" I cleared the emotion from my throat. "The other option is… well, sometimes when there's only one parent, they put their children in orphanages so they can work. But how on earth could I do that to Evelyn?"

He looked horrified. "Of course you can't. She's lost so much already."

Talking to Neil, getting his perspective, only confirmed my decision—if he was still amenable—that he was the right choice. While I had a hard time trusting that something could be this easy, this simple, marrying him was a solution to a lot of things.

After a long moment of silence, I looked up again. "What do you intend to do after the war? Will you practice back in the valley?"

His gaze sharpened, and he hesitated. "I don't know. It would depend on a lot of things."

"Like if there was a house in Chester, already paid for?"

He stared at me, surprise blanking his face as what I had said, and what I hadn't, sank in. "Nora, if you think I proposed because of the money—"

I shook my head quickly. "No, of course I don't. I didn't word that well. What I mean is…" My heart was beating a staccato now, like a hummingbird's wings behind my ribcage. "Would you consider practicing in Chester? Or nearby?"

The air grew thick and heat rushed up my cheeks as we stared at each other. "Neil," I began, "your friendship has come to mean a lot to me. You arrived on the worst day of my life, and you've been steadfast and kind. Now that Jimmy is gone… I look at that little girl upstairs and know everything I do has to be for her. I guess I just don't understand what you would get out of this arrangement."

He looked at me evenly and his voice was warm and sure. "Why, I'd get you, Nora. A woman I admire. And Evelyn, and the new baby, too. And… perhaps a way to make my own life, rather than settling for what is comfortable back home."

I looked away, trying to make sense of all he'd just admitted. Could it be that Neil was searching for something, just like me? From what I gathered, before the war he'd been going into practice with his father. Perhaps, as a man, he had more choices available to him than I did, but the burden of family expectations weighed on a person, too. Clearly neither of us liked disappointing the ones we loved.

He took my movement for rejection, but as he started to rise I reached out and put my hand on his arm. It wasn't romantic, but wasn't that a good thing? There were no false illusions. We would have companionship and support. And as he said on

Christmas Eve, many marriages had been built on less and succeeded.

I had to be honest. "I'm not in love with you, Neil, but I care for you. I like you and I respect you."

"I feel the same about you."

"And you must understand I'm still…" Humiliation burned behind my eyes. "I've given up on Alley. Let me be clear about that. But that doesn't mean I don't still have feelings about what happened."

"He broke your heart."

"He broke my faith," I corrected, "and that's worse, I think."

Neil nodded, relaxed in his chair again. "Nora, that's one of the things I like about you. You have so much integrity. You expect people to treat you the way you'd treat them, and you're hurt when they don't because you have a huge heart. You are kind and loving and smart and you work so hard. Why would I not want to marry a woman like that?"

My lower lip wobbled. What a speech, and despite having my trust tested, I believed every word. Out of all the options I'd considered, this was the one that seemed the most palatable. Keeping my family together. Food on the table. Most important of all, a solid, secure future for the children. Any other alternative would be selfish, wouldn't it? A mother put her children first, always.

"Then will you still marry me, Neil McLeod?"

God help us both.

Chapter Twenty-One

NORA

February 9, 1918

I'd wanted the wedding to be a quiet, no-fuss affair. It was, at its core, a marriage of utility. But it seemed that my wishes didn't count for much, as there was an air of celebration that Saturday morning as I woke in my bed—the bed that Neil would share with me tonight.

We were to be married. How on earth could Neil remain in his own room after that? He couldn't. Mrs. Thompson had already mentioned the possibility of taking in another boarder. So many in the city were still homeless after the explosion. It didn't make sense for a perfectly good room to go to waste.

I knew she was right. But the thought of having Neil in the bed beside me made a ball of anxiety sit right behind my breastbone.

Yesterday I'd gone through my dresser and made room for some of Neil's things. He didn't have much; uniforms and underwear, knitted socks, a handful of books he'd brought with him. He was now on permanent assignment to Camp Hill, which meant that at least until the end of the war we would be in this house. A house that suddenly felt much smaller than it was.

Married.

I was still lying in bed, considering it all, when a knock came on the door. It was Mrs. Thompson with a tray of tea and toast. "Good morning," she said with a warm smile. "Breakfast in bed for the bride."

"Oh, Mrs. Thompson. You shouldn't have, but thank you. This is lovely." No one would ever take my mother's place, but Mrs. T was like that kindly aunt that you couldn't help but love.

"Your grandparents are coming on the morning train, yes?"

"Yes. I'll eat this and then come down to help you. It shouldn't be all up to you to prepare a meal for everyone."

"Don't be silly. I never had daughters of my own to do for, dear. I'm so happy to do it. You and the captain are dear people."

My stomach rolled. "Mrs. T…"

"I know. I know what this is and what it isn't, but I'm going to say a prayer that love finds you both anyway."

Mrs. Thompson had pursed her lips and slammed things around the kitchen for a few days after Neil and I shared the news that we were going to marry. I knew it was about the situation and not about us as people, and I felt I'd disappointed her, too. It wasn't until we sat down and had an honest chat that she'd come around. Especially when I told her that Neil had initially proposed back in December. It hadn't been a rushed, impulsive decision, but rather one we'd mulled over at length. It was practical, but as Mrs. T had summed up, sometimes practicality was a saving grace.

I lifted my mug and hid behind the rim. After a hearty sip, I casually asked, "Where's Neil?"

"He's gone to the station to pick up his parents."

I had trouble swallowing my second mouthful of tea, and I coughed, clearing my throat before looking up. "So soon?"

"He asked me to tell you that he's taking them on a tour of the hospital first."

It would give me a little reprieve to prepare myself. Since Neil's father was also a doctor, it made sense he'd be interested in the newest hospital in the city. "Right. Well, there's no sense in grass growing under my feet now, is there? I'll be downstairs shortly."

"Take your time," Mrs. T offered warmly. She paused at the door and looked back. "And Nora, try to enjoy your day. You're a bride. This only happens once. It's all right to let it be special. You're marrying a fine young man."

She went out and shut the door while I closed my eyes. That was just the problem. Or rather, two problems. I was a bride... this decision was life-altering and permanent. For the briefest of moments, I considered backing out and calling it all off. But Neil *was* a fine young man. And he was offering a solution, no matter how much I hated needing it. That wasn't to say there weren't misgivings. Despite what anyone said, Neil was riding to my rescue, and I hated that. I didn't think he liked it much either, because despite his sweet words, the night we became engaged he disappeared into his room. The next morning his eyes were bloodshot, and he smelled like old man McDonald's still.

But here we were, a week later, going through with it. I ate my toast, licking the sweet jam from my fingers. Normally we conserved and used a skim of it on top, but today Mrs. Thompson had been generous. I rose and dressed in a regular day dress, then headed downstairs to help Mrs. Thompson, taking my tray with me.

The kitchen was a flurry of activity. Both John and Marvin were working today, but Evelyn was already up, dressed, and had been put to work rolling little pats of dough for cookies. Her pink tongue peeked out from her teeth as she worked, placing each little ball precisely on the pan.

"What can I do?" I asked. The wedding was to take place at eleven, as long as the train was running on time. The minister from St. Andrew's Presbyterian had agreed to perform the ceremony in the parlour. I hadn't minded. I'd been raised in the Anglican church in Chester, and Jane and I had attended St. George's here in Halifax most Sundays. But the church had been damaged in the blast, and when Neil had suggested a Presbyterian wedding, I found I didn't much care either way.

Mrs. Thompson set me to work making sandwich fillings while she slid the tray of cookies into the oven and began making little tea biscuits. At some point she disappeared next door and returned with her best china tea set and readied the cups and saucers. I was sent to double check the parlour was just as I wanted it.

The furniture had been moved to each side to provide room for everyone, and it was meticulously cleaned. The beeswax and lemon scent of Mrs. Thompson's furniture polish hung in the air; even the dark woodwork gleamed from a fresh polishing. The doilies that Jane had insisted upon were freshly starched and pressed, and a fire was laid but not yet burning. It would do nicely.

But there would be no walk down the aisle on my father's arm. No flowers or organ or even a white dress and veil.

I'd put my foot down about that. Why have a real wedding dress when this wasn't going to be a real marriage?

I jumped when a door slammed, followed by voices. *You've been pretending for weeks now,* I reminded myself. *It's just one more day.*

And so I let out a breath, dropped my shoulders, and adopted a welcoming expression with which to greet the couple who would be my mother- and father-in-law.

At five minutes to eleven, I smoothed my hands down the dark-blue fabric of my skirt, then tugged where the line of white buttons ran from my left hip down towards my thigh. I'd bought the skirt early last fall, wanting something new for church and for going out, but still serviceable. The shorter skirt had called for heeled shoes instead of boots, and for my birthday Jane had bought me a new blouse, a gorgeous one of ivory with white lace trim at the cuffs, collar, and down the front where it fastened with dainty white buttons. It wasn't exactly wedding attire, but it was the fanciest outfit I owned.

Gram stepped forward and fiddled with the tucks of my blouse before stepping back and smiling. "You look lovely, Nora. Though you know you could still wear Jane's dress if you wanted."

Gram didn't know about the baby yet, and my conscience wouldn't let me wear my sister's ivory silk wedding dress. If it would even fit… "This is fine, Grammie. It's almost new, and it's just a small ceremony anyway." Nor could I justify the expense of buying something new and then wear it only once, as soon I'd need different clothes and then styles would change.

"Sometimes, Nora my love, you are almost too practical for your own good. But I did bring you something." She reached into her handbag and pulled out a little box. "It's your mother's pearl brooch. It can be your something borrowed."

My eyes stung as Gram took out the circular brooch and pinned it at my throat, just below the lace on my collar. "Thank you, Gram."

"And something new." The older woman smiled a watery smile and held out a folded cotton square. "Every bride should have a handkerchief just in case."

I wanted to scream that this was all a fraud. Part of me wanted to rush down the stairs, out of the house, and away from everything in the last five months that had led to this precise moment. I wanted, I realized, my innocence back. It had been taken from me in more ways than one. Or rather, I'd squandered it.

But running away wasn't who I was. I reminded myself for the hundredth time that I'd pledged to do whatever it took to ensure Evelyn's happiness and security, and that of my baby, too. "I love you, Grammie."

"I love you, too." Those weren't words that were said often, but perhaps now it was easier because we both knew we'd never have the chance to say them to those we'd lost. Gram leaned forward and kissed my cheek. "We knew when you brought your captain home with you that he was someone special. We're so pleased for you, Nora."

I nodded, trying not to cry, wishing my heart was not so heavy.

"Now I must go. It's time. Your grandfather will be at the bottom of the stairs."

She departed, leaving the bedroom door open, and I took a final few seconds to make peace with my choices.

Then I walked out of my bedroom—the last time as an

unmarried woman—and made my way to the bottom of the stairs where Grampie waited.

His smile was wide as he held out his arm, and I took it. Each step took me closer to the parlour. Each step closer to Neil, standing so handsome and straight in his uniform, waiting for me by a now-crackling fire, joined by the minister. I reminded myself to smile as I made my way the short distance past Dr. and Mrs. McLeod, past Gram and Mrs. Thompson, a beribboned Evelyn between them. And then I was at Neil's side, and we were going through with this… farce. No, not farce, because there was nothing laughable about it. This arrangement. This very practical solution to my problems. Guilt crowded in around my heart. Then I glanced over and saw Evelyn's happy face, Neil's satin ribbons in her hair, and resolutely repeated whatever the minister asked of me. Before long it was all done. No muss, very little fuss, and I was Mrs. Neil McLeod.

The rest of the day passed in a blur. Following the ceremony, the men put the furniture to rights and Mrs. Thompson served a delicious tea of sandwiches, sliced chicken, deviled eggs, pickles, and sweets that must have used all our rations for weeks. Real coffee and pots of tea were brewed and consumed. There was chatter and laughter and sometimes I even found myself enjoying the celebration. But by mid-afternoon the McLeods departed to meet their train, and my grandparents followed suit not an hour after. Evelyn was exhausted and I had sent her for a nap once the excitement was over, and before I went to the kitchen to assist Mrs. T in the washing up, I pulled Neil aside.

My cheeks heated as I looked up at him. "I, um… I made space in the bottom two drawers of my dresser for your things."

"Oh. Oh, I see." He blushed too. Heavens, how were we ever going to get through the night?

"Neil, I…" I sighed. "It'll be fine, won't it?"

He took my hand. "Of course it will. I'll be a perfect gentleman. I promise."

He was perfectly supportive. Very dashing in his uniform and always seemed to know the right thing to say. I was beginning to wonder if I'd ever move past feeling like he was miles too good for me.

"All right. I must help Mrs. Thompson."

I turned to leave, but he held onto my hand. "Be sure to thank her for me, too, will you? The meal was lovely, and she made my parents feel very welcome."

"Of course I will."

He let me go then, and I escaped to the kitchen where the mess was substantial. I put an apron over my dress and rolled up my sleeves, determined that Mrs. T would not carry the weight of the whole day on her shoulders. Together we worked to clear the table, wash the dishes, and put the trays and cups away. The tea set was stacked together, awaiting transport back to Mrs. Thompson's house. We'd just finished and I had sent Mrs. Thompson to rest when John and Marvin returned from work. There was plenty of food left, so I fixed them each a full plate and put a plate of cookies and squares in the middle of the table.

John looked at me with one of his old smiles. "Thank you, Mrs. McLeod."

It gave me a start, the first time someone referred to me as a Mrs. My expression must have showed my alarm because John started laughing as he reached for a sandwich.

"I'm still Nora, so just you mind that," I ordered, putting the milk jug on the table.

"Don't mind him," Marvin said. "We're just right happy for you, that's all. The captain's a good man."

"Stepped up for sure. More'n some men, and that's all I've got to say about that."

I stared at John. It was the first time he'd directly referenced my situation, and the grumble that came from his lips told me exactly what he thought about Alley.

"He is a good man," I whispered.

At that moment, Neil appeared in the doorway, a just-awake Evelyn on his arm. "Someone said she thought there were cookies left."

I shifted my attention, though I was still recovering from John's statement. "There are cookies, but before cookies there are biscuits and butter and milk and maybe some strawberry preserves."

"Aw, Auntie Nora…"

"Gentlemen, did you know Evelyn helped make those almond cookies?"

"I don't believe it," Marvin said, feigning shock. "Such a little thing, making these fancy cookies?"

"I did, I did!" Evelyn cried, scrambling to get down while Neil chuckled at my blatant manoeuvring.

"Well," John said, a little slower, "I'm going to have to have one. Or maybe two. But not until I finish my supper."

"That's right," Marvin agreed. "But just enough supper so I have room for dessert."

Evelyn turned to me. "Auntie Nora, can I have my supper? But maybe just one biscuit with jam? And… a little chicken?"

I stifled a smile. "That sounds lovely. Coming right up, Miss." I fixed a small plate and poured a little cup of milk from the jug, then put it before Evelyn at the table. Marvin looked up and gave me a wink, and my lips twitched.

Neil was still in his uniform but had taken off the jacket and was now in his shirt sleeves. "Are you hungry, Neil?"

"Not very. I can see I'll have to postpone my cookie sneaking until later. I thought I'd read for a while."

I had been planning to escape to the parlour to knit. Somehow we were going to have to not avoid each other…

In the end, I stayed busy. First, I tidied up again after the meal. Then I entertained Evelyn while the men set up a cribbage game, and before long it was Evelyn's bedtime. While Neil socialized with John and Marvin, I took a deep breath and remade my bed with fresh sheets. As I smoothed the cotton over the mattress, my stomach clenched as I thought about sleeping here with Neil later.

I'd done the most intimate thing with a man possible, and yet the thought of simply sharing a sleeping place was currently more terrifying. What if I snored? Made noises in my sleep? What if he did?

The last hour before bed I spent in the parlour, darning some socks of Evelyn's—a task Jane would have done but now fell to me. I paused my needle. This was who I was now. A wife. A mother.

It wasn't bad, but it didn't quite sit right, either. Domestic life was no replacement for the hospital, and I wondered if I'd always miss it.

I counted down the minutes by the clock on the mantel. At ten, the men finished their game and bid everyone goodnight. Mrs. T wound up her ball of yarn and stoked the fire in the kitchen. Neil stood in the parlour doorway, and I was so unsettled, I thought I might throw up.

"Ready?" he asked.

I wasn't sure I'd ever be ready, but I smiled, rose, and we went upstairs together. "You should use the bathroom first," I suggested.

"If you wish."

When he returned I was already changed into my nightgown, the soft cotton covering me from my neck to my ankles. I scooted by him to the bathroom, trying to calm my pounding heart. When I returned, he was already in the bed, the covers up to his armpits. He didn't wear a nightshirt, I realized. His chest was naked under there. Good heavens, hopefully the rest of him wasn't.

"I don't know what side you like," he said quietly. "So I can move over if you want the one closest the door."

"I've never had to choose a side," I replied honestly. "I don't think it'll matter."

I scurried across the floor to the side of the bed, reached over to the little table, and turned down the lantern, casting us in darkness. Then, because I was cold and couldn't put it off any longer, I turned down the covers and got into bed.

The mattress felt different, with his weight on the other side, and I nearly huddled into myself trying to make sure we didn't touch. For a few minutes we lay there so stiffly, I was sure one of us would crack. And then Neil started to chuckle.

The sound was soft and warm and before long I found myself laughing, too, at the sheer absurdity of it all.

"It's going to be awfully awkward if we go to bed like this every night," he stated, turning his head to the side to face me. "We should both relax. We need rest."

I turned my head and found his eyes sparkling at me in the grey light. "Neil, I'm sorry, but I have to ask. Are you… wearing anything?"

His eyes widened, and then he burst out laughing, not the soft chuckles of before but a full-throated whoop, and then I started again until we were both wiping tears from our eyes.

"Yes," he finally answered. "Lord, yes, Nora. But my God. What a question."

I snorted, laughing again, realizing that just because we'd married didn't mean we weren't friends.

Besides, we *were* married. We either had to navigate this or founder, and I knew which I preferred. Till death us do part was a long, long time.

"Goodnight, Captain McLeod," I said, closing my eyes.

"Goodnight, Mrs. McLeod."

And surprisingly, blessedly, we slept.

Chapter Twenty-Two

CHARLOTTE

February 11, 1918

When I came home to Beech Street after work each evening, the scent of the day's special at Gammon's Café tended to follow me. Working as a kitchen girl wasn't glamorous, but it wasn't that hard, either, and as my leg continued to heal I didn't mind the walk to Argyle Street so much. I'd found the job shortly after Christmas. Winnie and I had come to an agreement. Aileen would stay with her during the afternoon while I was at work. I didn't begin until noon, so I watched the children in the morning so she could attend the various committees and activities she'd taken on in support of the war effort at home. I also gave her half of my earnings toward my board. I wasn't sure it would even cover our food, but I wasn't going to live off her charity forever. The other half I put away, because at some point I had to look for a way to support both Aileen and myself. Edward was helping me sort through the tangle of compensation. There was assistance for those who'd lost their homes, and once everything was sorted, if I was careful, I knew I could make things work.

Aileen was still awake when I arrived home. It was a Friday night, and the café had done a steady business all day. The tables had been crammed with khaki-coloured soldiers and many had a girl on their arm. Construction workers often stopped by for a hot meal. Getting out of the house and into the city had been a shock. I thought Halifax had been busy before, but now, in addition to being a wartime port, the city was being rebuilt. It was a going concern and no mistake.

The Beech Street house was an oasis of calm and comfort, and though I was exhausted, I gathered Aileen in my arms and took her upstairs to get her ready for bed. She patted my mouth with a pudgy hand, and I blew a kiss on it. It was a game we used to play, and usually she dissolved in giggles, the big baby laughs warming my soul. But now she gave me a toothy grin and babbled something incomprehensible before curling against my shoulder, and I frowned. Why didn't she laugh anymore?

Maybe I was just tired. Or maybe she was. It just seemed like since I started working, she was… It was odd to think, but at times my sweet baby felt like a stranger.

When I first brought her home, I'd felt complete. My fears had eased and my heart was at rest. Seeing her in that hospital, feeling her weight in my arms had made everything right again. For days I'd been out of my mind with worry and fear. In that moment in New Glasgow, I knew it was all going to be all right.

So when Christmas became New Year's, and I felt well enough to look for work, I thought it was all going to go perfectly. So why wasn't it?

I changed Aileen's diaper and got her ready for bed just as I had for the last year, only I took care to avoid the mark on her tummy, one that hadn't been there before. It was darker than the rest of her skin, not pink but instead a brownish colour. I wondered if she'd been burned somehow, to leave such a strange little scar. Goodness knew there'd been embers and flying debris during the explosion. I wasn't sure if it was tender, so I carefully pinned the diaper and then dressed her again for bed, thankful that whatever had caused the mark seemed to be the worst she'd suffered.

Winnie had put a rocking chair in my room, and I bundled Aileen in a soft blanket and sat, gathering her close. She was clearly tired; she rested her head on my shoulder and popped her thumb into her mouth. But that was different, too. Aileen had never been a thumb sucker.

Why did everything feel so different? Had Aileen changed, or had I? All I knew was that there was an odd distance between us that hadn't been there before.

Her lashes rested on her cheeks as she fell asleep, and the unsettled feeling grew, sitting right behind my breastbone. What on earth was wrong with me? Mrs. Campbell's words echoed in my brain, the ones saying I had no mothering instincts. Was she right? Shouldn't I be thrilled, overcome with tenderness and love? Why was there still a part of me that was dead inside?

I closed my eyes, too, and said a little prayer. The doctor at Camp Hill told me I'd hit my head, and I thought that just meant I'd have headaches for a while. But what if it was more? What if it had changed the way I thought, the way I felt things? Why did I feel as if I were in a fog some days, and perfectly fine on others?

And it wasn't like I could talk to anyone about it. They'd think I was going crazy. I ground my teeth together. Part of me was horribly afraid they'd be right. And afraid they'd take Aileen away from me again if I voiced my thoughts.

Maybe we just needed to get out of Halifax. Get a new start. Just thinking about it made the knot in my chest ease a little.

Aileen was sound asleep now, so I tucked her under the blanket and looked down at her for a moment, wondering why this time felt so different. Why it felt like there was this wall around my heart…

Maybe I'd just lost too much.

I tiptoed out of the room and shut the door behind me with a light click. I wasn't quite ready for bed myself; it was still early and I could use a cup of tea and a sit down. Lately I'd started knitting, too, a way to keep my hands busy in the long winter evenings. There was always a call for socks for our men in uniform. I'd grumbled about my mother-in-law's constant knitting, but I understood now the need to keep busy and feel as if you were doing something instead of feeling helpless.

Winnie was in the parlour, sitting next to the fire with a book, and she looked up as I entered. "Charlotte! I was wondering where you were. Did Aileen get to bed all right?"

Charlotte was always so cheerful. What would she say if she knew of my earlier thoughts? They scared me, so I shoved them down—as usual—and forced a smile. "She did. I stopped to make a cup of tea. It was so busy today, I'm still wound up like a top."

She closed her book and put it down. "You don't have to work so much, you know."

"Is Aileen a bother?" I was well aware that I was still taking advantage of our friendship. Even though I paid for some board, Winnie was doing me a kindness. I'd already been here a month and a half.

"No, not at all. Besides…" She beamed at me. "Oh, I might as well tell you. Eddie is going to have a little brother or sister."

It was happy news, so I was surprised when the old flare of resentment flickered to life in my breast. Winnie was a lovely woman and a generous friend. I hated that I was jealous of her comfortable life, loving husband, perfect little family. What kind of friend did that make me? I pushed the feeling down and smiled at her. "Oh Winnie, that's wonderful news," I said, and somewhere deep down I meant it. I put my tea on a little table and picked up my knitting. Maybe if I kept my hands busy…

"We're pleased, of course. And of course I understand you need to work. But you needn't feel any pressure from us, you know. You're welcome as long as you like." She looked at me closely. "Besides, I already think of you as a sister."

I counted stitches, overcome by the emotion of her statement. It made what I needed to say that much harder, but the more I thought about it, the more I knew I needed to get out of Halifax. Somewhere fresh. "As do I, Winnie. But I can't live on your goodwill forever. Now that I'm getting my feet beneath me, I was thinking I'd look for a job outside the city somewhere. Make a fresh start for the two of us."

Winnie's face fell. "I knew you were going to say that. And I can't say as I blame you, because if I were in your shoes…" She smiled a little. "Selfishly, I want to keep you nearby. You're the only one who knows me as, well, me, instead of as Ed Slaunwhite's wife."

"There's no rush yet. I haven't even begun a search for a new position. I'm thinking if I could find domestic work, somewhere I can take Aileen…" I sighed. "I always resented keeping house for the Campbells, but at least this way I'd be getting paid to do it. It wasn't the work so much as the… obligation, I suppose."

"Let me send out some inquiries, mention it to the other ladies."

"You don't have to—"

"I know, but I want to. Of course, I'd love to have you here, but if I can't, I can at least help you find a good place."

My resentment from earlier fled. "You're a good person, Winnifred. The best friend I've ever had."

Winnie got up from her chair and came to stand before me, then bent and gave me a tight hug. "Likewise, Charlotte. No matter what, we must not lose touch with each other again."

"I promise," I said, and meant it.

Three weeks later I found an advertisement looking for a housekeeper for a family in Chester, a short distance away by train. By the middle of March, I'd quit my job at Gammon's Café, packed our few things, left the destruction and memories of Halifax behind, and headed to a new life.

Chapter Twenty-Three

NORA

June 27, 1918

Spring had come and gone, and summer was on the doorstep. At first I welcomed the warmer days and bright sunshine, but as my due date drew closer, the heat was cloying and it was harder and harder to get comfortable. Especially in bed at night. I was always aware of Neil being close, sleeping, and was afraid my constant shifting would disturb him or that I'd wake up and find myself pressed up against his body. Neil had been true to his word since the wedding. He'd been a complete gentleman, and he hadn't pressed for anything physical between us. He'd even stopped drinking so much, and we spent our evenings catching up on our days, sometimes going for little walks in the soft purple light. It was calm, harmonious. Like being married to a best friend.

Some days it drove me mad.

I finished tidying the breakfast dishes and dropped a hand to the massive mound of my belly, rubbing it absently, rewarded with a solid kick against my palm. I would soon be a mother—not that I wasn't already to Evelyn, but to a newborn baby. I was terrified. I didn't have Jane or my own mother here to help me, and Mrs. Thompson was wonderful, but she'd never had any children. All of my friends here in town were nurses, not young mothers. The closer I got to delivering, the lonelier I felt.

Evelyn came into the kitchen, carrying her doll. "Auntie, Muriel wants to go for a walk today. Can we?"

I decided to ignore how ungainly I felt because the idea of fresh air and sunshine and a bit of exercise sounded like manna from heaven. "We might be able to, once the chores are done." The beds still weren't made, and the kitchen floor needed sweeping.

"Aw, when will that be?" A pout darkened the sweet face and I wanted to laugh. Adjusting to being a housewife had been difficult at times, and I still missed the vitality of the hospital, but Evelyn's expressiveness was a particular bright spot.

"Not long," I assured her. "Beds and sweeping."

Neil entered the kitchen, enjoying a rare day off. "Did I hear something about a walk?"

Evelyn nodded, her curls bouncing as she bobbed her head up and down. "Auntie said yes! But chores first." The last sentence was delivered with a put-upon sigh.

"Well, the beds are all made, so what does that leave?"

I brightened. Neil worked long hours but lately he'd begun helping around the house if he saw something that needed doing, usually without being asked. "You didn't have to do that."

He chuckled. "I was upstairs. Thought it would save you the trip. Anyway, I think a walk sounds lovely. Why don't we make a day of it? A walk in Point Pleasant, perhaps lunch out as a special treat?"

Evelyn was now jumping up and down, making us both laugh.

"No teasing me about how slow I'm going," I warned. "I'm carrying a whole other person." But the idea of a special day out brightened my spirits immensely.

Mrs. Thompson had moved back to her own house in February, though she came by in the afternoons to help with dinner and eat with the "family". She said it was to help me, but deep down, I thought it was because the older woman found herself lonely after being part of the "family" for two months. Either way, I was grateful for the help and for the companionship, and I was sure everyone else was relieved that she took the time to help me improve my cooking skills. It was odd being the only woman with four men in the house—we'd taken on another boarder when Neil moved into my room. Matthew had returned from the front with a leg injury and had found a job doing deliveries for a shop downtown.

Halifax was still in the throes of being rebuilt, and the war dragged on. While Neil still worked at Camp Hill, I had begun volunteering, helping with fundraisers and then putting together packages for those overseas with toiletries, gum, pencils, bootlaces, and whatever else was in demand. I'd finished the baby blanket and switched to socks, cursing the heels which I never seemed to turn correctly, but persevering. Men always needed socks, but I prayed that the war wouldn't go through another winter, and other knitted goods wouldn't be needed.

I'd even planted a Victory Garden in the back yard. I hadn't inherited my mother's green thumb, but Mrs. T was helping me with that, too, and the plants had begun pushing through the soil, reaching for the sun.

But today was a day off, and a welcome one. In a few weeks, there'd be a new baby to occupy my waking—and non-waking—hours.

We ended up splurging on a taxi to Point Pleasant, since Neil said he didn't want me to tire before the walk even began. Evelyn was wide-eyed in the car, exclaiming at everything while Neil and I shared amused glances over her head. At the park, Neil offered me a hand out of the vehicle, then gave his other hand to Evelyn, who took it without hesitation. My heart softened. He'd stepped in as a father to her so naturally—more naturally than being a husband. I couldn't imagine him loving the little girl more if she were his own.

Sometimes I wondered if my feelings toward Neil were changing, but he was maddeningly platonic. Our kiss on our wedding day had been our one and only, and lately I'd been thinking about it more and more.

"Auntie, look!" We'd barely started down the path when Evelyn darted to a clump of daisies. "A butterfly!"

And so the morning went… sauntering along, soaking up the sun, listening to Evelyn's chatter. A light breeze flickered through the leaves and birds sang while squirrels darted across the path, chasing each other, then scolding from the leafy canopies of the hardwoods. The sunny day was just what I needed, but the walk was proving tougher than I anticipated. My back ached, and after a while the exertion caused the muscles along my abdomen to tighten.

There were times I'd loved being pregnant, but this last month was proving to be a bit of a trial. Aches, swollen feet, feeling like an elephant… I'd be glad when this was over.

"Evelyn, why don't we watch the ships coming into the harbour?" Neil suggested, giving me a sideways glance. He nodded toward a nearby bench. "You look like you could use a rest," he said quietly, squeezing my arm. "Take a few minutes. I'll entertain Ev."

I sat gratefully and gazed out over the ocean as Neil took Evelyn off the path and closer to the water. He pointed out the different ships to Evelyn, who proved an enraptured audience. Seeing them together never failed to remind me I'd done the right thing in marrying him. Evelyn was thriving, happy and secure. My sliver of discontent was inconsequential in comparison to her happiness.

I'd hoped the backache would ease while I rested, but instead it intensified and I shifted on the bench, trying to seek some relief. The band of muscles in my pelvis tightened again and I let out a slow breath, trying to relax them. It was then I realized what was happening... for heaven's sake, I was a nurse, and I hadn't noticed the signs for the last hour and a half. It was still two weeks early, after all. Maybe it was just over-exertion... Regardless, I was having contractions and we still had to walk to the entrance of the park at the very least, even if we did manage to take a taxi home.

A familiar fear seized me. I was not ready to have this baby. Tears pricked my eyes. Jane should be here. Mum should be here.

"All right?" Neil asked, appearing beside me. His face fell into one of concern as I looked up at him through blurred tears. "What is it?"

"I think my pains have started," I whispered. "I'm so sorry."

"Why are you sorry? Don't be silly. You should have hours yet. We'll take our time, get you back to the house nice and comfortable, and Mrs. Thompson will take care of Evelyn." The plan had been in place for weeks. "It might be a false alarm anyway, from the walking. Don't fret, Nora."

I relaxed a little at his calm reassurance. "All right." I met his gaze. "Oh, who am I kidding? I'm frightened, Neil. Which is ridiculous. I'm a nurse. I know how this works and that most babies are born without incident."

He smiled, touched my arm. "Well, it's different when it's yourself, I would expect. But I'll be with you. They teach us how to do this in medical school, you know."

"You'll call the midwife?" Neil had insisted we install a telephone for emergencies last month, and I hadn't argued.

"Certainly." We'd agreed ages ago that unless he was needed, a midwife would attend the birth. I simply felt it too… personal to be so exposed to Neil. Which in normal circumstances would be odd with one's husband. But then, everything about this situation was odd.

I explained to Evelyn that I was very tired and perhaps we could cut the walk a little short. The pains were now coming regularly, spreading along my pelvis and to my back, holding for a minute or so and then easing. I found myself stopping and waiting the pains out, walking again when they went away. Evelyn's eyes were wide, and she'd stopped her regular chatter, sensing something was happening. When we finally reached the exit and Neil went to hail a cab, I took Evelyn's hand and squatted down to look her in the eye.

"Sweetheart, I think the baby is going to arrive today. I'm sorry we have to miss lunch, but I'm going leave you with Mrs. Thompson, all right? And when we come to get you, hopefully you'll be able to meet your new cousin."

Evelyn's eyes widened further. "Today?"

I nodded. "Can you go to Mrs. Thompson's and be a good girl?"

"Yes, Auntie." But worry creased the corners of her eyes.

"Evelyn, nothing is going to happen to me. You don't need to worry." It hurt my heart to know that Evelyn still feared losing those she loved. Perhaps that would never go away. Squatting hurt, so I put my hands on my thighs and pushed myself to standing, gritting my teeth as another contraction rippled across my belly. "Uncle Neil is going to make sure of it."

"All right, Auntie."

But the ride home was sombre. As soon as we arrived back, I went inside while Neil took Evelyn next door. By the time he returned, I had called for the midwife to come. The pains were more frequent now and growing in intensity.

It felt strange to be the patient. I found it difficult to acquiesce when Neil took over readying the bed and then helped me replace my dress with a more comfortable nightgown, my cheeks flaming with embarrassment. He suggested I continue walking to keep things moving along, and then found a towel to clean up when my water broke on the bedroom floor. I shed my soaked drawers then, and for a few moments was left alone when he went to answer the knock on the door. Seconds later Edith Baker arrived, looking fresh and cheerful with her bag of supplies.

"Ah, Mrs. McLeod. Captain McLeod tells me your waters have broken. All right, let me have a gander so we can bring this baby into the world."

Neil glanced at me. "I'll bring you some water." Then he left to afford us some privacy. If the midwife found it strange, she didn't comment. Instead, she put all her focus on the patient.

I toddled my way to the bed and let the midwife do her examination. "Good, good," Mrs. Baker muttered. "You're halfway there, dearie. Doing wonderfully."

"It… doesn't… feel… wonderful," I answered, panting as another pain overtook me.

"Ah, but worth it in the end. You two are going to have a grand start to your family."

As the pain waned, I thought of Alley. How he should have been here. How he could have been a part of this if he'd chosen.

He was the one missing out now. I would love and have the love of our child—something he would never know. I actually pitied him.

In March, a month after our wedding, I'd seen his name on a wounded list. He was alive. Had been alive… and had chosen not to write. I suppose at least I had my answer, and I could let go of the what if. I'd spent months wondering if he'd died. Months waiting for him to write. It was impossible to think that not one of my letters had got through; I'd sent over a dozen. In that moment I'd finally accepted that life was a series of choices, and he'd made his choice that didn't include me or our child. I could only make my own choices and find peace with them. Like my marriage to Neil. It wasn't perfect. But it was based on kindness and respect and caring. It was a good life, and while this wasn't what I'd planned, I discovered, to my surprise, that I had no regrets. I'd done what I needed to and for the right reasons.

Another pain gripped me and I cried out. "Coming faster now," Mrs. Baker said, patting my hand. "Nice slow breaths if you can, dearie."

Neil returned with water, which I sipped gratefully. I was no longer sure what time it was, only that the pains came and went. Walking was no longer an option; I remained on the bed, propped up by pillows. When a sharp pain came, Neil held my hand and let the midwife do her work. When my nightgown was soaked with sweat, he was there to help me change into another, modesty forgotten. There were sounds of voices and thumps from downstairs; the men were home and Neil left for a few minutes to explain the situation and then returned. Mrs. Baker checked me again and said if I felt the need, I could start to push.

Exhaustion threatened and I rested against the pillows, breathing heavily and trying to gather my strength. I wouldn't fight my body; all my training told me to let nature take its course. When the urge to bear down came, I gathered what power I had, rolled forward a little, and pushed, letting out a low growl.

"Good, good," Mrs. Baker encouraged. "Not long now. You'll have your little one soon, Nora."

The urge to push came in waves, and all I could do was ride them and work with my muscles to expel the baby from my body. Sounds came from my throat, sweat drenched my body, and Neil held my hand and brushed my hair from my face. "That's it, that's it now!" Mrs. Baker looked up, her smile wide. "Baby's crowning now. Nearly there." A moment later she ordered, "Head's out now. Don't push for a moment, dearie. Don't push…"

I tried valiantly to not push, but my body wasn't listening. There was a burning pain and a massive push and then suddenly Mrs. Baker was grinning. The baby in her hands let out a thin cry, and Neil was laughing and wiping a tear from his eye. All I could do was wilt against the pillows as my body cried out in relief that it was over.

"It's a boy, Nora. A perfectly healthy baby boy." Mrs. Baker brought the baby forward and placed him in my arms, so small and perfect and not yet bathed. My heart exploded then, with love and awe and fear that this tiny human was my child.

Neil clamped and cut the cord, his grin wide and triumphant. "You were an utter champ," he whispered, dropping a kiss on my forehead. "Rest now. Mrs. Baker will take care of you, and I'll take care of this little one."

"He needs a bath," I said, then snorted. "You knew that already."

"I'll bring him back soon. Mrs. Baker, is there anything you need?"

She shook her head. "We're all set here, Captain."

I watched Neil leave the room, my son in my husband's big, capable hands, and a wave of love swept over me for them both. How could it not, when he'd stayed by my side the entire afternoon, when he'd tenderly taken another man's child from my arms as if it was his own? This past year had seen such horrible loss, and yet right now I was filled with startling, brilliant joy. I started to cry, then shook my head, abashed at being so ridiculous, until Mrs. Baker laughed and reassured me.

"Lots of emotion after a birth. Natural as a spring rain to cry, dearie. Now, let's look after the rest of this business so we can put baby to breast, hm?"

Twenty minutes later I was washed and dressed in my third nightgown of the day. The bloodied sheets were removed, and fresh ones put on the bed. The midwife gave instructions for the bleeding and swelling that I would experience for the next several days. She tidied the room, then invited Neil back inside with the baby.

My son. He was now clean and pink with scrunchy eyes and a pert little nose, a dusting of dark-blond hair on his head. The rest of him was swaddled in a soft flannel blanket. "He's ready," Neil said softly, placing him in my arms.

"Captain, why don't you make our new mother a cup of tea and some toast?" Mrs. Baker suggested.

"Of course," he replied, and with a lingering, awestruck look at the baby, he left again.

Mrs. Baker smiled. "That is a man in love with his son if I've ever seen one," she remarked. "But I find new mums do this next part best without someone hovering. Let's put him to your breast. It often takes a bit of guidance and practice at first."

With Mrs. Baker's help, the baby was soon fed and content and asleep in my arms. I felt utterly shattered yet knew I would be unable to sleep. Mrs. Baker packed up and promised to return in a few days, and as she was leaving, Neil came back bearing a tray with tea and two of Mrs. Thompson's light-as-a-feather scones and fresh strawberries.

As I ate, Neil went to Jane and Jimmy's old room and retrieved the cradle. I had thought I had a few more weeks, so I hadn't yet made it up. But now, with my son lying nearby on the bed as I sipped the tea, I watched Neil place the cradle near my side of the bed, adding the soft mattress and warm blankets with gentle care.

"Thank you, Neil."

"He's a miracle, isn't he?" His voice was soft, like the summer evening light filtering through the window. He sat on the edge of the bed, staring at the baby. "Do you know what you're going to name him?"

"Do you have any ideas?" I asked.

He looked at me, startled. "Me?"

I nodded. "You're my husband, Neil. You're his father."

He looked away and I saw his throat working, as if overcome by emotion. He cleared his throat before speaking. "You should pick his first name."

"I was thinking James. After his Uncle Jimmy."

Neil turned my way and met my gaze. "Not Alton?"

"No." I didn't say anything else. Just the simple no. It was time to embrace the future and stop worrying about the past.

"Would it be all right if his second name was Cameron? After my brother?"

His brother who was still fighting… Neil rarely spoke of him, but I knew worry weighed on his mind, now that Cameron had recovered and was back on the front lines. "I think naming him after his two brave uncles is fitting," I agreed. I handed Neil my teacup and then reached for Baby James, lifting him in my hands and holding him close, feeling his warmth and weight. "Happy birthday, James Cameron McLeod."

"By God, that's a fine name," Neil said, his voice thick as he reached out and touched the blanket.

And as we sat there, the three of us linked, I knew without a doubt that this moment marked the start of truly moving forward as a family. That somehow, the four of us—Nora, Neil, James, and Evelyn—had to stay together and make a home. That despite our disjointed beginnings, this would only work if we were all together.

But that happy thought crumbled when Neil came to bed late, smelling of spirits. Oh, he was careful to not disturb me or the baby, and he wasn't so far gone that he had trouble undressing and getting into bed, but I smelled it on him and my heart sank. I had found a new contentment today, but it seemed like Neil had not. I'd thought earlier that I had no regrets, but I did have one. I regretted that Neil was not as satisfied with our life as I was, and I placed that blame squarely on my own shoulders.

The next morning, Neil rose at dawn and got ready for work, none the worse for wear. Mrs. Thompson was back in the kitchen bright and early, ready to take care of the house and Evelyn so I could rest for a few days. And when the paper came, I learned that on the day I welcomed a new life into the world, the Llandovery Castle, on a return voyage after delivering wounded soldiers to Halifax, was torpedoed and sunk off the coast of Ireland, killing fourteen of my fellow nursing sisters.

That there should be such joy amidst such sorrow and suffering was something I wasn't sure I'd ever understand.

Chapter Twenty-Four

CHARLOTTE

July 12, 1918

Leaving Halifax in March had been the right decision. Not just to get away from the memories, not just to regain my independence and not feel beholden to friends. But because not long after I began working for the Zwicker family, I realized that something was horribly wrong.

I think I somehow always knew but pushed it aside as nonsense. No, not just nonsense. Something so big and shameful that I would do anything not to face it. I just pretended everything was all right, came up with explanations and justifications for everything until I simply couldn't ignore the truth any longer.

Right now, Aileen was inside napping while I took clothes off the line in the summer sun. This job was a good one. The

Zwicker family was kind, their three children were school age, and while there was plenty of work, I felt appreciated. We had a roof over our heads, good meals each day, and I earned a wage to purchase our necessities and put a little by. It should have been perfect. And maybe that was why everything suddenly got turned on its head. Without the stress of the last few months, my mind was free to see things clearly. To… heal. It was like the veil of pain and shock had finally been lifted, allowing me to see clearly. And what I saw was nearly incomprehensible. I'd done something truly awful. I didn't know how to reconcile it with myself, let alone the rest of the world.

Because I'd come to the startling realization that the child sleeping on my bed at this moment was not my daughter.

I don't know how it happened. I looked back to those days in December, just out of the hospital, coming to terms with everything I'd seen, so frantic to find Aileen… Had I been so very desperate to find my child that I honestly thought she was mine? Had my mind played a cruel trick on me, making me see Aileen's sweet face in another? When I thought back to those days, I realized I had barely been eating and I laid awake each night, my thoughts turning over and over in desperation. I remembered the dark hole of hopelessness that threatened to suck me in, wishing I'd been killed, the bleak thoughts scaring me so much, I replaced them with a fearful determination that she was alive, and I would find her. The night I'd mistaken baby Eddie for Aileen. Then seeing that notice in the paper… Being so certain this was the moment I'd been waiting for. Walking onto that ward, spying the blond curls, fainting. Good God, had I been so delusional, I'd actually looked at her and seen my sweet baby? Looking back now, something had snapped the exact moment my gaze had landed on her. I thought it was everything going right in my world, but now I suspected everything had gone horribly wrong.

There was no other way to explain it. And certainly no way anyone would understand.

Even in the bright July sunlight, a cold shiver ran down my spine. I took the laundry basket inside and climbed the stairs, wanting to look in on Aileen to make sure she was still asleep. I looked down at the innocent face sleeping on my bed and guilt crawled through me, dark and poisonous. I'd sensed things were off for weeks back in Halifax. She felt different, didn't laugh, didn't like the same foods she'd loved before… All of which I'd explained away by blaming it on her injuries or our being separated for a while. But last week something had happened that crystallized it all into that one moment I couldn't ignore.

That mark, the one I'd seen a thousand times, changing her diaper… that mark wasn't a bruise. A bruise would have gone away. And it wasn't a burn, either, for wouldn't it fade over time? It was a permanent mark. It was the kind of mark a child had from birth.

My Aileen didn't have a birthmark. But this child did, a light-brown stain the size of my thumbnail. I froze in that moment as everything rushed forward, all the moments that I sensed something was wrong and pushed the feelings down, down, down, only to have them come crushing back with paralyzing certainty: *this baby is not my Aileen.*

Aileen—not Aileen—had looked up at me, her wide blue eyes holding mine, and I wanted to crumble. This little child trusted me… why?

How had I pinned her diaper without my hands trembling? I didn't know. But I did it, and I fed her breakfast, and I somehow ate while everything inside of me was in turmoil. Surely I'd seen that mark in the weeks that followed her coming home with me. The sheer force of my powers of denial was mind-boggling. The need to believe the delusion had been complete. I suppose it was self-preservation. The only other option for me was to blurt out what I'd done and lose the tenuous hold I had on living. Because the one thing that was clear to me was that in the days following the explosion, I could not have been in my right mind. No one in their right mind would have done what I did, let alone believed they were entirely right. I'd looked at this girl's blond curls and had seen Aileen's. Looked into her eyes and saw my precious baby. I'd been insensible with grief.

For the past several days, I'd turned this information around in my head, looking for answers, and all I had were questions and a healthy amount of fear.

If this child wasn't Aileen, who was she?

If this child wasn't Aileen, what had happened to my baby? Oh, that question had the power to make my stomach clench with dread and guilt and shame. Should I look for her again? Was she truly dead? What would happen if I confessed to what I'd done? Would I be arrested and put in jail? At the very least, I'd be left alone again. No family. No child. No nobody. Maybe it was what I deserved.

But what if this child's family had been killed and she was an orphan? After all, she'd been in a hospital for over two weeks. Until me, no one had come for her. Maybe she needed me as much as I needed her. Would that make what I'd done all right? Was I grasping at straws, trying to justify my actions?

Worse, though, was that I knew I could never have answers to any of those questions without admitting my own culpability. No one could ever know what I'd done. And so leaving Halifax had definitely been the right decision. No one knew me here. No one would recognize her, either. As long as I kept my mouth shut, we were safe. I was safe. Eventually, I'd make peace with what I'd done.

So I went day to day, doing my chores, cleaning and cooking

and doing laundry and caring for my… my daughter, with all of this weighing inside of me. I remembered that time, remembered my thoughts so clearly. I'd honestly thought that my reality was… real. That was the most terrifying thing of all.

"Mrs. Campbell, Mrs. Campbell!" The two youngest Zwicker children came barreling up the stairs, all the way to the top floor, where Aileen and I had our rooms—a lovely large bedroom and our very own water closet. Aileen was awake now and sitting up on the bed, playing with a handful of clothespins as I folded the clean-smelling laundry.

"Slow down," I advised. "You sound like a herd of elephants."

"We're back from Nan and Gramps's house, and guess what we did there?" Elsie was six with nut-brown pigtails and blue eyes that snapped with energy. "We went hunting for frogs!"

I glanced at her dress. It was clean except a little dirt along the hem, so I guessed she must have worn an apron. The two little girls were always having adventures at their grandparents'.

"Fwogs," echoed Constance, who was three and still struggled with her *r*'s. But her smile was equally wide. "And then we had cookies!"

"I hope you washed your hands first," I said, hiding a smile.

"Uh huh," Constance said.

"Mummmummumm," said Aileen, and my heart turned over. I had a life I was growing to love here, with this baby, and with the children who lived here. It was the nicest house I'd ever lived in. And while the Zwickers were certainly well off financially, they were also kind, decent people who treated me well. Mr. Zwicker was home after having served in France and losing a hand in battle, but on his return he'd rejoined his father's shipping business. When I'd applied for the position and explained about Aileen, they hadn't thought twice. "Of course, you must bring her," Mrs. Zwicker had said kindly. "We're happy to be able to help a war widow. Besides, the girls will dote on her." Their son, Alan, was eleven and had already begun helping out at the shipyard when he wasn't in school. But he was smart and polite and seemed to take his role as eldest quite seriously. Mrs. Zwicker said it was because Mr. Zwicker had been gone for three years, and Alan had wanted to become the "man of the house".

How many children had grown up too soon because of this awful war?

Now Elsie and Constance were practically dancing in front of me. "Mama said to ask you if we could play with Aileen if she was done nappin'." Elsie looked up with big, pleading eyes. "Can we? We want to have a tea party with our dollies."

"Of course you can, as soon as I finish folding the laundry." I smiled at them. "I'll have to come down to start supper, so I'll bring her down with me and you can play while I get things on the go."

"Thank you, Mrs. Campbell!" That came from Elsie, who was already making a beeline for the door. "C'mon, Connie. Let's get our dollies and get everything ready."

"Dolly," Aileen echoed, and giggled.

Tears filled my eyes as I took a moment and sat on the bed with her. How was it that I could wonder about my own child that I'd… abandoned, and yet still feel so much love for the little girl in front of me? She was walking now, toddling along fairly steadily with only the odd bump or fall. She'd started saying some words, too, and calling me Mum, most often "mumumumum" in four syllables.

How did my heart manage to hold both grief and love at the same time? How could I betray my daughter like this, but how could I not love this beautiful child? It felt as if God had entrusted her to me, knowing I had this love to give, that I needed to give it.

Perhaps I'd done something good after all, to end up in a place such as this.

"You want to have a tea party with the girls?" I asked Aileen.

"Dolly," she said again, her eyes sparkling.

"Yes, dolly," I agreed, and then I gathered her close. Maybe my Aileen was gone. But this little one was dear to me, so very dear. And when the guilt and fear threatened to take over, I reminded myself that she and I had been brought together for a purpose. We needed each other.

No one ever need know the truth.

Chapter Twenty-Five

NORA

September 3, 1918

I brushed the hair off my face and wished I'd put on a hat. It was unusually hot, and I'd been working in the yard for over an hour, tackling weeds and picking vegetables from our Victory Garden. Jane had begun it in 1915, and I hadn't really had much to do with it while I was studying and then working. But now I was home, there was no Jane, and tending the small plot fell to me.

I was definitely a better nurse than a gardener. But I was learning, and I took pride in the little achievements. With every jar that was filled and sealed and processed, I felt a sense of accomplishment. It wasn't quite as satisfying as my work as a nurse, but at least I felt I was doing *something*.

Today there were more peas ready to be picked, beans hanging heavily on the vines, and a second crop of cucumbers that would become some sort of pickle or relish once they were harvested. Anything we grew for ourselves meant more foodstuffs were available to our men in uniform.

But it wasn't food shortages and entertainments that weighed on my mind these days. Or even the end of the senseless conflict. It was a less discriminate enemy—the Spanish Flu. Every day it seemed there were tales of it ravaging the ranks of soldiers who survived battles only to succumb to illness, making its way into cities and towns, leaving scores of dead in its wake.

It was only a matter of time before Halifax found itself in its grip. The port was too busy and there were too many soldiers going to and fro to avoid it forever. Neil brought home horror stories from elsewhere, while I wished he wouldn't. Some nights they caused me to lay awake, listening to James's newborn snuffles in the dark, praying the virus didn't make it to our little corner of the world.

James was having his morning nap, so I took advantage of the quiet time to work among the plants. I wanted to pick whatever was ripe before it got even hotter. I was more than ready for the crisp, cooler days of fall.

"Nora?"

I gave a start, standing and looking over my shoulder. Neil was on the back step, James on his arm. The baby had been growing well, but still looked so small tucked into the crook of Neil's elbow. My husband was in his uniform minus the jacket in deference to the heat, and he looked handsome standing there, though his face seemed unusually serious.

I wiped my dirty hands on my apron. "Goodness, you're home early. It's barely eleven."

"I came home to talk to you about something."

"That doesn't sound good." Unease trickled through me, but I pushed it away. As Grammie always said, there was no sense borrowing trouble until trouble borrowed you.

He shrugged a little, then smiled. "Plus this little guy was awake. I think he might be hungry."

I was glad I was already warm because otherwise my blush would be noticeable. With so many men in the house, I'd taken to nursing James in the bedroom, making use of the rocking chair Jane had used for her babies. But at night, when Neil was asleep, I was sometimes too tired to get up. I unbuttoned my nightgown and tried to keep things as modest as possible. If Neil had ever seen anything, he did the gentlemanly thing and never said.

"Let me wash up first." I lifted my basket. "The beans just don't stop coming. There are still peas, too. Hodge podge again tonight." I gave a little laugh. "I'm not much of a gardener. Thankfully Mrs. T has been helping me along."

"That's all right. It's a favourite of mine, anyway."

Good thing. The summer dish of peas, beans, and potatoes in cream meant saving meat rations for another meal.

He looked around. "Where's Evelyn?"

I grinned. "Next door. Mrs. T took her over to sort her button box while she makes over a dress for me. That woman is a miracle worker with needle and thread." Nothing was wasted these days. Making things over to suit the new styles was common.

I followed Neil into the house and went to the sink to wash my hands with the brick of soap by the faucet. When I was done, James was tuning up, so Neil disappeared with him for a few moments and changed his diaper. Not many men would do such a thing and I appreciated Neil even more. Despite our marriage being unconventional, at least we were partners in the endeavour.

He returned, James on his arm, a tiny fist jammed into his mouth, little sucking noises filling the kitchen as he gnawed in hunger. "I can wait if you want to feed him first," Neil said, but I shook my head.

"It's all right. Just, um, turn away until I get him settled."

Neither of us remarked on how odd it was. It was the nature of our dynamic, and that was all.

I took James and sat in one of the kitchen chairs. Then, while Neil got himself a glass of water, I unbuttoned my blouse and settled the baby at my breast. Once he'd latched, I took a soft flannel and draped it over his head. "All right," I said softly, and Neil turned around, taking in the sight of the "tent" around James's head with a smile.

"You're a good mother," he said gently, taking the chair opposite me.

"I try. I'm tired, and I feel like I'm probably doing so many things wrong."

"I expect every new mum feels that way," he offered. Then he looked at me a little more closely. "And are you happy?"

"I am." The answer came readily, because it was true, but it surprised me just the same. "Oh, I'm tired and unsure of myself, but I love James and I certainly love Evelyn. Do I miss nursing? I do, very much. Perhaps I always will. But that doesn't mean I'm unhappy." I met his gaze. "When Jane and my parents died, I realized how much I loved and relied on my family. There was—and still is—an empty place inside me, missing them. But now I have my own family. It's overwhelming but also wonderful. So yes, Neil, I'm contented."

He nodded, his face sombre, and I wondered why my answer

hadn't put him at ease. Worry clawed at my heart. "Are you not happy?"

"Oh, no, I am," he rushed to assure me, nodding his head, perhaps a little too quickly. "It's not that. I mean, I know our marriage is unusual..." He looked away briefly, as if embarrassed. I understood. Ours was a true marriage in every way but one, but it was a glaring omission.

"Then what is it? What did you want to talk to me about?"

He took a moment, sighed, then looked me in the eye. "You know the general feeling is the war will be ending soon. Right now, there's an equal worry about the Spanish Flu. It would be foolish to think it's not going to make its way here." He wrinkled his brow. "Boston is dealing with it now."

I had kept up with the news. The cases from Massachusetts were multiplying by truly staggering numbers. It wasn't bad enough that the men in uniform had to face battle every day. This was a faceless enemy that showed no mercy, and it was making its way to home shores. Even Neil's brother, Cameron, had had his share of bad luck. He'd contracted it, though his latest letter had found him nearly recovered. Neil had started calling him a cat with nine lives.

"What are you saying? Are we seeing the beginning of an outbreak here, too?" The nurse in me wanted to dig out a uniform, roll up my sleeves, and get to work. The mother in me was terrified. In July the *Araguaya* had been quarantined in the harbour because of sick soldiers on board. It would be foolish to think the flu could be completely contained. It was far too contagious.

"Not yet," Neil said. "But there are rumours that we're going to send some nurses to Boston to help out. And learn."

"I see," I replied cautiously. James coughed, dribbling milk down the curve of my breast, and I took a moment to settle him again before looking up and meeting Neil's eyes. Even suspecting what he was going to say, it came as a shock when I heard the words.

"A few doctors might go as well. I want to volunteer."

I blinked as emotions thundered through me. After what we'd been through, after what we'd witnessed… why on earth would he put himself in further danger? Because it *would* be dangerous. There was no real treatment or way to keep from contracting Spanish Flu. One could only practice good hygiene and hope for the best. "But you're needed. Here." I wanted to say that I needed him, but it seemed presumptuous and too… personal. But it was true, even if I didn't want to admit it. I was extremely competent and could manage things at home. But there was also something about Neil coming home at the end of the day. He brought companionship, security, and calm with him. He steadied me when I wobbled. He always had, from the first moment he'd complimented my stitches at the hospital.

"Camp Hill is still busy, that's true. But I feel the need is greater in Boston. Besides, I'd be able to bring back what I learn and use it to help guide our public health response." His gaze sharpened. "It's a matter of when, and not if, Nora. Our first Nova Scotia death happened two days ago, in Cape Breton."

James broke off again, finished eating, and I handed him to Neil before hastily buttoning up my bodice. I put the flannel on my shoulder and then reached for the baby again, positioning him and patting his back, trying to coax out a burp. My jaw was tight, though, and my little thumps were faster than normal. "I know people are going to die," I whispered sharply. "But I don't see why you have to throw yourself into the middle of it."

"Don't you?" he asked, and rose from his chair, pacing toward the stove then turning back again. His eyes were troubled, and his lips turned down, so unusual for a man who seemed to always be smiling. "We were both there the day of the explosion and in the days following. You were right there with me, determined to do your duty. That's what this is, Nora. It's my duty."

"No, it's not." James let out a rumbling burp, then there was a wet sound as he spit up on my shoulder, the slightly sour smell tainting the air. I adjusted him, deftly wiped his face with a corner of the flannel, then folded the material up to wash later. It was crumpled in my fist as I faced my husband. "This is your..." I struggled to find the right word as fear for him—for all of us—rippled through me. "This is your need to save everyone. You rush in with no thought to yourself, this big, self-sacrificing hero. Well, you have other responsibilities now, Neil. It's not just you anymore. It's..." My face flamed and I looked away, swallowing the words that had come unbidden to my tongue. "It's the children. You have a family."

Silence fell, awkward and full of so many things we'd never said. Perhaps even things we didn't understand. We were married and shared a bed, but our union had never been consummated. We were parents to two children, but neither were his. We were friends and cared about each other deeply, but Lord above, we avoided the word *love* like it was diseased. He offered stability and legitimacy to me and the children, but it was more than that, too... and yet it wasn't. For as I stared at him across my sister's kitchen, I realized that despite whatever vows we had spoken six months ago, I had no right to tell him what he could or could not do. He'd upended his life for me. And damned if I didn't resent him for it sometimes, even as I was grateful. Even though I had played an equal part in this choice.

"Everyone has a family. Can't you see," he said, stepping

forward, "that I have to go because of the family? Because what I learn might help? That it will protect our family?"

His voice had sharpened and taken on a tone I'd never heard from him before, even on the days when he'd been exhausted and worn thin from the long, arduous hours of treating the wounded. And still, the fear of losing him—my anchor in the storm that had been the past year—dictated my next words.

"What I see is someone who constantly rushes in to be a saviour," I snapped. "Someone who needs to be needed, no matter who gets left behind."

"That's not true."

"Isn't it? Look at you. Serving at Aldershot. Hopping on a train to Halifax, working day and night. Offering to marry me out of pity—"

"That was not what I did!" We were nearly shouting now, and his cheeks were ruddy with… anger? Frustration? Was it horrible that this argument had me feeling more alive than I had in months?

A muscle ticked in Neil's jaw. James was in my arms and holding his head up now, watching the two of us but not fussing. Perhaps he was surprised at Neil's loud voice, as I was.

"I did not marry you out of pity," he said, a bit quieter. "I married you because I've never met anyone like you, Nora. And I thought that if you married me, you might come to feel the same." His eyes flashed. "It was always you, from that first time I walked into the hospital and saw you with your tongue between your teeth, stitching that wound. But it's been months and I've had to lie next to you in bed each night, not touching, not… anything. I've given you everything I am and not asked for a single thing in return."

It felt as if my stomach dropped to my feet as my brain raced to reject what he was saying. It couldn't be. I did not want him to love me. Care for me, certainly, as I did for him. But not love. Not… My body trembled, afraid. Not of Neil, but because the kind of relationship he was describing was what had set this whole thing in motion. Not losing my family, but my impulsiveness with Alley had taken away so many of my choices, altered the path I'd wanted my life to take. That was my burden to bear, for no one had made the decision to be with Alley but me. There was no way I was going to lose myself further because I'd been loose. Shameful.

"That was not our agreement."

"Damn that agreement," he shot back, running a hand through his hair. "I wish I'd never made it."

I recoiled, cut to the quick. I'd always known deep down that one day he'd regret marrying me, but I'd never expected him to say as much and so plainly. I clenched my teeth and refused to cry over it. I was stronger than that now. "But you did make it, and so did I. Don't you think I know you got drunk the night we got engaged? And the night that James was born? How do you think that makes me feel?"

"Dammit, Nora!" He rarely cursed, and his cheeks were flushed. It was, in six months of marriage, our first real argument. Perhaps we needed to get some honesty out in the open. "I did that because I couldn't have what I really wanted!"

He sighed, turned away from me, and braced his hands on the edge of the sink. After a moment he hung his head. James curled into my shoulder, leaving a wet mark on my neck. The calm, accepted pattern of our days had just been shattered, and all because Neil was determined to put himself in the middle of a deadly pandemic.

The thought of him getting ill or, heaven forbid, dying made my stomach tighten with dread. No matter our agreement, to lose him too, after losing so many others…

But now that he'd voiced his regret at our marriage, I kept my concern and fear to myself, while tucking away the knowledge that he'd been dishonest about his feelings. I wasn't sure what I was supposed to do with that. Especially when my feelings seemed to matter so little.

"When would you leave?" My voice was soft now, resigned. The agreement didn't matter, in the end, because I knew he was going to go whether I wanted him to or not. And that stung.

"I don't know. Probably October. There's time yet." Oh, how it hurt to look into his face and see regret and defeat there. The words could not be taken back, not for either of us. And I knew that our marriage—which had been balancing on a delicate tightrope for months—would never be the same.

I nodded.

"I should get back." The emotion was gone from his voice, and that hurt almost as much as the hastily blurted words of only moments before. "I'll be home for supper."

"All right," I answered.

Neil turned on his heel and headed for the front door, not even saying goodbye or giving James a kiss, which he normally did. When the door closed behind him, the house was silent and oh-so very empty. The boarders were at work, Evelyn was next door, and it was just me and James in the big, rambling house. The voices of those who were gone seemed to echo softly in the corners, and I sat in a kitchen chair and rested my forehead on my free hand, James still snuggled into my other arm. I had never felt so alone, not even when Jane and our parents and Clara had died. Then I'd felt others rally around me, but not now. Maybe marrying Neil *had* been a mistake. Had it been the easy route instead of determining to do this by myself?

Homesickness flooded me in a devastating wave. What I'd give to feel my mother's reassuring arms around me, telling me it was going to be all right. To see her hold baby James in her arms, a wide, proud smile on her face at having a grandson to spoil. And Jane, too, the most steadfast and loving of sisters. The woman who'd held all my secrets and loved me just the same. We could have brought our children up together… cousins, close as siblings…

James began to fuss at being held so awkwardly, and I sat up, adjusted him in my arms, and looked down at his sweet little face. Sometimes when I looked at him, I saw Clara in his blond wispy hair and the pert tip of his nose. But then I could see Alley in his eyes and the shape of his lips. He was so, so dear, and I loved him wholly. As I kissed his warm, soft forehead, I knew it was possible to love him and still have regrets. It was possible to have him and Evelyn and even Mrs. Thompson and still feel so very alone.

I wanted to go home. For the first time since moving to Halifax for my studies, I had a soul-deep longing to be back in the Chester house, with its familiar furnishings and the back door that squeaked and the drafty kitchen window that coated with frost on frigid winter days when the wind came howling off the ocean and went right through your bones.

The walls of Jane's house felt as if they were closing in on me. Staying here without my sister had suited in the beginning, had made perfect sense. Neil's work was here in the city, and I had come to rely upon Mrs. T and the other boarders to fill a void. It had been familiar in a time of chaos. But what was I doing? Living Jane's life instead of my own? It had nothing to do with Evelyn—of course I would raise the little girl who was as dear to me as my own child. But it had everything to do with the life I'd built and discarded when I'd stepped into my sister's shoes… her kitchen, her garden, her everything.

This wasn't my home. Not deep inside, where the idea of

home should feel like roots and warmth and comfort. My old life was gone. Jane's life didn't fit, like shoes that were the wrong size. I needed to find a new life, one of my very own.

A wet spot from James's drool spread on the light cotton of my dress, and I looked down to find him asleep again, comfortable after having his diaper changed and his belly full. Neil would be leaving us soon, and I knew I'd been relying on him too much. For almost a year now I had been swept along by circumstances that guided my decisions, either forced by events out of my control or consequences of my own making. Maybe this was the perfect time to move to the house in Chester. I'd be close to Grammie and Grampie during the winter, and to my brothers, too. And Neil…

My throat tightened. Neil. He wouldn't be in Boston forever. But maybe… maybe it would be for the best if I stayed in Halifax and managed the house.

Maybe it was time to stop pretending our marriage was more than it was.

When Neil came home late, I was already in bed, a light sheet covering my nightgown while James slept in the cradle. Neil tiptoed in and undressed, hanging his uniform over a chair before slipping under the sheet. I rolled over and looked at him, regret heavy in my heart. What a mess we were in. I'd said I was contented, and it wasn't untrue, but the words of earlier today couldn't be taken back. A new wall was between us now, even here, in the dark, in the bed we shared and in the bodies we didn't. He'd given me everything, he'd said, while asking for nothing in return. It was true. I just hadn't expected him to resent me for it.

"I was thinking," I whispered, "that I might go to the house in Chester for a while. I'm… I'm homesick, if I'm honest."

"I see."

I couldn't make out his facial expression in the dark, but the words were flat. He was still smarting from our fight, then.

"I-I think I avoided it for a long while. Because of Mum and Dad, and, well, everything. But I miss my family, Neil, and the only family I have is there."

If it were possible to sense him withdrawing further, I did. The air cooled between us, the space widening. He was my husband, but I realized I'd just said he wasn't my family. Tears stung the backs of my eyes. How many ways could I hurt him today—could we hurt each other?

"If that's what you wish. Perhaps Mrs. Thompson will be willing to take on managing the house. I would hate to leave the boarders stuck looking for a new place to live."

He wasn't even going to try to convince me to stay.

"I'll speak to her tomorrow. And write to Grammie." The hollow feeling that came from this moment, the knowledge that everything was about to change again, mixed with a sense of relief at the thought of home. Perhaps if I went back there, I could truly find my way and start over. Perhaps when Neil returned he would decide to make a home there with me, as we'd spoken of in the beginning. The fact that we were married would not change. But we did need to decide how we were going to navigate the years to come.

He was a good man, and he had once said that what he got out of the marriage was me. It hadn't occurred to me that it wouldn't be enough. That he wanted more, when he'd insisted he didn't. Once again, I felt as if I'd failed, even though my intentions had been to put my own needs aside and provide a stable and secure home for the children. How foolish I'd been to think that my dreams—and Neil's—didn't matter.

The bed creaked beneath my weight as I rolled onto my back, blinking hard to keep from crying. I loved James, but if I could turn back the clock and take back that night in the hotel room, I would.

Chapter Twenty-Six

NORA

October 10, 1918

Autumn brought news that the tide of the war was changing, and the Germans were close to surrendering. Canadian forces had gained significant ground in northern France; the papers shouted new developments in the headlines every day. Neil was in Boston. I had received a letter after his arrival, letting me know he was there safe and sound. He'd also said that if anything happened to him, I would be taken care of as his wife. I'd cried when I read that, wondering if he thought I didn't care at all. And then I'd dried my tears, and the children and I went to Chester and settled into the house.

It was so good to be home.

And yet the spectre of disease followed us everywhere. New cases of the Spanish Flu were being reported throughout Nova

Scotia. It wasn't just soldiers bringing it home. Fishermen came into port along the south shore, in Yarmouth and Shelburne. Late in September, a vessel from Massachusetts had docked in Yarmouth, and two of the sailors had died there. Life in Chester went on mostly as normal, but it was as if a pall hung over its residents, waiting for the worst to happen.

Surprisingly, I was happier than I'd been in months. I realized that in dealing with the fallout from the explosion, I'd simply been going through the motions, stuck in grief and worry. But here, all that started to fade, and the weight on my shoulders lightened.

I took a pan of hot biscuits out of the oven, frowning slightly at the golden brown, slightly lumpy tops. I hadn't mastered my mother's recipe yet, and perhaps never would, but the biscuits improved with each batch and certainly tasted just fine slathered with fresh apple butter. Evelyn sat at the table, entertaining James who sat in Clara's old highchair. Evelyn built up blocks on the table, then knocked them over and made James giggle, the baby belly laughs putting a smile on my face. A pot of vegetable soup simmered on the stove. We would have a hearty meal later, and there was a bowl of yellow-red apples on the counter that Grammie had delivered just yesterday. I had already cooked several into applesauce, and given James a tiny taste, his lips smacking at the sweetness.

Buttons was curled up in front of the stove where it was toasty warm. Mrs. T had offered to part with him so Evelyn wouldn't have to leave him behind. The house, once I had given it a thorough cleaning, was just as warm and homey as I remembered. Three bedrooms upstairs, with sturdy beds covered with quilts carefully pieced and stitched with love. A parlour, pantry, and kitchen downstairs, with a cozy front porch and an addition at the back, which housed a modern bathroom. It wasn't an overly large house, not like the one back on Henry Street, but it was perfect for my little family. I felt closest to those I'd lost here, too, even though at times the memories were painful and sad. There was only one thing missing. Or rather, one person. Neil.

"Auntie, look, James is laughing at me!" Evelyn called from the table, her blue eyes sparkling. "He thinks I'm funny."

"Of course you are," I replied, putting down the pan and going over to kiss Evelyn's head. "You're a wonderful cousin. He loves you." Evelyn's smile faded as she looked down at the table, strangely subdued as her lips curved downward. "What is it, Evvie? Where did your smile go?"

Evelyn shrugged, so I took the chair next to her, concerned at the sudden change of mood. Was she feeling all right? I put my hand on her forehead, fear sliding down my spine. "Are you feeling ill?"

"No, Auntie. I just got sad all of a sudden."

I exhaled in relief, then looked up. "What are you sad about, sweetheart?"

"Auntie, I love baby James. I-I want him to be my brother, not my cousin. Can't he be my baby brother?"

Oh. *Oh.* It made perfect sense, really. Maybe some would frown upon it, but I didn't care. Evelyn had lost her only sibling and her mother. Who could possibly deny her this?

"If you want to think of him as your brother, then that's all right, sweetheart. He loves you very much, and so do I." I kissed Evelyn's hair, closing my eyes. We had to hold onto each other now.

"If he's my brother, then you could be…" Tears glimmered on Evelyn's face. "My mummy. Can you be my mummy, Auntie Nora? I—" She started to cry a little, tiny hiccups that melted my heart. "I miss having a mummy."

"Oh, my love," I said softly, pulling Evelyn over onto my lap, missing Jane desperately and yet also feeling incredibly privileged that I was raising her sweet daughter. Moving here had allowed us to start letting go. Oh, not forgetting. Never that. But perhaps I was beginning to feel less of a stand-in and more of the real thing.

"Remember when I promised you I would love you and care for you always?" Evelyn nodded against the front of my dress. "That's what mummies do, sweetheart. They love you, no matter what. You always have a home with me and with James, because we're a family. Whether you call me Auntie or Mummy, that will never change. I promise."

Evelyn's arms came up around my neck and squeezed, while James patted his hands on the highchair, babbling. I hugged her back, my heart overflowing. The life I'd never wanted was mine, and in Halifax I'd resented it. As much as I'd told Neil I was contented, I hadn't been. Not really. A part of me wanted to be back in my blue-and-white uniform, with that horrible nursing veil, putting in long days at the hospital. But here, at home… it was different. It had taken going away and perhaps even losing my loved ones to make me realize this was where I belonged.

"Auntie?" Evelyn didn't call me "Mummy"—not yet. The little girl sat up straight, her curls damp around her face from her tears. "If you are my new mummy, can Uncle Neil be my daddy?"

It was an unexpected question, and it released a torrent of emotion in me. I missed Neil more than I cared to admit, and being away from him now forced me to see things a bit more clearly. I didn't like what I saw in myself and my past actions. I had held myself back from my husband because I'd committed myself to an idea of an agreement rather than a marriage. I'd taken Neil utterly for granted. And now he was in Boston, in the middle of an outbreak, and I was worried sick about him.

What I'd had with Alley wasn't love. I'd been swept away, just like my hat that had been tossed by the wind and landed at his feet that fateful day. But love… it was steady, not blown away by an autumn nor'easter. It was like the lines in that sonnet I'd heard recited at a war bonds fundraiser, by one of the students from King's College:

O no! it is an ever-fixed mark
That looks on tempests and is never shaken

That was Neil. Always steadfast, the calm in a storm. He cared for Evvie so much. I just knew he'd be touched that she wanted to call him Daddy. "Why don't you ask Uncle Neil when he gets home?" I suggested, offering a smile.

"When will that be?" she asked, affecting a pout.

I sighed. "I don't know, exactly. Hopefully not long, Evvie. Do you remember how we told you the people of Boston sent so much help to Halifax last winter? Right now those people are having some troubles, so Uncle Neil has gone to repay the favour and help them, too."

"That's a nice thing to do, isn't it?"

I smiled. I'd given him such a hard time about leaving us, but the truth was, I'd been afraid. Was still afraid. But also so very proud of the man he was. "It is."

James started complaining since he had stopped getting attention. Evelyn scrambled off my lap and went up to James's chair, affecting a funny face. James immediately started giggling again. At three and a half months, he was really becoming responsive, with a jolly personality. How Neil would enjoy him now…

Neil was the final piece of the puzzle, and the more I started to love my life, the more I realized I needed him in it. But would he want to leave Halifax behind and move to Chester? Besides, the war wasn't over. He would be at Camp Hill until then, wouldn't he? And before all that, he needed to come home from Boston…

That night I went to bed and rolled over, curling into a ball beneath the covers, huddling to stay warm. I even missed him in the bed, with his warmth and steady presence. After that day we'd argued, he'd been withdrawn and cool, but I still remembered everything he'd said that warm September afternoon. That he'd wanted me. That it had always been me, and he'd never asked for anything in return. He'd been patient with me, so very, very patient.

I tucked my knees in close and closed my eyes, wondering what he was doing right now. Was he all right? Sick? Tired? Missing me, or fulfilled with his new role and challenge? Would he even want to come back? If he did, could I be brave enough to tell him how I felt… that in his absence I'd realized I wanted a real husband and marriage?

That instead of him staying on his side of the bed, I wanted to be held in his arms? That I wanted his touch, his love? Why had it taken me so long to see sense?

At first, it had been impossible to imagine Neil's hands on my body, doing with him what I'd done with Alley. But now my fingers skimmed down my ribs, over the taut peak of my breast, and I felt that longing… for Neil.

Please come home, I thought. *Please still love me. Don't let it be too late.*

When the sun came up the next morning, I rose, dressed, and set about lighting the fire in the stove. I mixed up bread and set it to proof, then changed and fed James. By that time Evelyn was up, and the little girl got the three-legged stool that Jane and I had once used and stood at the cupboard to retrieve bowls and cups for breakfast. Today I would go to the post office and send another letter to Neil as well as one to Mrs. Thompson, and then I'd stop at Gorman's for some sewing notions. I planned to spruce up an old dress for a Red Cross benefit on Saturday. In addition, I had found several sewing projects amongst my mother's things, and I'd been spending my evenings embroidering pillowcases and crocheting doilies to add to the craft tables, my skills a little rusty but adequate, finding unexpected fulfillment in these little acts of service. So far, everything for the event was going ahead as scheduled, though I watched the papers with growing concern. If an outbreak happened here, Chester would likely restrict public gatherings the same as other communities had already done, Kentville being the most recent.

There was a knock at the door and my brother, William, poked his head in. "Good morning," he called, and I turned around with a smile and a bowl in my hand.

"Hello, Will. You had breakfast yet?"

"Not yet," he confessed. "I thought I'd come over and see if there's a little girl who would like to pick apples with Grammie today."

"Me! I'd like to!" shouted Evelyn, popping out of her chair.

I laughed. "All right, sit down, both of you. I'll cook you some eggs. Evvie, you have to eat your breakfast before you go. I'll walk over to get you after I run my errands today." It was one of the many benefits of being back home—spending time with Grammie and Grampie Hirtle, seeing my brothers again. While there had likely been a few whispers about my coming home with a baby when I'd been married such a short time, few questioned it since Neil had attended the funerals with me in

December. As far as anyone knew, Neil was James's father. I had since stopped feeling guilty about the deception, for he was a father in all the ways that truly counted, and it was no one's business but ours.

William pulled out a chair and sat. He'd finished his year in school but hadn't gone back, choosing to work instead, especially since so many of the local young men were off soldiering and he still had another year before he could enlist. "You're working today?" I asked, whisking eggs and pouring them into a hot pan.

"I am." William made funny faces at James. "Still a few weeks of apple picking left. And I'm going to be kept on for a while at least, fixing machinery and the like." He took the milk jug and poured Evvie a cup of milk, and I marveled at my little brother's comfort and confidence, which had only grown in the last year. "I like farming. More than I expected. I might like to save up for my own place."

I cut through a loaf of bread, pausing to look up at him in between slices. Goodness. He'd grown at least an inch over the summer, and he was becoming a man. How I wished Mum and Dad were here to see it. To guide him. Now it was up to me, and our grandparents.

"If it will make you happy, you should," I agreed, scooping up food and putting it on plates. "There's nothing wrong with farming. You're sure you're not interested in the shipyard?" There was a booming business on the docks these days. William would never be without work or be at the mercy of poor crops or falling prices.

"I like the outdoors," Will said simply. "I like helping things grow, and harvesting." He gave a crooked smile. "I don't know where I get it from, since there's not a farmer in our family tree."

But I smiled. "There is if you go back a few generations. It doesn't matter anyway." I ruffled his hair as I put the plate in front of him. If I'd learned anything the last year, it was that life was too precious to waste. "If working the land makes you happy, then I say do it."

"What about you?" he asked, speaking around a mouth full of fluffy eggs. He swallowed. "Are you going to be a nurse again?"

"I don't know, Will." The question didn't cause me as much pain as it might have a few months ago. "Right now, I have my hands full with Evvie and James. But I did love it, so who knows what the future might hold?" Maybe one day I'd nurse again. Maybe I wouldn't. But I was sure I'd find a way to be of service somehow.

When breakfast was over, William disappeared with Evvie, who was excited to be going to Grammie's for the morning, and I bundled James into the carriage, tucking a knitted blanket around him for warmth. The morning had a chill, and that crisp coolness that only October brings. The light shape of the moon was still visible in the pale sky, while the sun bathed the grass in a rosy hue. A year ago, I'd been gallivanting around Halifax with Alley, strolling through Point Pleasant, spending my days at the hospital. What a difference a year could make. James gurgled and I peeked down into the carriage, my heart lighter than it had been in months. Surely the war would end soon. And eventually the flu would run its course, Neil would return home, and life could begin anew. Sometimes I wished I could return to the days when my family was still here and I had purpose and accomplishment. And yet the last month had awakened something that had been sleeping inside me since last December sixth, buried under despair. Hope. Hope for the future, and a desire to build on the happiness that was burgeoning once again.

My first stop was the post office on Duke Street. The little bell tinkled above the door when I walked in, and the postmistress offered a cheery hello.

"Good morning, Mrs. McLeod," she said, a smile lighting her face. "And Master James. Lordy, he's growin' like a bad weed." She came around the counter and made a fuss over James, who stared at her with wide eyes and let out a little giggle and squeak.

"I'd like to send a letter, please," I said, reaching into my bag and withdrawing an envelope.

"Ah yes, to Halifax." The postmistress raised an eyebrow as she looked at the name. "Still running the boarding house?"

"Yes. It'd be a shame to leave our boarders with no place to live. We became like a family after the explosion."

"Maybe you and Dr. McLeod will go back there… after." Everyone in Chester seemed to know that Neil was off doctoring in Boston, and the innocent sentence sounded a lot to me like digging around to see if we intended to stay in Chester.

"Right now, I'm just hoping he's able to be home soon." I smiled, paid for the stamp, and handed over the letter. "And will you be going to the benefit on Saturday?" I asked, changing the subject.

The Red Cross benefit was at the Hackmatack Inn on Saturday night; Gram had offered to stay with the children while I joined with other local ladies to serve punch while the audience enjoyed an evening of music and elocution. With the news of infection becoming more grim each day, it might be the last one for a while. "Of course," came the answer, and after a few more moments of niceties, I was back outside again.

The air was clear with the ever-present tang of salt that came from living by the ocean. I filled my lungs with it, then began walking again, toward Gorman's store with a list of necessities like thread and perhaps some new lace or trim to update my green dress that was a good three years old and slightly out of style.

I was thinking about how I might alter it when a woman turned the corner, a small child in her arms.

I froze as any thoughts of the dress disappeared.

The woman was about my age, perhaps a year or two younger, walking with a slight limp. Her hair was a shiny and soft dark blond, her smile wide as she looked down at the little girl in her arms.

But it was the child that drew my attention and made my insides freeze with recognition, disbelief, and dread. For the girl had Clara's blond curls, her blue eyes, and the deep dimple on her right cheek as she smiled up at the woman.

It couldn't be Clara. It couldn't. Logic dictated that this was not my niece but a trick of the light, a trick of my brain. It had been nearly a year since the explosion. The entire family had been killed… a tiny child couldn't have survived when everyone with her had perished. No, this was just a small girl who resembled Clara.

And yet… there had never been a body. Was it… oh, Lord in heaven. Logic gave way to the call of my heart. Was it possible that this woman was holding Jane's daughter? Evvie's baby sister? For this child, even after ten months, looked exactly like Clara.

The woman looked up and saw me standing there, and her face lost all its colour despite the morning's chill that put roses in the baby's cheeks. The woman's eyes widened and reminded me of the time I'd stepped outside the house with a lantern and found a deer nibbling at my lettuces. Surprised and scared.

Before I could call out, the woman wheeled away in a swing of grey skirts and headed in the other direction, tucking the child close to her shoulder.

Shaken, I stood on the street for several seconds, trying to come to grips with what I'd just seen, trying to understand if it was real or even possible… and then asking myself what I was going to do about it. I'd been back in Chester for a month, and it was a small town. How was it I had no idea who this woman was? Her dress had been plain—a work dress. And she'd been pretty and well-kept, but not embellished in any way.

And the child… the child looked to be the age that Clara would be now. But I pressed my hand against my belly and let out a big breath, trying to steady my thoughts. It wasn't just the age. It was the child herself. The hair and the eyes and the dimple. The smile like Jimmy's and the pert little nose like Jane's.

I hadn't imagined that.

With renewed determination, I wheeled the carriage down the street, following the path the woman had taken. Right or wrong, I'd go crazy from wondering if I didn't get to the bottom of it.

Chapter Twenty-Seven

CHARLOTTE

She knows.

Those two words bounced around inside my head as I reversed my route, walking as fast as I could down Duke Street and in the direction of the Zwickers' house. My heart raced double time, my breaths short as I cursed the limp that had never quite gone away even though my leg was healed. Ever since I'd realized that Aileen wasn't my daughter, we didn't go out often for this very reason. Whoever that woman on the street was, she'd recognized Aileen. And instead of me keeping calm and meeting her smile, I'd panicked. The only thing for me to do right now was go back to the house and get out of sight. Once we were safe, I'd consider what to do next. Everything in my body was screaming *RUN*.

I wanted to walk faster, but it was impossible, what with the limp and carrying the baby in my arms. Aileen had wanted to walk today, holding onto my finger, and I'd relented. She was old enough now that she balked at the carriage when I did need to go somewhere, so today I'd given in, even knowing her little legs would tire before we returned. Today's errand had been easy: a quick trip to the store for cream of tartar that had been missed in the last grocery delivery. Small enough that I could tuck it away in my coat pocket and have both arms for carrying Aileen when she tired.

Except now I was even more unsteady between my limp and the extra weight in my arms. There was still the hill to climb, and my steps slowed—better to slow down than fall, taking her with me.

"Excuse me! Excuse me, ma'am…"

Panic raced down my limbs as the woman's voice called out behind me. I ignored her and tried to quicken my steps, pain shooting from my knee to my hip. Hobbling now, tears burning my eyes, I was helpless to keep the terror out. I'd been found out. I could be accused of kidnapping, couldn't I? I could go to jail. I would be all alone…

Those thoughts cascaded through my mind in a rapid spiral as I registered the sound of little wheels bouncing over the street—it was her, pushing her carriage with a baby inside. "Please, stop!" she cried out, but her voice was closer now, and I didn't trust my leg to hold up for one more hurried step. Heart pounding, body trembling, I halted and slowly turned around.

She came rushing up, the carriage springs bouncing. Her eyes were wild, her dark hair coming undone from its pins. She looked at me for a moment and there was something about her that jarred in my memory. I tried to place her face, but before I could, her gaze dropped to the child. There was no doubt in my mind that she recognized Aileen. It was my worst fear come to startling, devastating life.

I knew, in that very second, that I had two choices. I could either confess all and admit what had happened, or I could pretend ignorance. And God help me, self-preservation won out. I couldn't possibly know what she was thinking. My only defense was to deny everything.

Somehow I gathered the fortitude to lift my chin, ignored the quivering of my body, and met her gaze.

Her eyes kept shifting between me and Aileen. "It really is her. Clara. Oh, Clara."

Clara. The name echoed through my head as I held my daughter tighter, tighter. She squirmed in my arms, resisting the cinch of my embrace. "Shhh," I soothed, loosening my hold just a little. But I wouldn't put her down. Couldn't. I was terrified she'd run to this stranger; more terrified she would somehow recognize this woman, too.

"This is Aileen," I said, surprised at how strong my voice sounded.

There was a moment where confusion swept over the woman's face, and I thought I might have been convincing. But the expression only lasted a moment before her eyes narrowed again. "Her name is Clara," she said clearly.

The baby's head lifted, and she squirmed again. But it had been nearly a year. Half her life. Could she possibly remember this person, or what might have been her old name?

Deep inside me was a drum beat warning me to not let this child go. To do whatever it took to get through this chance meeting, and then run. Run as far away as possible, the faster the better.

"I'm sorry, but you're mistaken." My voice was brittle now. "This is my daughter. Leave us alone."

I turned to leave but she jumped forward and gripped my arm in her fingers, the tips of them digging into my muscles. "I'm not mistaken," she hissed. "This is my niece, Clara Boutilier.

She is two years old, and she's been missing since the explosion."

My stomach did a slow, sickening turn. "I'm very sorry for your loss," I offered, holding firm. "But this is not her."

She let go of my arm and I stepped back, but then she spoke, and I found I couldn't move. "Please, listen to me," she pleaded. "Her mother, my sister, was on the waterfront with our parents. They were killed. I saw the bodies myself, but not Clara's. I wasn't there… I was a nurse at Camp Hill. She has a sister, Evelyn, who now lives with me and… my husband. She has a family that misses her. A family that needs her." Her voice broke on the last words, shredding the fragile fabric of my resolve.

It wasn't hard to imagine the situation. This woman hadn't said much, but it was enough that I was taken back to those days again, the ones following the explosion. There was so much chaos. I had awakened at Camp Hill, frantic that Aileen was missing. The nurses had cared for me tirelessly… this woman had been one of them, I realized with a shock. Her face seemed so familiar, and there was something about her voice that stuck to the edges of my memory, firm but compassionate. I could easily see myself in her shoes, losing her family, not knowing where her niece was, because that had been me, searching for Aileen, and it was very likely that what she was saying was true.

But I couldn't just hand my child over. I loved her. I'd cared for her for nearly a year, and she was as dear to me as Aileen had ever been. I knew her moods and her likes and her dislikes. I knew how she loved to be cuddled, knew what sounds she made in her sleep, knew that missing an afternoon nap made her unbearably cross. I loved when she called me Mum and the other few words she had begun speaking. In all those ways she was my daughter. My heart wouldn't let her go. And neither would my head. Because if I did, it would mean

I'd taken a child not mine, it would mean I'd deprived a family of their baby, and it would mean *people would know what I'd done.*

"Her sister is five," the woman continued, her voice softer and pleading now. "Her father was killed overseas. She has great-grandparents and uncles right here in Chester."

"Her name is Aileen Campbell," I replied, my voice tight.

"Why are you doing this?" she asked, and the broken sound of her voice was like ground glass in my belly. "She is not yours!" The woman began to back up, shaking her head as she went. "I must report this." She put her hands on the handle of the carriage and moved as if to leave, and I knew I couldn't let her. I had to somehow convince her she was wrong.

"No, don't!" I said, jumping forward. "Please. Listen. I was there too, you see? I was with Aileen, and we were walking, and when I woke up, I was in the hospital and she was missing. I finally found her just before Christmas, in the hospital in New Glasgow."

Her expression didn't change, so I added, "I was at Camp Hill, too, a patient. Perhaps that's why I look familiar."

She shook her head, but doubt had crept into her eyes, and I pushed on. "We stayed with a friend on Beech Street, and then I found a job here in Chester where I could work and keep Aileen with me as well. We've made our life here. I truly am sorry for the loss you've suffered. I, too, lost my family. My husband—Aileen's father—was killed at The Somme. His family was killed in the explosion. But the two of us… we're building a new life." I tried for a hopeful, optimistic smile, but had a feeling it simply came off as desperate. Because I was.

There was silence between us for a long moment, and then she shook her head. "I feel horrible that you lost so many people, too. I truly do. But that doesn't change that this child is my niece.

For heaven's sake, I know my own family. I lived with her every day. She is not yours."

"You can't possibly prove that," I challenged, then held my breath. Unless she could. If she recognized this child, there might be others in her life who could as well. Or if she knew—

"She's got a birthmark on the right side of her abdomen. It's about the size of a thumbnail, and it's the colour of tea with milk in it."

My heart fell. The mark. The mark I had told myself was some sort of bruise or scar from her injuries, that had never gone away. The mark that had finally made me realize that this beautiful little girl was not my Aileen after all. My chest tightened as I began to realize this was not a battle I was going to win. The past ten months crowded around me, all the pain and fear and loneliness piling on until I could hardly breathe. This woman was going to take Aileen away from me. The need to escape was overwhelming, but I knew there was nowhere to go. "Please." I wasn't above begging. "Please don't do this. She's all I have."

The fact that this woman didn't reach out and grab Aileen—Clara—out of my hands surprised me. Instead, she looked at me with pity. Possibly compassion. It was impossible, but for the briefest moment it felt as if we were joined together—by tragedy and sorrow, perhaps, or by realizing that no matter what, one of us was going to walk away missing a sweet little girl.

"Why?" Her voice was hoarse. "Why would you take a baby that wasn't yours?"

We'd been talking long enough that my arms ached from holding Aileen, and she was restless from being still. Reluctantly I put her down, and this woman—I didn't even know her name—knelt down.

"Would you like to see the baby?" she asked Aileen, and I

watched as the woman smiled, her eyes hungrily taking in every detail from Aileen's curls to her tiny shoes and little brown coat, which was a hand-me-down from Mrs. Zwicker.

Aileen nodded and toddled to the edge of the carriage, peering over the top to look at the baby. He had fallen asleep, but that didn't stop Aileen from being curious. A pair of women approached and went by, nodding. "Good morning, Mrs. McLeod."

"Good morning," the woman said, standing and smiling as if nothing in the world was amiss. "It's a beautiful day."

"It certainly is. Will we see you on Saturday evening?"

I stood back a bit. I didn't know these women and they didn't know me. I'd deliberately kept things that way, but now it put me at a disadvantage.

"Oh, certainly! I wouldn't miss it. I'm volunteering for refreshments." She didn't offer anything more, though, and the pair went on their way, skirts swishing and heads together. She turned her attention back to me then, her expression not unkind, but definitely wary. She kept her voice low. "What in the world possessed you to take a child who wasn't yours?" she repeated, and the temporary reprieve was over.

"I swear, I thought she was my daughter." I tried to explain, but it sounded weak and unbelievable. I pushed forward, desperate. "You must understand. I checked all the hospitals, the papers, the orphanages, anywhere children were being cared for who were missing their parents. When I saw her, it *was* her. I swear." I lowered my voice, remembering that we were out in public. The last thing I needed was anyone hearing our conversation. "She lifted her little arms to me and everything was all right again." My throat clogged with tears, but I had to make this woman, this Mrs. McLeod, understand. "I didn't know. She was Aileen to me. I had no home, no husband, no family, but

I had her, and she had me, and I knew we would be all right. I thought she was… I didn't realize what I'd done until…" I stopped talking, my breath coming in small gasps, putting myself at the mercy of this stranger. "I don't even know your name," I whispered. She held my life in her hands, and I didn't even know her name.

"I'm Nora McLeod," she said, and to my surprise, she held out her hand. "Mrs. Nora McLeod. My husband is Captain Neil McLeod, a doctor at Camp Hill."

"McLeod," I repeated, and another memory slid into my consciousness. "Blond hair, blue eyes, tall." I met her gaze. "Kind and gentle."

Her face softened. "Yes, that's him."

"He…" I thought of that day I'd awakened. "He cared for my leg. He seemed like a very nice man." I met her gaze and swallowed. "And you, too. I remember you in your blue uniform. You… I mean the people at the hospital… you saved my life."

I stopped again. What on earth was I to do? I couldn't just hand over a child to a woman I didn't know. And I didn't want to. I wanted Aileen—Clara—it was all so confusing—with me. "Mrs. McLeod, we aren't going to solve this today. I can't just hand her over to you because you say she's your niece. That would be—"

"Like what you did?"

The barb hit its mark and I flinched. She was right, of course. I was the one in the wrong, but I didn't know how to make her understand that at the time I truly believed Aileen was my missing baby. I didn't know how to show her how lost I was and would be again; that I wasn't a bad person. What I knew for certain was that I wouldn't survive losing a child a second time. I couldn't do it. This little baby had saved me and given me a reason to go on. Without her, I had nothing.

"Sunday," I blurted out. "A few days is all I ask. You must provide proof this child is your niece." I forced myself to be strong. "I cannot just take your word."

She hesitated, and I saw a shadow pass over her face, but it cleared again quickly. "Sunday," she agreed. "But I must know where to find you."

"I work for Mr. and Mrs. Harold Zwicker, at their house on Pleasant Street." Aileen had since tired of looking at the baby and was now back at my side, clinging to my skirts. She didn't go to Mrs. McLeod, but instead looked up at her with a thumb in her mouth. She hadn't sucked her thumb in such a long time. I took heart that maybe this woman was Aileen's aunt and maybe she wasn't, but it was me Aileen turned to. I reached down and scooped her up. "But I don't want to meet you at my place of employment."

"At the Anglican church, then? I'll meet you at nine o'clock, before the service." Mrs. McLeod tugged at the wrists of her dress. "We will sort this out then, Mrs. Campbell. I am trusting you to keep your end of this bargain, and when we next meet, we will decide what to do."

My mouth dropped open in surprise. "You mean… you're not taking her?"

Mrs. McLeod's eyes sharpened. "I didn't say that. But I'm not unsympathetic to your situation. I am not going to turn you in. At least, not yet. Please don't betray my trust."

"I won't," I answered automatically. The baby in her carriage started to fuss, probably from being stopped for so long. I saw a corner of the blanket and it reminded me of all the days Aileen and I had gone walking, the miles we covered, and how beautiful those days had been. I was horribly jealous that Mrs. McLeod seemed to have it all—a husband, a new baby, a life that was her own. Now she was trying to claim mine, and I wanted to be angry about it, only she was being far more generous than she might have been under the circumstances. Someone else might have had me in handcuffs already.

"At nine," she warned. "And Mrs. Campbell, if you are not prompt, the next visit will be at the Zwicker house with the authorities."

I nodded.

Two days. I had two days to come up with a plan to keep Aileen at my side.

Chapter Twenty-Eight

NORA

I barely noticed the chill in the air as I walked back home with James, the sewing notions forgotten. There was no doubt in my mind that the little girl I'd seen today was Clara, and the mention of the odd little birthmark had clinched it. I'd seen the look on Charlotte Campbell's face when I'd mentioned it, full of surprise and guilt. I probably should have insisted that Clara come home with me immediately, but something held me back. It seemed, on the surface, to be simple. Clara was my niece, Evvie's little sister. She belonged with her family.

But I remembered this woman. Oh, not specifically, but I had clear images in my head, ones that would never go away—of women at the hospital, bloody, bruised, and dirty, waking without their babies, weeping for their dead or missing children. I'd had to harden myself against their tortured cries, building a wall around myself to withstand the heaviest emotions of that horrible time. But now that I was a mother, I couldn't imagine what I would do if suddenly James was torn from my arms. Maybe this Mrs. Campbell was telling the truth and she'd truly been so traumatized that she'd believed Clara to be her child in the days after the explosion. Or maybe she'd been so desperate, she'd taken the child to replace the one she'd lost. Either way, it was clear she hadn't been in her right mind, and instead of being angry, I was filled with pity and understanding. I had my own losses, but I hadn't lost my only child and my home all at once.

The house was empty when we returned; I had forgotten my promise to collect Evelyn from Grammie's and would have to get her later. Buttons was curled in front of the stove, dozing. It was quiet, too quiet. James looked up at me with wide, innocent eyes, and I suddenly gathered him close, closing my eyes while my lip quivered.

I couldn't help but put myself in the other woman's shoes, waking up and in pain, not knowing the fate of her child. Now I was going to take another child from her, when clearly all this woman wanted was to be a mother. Could I really be responsible for hurting another human being that way? It seemed so very cruel.

But the child wasn't just any child—she was my flesh and blood. Evvie's sister. I owed it to Jane to keep the girls together, to raise them together.

A year ago, I hadn't even been pregnant. I'd been full of purpose and dreams, thinking of the possibility of pursuing medical school, happy to be single and independent. If Clara came home with me now, I would be a mother of three. Three. And there was Neil to consider. How would he feel about having another mouth to feed, another child to raise that wasn't his? How could I ask him to take that on, especially after the way things had changed before his departure?

Oh, how I wished I could talk to him about this. I went to the kitchen rocker and sat, settling James at my breast and then leaning my head back against the solid oak and closing my eyes. Neil would know what to do. From the beginning, I'd been able to confide in him. He'd been a steadying presence, never judging, never criticizing. In fact, the only time he'd criticized me at all was the day I'd berated him for leaving.

I ran a finger over James's downy head as a tear crept down my cheek. I'd been so angry with Neil because I'd been afraid. I could admit that to myself now. I was still afraid. Afraid of the war, afraid he might contract this awful virus, afraid of my own feelings and worrying I might have destroyed what regard he had for me. But then I remembered what he'd said about why he cared about me. He'd called me the strongest woman he'd ever known, and I decided right here and now that I would live up to that praise.

And that meant bringing Clara home where she belonged.

October 12, 1918

I brushed my hands over my skirt and affected a smile as I poured cup after cup of punch for those gathered at the Hackmatack Inn for the Red Cross benefit. Gram was staying with Evelyn and James, and to my surprise William was in attendance with Amelie Payzant on his arm… Goodness, seventeen and he was courting. He looked dashing, all spit and polished, and Amelie wore an adorable blush as he leaned close and spoke to her. Her dress was plainer than some of the others but lovely just the same. My sharp eye picked Amelie's parents out of the crowd, and I gave them a nod. The couple was so very young, and that worried me a little. And yet a part of me softened, because there was something so innocent and sweet about young love.

"Punch?" I asked an older couple I didn't recognize. These days people easily traveled from Halifax to escape the city. The train made things so convenient, and Chester was a beautiful little town. There were a number of hotels that catered to guests from the city and from New England. And why not? This was a beautiful time of year, with all the trees showing off their brilliant colours next to the steadfast blue of the Atlantic. But as I looked around at the gathered crowd, I decided it was the last social event I'd attend for a while. I worried that every man and woman I didn't recognize might be carrying sickness. My children needed me. Three of them, now that Clara would soon be home.

"I'd love some punch," the woman answered, smiling. "What a lovely event. I just adored the soloist from Montreal."

I handed her the cup and smiled. "It was a lovely rendition of 'Keep the Home Fires Burning'," I admitted. "Hopefully this will soon be over." I thought of Neil and added, "And hopefully our men will return home soon."

"Is your husband overseas?" the man asked, also accepting a cup of punch.

"He's a doctor with the medical corps," I said, "and currently working in Boston. Before that we both served at Camp Hill Hospital in Halifax."

The woman's face lit up. "You're a Bluebird, aren't you?" she exclaimed.

"Was," I said, pleased nonetheless that the woman seemed happy to make my acquaintance. "I had a baby in June."

"Our congratulations to you both. We should take our seats again. Apparently there is an elocutionist from Charlottetown reciting 'Channel Firing'. It's a particular favourite."

The crowd settled once more, and I stepped back from the table and snuck close to the door of the room adorned with flowers, flags, and chairs for the audience. It was there I listened to the words of Hardy's poem, there I pressed my hand to my heart, vowing to somehow bring my family together. Not just Clara, but Neil, too, and perhaps a child of our own, raising them all as brothers and sisters, joined not only by blood but by love. I'd been so blind. I'd thought love meant settling and perhaps even boredom, but the reality was so different. It was kindness and patience and steadfastness. It was knowing what the other person needed and doing it with a glad heart, not for any sort of reward other than love itself. Neil had given me that from the start, and when he came home, I would do the same for him. Alley had been fun and adventurous and exciting, but that wasn't love. It never had been. And it killed me that Neil had to go away to make me wake up—and grow up.

Will had driven Amelie in the car, and the two of them drove me back to the house before Will delivered Amelie to her door, seeing her home properly. When I went inside, all was silent and dark. The children were in bed asleep, Gram was tucked into Evelyn's bed with her, old and young, wisdom and innocence together in a hand-bound quilt. Tomorrow I would add one more to this little house. All I had to do was meet Mrs. Campbell at the church at nine. The woman had no choice but to relinquish Clara, and our family would be complete.

Chapter Twenty-Nine

CHARLOTTE

October 12, 1918

It seemed as if half the town was at the Hackmatack for the Red Cross event, which made it the perfect time for me to reach the train station. The chances of me running into anyone I knew, or anyone even taking notice, were greatly reduced. I carried Aileen on one arm and a single bag with my other. Just the bare necessities, and all the money I'd been putting aside.

Tonight we were traveling to Halifax. Tomorrow morning we would continue on to Saint John, New Brunswick, and from there, I didn't know. Maybe we'd go to Ontario. Maybe we would cross the border and start a new life in the States. We would change our names and start over, a brand-new life. I'd get a job. We'd manage, and we'd never be separated.

I refused to look at the agent as I purchased my ticket. It was nearly dark now, each day shorter than the last. Aileen wanted down, then fussed—she was tired. It was close to her bedtime. She could sleep on the train, I assured myself. It would be fine. By the time Mrs. McLeod looked for me at the church, we would be long gone. I shoved down my guilt.

"Mummy," Aileen whined, throwing her weight against my leg. "Tired."

"I know, darling, I know. The train will soon be here, and we'll be on an adventure."

She gave a little cry. "No want."

My nerves were already frayed; hearing her fret set them further on edge. "Hush, now," I said, my voice low. There was not another soul on the platform and for that I was grateful. "Be a good girl, Aileen."

She was two and talking more and more with each day. I was glad we were leaving now, when she was so young, when I didn't have to worry about her speaking to others and revealing details. Disappearing was going to be hard, but I'd learned my lesson. Chester hadn't been far enough. We needed to go far away where no one would ever be able to recognize us.

"No, Mummy!" Aileen whined again. "Clara."

I whipped my head around and stared at her, but she was rubbing her eyes with one hand and held my skirt in her other fist. "What did you say?"

She didn't answer, just cried a little. I knew this was simply because she was overtired, but had she actually said "Clara"? Or was my mind playing tricks on me? I gathered her into my arms and tried to soothe her, but my heart beat faster as worry and doubts crowded in. This wasn't the same as before. Not the same as last December, when I had honestly and truly believed it was my daughter in that hospital crib. I knew now that her name was

Clara, and that her mother and father were dead. She was an orphan.

I settled her on my knee, cuddling her close to reassure us both. I hadn't been wrong when I'd told myself that she needed me. That her mother wasn't looking for her because she was dead. Those things were all true. She'd been sent to me for a reason.

I held her close, hanging onto more than just her sweet, small body. I had to hang onto my rationalization because if I didn't, I'd have to face that she might be an orphan, but she wasn't without family. She had an aunt. A cousin. A sister. Uncles, great-grandparents. The horrible, selfish truth was that I needed her far more than she needed me.

"I love you, Aileen," I said, kissing her soft head, knowing she wasn't Aileen, knowing that fact and yet unable to sever that identity completely.

"Wuv you, Mummy," she whispered back.

Tears slid from my eyes and I let them, though I held back the sobs that were building inside, screaming to get out. Who was I? Who had I become? Had I been so lonely, so desperate, so broken that I could justify this lie and still sleep at night? The child curled her hands about my neck, comforting me, and all I could think was that it was just so wrong. So horribly, horribly wrong. That woman—Mrs. McLeod—had lost her sister, her parents in the same explosion that had nearly taken my life and most certainly taken that of the real Aileen. She knew of the birthmark. She could provide this child with a beautiful life that wasn't a lie, wasn't on the run with a mother who would always be looking over her shoulder, wondering if today would be the day she'd be caught.

Leaving tonight wasn't in Clara's best interest. I had to start thinking of her that way, didn't I? Running was the ultimate act of selfishness for my own ends, but not hers. And what kind of mother did that make me? A mother never, ever put herself before her child. But that was exactly what I'd been doing for months now. I'd been protecting myself instead of doing what was right. Frank… Oh God. Frank would be so ashamed of me. I was ashamed of myself.

Clara had fallen asleep in my arms, and I held on for precious minutes. She was so tired she never stirred, even when the train arrived and departed again in a puff of black smoke and a burst of the whistle. Darkness fell completely and the stars poked through the inky blanket of sky, one by one as the half moon shone, casting a faint light over the town I'd come to call home. I didn't want to rise; I knew when I did that this was over, and so very final. And yet it was cold, and I couldn't sit on a bench at the train station forever. I had to do what was right, even as I knew it would devastate me yet again.

Finally I got up, went to the station master, asked if I could leave my suitcase there until the morning, and exchanged my ticket. He stared at me curiously but obliged, locking my case away. Then I began the walk toward Victoria Street and the house with the little front verandah and the blue door. The house where, according to Mrs. Zwicker, the Crowells had lived until last December sixth, when Mr. and Mrs. Crowell had died in the explosion and their two sons had gone to live with their grandparents. How they'd also lost a daughter in the explosion, but their surviving daughter, a nurse, had returned from Halifax with a husband, her niece, and a baby. Nora McLeod was known in this town. Her family was respected. And they lived on Victoria Street in a house with a blue door.

My arms ached as we shuffled along, my limp present but not paining. I absorbed each sweet flutter of breath against my neck as Clara slept, drew in the scent of her hair and a hint of cinnamon from the cookie she'd eaten only hours before. All too soon I stood staring at the house, the windows dark even before blackout hours. For the briefest of moments, I reconsidered. We could still take the morning train. Escape the province and I would never have to be alone again.

But it was wrong. And I'd been in the wrong for so long, it was time for me to make it right. To be the woman Frank married—even if it pained me right to my very bones. To right the wrongs I'd committed in the name of pain and of love and of loneliness.

I shifted Clara in my arms and climbed the front steps one at a time. Raised my hand, swallowed around the gigantic lump in my throat, and knocked on the heavy wood. Once, twice, three times. I waited a few moments and then knocked again. The sound matched the heavy beating of my heart. If she didn't open the door, maybe it would be a sign…

The door opened and she stood there, this Mrs. McLeod, her hair loose about her shoulders and a knitted shawl over a simple cotton nightgown. "Mrs. Campbell," she said in surprise, her gaze dropping to the slumbering child in my arms.

I took a breath. Let it out. Took another, lifted my chin. "She should be with you. With her family. I'm so, so sorry. I thought she was… I needed…" I stumbled around the words, tears in my throat. I struggled to clear the blockage, but my lip quivered, and I couldn't stop it. "I never intended for any of this to happen."

To my surprise, Mrs. McLeod reached out and put her hand on my arm. "None of us did. We've all lost, haven't we? Oh, Mrs. Campbell, I wish there was a way we could both walk away from this whole."

It was more generous than I deserved. Mrs. Zwicker was so right; this family was good people. "Her sister… she's here?"

Mrs. McLeod nodded. "Upstairs, asleep with my

grandmother." She opened the door wider. "Would you like to come in, Mrs. Campbell?"

I shook my head quickly. This was hard enough without stepping over the threshold into what would be Aileen—Clara's—life. One world into another, a life in which I didn't belong. I needed to go. I didn't want to, because the moment I walked away I knew I would never see this precious little girl again. But prolonging it was just as painful. I moved forward to shift Clara out of my arms and into those of her aunt. She roused a little, but didn't register the change in embrace, instead curling into her aunt's shoulder as I withdrew my empty arms.

"You don't want to say goodbye?" she asked softly.

I shook my head. "She wouldn't understand. I don't understand. It would only upset her. The kindest thing I can do for her is let her go without that pain."

Pain that was right now slicing my heart in two. I'd lost my child not once, but twice. I remembered waking in the hospital and thinking if I didn't have Aileen, I had no reason to go on. This little girl, with her curls and sparkling eyes and sweet smile, had given me that reason for ten precious months.

"Mrs. Campbell…" Nora McLeod's voice was soft in the cool night. "This must be so hard for you. Please don't think I'm ignorant of how horrible this is. I'm so very sorry for your losses. We've all lost so much. I just want you to remember something."

I lifted my gaze to meet hers, amazed at the strength and compassion I saw there.

"I thought Clara was dead. If you hadn't taken her from that hospital… well, I might never have known she was still alive. I don't know if you're a religious woman or not, but it feels like you were meant to have her… to bring her back home to us. I'm just so sorry that the cost to you is so dear."

I was crying now, cold tears slipping down my cheeks as I nodded, too overcome to try to speak.

"Thank you with all my heart," Mrs. McLeod whispered. "And good luck to you, Mrs. Campbell. I'll be praying for you. I hope you find happiness."

I had to go. I was hanging onto my composure by a tenuous thread, so tempted to reach out and hold Clara once more, to pretend that she was Aileen in my arms, to pretend that my daughter hadn't died that day and ignore the fact that I would never know what had truly happened to her.

"I love her," I managed, the words strangled. "You must know that."

"I do," she answered. "Because you are doing the right thing for her, not for yourself. That is what we do as mothers. We put our children first."

She was right. I had always tried to do what was best for Aileen. Except I'd failed to keep her safe. With that knowledge sitting heavily on my heart, I turned around and hobbled away.

I couldn't look back. The door clicked as it closed, and inside a woman was reunited with her niece and in the morning a little girl would have her sister back. My steps took me down the hill, Back Harbour on my right, the fresh, salty air beckoning. The moon still hung in the sky, lighting my way, even as the rest of the town was dark. In the morning, the Zwickers would realize I was gone. There was not a single soul in this world who would miss me. The grief in my soul was now so deep, so profound, that even tears failed. Instead, I walked, one halting step after the other, toward the shoreline.

Were there U-boats lurking out there somewhere, lying in wait? Or had they retreated across the ocean, now that the tide of the war had turned? Oh, if only Frank had survived, and we could have begun again. Or my parents, providing a safe haven for me to heal and start over. But I had no one. No one but Winnie, and a friendship only went so far. Winnie would never understand what I'd done. Aileen was dead, and I could only hope that heaven existed, and Frank was somewhere looking after her until I could join them.

Despite the autumn chill, I took off my shoes and my stockings, then lifted my skirts and waded into the frigid water of the North Atlantic. The cold was like needles in my feet and calves, and I lifted my head to gaze at the moon once more.

There was no one to miss me at all.

Chapter Thirty

NORA

October 13, 1918

I skipped church on Sunday to deal with the change in the family. Clara woke disoriented and upset. She didn't remember me and cried for Mrs. Campbell, inconsolable as I tried everything I could think of to soothe her—breakfast, toys, even Buttons didn't distract her from her distress. Snuggling her was out of the question; she saw me as a stranger, and why wouldn't she? Evelyn was only five and didn't understand anything—why her sister had been alive and not dead, and why she was with us now. She was excited and subsequently disappointed when Clara didn't seem to remember her, either.

In addition to trying to get Clara to settle, there were explanations to make to family, starting with my grandmother who awakened in the morning with no idea what had transpired the night before. I had James to tend to, and it was all so exhausting, I just wanted to have a nap. But the worst was when news spread through the town grapevine that a pair of shoes and stockings had been found on the shore of Back Harbour, and that it was suspected it was the maid for the Zwickers, who had awakened to neither an employee nor her baby. When I heard that, I sat down and cried, feeling horribly responsible. I should have insisted she come in. I should have… helped her more instead of letting her walk away.

The fact that said baby was now at my house meant more questions, but I was determined from the start that I would not malign the poor woman who had, most likely, taken her own life. When the time came, I would explain that Charlotte Campbell had adopted Clara, thinking her an orphan from the explosion, and when the truth came to light, she did the right thing and returned her to the arms of her family.

It was close enough to the truth. The least I could do was not villainize a woman who had simply been in pain and desperate. Another mother who had lost her child.

That had been Sunday. By Monday morning, I hoped that things might form some sort of new normal. When Clara still cried and barely ate, I realized that this process was going to take time and a whole lot of patience. But eventually Clara would adjust, the gossip would die down, and I would get used to now having three children under five to care for on my own. Gram was nearby to help, and I wasn't too proud accept her assistance. I also wondered if inviting the Zwicker children to visit would help. Surely familiar faces would put Clara more at ease.

But first I had to find a way to explain everything to Neil, who was definitely not expecting to come home to three children.

Not that I thought it would be a problem. Neil loved children and this was my niece—a miracle, really. Still, it might be nice to warn him and not spring it on him when he returned. I wasn't even sure where we stood as husband and wife. All I knew was that this… silence between us had to end. Nothing could be solved without talking.

I'd write tonight, after everyone was in bed and the house was quiet. It was my favourite time of day, when I could sit with a cup of tea, enjoy the quiet, and knit or read. I'd also write to Mrs. Thompson, who would be thrilled that Clara was indeed alive and back where she belonged. The thought cheered me, helped me deal with the frustration of Clara continually pushing me away.

It was, all in all, a solid plan. Until the mail arrived, and there was a letter from the hospital in Boston. It wasn't addressed in Neil's handwriting, though, and my stomach knotted looking at the unfamiliar script.

James was in his highchair and Evvie was trying to entertain Clara by showing her the doll, Muriel, and the clothes that Mrs. Thompson had sewed out of scrap material. I sat in a kitchen chair and opened the letter.

Dear Mrs. McLeod…

I bit down on my lip.

The rest of the words blurred together, and I read the letter twice while resting my forehead on my hand. He was alive, thank God, but the letter was dated four days earlier and I knew that might have changed. The very virus he'd gone to fight had struck him at the hospital and he was now in quarantine. This was exactly why I hadn't wanted him to go. Fear gripped my heart. What if he never came back? What if I never got to tell him how I actually felt about him?

He had to be all right. He must, for I couldn't contemplate

otherwise. Not now, not after we'd been through so much and now that Clara was back where she belonged.

I made myself a cup of tea and gave myself a stern talking-to. I'd been wrong to be angry about him going to Boston. Neil would have been in the thick of it, no matter if it was Boston or Halifax, because Neil went where the need was greatest. And yes, perhaps if he'd stayed in Halifax, I could have been near him, perhaps could have cared for him while he was sick—so many of the doctors and nurses contracted the disease—but what if I also got sick? There were the children to consider… Neil would have made me stay away.

There was only one thing I could truly do right now, and that was write back. Tell him I was no longer angry. That I admired him for what he was doing and supported him—the way he'd supported me every step of the way since the moment we'd met. The news about Clara could wait. What he needed most was to know that he was wanted—needed—at home.

I just hoped it reached him in time, and perhaps gave him the encouragement he needed to recover.

Hastily, while the children still played, I wrote out a short but heartfelt letter and then prepared the children for the walk to the post office. Clara kept looking around, fearful, as if searching for the woman who'd been her mother for nearly a year, and I kept up a cheerful chatter as I tucked Clara's arms in her little coat and slipped shoes on her feet. Evelyn helped, which allayed some of the fussing as Clara was already warming to her older sister. I got out the carriage for James and before long we were on our way through town.

As I advised the two older children to hold hands, I shook my head and marveled. How I wished Jane were here to see her two daughters together once more. Raising them, being able to see them grow up, was now my privilege. Never easy, but such a profound gift.

We mailed the letter. I took the children to the shop and treated them to a sweet—there was much to celebrate, and Clara's reticence began to melt like the chocolate drop she'd put in her mouth. When we arrived back home, the small ones tired from walking and with sticky fingers and cheeks, I took a moment to say a little prayer for Neil. Could I do this without him? Absolutely. I was strong and resourceful. But did I want to? No. I loved him. It had snuck up on me so slowly, but there it was. I loved my husband. I hadn't on the day we took our vows, but I did now, and I longed to tell him so.

"Please come home, Neil," I whispered, closing my eyes. "We need you. I need you."

Perhaps if the letter didn't reach him, my words might somehow.

October 30, 1918

I hung the sheets on the clothesline and prayed for the fine weather to hold. I was up early to get the wash started and could see my breath in the air, but the rising sun and slight breeze promised a good drying day. James had been up early and fussing—I suspected he had a tooth bothering him as he was drooling incessantly, and his top gum was swollen. He was now down for a rare morning nap and the girls were playing in the yard while I pinned the sheets to the line, their giggles a happy sound on the air.

I paused for a few moments, watching them. Evelyn had a ball that she tossed for Clara, who, instead of picking it up and throwing it, insisted on kicking it, sometimes hard enough that she fell onto her bottom. Evvie would laugh, then Clara would join in, the sound of the laughter like bells echoing in my ears. It had been more than two weeks since Clara had come back to us, and while she was still a little reserved with me, she adored having a playmate in Evelyn. I was smiling and reaching for a pillowcase when I heard my name.

"Nora?"

I froze. My name, spoken by a voice I hadn't heard in such a long time, gruff and with just a hint of south shore softness on the *r*. My heart clubbed against my ribs as I slowly turned and saw a man standing maybe twenty feet away, in uniform, but so thin it hung on his frame and an eyepatch covered his left eye.

"Alley," I breathed, shock keeping me rooted to the spot. My gaze darted to the children, who hadn't yet noticed his presence, and to the back door of the house, beyond which James slept. Our child.

"It's good to see you, Nora." He smiled a little, his lips tipping up at the corners, but it was a ghost of the charming smile he'd always aimed my way. As I grew accustomed to the surprise of seeing him here, in the flesh, other emotions trickled in. Disbelief. Dismay. Anger. Relief, too, that he was back on Canadian soil. Letting him go hadn't meant wishing any ill upon him. Now that he was standing here, right in front of me, I didn't know what to feel at all.

"You're back."

He stepped forward, pointed at his eye. "Earned myself a berth on the *Araguaya* and docked two days ago."

And now he was here. In Chester. At my house. Why?

Alley frowned, took another step forward. "I went to the house on Henry Street. The woman there told me where to find you. I was surprised it wasn't your sister. Though she never did like me." Another faded smile touched his lips.

I swallowed, unsure of what to say. So many questions sat on my tongue; so much had happened, I didn't know where to start. I decided on the most relevant to his last statement. "My sister died in the explosion last year."

His face fell—well, as much as it could. I noticed now that there was a puckered scar peeking out from behind his patch, and his skin had a wrinkled texture from his temple down to his neck. Burn marks? Scarring? I didn't plan to get close enough to examine it.

"God, Nora, I'm so sorry."

"My parents, too." I realized the girls had stopped playing and were regarding us curiously. "Evvie, take Clara into the house, won't you, sweetheart? You can each have a cookie. I'll be there in a minute."

"Come on, Clara!" Evelyn reached for her sister's hand. "We can have cookies!"

"Cookie," parroted Clara, taking Evelyn's hand and toddling a little behind, her shorter legs churning to keep up.

"Your nieces." His gaze followed their progress to the house. "You're caring for them?"

I nodded. "My brothers are with our grandparents nearby. We moved into the house in September."

"But the hospital…"

I looked away from him. "I finished nursing in January."

"A lot has changed."

More than you know, I thought, but kept the comment to myself. Old resentment was resurrected as I slid my gaze to him again. He might have known about all these things if he'd bothered to write. If he hadn't just disappeared and left me alone, worried. I thought of James, his son. I should say something. So why was I just standing here, silent?

"Do you hate me, Nora?" he asked, his voice soft and entreating. It reached in and touched a part of me that had responded to him a year ago, a part that had looked forward to fun and gaiety and escape. No, I didn't hate him. Though it would be easier, perhaps, if I did.

"Of course not," I answered, my voice barely above a whisper. "Why are you here, Alley?" I lifted my chin. How many times had I wished to have an opportunity to ask him why he'd disappeared? I wouldn't squander this one. "Why are you here when you couldn't have been bothered to write to me, not once, in all those months?"

His gaze shifted. "But you said you've been living here."

"Only since September. Almost a year after you left. I wrote you every week, sometimes more. Didn't you get my letters?"

I wished I could take the last question back. He could easily say he'd never received them, couldn't he, and get himself off the hook? But it was out there now, and I waited for an answer.

"I did," he confessed, crossing his arms in front of his chest. "I just…"

Then nothing. He just stopped talking, looked horribly uncomfortable, and I turned away, disgusted.

He wasn't a coward. The man had joined up, fought a war, been wounded. I wouldn't call him a coward about that. But he was on this point. I went to him, standing so close there was no way he could avoid me. "All I want to know is if you intended that all along. To step out with me, to do… that… with me, and then leave me behind."

His face was red now, and the blush accentuated the wound that rippled along the side of his cheek. "I-I did," he stammered. "It was wrong of me, and not gentlemanly at all. I was afraid of going overseas, and I wanted to live each moment in case I didn't make it back. Not that I didn't care for you," he hurried to assure me. "I did. I had so much fun during our time together. But when I left… I didn't intend to come back for you."

"Even though you lied and said you loved me."

"Yes, even though I said that." His throat bobbed as he swallowed. "What do you want me to say? I'm not proud of it, Nora."

Once again words sat on my tongue. Words like "Even though our night together could have left me with your baby" hovered there, begging to be spoken. He'd admitted to receiving my letters, so he had to know about James, but hadn't asked me anything about our child. Could he pretend our baby didn't exist, or did he plan to stick around, a constant reminder of my gullibility, my carelessness, a thorn in the side of the life I was building with my husband?

I had often wondered what would happen if I saw Alley again. The truth was surprising. Nothing. I felt nothing. I had a husband now, a man who not only cared for me but stepped up with no hesitation whatsoever. A man of honour and integrity. The feelings I'd had for Alley paled in comparison to those in my heart for Neil.

And yet Neil hadn't written. Two weeks had passed since I'd read the letter about his illness, and there'd been no word. I kept writing to him, though, and tried not to think that he hadn't written because he'd stopped loving me. Perhaps he was still too sick. Perhaps the nurses simply didn't have time to pen messages to relatives. If something dire had happened, I would have heard something.

Amazing. Despite everything, I still had faith. Neil was not Alley and never could be. I trusted him. Our marriage was not without difficulty, but Neil had proven time and again that he was a man of principle.

I reached up to tuck a piece of hair behind my ear, and Alley's gaze followed before sliding back to my eyes. "You're wearing a ring." His voice was flat, and the hint of sparkle left his good eye.

"I'm married," I replied, and I smiled as a warmth filled my heart. I was surprised and pleased that all I truly wanted was for Neil to walk into the back yard while the kids were playing, to share his warm smile, to lay on his side in bed and share bits of his day with me. The hot flush of my whirlwind romance with Alley had cooled, but the life I shared with Neil—the life I wanted to share with him, with our family—that was everything.

"I hope you didn't come here hoping to pick up where we left off," I said. "Alley, I'm glad you're home and that you're safe. Of course I am. But when you left, when you never wrote, when the only information I had was from a casualty board saying you'd been wounded, you can hardly blame me for moving on."

"Of course not." He took a step back now, his good eye looking pained, his lips set in a thin line.

"Mummy, can I get Clara and me some milk?"

We both turned toward Evelyn, whose lips held traces of cookie crumbs as she stood in the doorway.

"Just a small cup, and be careful, please."

"I will! Thank you, Mummy."

Alley looked back at her. "Mummy?"

I shrugged. "The explosion changed everything. I've been that little girl's mother since December sixth. She asked a while ago if she could call me Mummy instead of Auntie Nora. She's my niece but she's also my daughter, Alley. As is her sister. I'm sorry. When you left, I was a single working woman, only responsible for myself. Things change. I have a husband and children now."

Guilt gnawed at me, but I still hadn't mentioned James. Neither had he.

"There's no hope for you and me, then," he said, and he lifted his chin and looked away, almost as if he were pouting.

"You left me. Did you really expect there to be?"

His expression iced over and he stepped back, shoving his hands into his pockets. "No, I suppose not. I won't trouble you any longer, Nora." Then he turned away and started walking toward the front of the house again, and the street beyond. He had to know. If he'd received my letters, he must. But he wasn't even going to ask, was he?

"Alley, wait!" I called out, taking a few steps in his direction. He spun around and I stared at him for a long moment, needing to somehow imprint how he looked on my mind, using it as a permanent marker of the end of our association. "I asked if you expected there to be hope for us. But what I want to know is… did you want there to be?"

He smiled his old, charming smile, though the light of it didn't quite reach his eye. "Sure, why not?" he asked. "We had fun together, didn't we?"

Fun. Yes, we had. And sometimes I missed fun. But there was so much more to life. Not just responsibilities but the richness to be found in meeting those responsibilities, to be found in gratitude and home and security. Fun was a rather fragile, transient concept on which to base a relationship or way of life. It didn't last.

And a man who looked at our relationship and said "why not" and "we had fun" wasn't the kind who wanted to settle down with a child. For the first time, I realized that things had worked out exactly as they were supposed to. Not just the good parts, but the losses, too. And sure, that still pained me every day. But it also made me appreciate the life I had.

"Goodbye, Alley," I said.

"Goodbye, Nora. Take care."

He turned once more and walked on. Just as he reached the corner of the house, he slid his hand out of his pocket, half turned, and gave a little wave. A piece of paper fluttered out of his pocket, but before I could call out, he'd resumed walking. When he was gone, I went to the thorny rosebush and plucked out the paper.

Then I looked up in the direction he'd gone. And down at the paper again.

Dear Alley,

I haven't yet heard from you and I worry about you all the time. But I have some news I want to share, and I apologize for how brief this is but I'm due at the hospital. I'm going to have a baby, Alley. Your baby. Please, stay safe so you can come home and make us a family. Please write when you can.

Affectionately, Nora

He'd known. The entire time he'd known and ignored my pleas to write, even though I'd told him I was pregnant. And today… today he'd known too, had actually carried my letter, but he hadn't let on, hadn't asked about the baby at all. Alley had shown his true colours. Part of me was angry at how easily he was able to shake off any responsibility. Another part of me was relieved that he wasn't a threat to the life I so desperately wanted to build.

And perhaps I should feel guilty about that, but he'd fooled me during our brief courtship, making false promises, taking advantage of my affections. I compared his behaviour to Neil's, who was willing to take on not one but two children and a wife. I'd accused him of trying to rescue everyone, but was that sort of duty and compassion truly a fault or just a way to keep him at arm's length? Neil, who had given so much and, as he said, got little in return.

I needed him to come home. I needed him to be all right. For as much as Alley had left me disillusioned, I knew one thing for certain. I would not expect the same behaviour from Neil. Alley's deception did not mean I couldn't trust anyone else. It only highlighted the strong relationships in my life. The people who mattered, who had stuck by me when everything had fallen apart. Neil. Mrs. Thompson. John and Marvin. My grandparents. Will and Stephen. They were my family. And while I did still miss nursing—perhaps I always would—I also knew that what was most important was home... and home was where I was right now.

"Mummy! Clara spilled her milk." Evvie popped out of the door again, her face wreathed in anxiety. "I'm so sorry. I was watching and then Buttons wanted some and—"

I laughed, my heart lighter than it had been in weeks. "It's all right, Evvie. No use crying over it. It's easily wiped up. Come on. Let's give a little to Buttons and then see if James is awake."

I held out my hand, Evelyn took it, and we went inside to the warmth and comfort of home.

Chapter Thirty-One

NORA

November 11, 1918

The bells rang out, clanging a victorious hosanna that drew people from their homes and created impromptu celebrations on the street.

It was over. I pressed my fingers to my eyes, trying to hold back tears and failing. Even though everyone seemed to know the armistice was imminent, until this moment it wasn't truly real. The boys were coming home. The guns were silent.

We had all lost so much. In the Chester area alone, over fifty had given their lives.

"Mummy, why are the bells so loud?" Evelyn tugged on my sweater, looking up with wide, inquisitive eyes. She looked so much like Jane, it gave my heart a pang. Evvie's hair was tied back with a green ribbon—still her favourite one from last Christmas—and she wore a new sweater that Grammie had knit in the same rich green. There were roses in her cheeks and the tip of her nose was pink from the cold.

"Because the war is over, sweetheart." I knelt and folded Evelyn into a hug, smiling through my tears. "It means the horrible war is over."

And yet I knew nothing would really change in Evvie's world. Her father wouldn't be coming home. Nor her mother. But I chose to look on the bright, sunny side. Clara had been miraculously returned to us. We had this house, and the damned thing was over before Will or Stephen could enlist. Thank God.

Clara toddled over in her navy dress and boots and one of Evelyn's sweaters from a few years past. The light-blue yarn made her blue eyes even brighter, and her cheeks were equally rosy as she reached up to take my other hand. James was sitting up in his carriage, looking around with wide eyes as we prepared to join the rest of the community in celebrations. And still the clanging from the Anglican church continued. My lip trembled. It seemed like the last four years all coalesced into this moment: the victories, the losses, the struggles, and the happy times in one big ball of emotion. I wondered what the celebrations were like in Halifax, at the hospital, where the soldiers could finally know that victory was theirs. Would they be happy, or would they mourn the friends and comrades who wouldn't make it home?

The bittersweet feeling surprised me, but I let it in. There was only one thing that would make today any better, and that would be—

"Nora?"

I whirled around and there he was, coming toward me, thinner than I liked, his face still pale and gaunt, but the same blond-haired and blue-eyed man who'd walked into my life during its darkest moments, holding me when I cried and making me smile when I had every reason in the world not to.

"Neil!"

I let go of Clara's hand, left the children in their little trio and ran to him, abandoning caution and flinging my arms around him. His right arm came around me as he dropped the bag he held in his left, and he squeezed me tightly as we clung to each other in joyous reunion.

"That's an unexpected greeting," he murmured in my ear, and I laughed, the feeling so happy and free, I didn't know what to do with it.

"Oh, I'm so glad you're home! Why didn't you write to say you were coming? All I had was the note from the hospital saying you were recovering. I was afraid you… after what I said…" I stepped back, but still gripped his forearms, as if afraid he would slip from my grasp.

"I wanted to surprise you. And I have things I want to say but I didn't want to put them in a letter. Instead, I've arrived in the middle of celebrations." He smiled then, the wide, warm smile I remembered. So genuine and unaffected and I laughed again, from relief and pure joy of seeing his face.

"I can't believe you're here. The celebration can wait. It'll be going on for hours. Come inside, Neil." I let my gaze hold his. "Come home."

He nodded, then looked over my shoulder at the cloverleaf of children watching the two of us with wide eyes and open mouths. I smiled. "Evelyn, Uncle Neil is home."

Evelyn took one look at him, started to cry, and ran to the house.

I looked at Neil, perplexed. Evvie loved Neil. She had from

the beginning, when she'd sat on his knee on Christmas Eve. Yes, he'd been gone, but only for a few months. Surely she hadn't forgotten him.

"We'll get to the bottom of it," Neil said easily, and then his gaze fell on Clara. "And who is this?"

I put my hand on his arm. "This is my niece, Clara. Oh, I have so much to tell you, and I also didn't want to put it in a letter. She made her way back to us, Neil. She came home the day before I got the letter saying you had contracted the flu. It's a bit of a miracle, really. And so you've returned to three children instead of two."

He shrugged. "What's one more? I'm lucky I made it back." He turned and cupped my face in his hands, his eyes haunted. "I saw too much death, Nora. Too many children. One more is a blessing."

"Does this mean you're home to stay?"

"Do you want me to be?"

I nodded. "I do." I started laughing again because the church bells didn't stop and the constant chiming added to the chaos of the day. "Let's take these two inside, sort out Evvie, and then talk, all right?"

"I'd like that a lot."

I picked up Neil's bag, then took Clara's hand. Neil plucked James out of the carriage, putting him on his arm and ruffling his downy hair with his other hand. James didn't fuss at all but snuggled in the way he'd done since the day he was born. I looked at the two of them and my heart overflowed. I would have to tell Neil about Alley's visit, but right now I just wanted to drink in the sight of him, to let in the relief of knowing he'd come home and had opened his arms to me.

Once inside, I went to find Evelyn. It didn't take long; the muffled sound of crying came from the girls' bedroom. I found Evelyn curled up on the bed with Buttons and Muriel, sniffling with tears on her cheeks.

"My goodness," I said softly, stepping inside. "What's wrong, sweetheart?"

"Nuffin."

But I knew it was a big ball of something, because I hadn't seen Evelyn cry like that since the day I'd had to tell her that Jimmy had died.

An idea started to glimmer.

"Aren't you happy Uncle Neil's home with us again?"

Evelyn sniffled, then gave a small nod.

"They why did you run off so upset?"

Evelyn hugged Muriel tighter. "I-I h-heard you t-talking to G-g-grammie that he was sick," she finally said. "You was cryin'. You t-told Grammie that Uncle Neil might d-die."

Oh, heavens. I had talked to my grandmother one night after the letter had come. I'd needed to confide in someone, wanted some advice. Not that I'd told Gram the intimate details of our marriage, just that I'd been upset with Neil for going to Boston in the first place and now he was sick. The conversation had not been meant for little ears, but Evvie had heard it just the same. "And that scared you?"

"I d-don't want Uncle Neil to die. Not like Mummy and Daddy and Grampie and Grammie. I w-want him to be my daddy."

"Oh, sweetheart. Come here. You need a hug. You've been through so much. Of course you were scared. I'll tell you a secret. I was scared, too. But now he's home, and the war is over, and we're going to be a family." I hoped I wasn't speaking presumptuously. The welcome hug from Neil hadn't exactly been platonic. It had felt very much like how a husband and wife would greet each other at such a moment.

Evelyn slid onto my lap and into my embrace.

"Evvie, you've had so many changes this past year. It's okay to be scared of losing those you love. It means you care for them very much, and they care for you too, and that's a beautiful thing, isn't it?"

Evelyn nodded against my sweater.

"Come out to the kitchen, now. We can all be together and you can help me cook a real celebration dinner." I lifted Evelyn off my knee and set her on the floor. "And Uncle Neil will be needing a big hug. He missed you, too."

Evelyn took my hand and we went to the kitchen together. Once there, she went to where Neil was sitting and climbed up onto his lap, then wrapped her arms around his neck and hugged him, hard. Neil closed his eyes and hugged her back. My heart expanded. He had such capacity for love, my husband.

After that, things relaxed and we set about enjoying the day. Evelyn helped me make an apple pie and we put it in to bake while Neil played with James and got to know Clara a little—she hid for a while, shy, but eventually showed him her toys, and that helped break the ice. Shortly after that Grammie, Grampie, and the boys arrived, filling the house with laughter and love. They brought with them a loaf of fresh bread and a mess of fish. I put potatoes on to boil and set about making mounds of fish cakes, opened up a jar of Gram's chow chow pickles, and heated up baked beans left over from Saturday's feed. There weren't enough chairs for everyone, but we made do, and the boys entertained the children while Neil and Grampie talked and Grammie and I washed dishes. It was growing dark when everyone went home. Finally, two exhausted little girls were tucked in, hugged and kissed, with Buttons settled at the foot of the bed.

Neil and I sat in the parlour next to the fire with cups of tea and as I rocked James I told him the story of Charlotte Campbell and Clara; Neil related tales from his time in Boston in low, sober tones. He also told me that his brother had used up the third of his nine lives, having been shot in the shoulder earlier in October, and the family would be relieved when Cameron was finally on home shores again.

Then while Neil took a hot, restorative bath, I nursed James until he fell asleep. James slept through the night now, and I had set up his crib in the "boys'" room, where Will and Stephen had slept during their childhood. I tucked him into it, covering him with the handmade crib quilt my mother had made for Evelyn.

I looked around me. Family was everywhere in this house. In the quilt, in the scratches on the woodwork, echoes of those who had left us in the cozy rooms and dusty corners. In the laughter of this afternoon when those who remained were all together; in the colour of Evelyn and Clara's eyes and the way Stephen gestured with his hands, so much like my father. There was so much I had once taken for granted but now cherished with every beat of my heart—along with the man who had come home today, opening his arms to me as I finally opened my heart to him.

I closed James's door quietly, the latch giving a small click in the quiet.

Neil had finished his bath and was in the bedroom, emptying out the bag he'd carried home with him. I took a few moments to get ready for bed, my heart beating now from nervous anticipation. It had been six weeks since we'd slept in the same bed. And in the month before that, things had been strained and conversation stilted.

When I returned to the bedroom, Neil was already beneath the covers and the lamp was burning beside the bed, casting a warm, soft glow over the room. He looked better, perhaps after a good meal and a hot bath—sometimes simple things provided the best medicine. I got into bed and turned to my side, facing him, and he did the same, and for long moments we lay there, smiling at each other.

"It's good to be home," he finally said.

"It's good to have you home," I replied. "Oh, Neil. I don't know where to begin."

"You were so angry with me for going to Boston. Are you still?"

"I was. But not truly angry. Afraid. But I had time to think, and the flu is going to spread. And you are you. You will always go where you're needed. It's one of the things I love about you."

"You love about me," he echoed.

I swallowed tightly. "Yes," I whispered. "I feel horrible that it took you going away for me to realize it. It was just… I felt I'd lost so many already, and I was afraid I'd lose you, too. And then I almost did. When that letter came…" I swallowed again. "It was horrible, thinking that I might never get the chance to tell you. Thinking about you so ill, and me not there to look after you." I laughed a little. "If it hadn't been for the children, I would have jumped on the next train and cared for you myself. I was so stubborn, and I was angry at Alley and life and resentful that I'd had to give up a job I loved. I was wrong, Neil. And I'm so sorry."

He reached out and touched my hair with gentle fingertips. "The flu is horrible, Nora. I honestly did think I might die. But I kept thinking of you and James and Evelyn and how I wanted to come home and try to make things right with you. I'm sorry I snapped at you as well. I'm sorry I blamed you when we'd made an agreement, and that I wasn't honest with you. I expected too much—"

"No, you didn't." I joined my hand with his, pulled it down between us. "I needed to grow up. And I needed to see what was right in front of me, but I was too stubborn to admit." I paused, not wanting to bring Alley into our bedroom, but knowing I must this one time if we were to finally leave him in the past. "Alley came here looking for me." I told him about our conversation, about how I'd discovered the letter that had come out of his pocket. "He knew about the baby and never even asked about him. He admitted he'd lied about loving me. I was so wrong about the kind of man he is."

I rubbed my thumb in a circle over his hand. "I thought I understood what love was, but now I know what it's not. It's not being swept off my feet and romanced, not about being reckless. It's about being with someone who sees you at your worst and loves you anyway. Who knows what you need and gives it unreservedly." A tear slipped out of the corner of my eye. "You have done nothing but love me since the day we met, and I fooled myself, thinking it wasn't romance. But I love you, too, Neil, and the whole time you were away I prayed it was not too late." I bit down on my lip and met his gaze. "It's not too late, is it?"

"Oh, Nora," he whispered, and leaned forward, touching his lips to mine. The kiss was soft and sweet, tentative and yet somehow sure, and I wasn't sure if I wanted to laugh or cry.

He cupped his hand along my jaw and sighed. "I was a fool to agree to that arrangement in the first place. I had had my heart broken and never wanted to go through it again. When we said our vows… I thought it could be enough. And then James was born and I just… fell."

Neil shifted and came closer, his bare chest brushing against my nightgown, the warmth of him seeping through the flannel. He kissed my cheek and pressed his forehead to mine. "I love you."

"I want you to know that whatever happens—if you must stay at Camp Hill for a while, or if you set up your own practice in Kentville—I'll go with you, Neil."

"But you love this house."

"I do. It's full of sweet memories. But it's not home without you. Today, having you here, looking across the room and seeing you… You and the children are what makes this home. I'm just sorry it took us such a long road to get here."

"I could stay here, you know, and open a practice." He ran his fingers over my cheek, sending shivers down my extremities. "I love your family, Nora. And home is where you are. If you wanted to nurse again, maybe we could hire someone to help with the children, at least until they are in school, and you could work with me at my practice."

I drew back and stared at him. "You'd do that?"

"I want you to be happy. You're a wonderful nurse. The least I can do is give you the choice."

Choice was not a thing many women had, I realized. Women were just starting to get the vote. Most often the choice was made to either work or bear children; rarely could they do both. I thought about working side by side with Neil, using my skills, helping other people, and my heart took a leap. Then I thought of the two of us spending time with our family… right now, a family of five, but maybe there'd be more…

Neil's child. Oh, wouldn't that be lovely…

Neil drew me close, wrapping his arms around me and tucking me into his embrace, our legs twining together beneath the blankets. "We have months of hard times ahead, Nora. This virus isn't done with us yet. But God willing, we'll use what we learned over the past year to deal with it. And we'll get through. We just have to hold onto each other."

"Then hold onto me, Neil."

And he did… until the lamp burned low, the moon slid across the sky, and we finally fell into a blissful, contented sleep.

Chapter Thirty-Two

CHARLOTTE

November 26, 1918

I'd been back in Halifax over a month. I was able to get my old job at Gammon's Café back, and I rented a room at a nearby boarding house. The work kept me busy and gave me a reason to get out of bed each morning. Starting over—again—was incredibly painful.

I looked in the small mirror in my room and fiddled with my hair, trying to smooth the soft curls of my newly bobbed cut. Today would mark the possibility of yet another new start; if I was wrong, I'd pack up my few belongings and leave Halifax for good. Start over one more time, hopefully the last time. Leave the ugliness of the war and the explosion behind me once and for all.

The night I left Clara with Nora McLeod was the lowest I had ever been. Lower than when Frank died, lower than even waking up in hospital without Aileen. For that night I'd had to face so many truths about myself, things I was deeply ashamed and even frightened of. I'd waded into the water of Back Harbour and considered going out, out, until the waves closed over my head and took away the pain that had been my constant companion. Away from the loss and guilt, away from the knowledge that I had been so out of my mind with grief that I'd taken another family's child and in the process, had given up on my own. I could slip under the dark, briny water and never have to feel that way again. I thought of my parents, and thought of Aileen, and instead of giving up and following them into whatever afterlife existed, I made the decision to honour them by living instead and doing something better with my life. Frank would have wanted that for me, and as the moon slipped behind the clouds it felt as if he was there with me, my guiding star, holding my hand and telling me to go on, that there was still something I had left to do.

So I abandoned my shoes and stockings on the beach and walked, through the cold night, in bare feet to the train station. The next morning I'd quietly boarded the train, carrying only my reticule with my savings inside, leaving my suitcase and my past mistakes behind, and chugged toward Halifax. If anyone noticed my bare feet tucked under my skirts they didn't comment, and upon arriving in the city I made acquiring footwear my first priority.

Then I'd secured a small room to rent, visited the café, and shopped for the bare minimum of serviceable clothing.

I refused to go to Winnie again. For one, I was through with accepting charity. I didn't deserve it. And for another, I wasn't ready to tell my friend the truth about Aileen and Clara. I wasn't prepared to see the horror and disappointment in her eyes.

Maybe someday I would seek her out, but for now I had to focus on getting my life to a place I was proud of.

Then two days ago I'd seen an article in the paper about the Halifax School for the Blind and the accompanying photo had made me sit heavily on my lumpy bed with my hand over my mouth.

The photo showed several girls at different worktables, all blind. At the middle table sat a girl I was certain was Alice, Frank's sister.

I had walked away from the Campbell family, thinking them all dead. The house had been abandoned for days, Mrs. Campbell's body inside. The men had been killed at the sugar refinery. But if I was correct about the photo, Alice had somehow survived—and had been alone all this time. She had, like so many others, suffered injury to her eyes.

Alice had been smug and miserable much of the time, but that mattered little now. She was Frank's sister, and she too was alone. That was common ground enough for me. I couldn't shake that this was the reason I'd walked out of the ocean that night. That this was the something I was supposed to do. So today I would venture to Morris Street to the school, and I'd soon know if the girl was indeed Alice Campbell.

The sky was clear and the morning cool but not too cold as I buttoned my coat on the way out the door. My leg still troubled me—at the end of a long day, when it was very damp and cold—but my limp wasn't too pronounced as I headed across Barrington Street. Though the war was over, soldiers still filled the city, returning home from the front. Reconstruction was still happening all over; if the girl at the school was indeed Alice, perhaps I could get us into one of the new Hydrostone houses going up in the north end since the destroyed houses had been razed. I gave a small smile as a soldier stepped aside and gave me a polite nod as I passed. Halifax was a military port, with all the benefits and detriments that came with it, but it had been my home for over twenty years. It was the scene of my happiest and also my saddest moments, and I wasn't ready to leave it totally behind me yet. Not if this was Alice.

At the school, I inquired about Alice Campbell and was ushered to a room where several students practiced machine sewing, knitting, and needlework. I marveled how each girl was so sure with her hands, seeing with her fingertips as she ran fabric through the machine or picked up stitches with her knitting needles.

I spied her immediately, sitting straight in a chair, her fingers probing the feet beneath the material as she carefully stitched a length of cloth. She finished her seam, pulled the fabric out a little, and using her fingers to see, snipped the threads.

"Alice?"

Her head came up, turning in my direction. I started toward her table, my heart hammering. It was her. Frank's little sister. The last member of his family. And, perhaps, my last chance to right all my wrongs.

"Alice, it's Charlotte," I said breathlessly. "Your sister-in-law."

"I know," she said softly. "I recognized your voice."

But her gaze was blank, devoid of sight or any kind of recognition. Pity washed over me as I thought about this young girl, without a family, without her eyes. "I didn't know you were here until a few days ago," I said, going to stand in front of her. "I'm so sorry, Alice. About your family. About your sight. Oh, about everything."

But Alice smiled, something far softer and more genuine than I remembered from the days before the blast. "I'm sorry too, Charlotte. But I'm so glad you're alive."

"And you're all right? Other than your eyesight?"

She nodded. "Would you like to have a cup of tea? I'm sure I can be excused for a little while."

The young woman before me was far more self-possessed than I remembered. She picked up her cane and slowly led me out of the classroom to a small kitchen. I watched, dumbfounded, as she began fixing the tea herself. "You're so… self-reliant," I commented.

She smiled. "I'm learning all sorts of things here. It's been hard sometimes, but… oh, Charlotte, I'm sorry I was so nasty to you. It wasn't you at all. I was… jealous. And I blamed you for taking Frankie away. He was the best thing about home."

"It's forgiven," I said simply, and meant it.

I was amazed at how easily Alice managed to make tea, putting everything on a tray. "Let me," I said, taking the tray to a little table.

We took our first sips, and I was thinking how odd this all was, when Alice said, "Charlotte, how is Aileen?"

I didn't know what to say. I had no answers, and I took so long that her smile fled, and her cheeks fell. "Oh," she said quietly. "Oh, dear."

"It's all right," I said, and realized it was. I had chosen to go on and now I understood why. "What's important is that you're here and you're all right." I reached out and clasped her hand. "And if you like, I'm going to help you, Alice. You're the only family I've got. Maybe we can rely on each other. Maybe even make a new home." A warmth expanded in my chest as I said, "You know, I always wanted a sister."

And when Alice twined her fingers with mine and squeezed, I finally stopped running.

Author's Note

I grew up outside Fredericton, New Brunswick, a picturesque city on the Wolastoq (St. John) River. Social Studies was of course part of our curriculum with a dominant Canadian component. I even took Canadian History in high school, filled with details on the fur trade, the Loyalists, Responsible Government in Upper and Lower Canada, Confederation. But surprisingly, it wasn't until I read *Barometer Rising* by Hugh McLennan in my Grade 12 Atlantic Literature class that I knew anything about the Halifax Explosion. And I suppose that follows a lot of my learning about history and why I love historical fiction: in losing myself in the characters, I also absorb bits of history from the backdrop that I never might have otherwise discovered. I never forgot that book, and when we moved to Halifax many years later, I was able to explore in depth what happened that fateful day. It seemed natural to set my first historical fiction during that time, when Canada was embroiled in World War 1 and suffered such a massive loss on home shores.

On December 6, 1917, a ship called the *Mont Blanc* entered the busy Halifax harbour. A relief ship, the *Imo*, was departing. Each blasted horns demanding the other concede the right of way. Course adjustment came too late, however, and the two collided, lighting the *Mont Blanc* on fire. This might not have been a cause for panic if the *Mont Blanc* hadn't been carrying highly incendiary material—2.9 kilotons of explosives were on board and for security reasons, only a few people knew its cargo. It was only a matter of time before the fire ignited the munitions, and at just after nine a.m. the *Mont Blanc* exploded, levelling an entire part of the city, killing nearly 2000 and injuring 9000 more. It was the largest man-made explosion in history until 1945 and the use of the atom bomb in Japan.

The importance of Halifax in the First World War was huge. The harbour doesn't freeze in the winter, it's deep, and the way it's shaped—in the book I compare it to the curve of a woman's waist—narrows in the middle (appropriately called The Narrows) and empties into the Bedford Basin. Ships entered the harbour, then gathered in the basin and formed convoys to cross the Atlantic with protection in numbers against German U-boats. There were defences all along the east coast of Nova Scotia, and Halifax closed the harbour to arrivals and departures of ships each night with submarine nets.

The *Mont Blanc* was due to arrive on December 5, but because the nets were already extended, it had to wait until morning to enter. The *Imo*, on the other hand, was delayed leaving because of a late arrival of coal. It really came down to a series of unrelated events leading to a collision course. While the initial inquiry placed the blame on the pilot and captain of the *Mont Blanc* (whose crew had abandoned ship), a later Supreme Court decision laid the blame equally. Interesting to note is there are still some conspiracy theories of German sabotage floating about.

As you can imagine, the sight of a ship on fire in the harbour was cause for excitement on that December morning. Many flocked to the waterfront to see the commotion. Others stood at their windows, looking down over the harbour. When the blast occurred, it leveled the tallest building on the waterfront, the Acadia Sugar Refinery, and reduced the piers and the Richmond area to rubble. Those watching from windows were hit with shattering glass, and dozens of people were left blinded. 206 lost one eye and hundreds more suffered ocular damage. In my story, an oculist, Dr. Cox, arrives from New Glasgow later that day to assist in treating the wounded, and his participation and the scene with the grotesque bucket of eyeballs is drawn from fact. This "mass blinding" eventually led to the birth of the CNIB—the Canadian National Institute for the Blind, as so many required assistance in adjusting to their new circumstances.

Camp Hill Hospital was a new hospital for convalescing soldiers and was partly sheltered from the worst of the blast by Citadel Hill, the star-shaped fort in the centre of what is now considered "downtown." In the hours after the explosion, the hospital built for under 300 saw over 1400 patients crowding its pavilions, needing treatment.

While the characters of Nora Crowell and Neil McLeod are fictional, I did draw on some real people to populate this section of the story. Jessie Smiley was a nursing sister at Camp Hill after graduating from the program at the Victoria General Hospital in 1915. Matron Cotton had indeed served overseas as part of the Canadian Army Medical Corps and served in Russia (Petrograd) before being transferred to Halifax and Camp Hill, even though I played with the dates slightly here to suit the story. Out of necessity, this mass casualty event changed the way nurses practiced. "Before the explosion, nurses could only do what doctors said they could do. After the explosion, the need was so great, they were doing things they had never done before, like removing glass, and suturing wounds. Nurses got together and said, 'We can do more.'" (Gloria Stephens of the VG Nursing Archives)

Relief immediately started arriving by train, with doctors arriving shortly after the news got out. Trains were stopped at Rockingham, as the devastation prevented them from getting further into the city, and they were left to make their way on foot. The Boston municipal government held a meeting that same day and was instrumental in sending immediate aid, including a fully staffed medical unit from Harvard. Halifax still enjoys a special relationship with this "sister" city and sends a Christmas tree each year that is lit on the Boston Common.

In my research, I discovered so many inspirational and miraculous stories of survival and goodwill that I couldn't possibly include them all, but the child who was rescued under an ash pan did exist and became famously known as Ashpan Annie. Entire families were wiped out in an instant; children were orphaned and subsequently adopted or went to live with extended family members. The ad that Charlotte sees about the child in hospital was a real advertisement, though the lack of detail meant I could take some liberty there, and sent her off to New Glasgow in search of her daughter. I also took a few liberties with smaller details like train schedules, in order to have them suit my timeline, as well as having Neil conveniently seconded to Camp Hill on a permanent basis.

In short, this novel has hallmark moments as historical seeds, but the characters are a fictional reimagining of those who were lost and how those who survived may have navigated this devastating event.

Writing a historical fiction was a huge departure for me

creatively, and I loved every moment. I've always adored it as a genre, but my fear of "getting it wrong" always held me back from actually writing one. Two things happened to jolt me out of that fear and into taking a chance. First, writing this story never would have happened if Charlotte Ledger hadn't emailed me asking if I'd considered writing Canadian historical fiction. I firmly believe in signs, and her email came at a time when the pandemic was creating some uncertainty in my family's financial situation and I was trying to decide what to do next. As an eternal optimist, I tend to look at things as opportunities, so I was immediately intrigued and wrote her back. Thank you, Charlotte, for reaching out and especially for all your hard work on this novel. You have been incredibly encouraging, and made the process so fun, helping me see the possibilities inside!

Second, when Charlotte reached out I was also nearing a milestone birthday, and I thought to myself, *if not now, when*? The older I get, the more I realize that it's okay to embrace risks and challenges. Not just okay, it's imperative! Fear shouldn't hold us back from chasing dreams, and failure is never final. The older I get, the less I care about "shoulds" and the more I want to just go for it. I don't want to look back with regret, thinking "I wish I would have…" Life is too short.

Of course writing—and life, for that matter—is never a solitary endeavour, so in addition to Charlotte, there are some truly wonderful people who helped me get this off the ground and also kept me sane in the process. Kimberley Young, publisher at One More Chapter… thank you for letting me spread my writing wings. One of the reasons I was so keen to explore this opportunity was because you were attached to it. Thanks to editor Laura McCallen for her insightful edits and *that* email that nearly made me cry! I also have to give a huge shout

out to the One More Chapter and HarperCollins teams… from editing, the art department, PR and marketing and everyone in between… teamwork does indeed make the dream work, and I appreciate your dedication to bring this book to bookshelves.

I absolutely could not do this without my writing besties, who are the best cheerleaders and brainstormers in the world: Barbara Tanner Wallace, Renee Ryan, Shirley Jump, and Jenna Bayley-Burke. Renee and Barb, you also brought me on board at Step Into The Story, where I'm able to grow and share my love for historical fiction, including fangirling over our guests and getting serious writer envy vibes from all the fantastic work. Michelle Helliwell and Genevieve Graham, extra thanks to you for taking the time to do early reads. Knowing you were casting your talented eyes on this story helped alleviate a lot of my accuracy anxiety!

I'm including a list of recommended reading at the end, but I must also thank the staff at the Maritime Museum of the Atlantic in Halifax, and the librarians at the Halifax Central Library. Your resources are so very appreciated!

Nora and Charlotte's stories revolve around one central idea —that family is everything. Darrell, you have never once told me not to do something because it was foolish or risky or the odds were against me. You've not only had faith in me but trusted me with my career decisions, and always make sure I look after myself when I start to get overwhelmed. Thanks to my eldest, Ash, for your exacting editing and feedback skills and for bringing your talents to Step Into The Story, and to Kate, who loves (or at least puts up with) brainstorming sessions to get me out of plot holes. And big thanks to both of you for your enthusiasm, even during the years when parents are supposed to be a source of embarrassment (I know I achieved that in other ways, you're welcome). You've always been proud of me, and I'm so proud of you both.

Most of all, this is a story about sisters… the sisters we choose, the sisters we lose, and the ones we treasure every day. This book is dedicated to my sister from another mister, Barb—the bestest bestie that ever bested; to Janet, the sister I'll always miss and who left us too soon, to my sister-in-law who has been a part of my life since I was a toddler—Sheila, who takes such wonderful care of my mum, and to Janell, who always seems to know exactly what I need, even if it's just a Kleenex and an ice cream sandwich.

Donna

Reading List:

Breaking Disaster: Katie Ingram
As British as the King: Gerald Hallowell
The Town that Died: Michael J. Bird
Nova Scotia at War 1914-1917: Brian Douglas Tennyson
Explosion in Halifax Harbour 1917: Dan Soucoup
Shattered City: Janet F. Kitz
Survivors. Children of the Halifax Explosion: Janet F. Kitz
Explosion in Halifax Harbour: David B. Flemming
Halifax: Warden of the North: Thomas H. Raddall
Canada's Atlantic Gateway: Frost
Shattered: Jennie Marsland
Barometer Rising: Hugh McLennan

Other Resources:

South Shore Sketches
Chester Municipality: A History
Nova Scotia's Part in the Great War
Camp Hill Hospital: 70 Years of Caring
History of Chester: 1759-1967 (225 Years in Chester Basin)

Book Club Questions

1. At various points in the book, different characters express attitudes about serving at home vs. serving at the front. Do you think one is more valid than the other?
2. Nora and Charlotte have different upbringings and live very different lives, yet both are tragically affected by the explosion. Did you relate to one character more than the other, and why?
3. We know much more about trauma responses and PTSD today than was known in 1917. How did you feel about the actions of the characters as they processed their grief and trauma? Were the soldiers' responses different from, for example, Nora's and Charlotte's?
4. How did you feel about Alley's role in the story?
5. The story recounts a pivotal event in Canada's history – the largest man-made explosion until 1945's bombing of Japan and a mass casualty event. Had you heard of

this event before? How did it change your view of Canada in wartime?

6. In the beginning of the story, we see Nora as an independent woman—or, as she says, as independent as a woman can be in 1917—who bucks tradition in favour of a career. Her choices—and the explosion—lead to some big life changes. Charlotte, on the other hand, begins the story entrenched in domestic life and then must find work. How did you feel about the changes in their circumstances? Is one life better than the other?
7. What role does community play in the story?
8. Do you see any parallels in the themes in the book with our lives today? What do you think is the most important message from the story?
9. Did you know about the "sister city" relationship between Halifax and Boston that stemmed from this event?
10. Did you find the ending of the book surprising? Satisfying?

YOUR NUMBER ONE STOP

ONE MORE CHAPTER

FOR PAGETURNING BOOKS

The author and One More Chapter would like to thank everyone who contributed to the publication of this story...

Analytics
Abigail Fryer
Maria Osa

Audio
Fionnuala Barrett
Ciara Briggs

Contracts
Sasha Duszynska Lewis

Design
Lucy Bennett
Fiona Greenway
Liane Payne
Dean Russell

Digital Sales
Hannah Lismore
Emily Scorer

Editorial
Kate Elton
Simon Fox
Arsalan Isa
Charlotte Ledger
Bonnie Macleod
Jennie Rothwell
Caroline Scott-Bowden

Harper360
Emily Gerbner
Jean Marie Kelly
emma sullivan
Sophia Walker

International Sales
Peter Borcsok
Bethan Moore

Marketing & Publicity
Chloe Cummings
Emma Petfield

Operations
Melissa Okusanya
Hannah Stamp

Production
Emily Chan
Denis Manson
Simon Moore
Francesca Tuzzeo

Rights
Rachel McCarron
Hany Sheikh
Mohamed
Zoe Shine

The HarperCollins Distribution Team

The HarperCollins Finance & Royalties Team

The HarperCollins Legal Team

The HarperCollins Technology Team

Trade Marketing
Ben Hurd

UK Sales
Laura Carpenter
Isabel Coburn
Jay Cochrane
Sabina Lewis
Holly Martin
Erin White
Harriet Williams
Leah Woods

And every other essential link in the chain from delivery drivers to booksellers to librarians and beyond!